The Beirut Conspiracy

by

John R. Childress

The Beirut Conspiracy

Copyright © 2004, John R. Childress

Printed in Canada.

For information address:
Durban House Publishing Company, Inc.
7502 Greenville Avenue, Suite 500, Dallas, Texas 75231

Library of Congress Cataloging-in-Publication Data
Childress, John R., 1947

The Beirut Conspiracy / John R. Childress

Library of Congress Catalog Number: 2003115787

p. cm.

ISBN 1-930754-55-8

First Edition

10 9 8 7 6 5 4 3 2 1

Visit our Web site at
http://www.durbanhouse.com

Acknowledgements

This is purely a work of fiction, and hopefully it will remain that way. The ingredients for this story, however, are all around us. The issue of Palestinian statehood is very much with us. Every passing day, more and more young people succumb to the illusionary glory of becoming suicide bombers. Those intent on profiting from international conflict grow stronger and bolder. The coffers of international criminals are increasingly filled with profits from the drug trade. It is no longer just a Middle East issue. It is a global crisis.

Full face transplants, as farfetched as they may seem, are today a medical and technological reality. The only thing, if any, keeping them from being commonplace are the ethical issues surrounding such a procedure. However, ethics have never stopped criminal organizations intent on profit. Lebanon, and Beirut in particular, remains a turbulent region. The Palestinian refugee camps continue to be a spawning ground for hatred that knows no antidote.

Many of the scenes and experiences described in this novel come from my own experiences as a foreign exchange student at the American University of Beirut in 1968. However, after thirty years, my memory is less than perfect, so I have added generous amounts of fiction to the actual events, first to fill them in, and secondly to make them more exciting. I have also contacted many of my friends from AUB to gather their impressions and input. I hope I haven't embarassed any of them as a result. Again, this story is purely fiction, a work of my imagination. Any errors or misrepresentations are purely my own. However, typos are not my fault. Blame my cat, Sally, who insisted on climbing into my lap and pressing on the keys of my computer keyboard.

Chapter One

Washington, D.C.

THE TARGET WAS IN PLAIN SIGHT. *Like the many others among the press the short figure, notebook in hand, elbowed toward the front. The bright press badge stood out clearly against the heavy wool overcoat. Necessary for the chilly January air, the bulky coat's main task was to conceal the mass of tightly packed plastic explosives inside a vest of deadly ball bearings. A human bomb waiting to unleash its terror. The smooth button of the detonating device was moist and warm from the perspiring hand that reverently cradled it. A practiced smile masked a racing heart and morbid fear that something would go wrong after all the years of preparation, all the sacrifices. On the outside an eager, smiling reporter. Inside burned an all-consuming hatred. The harbinger of death in Allah's just cause was in place.*

President Roswell Clayton Pierce shook hands with his old friend and personal physician, Dr. Andrew Norman. It was a perfect photo opportunity. The first of the New Year. The two men stood in front of the luxury brownstone, waving to the crowd and television cameras below. The president flashed his charismatic boyish smile, turned up the collar of his overcoat, and moved athletically down the steps. A jostling mass of reporters, cameramen, D.C. police and Secret Service agents pressed up against the tall iron fence.

"How was your checkup, Mr. President?"

"Float like a butterfly, sting like a bee." The 58-year-old first term president smiled. "I believe that's how Dr. Norman describes my fitness level."

"Dr. Norman? Dr. Norman? Can you give us an official statement concerning the health and well-being of the president?" called an attractive correspondent from Fox News. "Was this just a routine checkup, or is there some sort of health problem?"

President Pierce stepped back and gave the spotlight of the nation to his friend. "You're up, Andrew." A ripple of laughter spread through the crowd. Not since John F. Kennedy had a U.S. president enjoyed such an easy relationship with the press.

The elderly physician moved toward the fence, eager to field questions about the health of the President of the United States.

"In the name of Allah, Most Beneficent, Most Merciful!"

A high-pitched voice screamed loudly, but the explosion was even louder.

The black overcoat disintegrated along with bone, flesh, blood and viscera. Thousands of round ceramic projectiles rushed outward in all directions at the velocity of a rifle bullet. Those closest to the assassin were instantly torn to shreds, but the deadly balls kept spreading outwards in an ever-expanding circle of death and carnage. A large quantity of them slammed into the metal casing of a shoulder-held television camera, ricocheted off and decapitated the young cameraman. In seconds the street was littered with bodies, fallen as if stalks of wheat before a maniacal scythe. Blood, steaming in the crisp air, formed into rivulets. They moved towards the gutters, coalescing into larger and larger pools.

The first suicide bomber on American soil killed fifty-seven people that crisp, sunny January morning. Seventy-five others were seriously wounded. The pain and anguish unleashed that day in Washington, D.C. erased all hope for peace in the Middle East.

Sweet Briar College, Virginia

"MATT, MATT, WAKE UP. Something terrible has just happened in Washington." Kelly Stevens dashed from the kitchen, her plate of toast falling to the tile floor. Bare feet pounded as she ran into the bedroom of the modest wooden house on faculty row.

Matt Richards lay still, seemingly paralyzed, his nerves and muscles bound tight in an all too familiar alcohol-induced haze. But he had heard it. Familiar sounds of a press interview. President Pierce at his most ingratiating. Then the detonation. The sound of it shook his clogged brain. The memory, the fear, the terrible sorrow inundated him. The past, suppressed and locked away, surfacing unbidden at the damnedest times, kept in check with ample quantities of Scotch, now broke through the surface. He clutched his pillow. She would come at any moment, all over him, smudged lipstick, fresh face and breakfast crumbs. *God, I'm too old for this.*

She sprang onto the rumpled sheets of the wrought-iron bed, her tangled blond hair cascading into the face of her secret lover.

"Wake up," she pleaded, shaking him. "There's been a suicide bomb attack on the president."

"Score one for the rugheads." Dr. Matthew Richards, assistant professor of anatomy and human biology, rolled over and slowly sat up, legs dangling, head in hands covering blood-shot eyes. "And close those goddamned curtains. It's uncivilized for any decent human being to see the sun before noon."

"You only say that because you drink yourself into a stupor every night." Kelly smiled, somehow enjoying the unique opportunity to reprimand one of her teachers.

He watched her close the curtains, this lithe coed from his anatomy class, reaching, stretching, buttocks round and taut, a nymph in the slanting sunlight. Then the memories crowded in. She was about Kelly's age when she died.

"Here, have a puff of this. It'll keep your liver from shutting down." She exhaled and held out a thin wrinkled joint.

Never again. Matt shook his head. He reached for the remnants of his Scotch. Miraculously, one swallow was left. A quick gulp, and slowly the world came into focus. He looked down at his slim body, contoured with hard sinewy muscles, his skin tanned and weathered as a result of a lifetime of distance running, the last real vestige of an attempt at self preservation. He had the gaunt look of a well-worn movie cowboy, old and youthful at the same time.

"I'll stick with my liquid gold. I tried marijuana once, in Beirut. Actually it was hashish and it nearly killed me. Gave me hallucinations for two days straight. Now turn off that damned noise-box and climb in bed."

"But something important is happening. Don't you even care anymore?" She left the darkened bedroom for the kitchen and the blaring news.

Matt stared into the empty glass, at his empty life. The words of an anchorman floated in from the kitchen, hesitant, seemingly free of the teleprompter and the blandness of political correct broadcasting.

"We can now confirm that the president of the United States is alive. I repeat, President Roswell Clayton Pierce is alive, having sustained only superficial wounds as a result of a suicide bomber attack this morning outside the Washington, D.C., residence of Dr. Andrew Norman, his personal physician. The president, at this moment, is at Walter Reed Hospital, where he will remain under tight security as military doctors tend to him. At this time, all indications are that the president of the United States has escaped a suicide bomber attack in Washington, D.C., with only minor injuries."

Matt leaned against the kitchen doorway. The empty Scotch glass was warm in his hand.

"God, Matt, look at this. Can you believe it?"

He reached for the pinch-shaped Scotch container and half filled the tumbler. It hadn't just been Samir. There was Bedouina, intense, eager to right the injustices, passionately in love with Samir. And Maha. Ravishing red-hair, alabaster skin, beckoning green eyes. Drop-dead figure, totally in love with, melt your heart for Maha. Beirut. 1968. A magical year abroad. Study. Debate the world's problems. Party hearty. Stare into Maha's eyes. Run fingers through that soft red hair. Shit. Four lives shattered by a terrible explosion.

"While we now know for certain that the president of the United States is alive and safe, his personal safety is overshadowed by the horrible carnage that took place at 10:38 this morning on the lawn outside the residence and private office of Dr. Andrew Norman. Dr. Norman, personal physician to the president and one of his closest family friends, along with fifty-six others, mostly journalists, photographers, policemen, and Secret Service agents assigned to guard the president, were savagely murdered by a suicide bomber. Many of the dead were standing in close proximity to the explosive-strapped assassin and were killed instantly. Early reports indicate there are scores of casualties, many seriously injured. Dozens of ambulances have taken the wounded to hospital emergency rooms throughout the greater Washington, D.C., area."

"Shit," Matt Richards said. Trying to rebury the painful memory from thirty years ago seemed impossible now. He slumped down into the wooden kitchen chair. "I hate bombs."

"They've stopped showing the bodies. Now it's just long shots of the area." Kelly nipped out the joint, setting it aside for later.

"Political correctness moves in." Matt tightened the drawstring on his pajama bottoms.

"Look, something is happening. It's that up-and-coming CNN reporter, Angela Wu. This is a big break for her."

"I see cynicism isn't just reserved for us old geezers."

"You're not old, just ridden hard. Look how she's shaking."

The scene changed from the newsroom to a chaotic, tree-lined street. "This is Angela Wu reporting just up the street from the Washington, D.C., home of Dr. Andrew Norman, personal physician to the president, who, along with scores of others, was killed this morning during a suicide bomber attack obviously intended for the president of the United States. The police, FBI and Secret Service have cordoned off most of the area around the blast scene. It's a site of horrific carnage—blood and body parts scattered everywhere. When I first arrived on the scene, a severed head lay against the curb."

"She's gonna throw up," Matt said, taking another long pull on his Scotch. *I know how she feels.*

The camera held steady, following closely as she bent over. Sounds of retching mingled with the shouts of medics and blaring sirens. The camera swung away in a circle, panning over policemen, firemen, trucks, ambulances and more bodies. Frantic shouts carried.

"This one's still breathing." "Get a medic over here right now." "For God's sake, someone help me."

Then the strained face of Angela Wu returned. "...I was supposed to be here this morning, reporting on the president's routine checkup, but my car wouldn't start and, as a result, the crew left the studio without me. My colleague, Sylvia Stone, went in my place. She's out there somewhere. Ruthlessly cut down. Senselessly murdered."

The shrill sound of an ambulance siren caused the microphone to squeal in harsh protest.

"Stay on me. Stay on me. I've got to finish this."

"I've got you, Angela. Keep going. We're live."

Tears streamed unchecked. Lips quivered uncontrollably. "Who are these beasts, these criminals, these cowards? This isn't a noble political cause; it's just premeditated murder. The savage and brutal slaughter of dozens of innocent people. First we have the horrible destruction and mayhem of September 11, and now this, the first suicide bomber on American soil, attempting a cold-blooded assassination of the president."

Another quick panorama shot. Ambulances sped away. Paramedics zipped up black bags.

"When is this senseless killing going to stop? I'm angry, depressed, tired, and just plain sick of all this shit. The whole world has turned into a bloody battlefield. Is no one safe from the madness? What do we tell our children? Kill first before you're the next victim? What's it going to take to finally bring peace to the Middle East and put an end to these attacks? When is someone going to do the right thing and make the courageous decisions that will put an end to this madness?"

Her face was a picture of anguish for all that was going on around her. And inside of her. She looked straight into the camera and out at the world.

"That's it. I'm finished. I quit."

The camera held her, another casualty added to those strewn about the street. The world watched as she threw down the microphone, tore off her earpiece, turned around, and forced her way through the large crowd pressing against the yellow police cordon.

"Oh my God," cried Kelly. Cannabis intensified her tears.

"She'll be back."

"Jesus H. Christ, Matt. Don't you feel anything? Doesn't this move you even a little bit?"

More than you know. He wanted to say something. But what was the use? How could he help a privileged young college coed, pampered daughter of a senior U.S. senator, raised on first-class trips to Europe and monogrammed underwear, understand the pain and sorrow of something like this? To be really moved, he realized, you had to be close enough to feel the heat from the blast and smell the death.

The screen flashed back to the anchorman at CNN headquarters, looking quizzically to his left. Excited voices could be heard. Aware of the probing lens, he regained his professional demeanor and faced the camera.

"A senseless tragedy like this affects all of us in different ways. Even the most professional newscasters find it difficult to remain detached when something as horrible as this happens in our own nation's capital.

"We have just received some remarkable footage of the moments before the blast, taken by our CNN crew on location. Due to the graphic nature of this material, CNN has decided not to broadcast all of it. However, we are able to show the moments leading up to the assassination attempt."

Fade to black. Replaced a second later by images of President Pierce shaking hands with Dr. Norman, then moving down the steps of the Washington brownstone toward the reporters crowding the fence.

"Here we see the president emerging from the offices of his personal physician and coming down the front steps to make a statement to the press," the anchorman said, comfortable with tape and hindsight. "And here is the brief footage from one of our CNN cameramen whose job it was to film the crowd. If you look closely, you'll see a short figure wearing a large fur hat and a black overcoat, moving steadily through the crowd, trying to get as near the front as possible."

Someone in the newsroom drew a yellow circle, like the highlights on Monday Night Football, around a small figure in a large fur hat, pushing through the crowd. The hat purposely obscuring the face, but the intent evident. Squirming through the assembled mass, press badge in hand, finally standing at the front of the press corps. A voice called out to the president. The assassin looked up. The camera found its mark.

"In the name of Allah...."

The picture froze. Matt Richards stared. "No. It's... not possible." Matt fell. The chair crashed to the floor. Matt fell. Sour vomit spewed across the kitchen floor.

"Matt. Jesus. What's the matter?"

The deep voice of the newscaster came alive again. "While we currently have no information on the suicide bomber's identity, we can say at this time that the individual was of Middle Eastern origin, approximately forty-five to fifty-five years of age, with thick black hair." CNN enlarged the image on the screen. "And as you can see, a woman."

Walter Reed Military Hospital

ROSWELL CLAYTON PIERCE LAY STILL on the starched white sheets. His head throbbed, the bandage across the deep sutured gash in his forehead white against a perpetual tan. Several other bandages were scattered around his arms, legs, and hands. He could manage the pain in his body, but the emotional pain was searing. CNN was showing a rerun of Angela Wu. "I quit...."

As she threw down the microphone and tore off her earpiece, the president of the United States jabbed at the off button on the remote control.

His first visitor since the attack said nothing. He waited. He always waited. Van Ness was a counter-puncher, and a fixer of the highest order. A skillful player on a global stage.

"She's right, Karl. Someone should do the right thing. Make the tough decisions. And that someone is supposed to be me."

Van Ness stared at the scrubbed linoleum. "Anyone can make decisions, Ross. It's having everything in place behind the scenes that makes a decision stick. We have a little time yet."

His gray eyes found his mentor's. "Time for what? I'm the decisive president, remember?"

"Grieving for Andrew. And the others. Checking your motives for stepping back."

"He was keen to be in the spotlight. He practically ran forward to talk to the press."

"No guilt then? You can't face the nation, and the wolves, showing even the slightest bit of guilt."

Ross threw the remote against the wall. The freed batteries rolled across the floor. "You know me pretty well, Karl."

"Perhaps better than anyone." Van Ness felt the smooth outline of his faithful pipe in his coat pocket. "They're outside, waiting."

"I know. I know. CIA, FBI, Secret Service, Homeland Security. I can just imagine the denials and finger pointing." Ross Pierce touched the wound on his forehead.

"As always. But like I said, you have a little time. Get yourself together. The next few hours may well set the course of history. And your political career."

"It's a funny thing about being a Navy Intruder pilot, Karl. Every moment is filled with potential and real danger. Heat-seeking missiles, random fire from the ground, enemy aircraft, and night landings on a pitching deck. Shit scary. But none of these ever had a face. Christ, Karl, she was right in front of me. I saw her face. Twisted hatred and serenity at the same time."

Van Ness waited.

"Remember how back in New Mexico we talked about running for the presidency?"

"Over some excellent Napa Valley wine as I recall. Sundown in the desert is a good time for thinking."

"You've always been an excellent listener and sounding board. Look what we pulled off together: an enviable record as governor of New Mexico, then as a U.S. senator."

"You worked hard, Ross. And you fought hard. Just like all your posts along the way: the Navy, the construction business, the ranch. It was more your effort than mine, Mr. President. You're into your second year after a close race. And I have a feeling you may just pull off the biggest miracle of all."

"Forget the sales spiel. Neither of us believes it. The state of the economy and worsening conditions in the Middle East were my real allies. Anyway, I'm sitting here; sliced up by steel pellets from a suicide bomb, lucky to be alive, and soon I'll have to face the nation and the world. With answers. I will need your help again, Karl. Big time."

"Where's your tin cup?"

"You don't think I use it too much? It's important for me, just as much now as it was in the prison camp in Vietnam. Reminds me of my purpose. In an odd way it gives me courage, too."

Karl van Ness nodded. "It's certainly good theater, and every good politician needs a little theater now and then. But yes, you over do it sometimes, banging on the podium during the presidential debates to make your points."

"We're from different generations, Karl."

"I respect more than most what that tin cup means to you. I was one of those waiting on the tarmac in Hawaii after your release from the Hanoi Hilton. You looked like hell, but you were proud."

"I believe strongly in the importance of open communication. That's what the cups were to us in prison, our only means of communicating, through code banged on the prison bars. And open communication is what I've tried to provide throughout my business and political career. But it gets harder and harder as this world gets more and more complex and intertwined. Sometimes I feel like I don't have the fortitude anymore."

"Your mother still believes you do."

Ross smiled. "If I only had a tenth of her courage. She's a Quaker, and a good one. She actually says what she thinks and practices what she preaches."

Van Ness listened to the voices outside. Politicians, all of them. "Your dad made up for your mother's strengths," he said dryly.

"One domineering sonofabitch. A confirmed capitalist and product of the American dream. He constantly kicked my ass, but always in the right direction."

"Well, with all due respect, Mr. President, in this case the apple didn't fall far from the tree. So let's see if we can't use those attributes to get out of this mess."

Ross leaned back. He rubbed his eyes. "Just how the hell did she get a press badge? *The Israel Daily*, no less. Can't miss the irony there."

"Somebody was clever. And prepared."

"The first suicide bomber on American soil, and it happened on my watch. And I'm the big mouth who campaigned that he would solve the crisis in the Middle East – one way or another."

"Mr. President, it's not important what happens. It's how you handle it that matters. Now let's forget this self-serving 'on my watch' crap. It's time to put some backbone into this country. And those dithering advisors waiting outside."

"Check on Emily for me will you? She must be having a fit not being allowed in yet."

Van Ness grinned, an additional score of wrinkles surfaced on his weathered face. "Shall I tell her it was your decision?" He reached for the door handle. "I'll let the boys waiting outside know you're ready. Good luck, Mr. President."

Ross Pierce winced as he swung his legs over the side of the hospital bed and groped with his feet for his slippers. The ones with the presidential seal embroidered on them.

"The country is in chaos and someone still thinks of the image of the president." He smiled, straightened the bed sheet and waited. A gentle knock came from the other side of the door.

"For Christ's sake, come in. We've got work to do."

Polished shoes shuffled on the floor. Eyes darted around from uncertain faces, checking the political landscape.

"Only two chairs. Anyone want to sit on the bed with me?"

CIA Director Terry Finch looked quickly at the floor. "I'll stand, Mr. President."

"That's to your credit, Terry. I don't want the CIA in bed with anyone."

Tight smiles all around. "How are you feeling, Mr. President?"

Ross Pierce glanced quickly at the Secretary for Homeland Security. "Maybe better than you, Bill. You get attacked by a mad BIC razor?"

"We were in New York working all night. Just got to bed when the call came about the bombing." William McLaughlin gently touched the blood caked cuts on his face.

"To answer your question, I'm fine. Physically at least. But my heart aches for those poor people who didn't have a chance."

President Roswell Clayton Pierce looked at the tense faces of his security advisors. Time to move things along. Seize the day. "Okay. I take it you've all seen the Angela Wu piece as well as the CNN shots of the bomber?"

"We're on to tracing the bomber, Mr. President; computer search of a facial grid might turn up...."

Ross Pierce raised his hand, oddly commanding as he sat in his pajamas. "Let it go for now, Howard. I know all your agencies are working flat out, and I expect nothing less. But the real reason I wanted you all here together is to get something said, and something understood. Right here. Right now." He held each in his gaze as he looked around the tiny room.

"Okay, we fucked up on this one. A bomber got through all our best security, and she did it on national TV. They showed a severed head in the gutter, for Christ's sake."

The warbling P/A system broke the brittle atmosphere as a doctor was paged to surgery.

"And we lost people. Lots of people. Good people. Some we knew, some we didn't. No one's going to want to cover a presidential press event from now on. To hell with the president, they might get blown up."

Ross looked down at the floor, then up to the ceiling as he shaped his words. "Let me tell you how this is going to go from now on. First, no more fiefdoms. It's common knowledge among every terrorist organization, it's in all the newspapers. Our security agencies don't work together, don't coordinate, don't even communicate. That's the past gentlemen. It's over. Finished. From now on I want one joint report on my desk every day that each of you has contributed to and are willing to stand behind. We don't have time for second guessing and withholding."

Someone coughed nervously. All eyes turned to the CIA Director.

"Mr. President," Terry Finch began quietly, "we're always...."

"Knock it off, Terry. That bullshit line is over. Blown away. Like the safety of our country. Like peace in the Middle East."

The president poured himself a glass of water. "So, number one, you guys get your acts together. I want some facts that I can give to the reporters, and the American people, when they come after me ready to chew my ass off. Taxes are crippling the average American and with all the money spent after September 11, what do they get? A severed head on the streets of Washington, D.C."

"If I may, Mr. President?"

"Okay, Bill. What's the view from Homeland Security?"

"I'm grossly underfunded as it is. Guys work two, three nights in a row just checking out all the leads we get. I need ....."

Ross nodded, cutting him off. "It's a thankless job, I know. I'll see what I can do. Maybe your new partners here will give you some extra manpower?"

"Shit, Mr. President. We can't even get our databases to talk to each other. Different systems running on different software platforms." The bald head of the FBI Director beaded with sweat, but he was committed now. "Everyone agrees it will take at least another year to marry up our database systems."

"Look, gentlemen. Reality has just pitched us a big roundhouse curve. I definitely wasn't ready when that missile shot down my A6 Intruder, but I had to deal with it real quick. And that's what we're going to have to do now. Deal with it,"

"Just how are we supposed to...?"

"I wish I knew, gentlemen. I wish I knew. But it's your job, not mine. I've got to keep the world from blowing up."

Again the P/A system echoed in a faraway hall. Ross Pierce refilled his glass.

"Look, gentlemen. You know your jobs, your people. You're the best in the business. And you know the predicament we are in. If we don't find out how this happened and shut it down, every two-bit terrorist with a knife, gun or bomb will think it's open season on Americans. Whose head will it be in the gutter next time?"

Wearily he stared at the bed sheets. "I want your first joint report on my desk at 7 a.m. tomorrow morning. Something substantial for my address to the nation." He peeled off a bandage from his hand.

"And we will meet every Tuesday at 7 a.m. in the Oval Office from now on. You're my new cabinet on terrorism, security and the Middle East. I'll add a few more members, but keep it small. No substitutes. If you don't come to a meeting I'll assume you're dead or dying.

And you will be."

He reached out and shook each member's hand, holding it firmly, communicating his resolve. "And about that funding, I hear you, Bill. We'll get more money from somewhere. I guarantee it."

They all nodded, both hopeful and fearful. "Get some rest, Mr. President. I think we're all going to need it."

"Thanks, Frank. But I doubt if any of the Secret Service will be sleeping tonight. Nor will I."

The door closed firmly. Marine guards snapped to attention as the four senior directors quietly left the room.

Alone again. Ross Pierce picked at his bandages. Like in a jet fighter, timing was everything. Angela Wu arrived late at the press conference. She lived. He moved a few feet back behind Dr. Andrew Norman. He lived. Life and death, turning on the smallest of actions. But just what were the right actions from now on? Was there one right decision that could shift the momentum of the world from destruction to global peace? Could he find it? Could he use it?

He picked up the phone. "Nurse, I need to use the head." He listened. "I know that. Send her in, but I'm closing the damned door."

While the army nurse stood in the empty room, just next to the bathroom door, the president of the United States reached for a towel. When the tears overtook him, he buried his face, muffling the sobs. He slumped to the cold floor, his back bumping against the door.

"Are you all right, Mr. President?"

Roswell Clayton Pierce was fine, but he knew the world was running out of time.

Chapter Two

The American University of Beirut, Lebanon, 1969

"COME ON, SAMIR, I'M STARVING. Let's get something to eat." Matt Richards threw his pencil down on his dormitory desk and stretched. "We've been studying for three solid hours. My ass is flat, and my stomach is growling."

"You Americans, all you think about is your stomach. In the Koran it says prayer is the food of the righteous." Samir Hussein was a psychology major, Palestinian, and Matt's roommate.

"Well, in the King James version of the Bible it says the Lord helps those who help themselves. And right now I'd like to help myself to a bowl of humus, a mountain of tabouli, a big juicy lamb kebab and a couple of beers."

"You can afford to be casual about studying. In two months school will be out and you'll be headed back to your home in America."

A grin cracked Matt's suntanned face. "Yeah." A summer job in the fruit orchards outside of Seattle, then his final year at Harvard. "Don't forget med school, Samir. Next time we meet you'll have to call me Doctor Richards."

"Just like your father and older brother, Sam." After nearly eight months of living with him every day, Samir still wondered about his American roommate. Was he following his heart, or someone else's expectations? With a world-renowned heart surgeon for a father, who could ever measure up?

"No matter what I become, surgeon or bum, I'll never forget this year." Matt said. He studied Samir's intense face. Born in Jerusalem. At that time the independent state of Palestine. Soon to be lost forever in a sea of chaos and conflict. "This year has been the most influential of my life. I know it. I'll always remember the sights, the sounds, the smells, the food, the history. And the women. What can I say?"

"Speaking of women, are we going to meet up with Bedouina and Maha tonight, or are you going to give me one of your 'I love Beirut' monologues that puts me to sleep?" Samir stood up. Anxious fingers ran through his thick black hair. "Anyway, I think we're out of luck. It's past curfew and the school gates are locked. We're stuck. Besides, you've seen the guards carrying machine guns posted at all the University gates. They're loaded with real bullets."

"Don't be such a wimp. Ever since the attack on the Beirut Airport by the Israelis in December, they've had guards everywhere. Who cares? We'll just climb over the wall like I always do. You can do it. We'll be back in less than two hours."

"But you saw the burned-out Middle East Airlines planes scattered across the runway. The town has never been the same since. Armed patrols on the streets, guards at the University gates, fighting between the Christians and the Moslems, right here in the city."

"Screw that. I'm off. You coming or not?"

"Okay, Okay. I'll call and tell the beauties to meet us at the kebab restaurant at the end of Rue Bliss. If we're going to die, it might as well be in the arms of the lovely Maha and Bedouina." He dialed and spoke rapidly in Arabic.

"Shit," Matt said, searching for his windbreaker. "Why can't I pick up Arabic? I speak French like a native, thanks to my Mom, but that language totally baffles me."

"It's simple, blockhead." Samir laughed and punched his roommate. "By the way, I like these American terms you've taught me."

"So what's so simple?"

"Life is too easy here for you. French is one of the two official languages of Lebanon. And all the courses at the American University are taught in English. Do you really expect to learn Arabic?"

"It might help my love life."

"I'd say you're doing pretty well with Maha as it is." Samir said dryly. The relationship between Matt and Maha, a Jordanian with a fiery temper from an aristocratic family, couldn't last much longer. But he couldn't tell Matt.

Matt zipped his windbreaker. "Okay, it's 11 p.m., and I'm out of here. Put on a dark jacket. With all the street lamps smashed, we won't be spotted as we climb over the wall. Let's go, I'm starving."

A large red bougainvillea in full bloom provided the perfect ladder and concealment. They climbed over the high stone wall surrounding the university, carefully avoiding the broken glass imbedded along the top, and dropped to the street.

Samir grabbed Matt's collar. "Beirut may be the crossroads of the Middle East, but don't get killed crossing the street."

"God, this city mesmerizes me every time I step into these potholed, dusty streets. Smell the spices, the tang of the sea, the lamb roasting on charcoal?"

"You're just a hopeless romantic under that verneer of cynicism, roommate."

Matt sprinted across the busy street.

Dusty cars honked, dodging Matt and the other pedestrians. Cheap neon reflected off the windshields. Impatient bearded faces squinted against the glare. Everybody going somewhere. Above a modern cinema, a giant poster showed John Wayne in Green Beret fatigues. He looked down with his usual snarl. Matt pressed himself against a shop window. Several elderly men in long white robes passed by. He turned to look into the shop. The haute couture of Paris and Milan draped on headless mannequins teased Matt's student pocketbook. He slipped between sidewalk café tables, the thick aroma of espresso clinging to the air; animated conversations in French, Arabic and English competed with the horns of shiny Mercedes taxis and shouts of greetings. But the heady chaos was not only above the streets. Buried in deep vaults, the financial center of the Middle East kept pace with the activity above, bank notes rippling through counting machines, sterling, dollars, lire, and yen. Mounds of currency powered a vibrant trading economy, and unknown to most, it also powered a new industry, terrorism.

A FAINT BREEZE CARESSED HER CHEEK. A perfect crescent moon beckoned above the glassy Mediterranean. Maha Hammad sat facing the sea. Happiness and sorrow, anticipation and regret weighed upon her. She ran her long fingers through her red hair, coppery in the glow of the lights. The small table for four sat in the far corner of the cozy rooftop terrace overlooking the limestone cliffs of the Ras Beirut peninsula. It was here, in ancient times, that the Crusaders regrouped for their march into the Holy Land. It was the foursome's favorite meeting place.

"Where are those men? They're never on time." Bedouina's eyes narrowed, her dark black hair, cut short, stuck out at unruly angles. Intensity strained her face muscles. "They can't be late tonight, not tonight."

"Look, we've spent nearly three years at the School of Pharmacy studying like animals. Relax. It's almost over. Soon a new adventure will start."

Matt came up the terrace stairs, stopping in the doorway. He stared. "Oh my God. Can I ever get enough of just looking at her?" In the months following their first meeting last September, they had spent hours together learning about each other's lives and worlds. On the surface they were very different; at an inner level a deep connection and a strong bond of trust, respect and love bound them.

In contrast, there was Bedouina, a dark-skinned Palestinian with an even darker personality. Samir watched her. "She is tense tonight." He turned to Matt. "I promise we won't talk politics, not tonight."

"You say that every time, Samir, and somehow the two of you always climb on your soapboxes about one thing or another. I'm starved for food, not politics."

As the four of them talked Matt's hunger retreated. "How you guys eat all this great food and never get fat is a mystery to me," he said. Drippings from the lamb kebabs glistened on his chin. Maha used her to napkin to wipe them off. "Where am I gonna find tabouli and humus back in Boston? I may just wither away to nothing."

"I've got an idea." A devilish grin lit up Maha's lovely face. "Why not marry me and take me back with you? I'll be your official Middle Eastern chef, and I guarantee you'll never go hungry again, for anything."

"And your brothers would hunt you down." Bedouina sneered, shaking her dark mop at the foolish ideas of her Jordanian friend. "If only life were that simple. It would take a major cataclysm for our lives to deviate from the course Allah has set for us. You, Matt, will return to the United States and be a famous doctor. Maha will become a successful pharmacist back in Jordan and have a dozen kids from an arranged marriage."

Matt raised his arms in protest. "Whoa. This is the 20th century, not the Middle Ages. Maha is a modern woman, a pharmacist for Christ's sake, and the last thing she would agree to is an arranged marriage. Besides, I've got some ideas of my own for her." His arm gently caressed her shoulder. He planted an affectionate kiss on the forehead. Maha blushed.

"I dream of that," Maha sighed. "But actually, Bedouina is right; my fate has already been chosen." She looked at the moonlit sea. A tear glistened in the translucent light.

Matt changed the subject. "And what about you two?"

"Samir and I will die fighting to free Palestine, our rightful homeland, from the oppressive clutches of the expanding Zionist usurpers." Her words rushed out, a rote of unbreakable commitment.

"Hold it," Samir protested. "I believe in the freedom of Palestine. But I'm not ready to die just yet, not for a long time."

"Okay, time to go," Matt stood up. "Politics always ruins a good meal. It's getting late and we've all got to get ready for exams."

Bedouina shrugged, her ink-black eyes hard. "You Americans don't want to discuss anything serious, do you? Sometimes I wonder if America isn't just one big Disneyland."

They had all turned twenty-one during the school year. It was the beginning of adulthood, a turning point of their lives. And though Bedouina had suggested that soon they would part ways, Matt wasn't so sure. In the back of his mind, he sensed – beyond the question of what happened to him and Maha, and whether their love was strong enough to weather their differences – that their fates would be entwined for-ever. When, where, and how the four of them would cross paths in the future he couldn't foresee, but that didn't shake his hunch. Matt shiv-ered.

"You guys wait out front." Bedouina winked at Samir. "Maha and I need to freshen up. We'll be right out, and then you can walk us back to our dorms."

The glow from the Beirut nightlife reached up into the dark night, overpowering the smaller stars, but giving the larger celestial bodies an even more radiant glow. Waves from the warm Mediterranean Sea thudded against the cliff face like far-off ancient drummers sending out messages to distant gods. The sounds and smells of the vibrant exotic city filled Matt's memory to overflowing. He would never forget such wonderful evenings as this. Nor could he ever forget his special friends.

They crossed the street, Samir's hand on his shoulder in a sign of friendship. "We are so different, my friend, yet we have become so close. I know all about your family, your home, your hopes, your dreams. And I still like you." They both laughed.

"It's different for me, Samir. We talk about everything, yet I still don't understand your passion about this Palestinian thing. The Middle East is only a small part of the world. There's so much else going on that's positive and exciting."

"Yeah, like Vietnam."

"Well, besides that," shrugged Matt.

"This area may be just a small region at the moment, but if some-thing isn't done, then more and more people will be evicted from their homes, their land, their roots. All with the blessing of the western nations. It may even reach you in America. Disneyland would never be the same."

They approached a tall stone wall, parts of which were said to contain carved blocks from the original 12th century Crusader fortress in the Ras Beirut area. The twisted branches of a fragrant plumeria tree, bursting with waxy yellow flowers, spread over the wall from someone's garden on the other side.

"How long does it take to powder a nose?" Samir said, nervously glancing up and down the street. He checked the luminous dial on his wristwatch. "I'm going to hurry them up. You wait here." He walked across the street.

Matt inhaled the heady fragrance of the plumeria blossoms. The rich meal and the city lights added to his comfort and contentment. He watched Samir step onto the far sidewalk.

The door handle seemed jammed. Samir pulled harder. The flash came first, followed by searing heat, then the shock wave. The front of the restaurant burst into orange flame, and then disintegrated. For years afterwards, Matt's nightmares would replay over and over the scene as his roommate's hand tugged on the restaurant door. It couldn't have lasted more than a second, the deafening explosion and the brilliant flash, just before the huge orange ball of fire. Samir's high-pitched scream disappeared as he vaporized.

Matt couldn't move or cry out. Samir's death wail reached his ears, and his fiery image shimmered behind his closed eyes. Then the force of the shock wave hurled him against the stone wall. He lay unconscious and bleeding.

Chapter Three

Bald Eagle Estate, Blue Ridge Mountains

"THERE'S THE ENTRANCE TO THE CLINIC. Keep going, the Egyptian's estate is a half mile ahead. And slow down, the ice on this road is tricky at this hour of the morning." The ambassador sat back into the plush seat and looked out the darkened, bullet-proof windows. The driver and bodyguard, both armed, concentrated on the road ahead.

Turning left, they were waved through the gate, the guard not even coming out of his warm hut. "Wow, what a fortress." The body-guard studied the layout. "Most eyes would miss the electronic bullocks and tire-shredding spikes submerged in the road."

"You two know the drill," the ambassador said, buttoning his coat. "Park the car and wait. And keep on the alert. I should be only a half hour or so." His look skewered the driver. "And maintain radio silence. We're not officially here."

"Yes, sir."

The ambassador opened the door. A cold blast of morning air made him shiver. He hated the estate.

"Welcome, my friend," said Mohammed al Nagib, still in his warm-up suit, his white hair bright in the sun. "On time as usual." They shook hands stiffly.

"I see you've been out for a walk."

"As always. It gets the juices flowing and wakes up the brain cells. Must keep our wits about us during these, shall I say, interesting times."

"And your dogs? For protection?"

Al Nagib smiled. "Good companions. They never offer opinions, just loyalty."

"Such odd names," replied the ambassador, cocking his head. "Rough and Tumble."

"A little whimsy on my part." The host gestured toward the large double door. "Shall we go inside? On a crisp day like this, some hot Arabic coffee is in order. Or should I say Middle Eastern coffee?"

The Israeli ambassador to the United States looked back at his car, now tucked into a small space just next to the circular driveway.

"Ah. You are looking at my statue. Magnificent, isn't it?" The thirteen-foot bronze bald eagle, wings outstretched in full flight, dominated the circular driveway. Its wingtips shimmered in the brilliant cold sunlight. "It's the American symbol of liberty and freedom. Although Benjamin Franklin argued strongly that the turkey should be the national bird. Perhaps he was prescient." They both laughed, turned, and walked into the main house.

The warm, inviting aroma of bacon and eggs drifted in from the kitchen, just to the left. Silverware clattered. A maid giggled. Inside the colonial period breakfast room, the ambassador, a former Israeli Army general, pulled out a small electronic device, turned it on and slowly swept through a full 360-degree circle. All three lights remained green. He smiled, and then sat down opposite his host.

"We both have much to hide, Mr. Ambassador," said his Egyptian-American host. "Sadly, that is the way of the world. Politics makes strange bedfellows, and in our case, very strange indeed."

"On that we can easily agree."

"Let me assure you, you have nothing to fear here in my home. This room isn't bugged and we are perfectly alone."

"As per our agreement," nodded the Israeli, his back ramrod straight.

"I prefer the old-fashioned type of meetings," Nagib smiled, "where two people, both with as much to gain as to lose, look each other squarely in the eyes, make commitments, and keep them.

Nothing could be simpler, and it seems in today's crazy world, nothing could be more difficult."

Al Nagib picked up the silver pot. Steam furled from the spout. "Coffee, Mr. Ambassador?"

"Thank you, Mr. Nagib." He took a small sip of the thick aromatic coffee. "As always, excellent." The small cup met the saucer with a delicate *chink*.

"I asked for this brief meeting to make certain that everything was in order before we consummate our arrangement. I too believe in looking my partners, as well as my victims, directly in the eye. Is everything ready at the clinic?"

"Thanks to my modest funding and your exceptionally talented physicians, the new private wing at the clinic is ready and waiting. Tonight's reception in Washington will provide the occasion to welcome our first guests to the private wing."

"Splendid."

"Why thank you, Mr. Ambassador. And of course I have no need to worry that you have a firm commitment from the senator?" Nagib passed a large bowl of dried dates and figs.

"He is most anxious to support the cause of the United States against those who threaten its borders and its people. And he already has the first deposit in his new Swiss bank account. Ah," the ambassador held a date up, admiring it, "Medjoul dates from Jordan. We have a hard time getting them in Israel."

"Then this unruly terrorist cell will be discovered by your people?"

"There is an excellent possibility. And if all goes well, it will soon be under our control." The ambassador savored the sweet dried fruit.

"It is good that we have a common goal," Nagib said. "It proves that Israelis and Arabs can work together."

The Israeli's eyes narrowed. "Do not delude yourself, Mr. Nagib. My purpose is to safeguard the nation of Israel, at any cost. Your only purpose is profit."

A glass shattered in the kitchen. The ambassador turned with a start. Al Nagib remained motionless.

"Perhaps we differ in motivation, but not in the end result," the host laughed nervously, standing up to escort his guest out. The ambassador's car crept forward. As they walked out the front door, another cold blast of air buffeted the general. He shivered more deeply this time. The bodyguard held the door as the ambassador turned and nodded farewell. Mohammed al Nagib replied with a faint wave, then returned to the breakfast room.

"Demetrie?" Al Nagib's voice echoed.

Demetrie Antonopolis, brown hair tied back in a long ponytail, stepped through the glass doors facing the enormous garden. "I got every word clear as a bell from the pool house," he announced. "These new laser directional microphones are remarkable."

The Egyptian stared at the aging perpetual adolescent, international playboy, and professional assassin. "Process and file it with the other recordings, and send digitized copies via our secure network to the others." Nagib watched him closely. "We'll be leaving for London this afternoon. Make certain the Falcon is fueled and ready, and don't be late this time. And for your own sake, leave that hashish at home. If it weren't for your father, I'd consider you more of a liability than an asset."

Virginia, US Route 29

THE BRIGHT YELLOW PORSCHE BOXTER sped northeast through the afternoon haze toward Washington, D.C. Matt Richards sat slumped down in the narrow passenger seat, brooding.

"Please remember, Ms. Stevens, that I'm attending this stupid shindig under formal protest," he said above the revving engine. "And for Christ's sake, slow down. Porsches fly well, but they don't land worth a shit." Matt glanced over at his ardent admirer and secret lover, her hand firmly on the steering wheel. The wind whistled about the small car's windows.

"But Professor Richards," Kelly grinned, "you look so dashing in that tuxedo. Just like Harrison Ford, only more rugged."

This affair is absurd. Yet he needed company. Someone to hold him, to help him make it through the lonely evenings before the

Scotch took over, keeping the memories at bay. Images, past and present, cascaded like flickering TV screens across his brain.

"And I'm so excited about this evening," she said. "I want to get to the reception early to show you off to all the politicians and society people."

"The only good politicians are the ones in jail for life. And remind me again why we're going to a reception for the new personal physician to the president of the United States?"

"Because my daddy insisted I come along. He said it would be good for me to meet some of the VIPs there. Especially since I graduate this spring and his embassy friends can help me get a job." Tires squealed as they snaked around another sharp corner. "Besides, he wants to meet my new boyfriend."

"You told your father about me? Are you out of your sweet little mind? The illustrious senator from Virginia, Mason T. Stevens? He's one of the longest-serving members of Congress, chairman of the Senate Select Committee on Intelligence, and a very mean political son-of-a-bitch. You told him about us?"

"Yes."

"Jesus, Kelly. Think it through, for God's sake. He's going to kick my ass the moment he sees me. And he won't even have to get his hands dirty. He's got hundreds of professional assassins at his beck and call."

"Don't be so melodramatic." The engine purred as she downshifted through the gears. "You'll charm him, just like you did me. Besides, what can he do? I'm free, white and twenty-one."

As she pretended to pout, Matt asked himself again why he was so enchanted by her youthful vigor and naiveté. Or was he just an alcohol-soaked dirty old man? No, in many ways she reminded him of himself some thirty-odd years ago as he prepared to venture forth to Beirut, Lebanon—lifetimes ago, and a whole lot of empty Scotch bottles by the wayside.

"Famous last words, Ms. Stevens," he said. "Like those uttered by the historically insignificant and long forgotten General Spottswood. And I quote: 'Don't worry men. Their cannons couldn't hit the broadside of an elephant at this dist—.'" They both laughed. Matt gripped the armrest. "Now slow down. I'd rather die running from assassins than strapped into a pocket rocket going up in flames."

The late February afternoon faded to twilight as they crossed the Francis Scott Key Bridge. The Boxter wound its way through tree-lined residential streets into the exclusive community of Potomac. Lights in the large mansions set back from the road were just coming on. By the time they reached their destination, the home of the chairman of the National Institute of Health, it was dark.

"Now *this* is a palace." Matt muttered as Kelly gave the marine guard their invitation. "So who's the host?"

"Dr. Martin Thomas is an African-American Ph.D., a specialist in genetic research." She tucked a loose strand of blond hair behind her ear. "He founded several successful biotech companies and earned a ton of money before he entered politics. He's a heavy contributor to the Republican party." Kelly glanced over at Matt. "And I might add, a regular golfing buddy of my father's."

The Georgian mansion was set back from the road and surrounded by an immense lawn, brilliantly lit up for the evening affair. The yellow Porsche caught the light as they pulled up under the grand portico. It stood out among the sleek black and gray limousines.

Matt watched the limos discreetly deliver well-dressed elderly couples. "You know, these people could probably buy two or three of these mansions out of petty cash."

Kelly inspected her lipstick in the visor mirror. "What's eating you?"

"What are you talking about?"

"You've gone into one of your moods."

"Okay. I was just mulling over your African-American Ph.D."

"What are you talking about?" She stole a quick glance back into the mirror to check her lipstick.

"Well, I knew a Dr. Martin Thomas once. A long time ago. But I doubt if they're the same."

"Fine. Can we go now?"

MATT RELEASED HIS TIGHT SEAT BELT. "Well, whoever he is, by the looks of the obvious marine guards and the not-so-obvious Secret Service agents, this is going to be a well-attended and well-armed soirée. Just what I need in my life, more idiots with guns and attitudes."

Matt waved away the young marine in dress uniform about to open the car door for him. Kelly placed her hand on his shoulder. "Now, behave yourself and have a good time."

"Where's the bar?"

"Mingle and make small talk."

"That's what I do best."

"And please don't drink too much," Kelly bit her lip. "When I spoke to daddy this morning he wasn't in a great mood—try not to get into trouble."

"Who, me?"

"Remember your award-winning performance at the faculty party in September?"

"I'm trying to forget, thank you very much."

"Well, just do the opposite tonight and everything will be fine." She kissed him again and they both unfolded from the sports car.

Up ahead, a tall attractive woman was arguing with one of the security guards at the front door. Matt and Kelly passed easily through, showing their invitation and then moving up for a thorough and meticulous security check before entering. The woman stepped into the line behind Matt.

"No respect for the press." Her words spat out. "Even though I'm a real guest this time."

Matt turned around. He was nearly six foot tall. Their eyes met evenly. She was in her early to mid-forties, with light auburn hair piled on top of her head. Around her neck she wore a large diamond cross. Its ornate design reminded him of crosses he had seen on Coptic and Armenian churches in Lebanon and Egypt. Her nose, slightly too large for her face, somehow made her more attractive.

"The receiving line is through the left in the great room," a stocky marine lieutenant said after checking Kelly's purse. Matt and Kelly passed through the arch of the metal detector, which remained silent. Another marine admired the buxom young girl with a man more than twice her age. He raised his eyebrows, then firmly but politely suggested they move along so other guests could enter the hallway. Matt gave the marine a cheesy grin and followed Kelly toward the reception line. Behind him he could hear the same woman complaining again. "It's just my digital camera. Want me to take your picture?"

"This really is a unique appointment, you know?" A heavily bejeweled matronly woman stood in front of them, tugging on her husband's sleeve. "It was a very courageous move on the part of the president. Finally someone is trying to do the right thing and show some conciliation."

"Quiet, Grace, we're almost there." He eased her hand away.

"Well I'm just saying—"

"It's a pandering political appointment." His voice lowered to a whisper. "And the Jews are mad as hell."

Matt spotted Senator Mason T. Stevens up ahead in the reception line. Tall, slightly stooped, with shock white hair and a theatrical profile. At one time he must have cut a dashing figure as an up-and-coming politician. But the heavy travel, lack of exercise and far too many late night meals had extended his girth. The long hours on the golf course had turned his skin leathery.

"Well, if it isn't my lovely little girl," the senator said, when Kelly approached. "You've grown since I saw you last. Have you matured as well?" He offered his practiced political smile, at once urbane and warm, then kissed his daughter on the cheek. "I'm glad you decided to listen to your father for once. There are lots of people here I want to introduce you to."

Matt held back in line to observe the famous father and head-strong daughter. He remembered how his father would lecture him and his elder brother Sam about the benefits of hard work and respecting your elders—but this was different. Under patented smiles and feigned warmth, there was a steely, almost threatening edge to the senator's voice.

"And you must be Dr. Richards," the senator said, glancing his way. "I look forward to speaking with you a little later in the evening. I'm certain I'll find you hanging around the bar."

Matt, realizing he had been inspected, found lacking, and summarily dismissed, held his tongue.

"Matt? Dr. Matthew Richards? Is that you?" The elderly Dr. Thomas extended his hand. "I haven't seen or heard from you since Beirut. How are you, my boy? And what's your father doing these days?"

"Good to see you, Dr. Thomas," Matt said. "Dad's retired now, as you probably know. And thoroughly enjoying himself. In fact, I haven't seen him in two years. He's busy fly fishing in South America at the moment, I believe."

"I'm sorry to hear about your brother Samuel. He was a fine doctor and an excellent humanitarian. The world will miss him."

Matt was sorry too. Sam had always been the one who kept him from going off the deep end. Too late now. The deep end was where he lived.

"And what are you up to these days, Matthew?"

"I'm retired too, sort of. Just doing some college teaching at the moment." He felt claustrophobic in the tuxedo and the crowded room. "You'll have to excuse me. I hope we can talk a little later, maybe catch up on Beirut days?" He broke away and headed for the bar, leaving Kelly floating along through the receiving line, chatting excitedly with numerous dignitaries. Perspiration broke out on his upper lip. Why were these damned functions always so hot and stuffy? He reached down for the handkerchief that wasn't there.

The bar was located in the oak-paneled library. He quickly ordered a double Scotch, neat. The scotch swirled around the glass as his hands shook. A bad sign for a surgeon, but then he hadn't been in an operating theater for almost ten years. "I'm not even sure I ever was a real doctor," he said to no one in particular. He took a long sip from the crystal tumbler. The liquor began to work its magic, beating back the gremlins from his past.

"You seem to be enjoying that." A soft feminine voice from behind. "Can you order me one as well? Only much smaller, if you don't mind." The auburn-haired journalist came up beside him at the bar. A seductive fragrance of perfume mixed with the scent of warm skin reached him. "And whom do I have the pleasure of drinking with?"

"Richards. Dr. Matt Richards. I'm a professor at Sweet Briar College in Virginia," he said. His extended hand shook slightly.

"Nicole Delacluse, from the *International Herald Tribune*. I actually have a real invitation—I'm not here to snoop. But you never know. Leopards don't change their spots very easily." She belted down her drink, then gently placed the tumbler on the bar, her eyes locked onto his. "One needs a little reinforcement before mingling with this crowd," she said, drifting away as quietly as she had arrived.

Matt watched her weave through the throng, then drained his glass and ordered another. She was right, of course. You did need a little reinforcement with this crowd. But this wasn't his crowd. His had been Samir, Maha and Bedouina. And a long time ago, 1969, when they had discussed life, love, the future, and damned-politics beside the Mediterranean under twinkling stars. When Maha had offered her exquisite beauty.

He began to shake. Images of the female assassin, frozen on the TV screen, assaulted his mind. Blinding. Searing. Pleading. Bringing up old fears. The ice rattled against crystal. Why was this happening again? Matt took a deep breath.

The deaths of Samir, Maha and Bedouina in 1969 had destroyed his youthful naiveté. His self-confidence evaporated along with his friends. But however badly the explosion cracked his soul, on the surface at least he seemed to recover. Back in the States he was quickly caught up in the academic grind of his senior year at Harvard. An excellent student, he had his choice of several outstanding medical schools. "Not a real choice," he thought. There was no question he would attend Harvard Medical School, where his father had gone, and from which, just a few years earlier, his brother Sam had graduated.

"I should have made an effort. I should have tried to get closer to Sam." He spoke into his empty tumbler, his reverie now traveling a well-worn path. Not overly close, Matt and Sam rarely spoke as they went about building their professional lives. The first, last and only letter Matt ever received from Sam was postmarked Santarem, Brazil. After a distinguished career in orthopedic surgery, Sam informed everyone that he was resigning from his medical practice in Seattle and joining a Jesuit medical organization called Esperança, which meant 'Hope' in Portuguese. After years of fixing bones for the rich and famous, he wanted to do something for the poor of the world. Esperança ran a hospital boat up and down the Amazon River. On board was a small operating theater where visiting physicians from the United States donated their expertise to fix cleft pallets, deformed

hips, club feet and other surgical problems. In addition, the organization trained nurses and healthcare workers to deliver primary and secondary care in the remote regions of the Amazon.

A burst of laughter erupted from the hallway. Matt jarred from
his mental meandering, then gulped down another drink. He looked
down at the polished bar. The letter ....

He recalled it was written only a few days before Sam's death.
He'd been helping secure the ship at a remote village when he fell
overboard and was crushed between the hull and wooden dock. The
letter was full of enthusiasm. "I've finally found a home," it began, in
Sam's neat script, so unlike a physician's typical scrawl. "The Esperança
organization has shown me there is much more to medicine than healing wealthy patients and writing articles for medical journals. At last I
feel as if I'm doing something worthwhile. And it suits my personality.
I never liked the doctor cocktail circuit."

Matt had read the letter with shock. His older brother, like Matt
himself, had labored under the burden of their father's high expectations. Unknown to each other, they had both borne the intense pressure to succeed in the lofty circles of medical greatness in stoic and
lonely silence.

Matt never showed the letter to his father. It would have sparked
an ugly discussion and he wasn't certain he had the courage, or the
confidence, to really speak his mind. But Sam's death crystallized a
growing uncertainty about his own path in life. A bitter divorce, and
having no one to talk to, sent him to seek sanctuary in a bottle of
Scotch. It was social at first. Then the crush of loneliness took his legs
out from under him. He quickly slid into insecurity and then depression. The pain of the past descended. Why didn't he have the same
courage as Sam? He kept asking himself that as his career took a bob-
sled ride downhill. After two botched operations in a row, his partners
in their successful Chicago medical practice gently but firmly eased
him out.

When he was on his fourth drink—or was it his fifth?—two arms
encircled his chest. "There you are, I missed you." Kelly whispered in
his ear, then flicked her tongue in and out quickly. Matt jerked his
head away, now fully back in the present.

"Are you behaving yourself?" Kelly went on. "I've just had the most interesting conversation with a gentleman from the U.S. Foreign Service. He said I would be the perfect candidate for an embassy job somewhere in the world. He even gave me his card." She held up the small white business card with the seal of the United States of America embossed on it.

Matt put down his empty glass. "You know what I wish?"

"What?" Her breasts pressed into his back.

"I wish you would stay at this age, just as you are, forever."

"But I want to grow older. Get a job. Make a difference. I've got to prove myself." She moved around to face him. Her face showed both defiance and hurt.

"What you don't appreciate, at your tender age, is that only pain, suffering and betrayal lie ahead. In a few years, out there," he jerked his thumb to indicate the crowd in the room, "you'll become like all the rest of us. Cynical, distrustful, and resentful."

"Oh Christ. You're drunk." Kelly looked around nervously. No one was paying attention. She looked over at the entrance to the ballroom.

"Come on, we have to hurry, they're going to introduce the guest of honor." She pulled on his arm and led him into the grand salon. He concentrated on walking.

"Holy shit. It's big enough to be a conference center." Matt found a spot near the buffet table along a far wall. From here they had a clear view of a lectern set up in front of the large bay window overlooking the back lawn. He gulped down a caviar canapé. His fingers smelled of fish. The rest of the guests noisily filed in. The room buzzed with expectation. Someone dropped a glass. Secret Service agents turned with a start, scanning the crowd. The Marines, stationed next to all the doors and windows, stiffened.

A hush descended over the crowd as Dr. Thomas stepped up to the lectern, which was emblazoned with the seal of the president of the United States. "Ladies and gentlemen, I'm pleased you were able to accept my personal invitation this evening to what I believe is a very special event." He paused as more people entered the already crowded room.

"As you know, many of us here this evening knew Dr. Andrew Norman personally, and our heartfelt prayers and wishes go out to his family. He was a unique individual, an outstanding physician, and a long-time friend of President Pierce and the first family.

"Dr. Norman carried out his duties as personal physician to the president of the United States with the utmost discretion and professionalism. Yet, in a twisted and savage act of terrorism his life, along with the lives of dozens of other fine men and women of the United States, was destroyed. But no act of terrorism, even this one on American soil, can stop the quest for freedom that all civilized individuals crave. The freedom to choose their own career, their own religion, to have access to education for their children, to receive adequate health care, to live in a secure home safe from outside threats and usurpers—to choose their own lifestyle. These are just some of the freedoms that make all of us here tonight dedicated to the noble American vision of democracy and world peace."

Matt looked around. The elderly crowd stood respectfully. Claustrophobia closed in on him again. He pulled at his bow tie. His breath was turning stale from the oily caviar and the scotch. He gulped down a half-empty glass of punch. The former owner had worn bright maroon lipstick.

Dr. Thomas lowered his voice. "Without this precious freedom, a young African-American boy, the fifth son of a poor but proud steelworker from Pittsburgh, could never have realized his dream of becoming a Ph.D. and a professor of genetics. Whatever my race, religion or economic background, this great country afforded me that opportunity. And we must continue to protect these freedoms." The assembled crowd clapped loudly. The sound assaulted Matt's senses.

"So this evening, I'm pleased to host this reception for the new personal physician to the president of the United States, Dr. Noubar Melikian. As you all know, this is a somewhat controversial appointment by the president. But it's one which I believe displays President Pierce's true greatness and courage.

"Some of my less visionary colleagues, and several loud voices in Washington and the press, say that appointing someone from the Middle East to such a sensitive position, especially in the wake of recent events, is political grandstanding. But to my mind, such an appointment rises above politics and petty prejudices. In fact, if we really want peace in all corners of the world, then the United States must take the lead in showing the decent people of the Middle East and the rest of the world that it is not them we are fighting against, but the terrorists, whoever they are and wherever they come from." Again a loud burst of applause.

Matt groaned. Kelly grabbed his arm tightly and glared.

"Dr. Melikian, who has practiced for the past twenty-five years in the Washington metro area, is eminently qualified for this position. He is a highly respected physician and a recognized specialist in skin cancer, a longstanding member of the AMA, an outstanding humanitarian and a vociferous advocate of a peaceful solution to the problems in the Middle East. Without further ado, it is my great honor to present Dr. Noubar Melikian."

Dr. Thomas stood aside as the robust, white-haired doctor stepped up onto the podium. As the African-American and the Armenian-American shook hands and then kissed on the cheek, Middle Eastern style, the room roared its approval.

Matt moved with a start. Kelly whispered. "What's wrong? You're not about to throw up, are you?"

"I'm okay. I just thought I recognized that man for a moment. But I guess not, or maybe I saw him at a medical convention some time ago." Kelly listened to the lie.

Dr. Melikian faced the crowd, his eyes twinkling as he held out his hand urging them to stop the applause. The warm welcome subsided. Dr. Melikian took a small sip of water. Then he looked up, excitement burning in his eyes.

"It's a great honor to be here this evening. But I must first thank our host, Dr. Martin Thomas, a colleague and friend, for supporting my appointment to this post. In fact, it was Dr. Thomas and several of his esteemed colleagues, along with my good friend Senator Mason Stevens, who initially urged me to consider this appointment. At first, I must admit I was skeptical. But their arguments eventually convinced me to take them seriously.

"Who would have ever thought that an Armenian boy who grew up in the nation of Palestine would ever be able to serve the world in such a meaningful manner? I thoroughly enjoy being a physician, but like all of you, I am also many other things—a husband, the father of three wonderful children, but not yet a grandfather, thank goodness." The crowd laughed. "I am a dedicated and hard-working physician. Too hard working says my wife." A few snickers of understanding and acknowledgment bubbled forth from the crowd, heavily populated with doctors and their spouses.

"And I am also an Armenian, born and raised in the Middle East. And to me that is very important. None of us can deny, nor should we, our heritage. It is the DNA of our past, present and future. Like many of your ancestors, mine suffered greatly. Between 1915 and 1923, over 1.5 million Armenians perished at the hands of the Ottoman Empire, nearly three-quarters of the population of my tiny country. And this horrible eradication of a nation was barely noticed. In fact, Adolph Hitler used the Armenian genocide in persuading his followers that a Jewish holocaust would be tolerated by the West. Who, after all, speaks today of the annihilation of the Armenians?" he asked.

Matt listened to the murmurs of acknowledgement and under-standing. "Pretty effective public speaker for a doctor." Kelly glared at him again. He looked down as Kelly turned back to listen. Matt slow-ly edged around the table, nodded at the Marine, and stepped out onto a terrace. The fresh air revived him a little. The doctor's speech could still be heard.

"Because of what is now called the first genocide of the modern age, Armenians all over the world are committed to opposing racism, bigotry and prejudice, wherever they exist. And like my Jewish broth-ers, who also know the horrors of genocide, our suffering has made us stubbornly passionate about freedom, liberty, and the personal respon-sibility that goes with these precious gifts." There were open expres-sions of agreement from the large Jewish population of doctors and other professionals in the crowded room.

"And I am also a Christian. Most people don't realize that in 314 A.D. Armenia became the first country in the world to declare itself a Christian nation. Everywhere Armenians fled during centuries of per-secution, they took the Christian faith with them. Even today there are pockets of Armenian Christians in Syria, Jordan, Iran, Iraq, Jerusalem, Lebanon, and the United States, where we have established over one hundred Maronite Christian churches.

"And most proudly, I am an American. I became a U.S. citizen two years after moving to Washington from Switzerland, where I studied medicine. It was one of the proudest days of my life, as I stood among other immigrants from all corners of the globe reciting the oath of citizenship and pledging allegiance to the flag of the United States of America. My wife and children are natural-born Americans. And I would venture to say that I am a pretty typical American. I have three cars, two dogs and a mortgage. Too big a mortgage for my liking." The crowd laughed its approval.

Matt walked back into the room. The voice was vaguely familiar. It bothered him, like the buzz of a mosquito, distant then near, close then retreating. Kelly took his arm again, this time tenderly.

"But there is no denying that I am also a man of the Middle East. I was born in what was then known as the state of Palestine. I grew up with Muslims, Christians, and Jews as my playmates. We stole candy and smoked our first cigarettes together. I hated the taste." He made a face which drew forth chuckles. "A good thing, too, because nowadays in America it's practically a crime to even think about smoking." The doctors in the room roared with laughter.

"Seriously, being from the Middle East gives me a unique vantage point in Washington, because I understand many of the feelings of the Arab world concerning today's precarious global and political situation. Only the insane want war and killing. Yet somehow a small yet active minority of terrorists have continued to drive a wedge deeper and deeper between the peace-loving peoples of the Middle East and the West. It is time this wedge was torn out and replaced with strong sutures sewn by skillful and dedicated hands.

"I've dedicated my life to two things: healing the sick and working toward a peaceful solution in the Middle East. I will continue to carry out these two commitments in my new post as personal physician to the president of the United States. Thank you for your encouragement and support."

Amid generous applause, a loud female voice caught the attention of the speaker. "Dr. Melikian? That was a tremendous and, I must say, moving speech. Can I ask just one or two questions?"

"I'm afraid I didn't expect a question-and-answer session and I'm not very experienced in these matters," he said. "I'm sorry, I don't even know your name."

"Delacluse. Nicole Delacluse of the *International Herald Tribune*, although I'm not here in an official capacity tonight," she was quick to add. "This is an important appointment by the president, and as you've said, there are skeptics. Is it true, Dr. Melikian, that you received several death threats after it was announced that you were one of those being considered for this position?"

"The truth is yes, but I'm not at liberty to say much about it other than that I'm not too concerned. It seems rock stars and TV news commentators are in much more danger from deranged individuals than I am."

"And is it true you've hired a security service to protect yourself and your family?" she said quickly, catching him slightly off guard.

"That's not quite accurate, Ms. Delacluse. The Secret Service, in recognition of the recent tragedy, has provided my family with a certain measure of security. That is what the president wanted, so of course I agreed. Now, since this is a reception and not a press conference, thank goodness, I'll turn my attention to the guests here this evening. But when I do have my first official press conference, I hope all the journalists are as professional as you." It was a polite but firm dismissal, after which Dr. Melikian shook hands with Dr. Martin Thomas and stepped down.

At the edge of the makeshift podium, Senator Stevens discreetly pulled over two men in dark suits for an animated conversation. They kept glancing in the direction of Matt Richards. The crowd had now descended upon the buffet table. Matt was slowly pushed to the side by the crowd. Presently the men nodded to Stevens and moved off. The portly senator stepped down and began working the crowd.

"Miss Stevens? Dr. Richards? The Senator would like a few private words with you both. Please follow me." A nondescript man in a nondescript gray suit stood in front of them. They nodded, sharing quizzical glances. Matt and Kelly followed him down the hallway, through an open door and into a dimly lit study. Persian carpets and red velvet curtains added to the richness of antique oak furniture. Ornate wall sconces offered hazy shadows. The walls were lined with books, diplomas and photos of Dr. Thomas with numerous dignitaries. Matt surmised this was Dr. Thomas's personal office. He wondered how many hours he spent here. The place was certainly conducive to relaxation and reflection. And it reeked of power.

The door closed solidly behind then. A gravelly voice from the far corner of the room boomed out. Senator Mason T. Stevens, his face red, stepped out of the shadows toward the center of the room. He pressed a button on a side table and the lights came up to full strength. Both Matt and Kelly squinted.

"So," Stevens said, "you're not only a cradle robber and a disgrace to the medical profession, Dr. Richards, you're a goddamned drunk as well." Shaking, he moved forward until he pressed up against Matt, backing him into the large desk of Dr. Thomas.

"Daddy, stop it. What's gotten into you? Can't we talk about this some other time? Please, Daddy?"

"You shut up." The senator's words tumbled out, but his eyes kept boring into Matt. "I'll deal with you later, young lady. You've had too damn much freedom at that sissy girl's school, and now you've gone way overboard. I've heard all about your drinking, the drugs, and now your affair with this loser. I've a mind to yank you out of that school for your own good." Kelly's tears caught the light. She collapsed onto the sofa.

"You fat son-of-a-bitch," Matt grated. The esteemed senior senator from the great State of Virginia never saw the roundhouse left that knocked him to the floor. Matt stood in a half-drunk stupor, hardly registering the pain where his knuckles had collided with the senator's teeth.

Kelly jumped up. "Daddy? Daddy? Oh God. What have you done? Get away from him." She pushed at Matt, then knelt on the floor, trying to stem the blood from her father's nose.

Secret Service agents and Marine guards materialized. Matt was gripped firmly from behind. He glared at them.

"Get the hell away from me. This is none of your business," he shouted. "I'm leaving anyway. You better attend to Mr. Big Mouth. His big nose is bleeding all over the expensive Persian carpet." When they let go he grabbed Kelly's hand, and started weaving toward the door. Kelly hesitated, gazed worriedly at her father on the floor, then helped Matt maneuver down the hall towards the front door. Her father's verbal onslaught and abuse still rang in her ears. She pulled away for an instant, then made her decision.

The Porsche was parked under the portico. The parking attendant quickly produced the keys. He gave the keys to Kelly, and the two of them helped ease a wobbly Dr. Matt Richards into the passenger seat. The attendant buckled the seatbelt. As the sports car turned left out of the big iron gates, a late model black Pontiac with tinted windows followed a safe distance behind.

"Well, Dr. Richards, you really are something, you know? Not only do you get stinking drunk, but you knock my father down. Why didn't you just screw an ambassador's wife or something? Then no one would have even noticed or probably cared." But her words fell on deaf ears—Matt was out cold, head slumped against her shoulder.

Turning onto the George Washington Parkway, the Porsche sped west, intending to link up with I-95 and the main road back to central Virginia. The parkway, a major commuter artery into and out of Washington, was nearly deserted at 10:45 p.m. The road was edged on one side by trees and forest, on the other by the Potomac River, which was at its high watermark from all the rain and snow that had descended on the area in recent days.

Kelly shoved him with her shoulder. "Matt, wake up. Someone's following us, wake up." After two more pushes she heard a moan, then a familiar, "God damn son-of-a-bitch. What time is it?"

"Thank God you're awake. A car has been following us ever since we left the reception."

"So?" he bent his neck from side to side to work out some of the kinks.

"It keeps getting closer."

Matt looked down and struggled with his seat belt. *I hate being confined.* It released with a strong click. "Goddamn belt. Now what were you saying?"

The black Pontiac roared up behind the sports car and banged its bumper into the rear fender. The little car lurched. "What's happening?" Kelly screamed. "I can't steer. They're trying to force us off the road."

Adrenaline pulled Matt around. When the second jolt came it was more forceful, more threatening.

"Speed up, Kelly," he said, gripping the headrest. "Drive as fast as you can."

She jammed down hard on the accelerator. "Jesus Matt...."

"Now listen to me," Matt said slowly. "When I tell you to slow down, do it quickly—*very* quickly, just short of slamming on the brakes. But don't slam on the brakes or we'll skid out of control. Just press down forcefully. At the same time, try to hold us in the center of the road. Do you understand?"

She was gripping the steering wheel, eyes on the road. "But what if they rear-end—"

"Do you understand?"

"Okay. Okay. Just don't shout." Her hands shook as she gripped the wheel.

"Do what I say. You have to trust me. Do you understand?"

Kelly nodded. Her face was a ghostly white.

Matt looked out the rear window. "Get ready. Alright then, now… *slow down.*"

She geared down hard and applied the brakes at the same time. The rapid deceleration caught the Pontiac off guard. It swerved, skidded back and forth, then slid off the road. Matt glimpsed the driver, his face contorted, trying to regain control, but it was too late. The car crashed through the guardrail and went rolling down the steep bank. Kelly screamed and floored the car. The black Pontiac plunged into the dark swirling waters of the Potomac.

"Okay, Okay. Let up, let up." Matt yelled, but her foot stayed hard down.

"I want to go home." Her upper lip quivered. "First you hit my father and now someone's trying to kill us." The car tore ahead, weaving back and forth.

Matt reached over. "For God's sake Kelly, slow down...."

She screamed, her eyes wide. Two large cars blocked the road. Men in dark suits with flashlights frantically signaled them to stop. Kelly panicked and slammed down hard on the brakes. Matt smashed into the windshield, then ricocheted back against the passenger seat. The last thing he heard before losing consciousness was the high-pitched squeal of Pirelli tires sliding sideways.

Chapter Four

Orly Airport, Paris, August, 1968

"THERE'S THE SIGN: '*AUB Junior Year Abroad Program*,'" Matt said. He and Todd Cummings, both from Harvard University, had traveled together from Boston to the meeting place at Orly Airport for the official beginning of their year-long adventure.

"Think the living conditions will be as good as Harvard?"

"Who cares? This is our year to live it up. See and do everything. To really live life." Matt punched his friend playfully.

"Yeah. Well I'm here because you wanted a familiar face around. And my parents thought it would be good for me to see the world a little. But I'm still not sure this is a good idea. I mean, being away from Harvard for a whole year. What if we don't learn anything?"

"Look, Todd. I know I talked you into coming along on this Junior Year Abroad program. But think of the things we can see and do. This is about as far away from Massachusetts as you can get. And I don't just mean in miles. What kind of students do you think have signed up for this year?" Matt eagerly strained his neck to look at the students milling about ahead.

Todd followed Matt through the crowded waiting area. "I hope they're not just a bunch of rich dope heads getting away from their parents for a year."

Matt laughed. "Don't be such a cynic, Todd. Not everyone in the world is as serious as you are, thank God. This is our year to really live life. 'See all and do all,' that's my motto for this year. It would be a relief to talk to a few beery souls after spending four days in Paris with you. I've seen enough museums to last a lifetime."

Matt slapped his traveling companion on the back good-naturedly. "Come on, Todd, let's go meet the others."

On the other side of the waiting area they could see a small group of students clustered around a banner. A short black man with horn-rim glasses and a pipe was at the center of the group.

"That must be Dr. Thomas." Todd moved ahead, curious. "He's a professor of genetics on sabbatical from Georgetown. He's our faculty adviser for the year. His photo's in the briefing packet."

"I lost mine. Is he our official den mother or something?"

"Very funny. He's a world-renowned geneticist."

"Who's the tall guy that looks like a banker?"

"That's William Fisher. He recently graduated from Yale. Middle Eastern Affairs. He joined the State Department and now he's moving to Beirut with his wife to be a cultural attaché at the U.S. Embassy. He'll be giving us several lectures on the Middle East during orientation week. The briefing packet says he speaks fluent Arabic. Think you'll pick up any Arabic?"

"I'll give it a try, Todd. But thank God I'm fluent in French. I hear French is the official second language of Lebanon, after Arabic of course."

Middle East Airways Flight No. 148 left Orly Airport at 3:25 P.M. for Beirut, with a brief stop in Athens to pick up passengers and refuel. She came onboard in Athens. As she walked down the aisle, her long red hair bounced and her fiery green eyes radiated confidence. "Excuse me. I believe I have the window seat." Matt and Todd stood up to let her slide in. They scrambled for the middle seat. Matt won.

A severe thunderstorm quickly took the spirit out of her. Amid flashes of lightning the plane rocked violently. Her alabaster skin paled as she shrank down in her seat, gripping the armrests.

Matt leaned over. "Are you all right? Why don't you tighten your seat belt and close your eyes? It's just a little electrical storm and these planes are extremely sturdy." He reached over and pulled down the window shade. "There, that's better. It'll keep out the lightning flashes."

The airplane shuddered. She gripped his arm. Her eyes shut tight. "Just make it go away, please."

"I wish I could. But I'm not God, just an American. Why don't we talk a little and try to distract ourselves?" He looked at her, absorbing her breathtaking beauty, only partially masked by her fear. Slowly she opened her eyes. He fell into their deep green pools. She spoke slowly at first. Matt was mesmerized by her accent and the soft power of her voice.

"My name is Maha Hammad. I'm Jordanian."

"What a beautiful name. Maha. Does it mean something?"

"In Arabic it means laughing eyes." She winced as lightning illuminated the cabin.

"A fitting name for such eyes, and such a beautiful face." He squeezed her hand with true care and concern.

She turned away.

"Sorry. I've made you uncomfortable." Matt leaned back in his seat, feeling foolish.

"He often does that to people," remarked Todd, leaning over to try and speak to her.

She looked directly at Matt. "I have been visiting friends in Athens," she said, her confidence returning. "But now I'm on my way back to Beirut for my third year in the School of Pharmacy at the American University. And what about you? Why are you traveling to Beirut?"

"I'm attending a junior year abroad program at AUB. I'll be going there for the entire school year. Along with my friend here. Todd. We're both from Harvard. It's my first time out of the U.S."

They talked long past the patch of turbulence until the jet touched down at Beirut International Airport five hours later. They agreed to meet three days later on the university tennis courts.

Matt floated off the plane and, thanks to serious-minded Todd, was able to collect all his baggage and join up with the rest of the group near the taxi stand just outside the main airport doors. The warm humid night air assaulted him as he stepped through the doors.

"Wow," Matt said.

"Wow, what?"

"Can't your feel it? Marco Polo and Alexander the Great passed through this country. This exotic Lebanon. Take a deep breath, Todd. The air is like nothing I've ever experienced. The sea, the mountain trees, the desert sands, exotic spices, smoke from cooking fires. God, it's an ancient aroma. This must have been what enticed Marco Polo and Alexander the Great to journey all the way to Lebanon. They were drawn here. Just like me." Matt dropped his bags and stood still, exhilarated at his first experience of the Middle East.

"Smells like diesel fumes to me," Todd said, "and open-air toilets. Maybe this wasn't such a good idea."

Before either of them could get their bearings, they were bundled into a battered Mercedes taxi with one other American student. After luggage had been precariously strapped into the open trunk and stuffed into the vacant passenger seat, the cab tore off.

"He's doing very well, don't you think?" said Matt, his hands gripping the seat.

"They said in the briefing packet that traffic signs are more like suggestions than rules," Todd said, wincing as they came to their first roundabout.

Matt and Anne-Marie, a student from Boston College whose parents were first-generation Lebanese American, screamed with delight. Flying along at 120 kilometers per hour on the pothole-filled tarmac roads, they survived the thirty-five minutes of exhilarating fear and screeched to a halt in front of the dormitory gates at the American University of Beirut.

Matt said an excited goodbye to Anne-Marie and Todd, then lugged his suitcases up to the second floor. He found room 24 and knocked. After a few moments, a light came on. Then the door opened. Samir Hussein, in boxer shorts and a sleeveless t-shirt, smiled as he grabbed one of the suitcases.

"You're obviously my roommate. Come in. Let me give you a hand with those." Matt liked him immediately.

After they shut the door, Samir put on his clothes. "Come on. You can unpack later. Let's go get a beer. There's no curfew until the official start of classes."

The beer helped quench his dry throat and wash away some of the fatigue from the long trip. But what invigorated Matt even more was the little club, tavern, restaurant, whatever it was. The place stood atop a cliff facing the Mediterranean. He could hear the waves crashing below, even though in the darkness he couldn't see anything except the myriad of stars in the sky. Arabic music, so different to his ear, played loudly over the speakers. The smells from the kitchen made him both curious and hungry. He looked around. He was the only Caucasian in the entire restaurant. This piqued his sense of adventure even more.

Samir was Palestinian. Something Matt didn't really understand, but he was a fount of knowledge about Lebanon, Beirut, and the University.

"Can you tell me about the history of this place? I was too busy working this summer to do any reading."

"My friends were right. What Americans know about the world wouldn't fill a hookah pipe."

"A what?"

Samir laughed, and Matt smiled back. Both took long pulls on their amber beer bottles.

"Okay. Let's start with our school. AUB was originally set up by American missionaries under an educational charter from the State of New York in 1866."

"You're kidding? It's that old?"

"It's the premier center for higher learning in the Middle East. There's a medical college, school of pharmacy, school of nursing, a teaching hospital, and all the academic departments of any modern university. I'm in the engineering department. How about you?"

"I'm studying biology. Destined to be a doctor, like my father and brother. Man, this stuff is good. What is it?"

"Hummus. A mixture of chick peas, garlic, olive oil and pine nuts. You eat it with flat Arabic bread like this." Samir broke off a corner of the round pita and used it to scoop up a glob of hummus.

"What about the campus. It's too dark to see anything. How big is it?"

"This is a beautiful place, Matt. Let's see, as I recall, it's about 75 acres that sits on the Ras Beirut peninsula, overlooking St. George's Bay. From the campus you can see the mountain range that runs the length of Lebanon. They have snow almost all year round."

"Snow? In the Middle East?"

"Yeah. You can ski in the morning and swim in the ocean in the afternoon."

"Now I know I'm gonna like it here." Matt took another sip of his Amstel beer. Suddenly he felt a shove from behind. His beer bottle landed on the floor of the sidewalk café with a crash. "What the hell."

"Hey Samir? What are you doing with a filthy American?" A small group of dark-skinned youths, about Matt's age, encircled their table.

Samir spoke roughly in Arabic. He stood up, his 6-foot frame towering over the others. They backed away. The leader, a thin fellow with a moustache and thick glasses, glared. He gestured at Matt with his fist and walked away. The rest of the group followed.

"What was that all about?" Matt tried to pick up the glass from the broken bottle. A waiter smiled and quickly cleaned up. A new bottle of beer appeared on the table.

"Things are getting crazy around here." Samir took a bite of his lamb kebab. "Some of the newspapers are trying to stir up anti-American sentiment."

"But why?"

"The Vietnam War and America's blatant support for the Zionists and Israel. Examples of American imperialism. I'm afraid it will only create more problems here and take the focus away from the real issue."

"Which is?"

"The return of the state of Palestine to its rightful peoples. They've even begun to have protests at the American Embassy. It's just outside the AUB campus."

"Well, I'm not going to let it spoil my year. Besides, I don't care much for politics anyway. Tell me some more about this place." A drop of olive oil ran down his chin. "God, this stuff is good."

"Did you know that Beirut was founded by the Phoenicians around 3000 B.C? Its location on the eastern shore of the Mediterranean, sheltered by a large sweeping bay, made it a perfect launching place for their ships. Whole fleets ventured forth, explored new lands, and traded with other civilizations."

"Wow. 3000 BC. That's as old as the Egyptians."

"The Phoenicians were clever, intrepid, and commercially minded. They amassed a great deal of wealth as well. And these ancient Lebanese left a monumental legacy to the world."

"What was that?"

"They invented the alphabet, my friend. In addition, the Phoenicians invented glass making and excelled in producing textiles, carving ivory, and working in metal, stone and wood. As a result of their ingenuity and trading fleets, Beirut became a thriving port and the crossroads between the exotic East and the developing West."

"I should have paid more attention in my history classes."

Samir pushed his lamb around the plate. "However, all this wealth and power came with a price. Inevitably, over thousands of years, numerous civilizations invaded the country—Egyptians, Hyskos warriors from Asia, Alexander the Great, Marco Polo, Romans, Muslims, Crusaders, Ottomans, and most recently the Shiites. But what's amazing about this country and its people is that throughout centuries of conquest and foreign domination, the Lebanese culture held steadfast to two things: their determination for independence, and their predominantly Christian beliefs."

"Samir?"

"What."

"I met an amazing woman this evening. A gorgeous red-haired beauty with seductive green eyes."

"She was Jordanian."

"How the hell do you know that?"

"She has to be Jordanian, Matt. What am I going to do with you? I'm talking about real history and culture, and all you can think of is a woman."

Matt grinned. "What say we get some sleep?"

"You won't sleep. The green-eyed goddess has you firmly in her grasp."

"Not yet," said Matt. "Not yet. But I hope it won't be too long." He stood up from the small table. "Thanks, Samir. It's been an absolutely great day, but I'm totally exhausted. Let's get some sleep. But tomorrow I'd like you to show me some more of this magical city."

It was Samir Hussein who first introduced Matt to the mysteries of the Souk, also known as the covered bazaar. "This reminds me of the *Souk* in Jerusalem where I grew up," Samir said as he took his new American roommate on a tour. "The *souk* is the heart and soul of every Middle Eastern city. This is where political ideas are born, discussed, argued, and often acted on."

Matt felt like he had been transported back in time. The narrow passages and dark alleyways of the covered bazaar beckoned to him. Samir had told him of the different areas within the Souk. The spice market and its aroma assaulted his nostrils. His mind reeled with exotic images of camel trains and cargo ships, all brimming with cargo and bound for the coast of Lebanon. Samir was still talking.

"Marriages are arranged here and disputes settled. World events are discussed in every shop and at every intersection. All forms of business are conducted in these narrow alleyways. In fact, the *Souk* is the center of news and information. Modern governments have tried to shift these activities to more formal institutions, like courts and houses of parliament, but the *Souk* is still the center of life for most Middle Easterners."

"Why are the shopkeepers and customers always arguing with each other?" Matt felt uncomfortable at the belligerence that seemed to be erupting from nearly every stall.

Samir laughed. "They're not arguing, they're negotiating on price. It's a custom in the Middle East. Unlike the States where prices are fixed, here they're fluid. Bargaining is a way of building relationships. A person who negotiates well is respected. At the end of what seems like a heated argument to you, if both the buyer and the seller are pleased with the price, the relationship deepens."

"But that's not fair. What if you don't know what a reasonable price for an item should be? You could get screwed."

Samir's dark eyes watched him. "If you learn anything from your year in Lebanon, Matt, it's that life isn't fair. You're blinded by the American concept of all people being created equal. The truth is, people aren't equal. Some are more gifted than others, some are born to rich families, some to poor shepherds, some are lazy, some dishonest, some kind, some cruel. It's the same the world over, only in the Middle East the differences are starker."

Matt said nothing.

"Is everybody in the West as naïve as you?" Samir said.

"I just assumed the whole world thought like we do, only they were a little behind in technology...."

"My father has a saying: If you don't understand your enemy, you can't defeat him. Ignorance of one's enemy is a fatal weakness."

Matt was about to ask why everyone in the Middle East seemed to talk about enemies rather than allies, but a shop caught his eye.

"Wow, this is a cool stall, Samir," Matt said, changing the subject. They squeezed into the tiny space where leather-bound volumes of all sizes and colors were piled high on brightly colored carpets. "I'd like a journal to record my experiences this year."

"Now you are talking more like an Arab—we are great believers in keeping journals to record our thoughts and our conversations with God. The written word is sacred, and learning to read and write is an important milestone in the life of young Arab men."

Samir greeted the shopkeeper in Arabic. "Here," he whispered to Matt, "I'll help you negotiate a price. Pick out two journals, one you like and the other you don't like. It's the way to get the best price, by negotiating for one against the merits and defects of another."

Matt never knew anyone could talk as fast as Samir and the shopkeeper while they were haggling. It was the verbal equivalent of a long, intricate wrestling match, with the two opponents in close contact, circling and shoving and pinning each other, and when it was finally all over, they stood back, shook hands and smiled. While the shopkeeper poured tea, Samir handed the journal to Matt, beaming at the reasonable price he had wrangled.

On the third day, Matt met Maha on the AUB tennis courts.

"Whoa. I've never played on clay courts before. We don't have many back in the states. It's slippery." Matt chased a return from Maha, slid on the ochre surface and tumbled into a heap at the baseline. Her giggle reached his ears and he began to laugh as well.

They abandoned the court and spent the next three hours sitting under a large banyan tree at the edge of the AUB grounds overlooking the Mediterranean. "Isn't this a beautiful campus? I just love it here, so different from Jordan. So peaceful."

"Tell me about your life, Maha." Matt listened as a whole new world was revealed to him.

During Matt's first week at AUB, he and the fourteen other American students were invited to the College Hall offices of the president of the University, Dr. Samuel B. Kirkwood, for a reception marking the official start of their junior year abroad. The students were from all over the States, from elite universities like Harvard and Stanford, to small choice colleges like Oberlin and Sweet Briar.

"So why are you here?" A lanky, sandy-haired student sat next to Matt at the back of the reception room at College Hall. Matt stared at the very expensive Nikon camera around his neck, complete with a professional flash attachment.

"It's a long way from Seattle and my father. Besides, isn't this the most exotic place you've ever seen?"

"It certainly is. All the ruins, the Cedars, the snow covering the mountains. And those dark alleyways in the bazaar. I've already shot ten rolls of film and it's only the first week." His voice had a nasal quality. "By the way, my name is Theodore Janus, from Ohio State. But everyone just calls me T.J. What's yours?"

"Matt Richards. Harvard." Matt immediately noticed the limp handshake.

"That's a pretty expensive camera you've got there."

"I'm a Geology major, but my real passion is photography. Dr. Mitchell is the head of the Geology Department and he already said I could use the darkroom any time. I'm looking forward to touring the entire country and taking pictures of the land and the people." He caressed his camera. "Are you into photography?"

"Not really. But I'm looking forward to seeing your pictures." Matt moved away slightly, uncomfortable at how close T.J. was sitting. "Think I'll get a beer from the refreshment table. See you around." Matt moved quickly across the room, nearly bumping into another student.

"If you can dribble a soccer ball and crash into people at the same time, then you're just the guy I'm looking for." He juggled his drink without spilling it. "My name's Brian Walker, from Berkeley." Their handshake was firm and each recognized the other's athletic abilities.

"Pele came to Harvard once, but saw me dribble, score from 75 yards out and he caught the first plane back to Brazil." Matt grinned. "Name's Matt Richards, from Harvard."

"Okay, big shot. We've got a tryout with the AUB soccer team on Saturday. It should be fun. What's your major?"

"Biology and medicine. My dad's a heart surgeon, and my older brother's already in med school. So I'm next. What's yours?"

"Political science and official Berkeley radical. My dad's a big corporate lawyer helping the fat capitalists exploit undeveloped countries."

Matt threw up his hands. "I'm ready to play soccer and drink some beer. But if you want to talk politics, I'm the wrong guy."

"Deal." During the next several months at AUB, Brian, in spite of his outspoken political views on Vietnam and American "imperialism," became an integral part of Matt's school and social life.

"Who's the gorgeous blond over there?" Brian asked, pulling Matt's sleeve and pointing in the direction of three female students huddled together.

"Only one way to find out." But his mind quickly centered on the thought of Maha, her red hair and green eyes. "I'm not a blond man. She's all yours." They walked up and introduced themselves, holding out fresh Amstel beers for the three women.

As they found out later, Susan Miller, a tall, blond-haired beauty from Michigan State was escaping from an abusive boyfriend and indifferent parents and thought it would be keen to spend a year in Beirut. She reminded Matt of a spoiled daughter of rich parents—he had met plenty of them during his two years at Harvard—but he liked her nonetheless. And Brian liked her even more. She and Brian became inseparable and formed a part of Matt's regular group for weekend trips and skiing in the mountains above Beirut.

"Hi, my name's Anne-Marie Khoury, from Boston College. We shared a taxi our first night, remember?" A dark-haired Middle Eastern looking young woman reached out for one of Matt's cold beers. "Any man bringing cold beer is either a mind reader or a saint."

"He's neither," said Brian, laughing. "He's a Harvard man."

Matt called over Todd Cummings, and they all sat down together. The official activities weren't scheduled to start for another twenty minutes.

"Are you Lebanese, Anne-Marie?" asked Todd.

"Sort of." She put down her beer. "My grandparents immigrated to America from Lebanon in the late 1800s. Thought I would come over here for my junior year. Curious I guess. I'm studying medicine and hope to become a doctor."

"Me too. Guess we'll be in several classes together."

They exchanged light talk for a few minutes, then Anne-Marie began an emotional discourse on the plight of Palestinian refugees who had been relegated to living in squalid camps in southern Lebanon. "It's a grave injustice. Their homes, their homeland, given to the Israelis by foreign decree, for God's sake."

"Ah. Sorry folks. Beer goes right through me. See you later." When Matt looked back, Todd and Anne-Marie were deep into an animated discussion. He headed for the refreshment table. T.J. intercepted, his Nikon and flash swinging.

"Oh, Matt. This is Dr. Mitchell, the head of the Geology Department." T.J. stepped back as Matt moved to the buffet table. "I was just telling him about you. He's also one of the scuba diving instructors, so if you want to learn to dive while you're here, he's forming classes in two weeks."

"Pleased to meet you, Matt." He was overweight and obviously gay. "Beirut is a remarkable place. It's got some interesting terrestrial and marine geology. The Med's like a bath tub and the marine life is spectacular."

Matt smiled politely and begged off. He stuffed a rolled grape leaf into his mouth. Garlic and olive oil filled his senses. "This is going to be a more interesting year than I first imagined."

Dr. Martin J. Thomas, adviser to the American students, stepped up to the lectern and welcomed the students to the American University of Beirut Junior Year Abroad Program. Matt moved into the large hall to listen.

"… after the welcome remarks by AUB president Dr. Samuel B. Kirkwood, we will be receiving the first of five lectures on the politics and economics of Lebanon and the Middle East by William Fisher of the U.S. State Department." Matt turned and walked out. He grabbed another beer and sat down on the steps of College Hall. He'd wait for Fisher's talk. A group of male Arabic students glared at Matt as they walked by. He smiled but they muttered something in Arabic and walked off.

As Matt returned to the large hall William Fisher, a tall, lanky man, strode up to the podium and began to speak. Matt found a seat among the other students.

"Most of you have never heard the word *terrorist* before. But by the time you're in your forties, *terrorism* will be a household word and your worst nightmare."

Thus began an hour and a half of the most riveting political and current affairs lecture Matt and the other students had ever experienced. William Fisher had a firm command of facts and drew conclusions about the future that, to his assembled audience of fresh-faced youth from America, were shocking and unsettling. Back home in America everyone believed the future would be prosperous and safe, thanks to years of economic and technological superiority and the benefits of freedom and capitalism. Even now they were ridding Vietnam of the communists and preserving peace.

"The greatest threat to peace in the next two to three decades will be the sudden and prolific spread of refugee camps. Right now the center of attention seems to be on the Palestinian refugee camps in southern Lebanon, but in the years to come there will be more and more concentrations of uprooted people living in poor and squalid conditions. Recognized by no country, they will have no legal citizenship, no adequate representation, and no hope. This is the deadly mix that will spawn a massive rise in terrorism, and it won't stop at regional boundaries—it will inflame the entire world."

Matt looked around. Todd was sitting next to Anne-Marie, who was sitting rigid, engrossed in what was being said. On the other side of the room, Brian and Susan were whispering to each other. He had his arm around her.

"When young people have no hope, no dreams, no outlet for their desire to create something positive, then out of frustration and anger they will focus their energy on ways to destroy. Youth who grow up in crowded camps are the perfect prey for sinister organizations around the world that wish to destroy any hopes of peace.

"And why would they want to destroy? For profit. They make money when peace is shattered and countries go to war." Fisher took a drink of water and looked out at the fresh young faces of America's youth. "Who are these people? They are the international arms dealers, the suppliers of traditional as well as chemical weapons, and of course the armed mercenaries. And there are secret organizations who stir up conflict to generate profit. By sponsoring regional and global terrorism, they can line their own pockets with millions and millions of dollars. They hold no allegiance to any country, religion or political doctrine. Their only devotion is to profit, their only allegiance, power."

Anne-Marie clapped. All heads turn toward her. Both she and Todd sank down in their seats. "And the thirst of angry refugees for arms and ammunition will lead to a rise in the growth, manufacture and distribution of illegal drugs, which will become the prime currency for funding terrorist activities. Terrorists may disguise their motives under a banner of religious or political injustice, but the organizations supplying them with arms don't have noble disguises. Their motive is greed—pure, unadulterated, transparent greed, and on a scale that the world has never seen before. Global greed."

William Fisher paused. Only twenty-eight years old and on his first assignment overseas, he was already one of the brightest stars in the State Department. He took a sip of water.

"Because of the weakness of President Helou and the current Lebanese administration, a deep divide is growing within Parliament. On one side are the Muslim Lebanese, who consider the Arab position in the Palestinian-Israeli conflict a sacred cause. Opposing them, the Christian Lebanese, who are fanatical about the continued independence of Lebanon and who worry about security in light of the rising tide of terrorism. This schism within the Parliament is the opening the terrorists and their financial backers need to dramatically increase their presence and support. I predict that the newly organized Palestinian Liberation Organization, and other so-called political action groups, will quickly transform themselves into ruthless global terrorists.

"I wish I could see a more optimistic future for this beautiful country, but I'm afraid all signs point to Lebanon as the battleground upon which terrorists, Israelis, the Western world, and surrounding Arab countries will wage war. And that war will escalate to engulf the entire world."

"Is there any good news?" Todd called out, waving his hand in the air.

"The best solutions often begin with the best questions, Mr. Cummings," replied William Fisher. "The good news is that there are various nations, including the United States, that are quietly trying to support President Helou and bring the two factions in Parliament closer together. We hope these efforts will prevent, or at least delay, the spread of terrorism. In addition, certain nations are working hard to gather information on terrorist groups and their supporters. The more we know about their plans, organizations, sources of income and arms, the better chance we have of preventing the deaths of thousands of innocent people around the world."

"You mean to tell us these terrorists will target civilians instead of the military?" asked Matt, dumbfounded at the thought of deliberately killing innocent people just to make a point on the world stage.

Anne-Marie jumped up. "Have you ever been to a refugee camp before, Mr. Fisher?"

"No."

"So you've never spoken with the mothers, the children, the abandoned old men, the eager young people who can't find work other than being garbage collectors, brick layers, housemaids, or kitchen workers? These people used to have homes, they used to have land. They once had a nation, Palestine. All of which was stolen from them by the Zionists, with the blessing of many of these same Western nations who you say are now so afraid of terrorism. Well, in case it slipped your mind, you guys helped create this mess." She pointed dramatically at Fisher, her hand shaking. "Why can't you see that the problem really lies with Israel and the West, and not the Palestinians?"

"Believe it or not, Ms. Khoury, I agree with you." T.J.'s Nikon flashed a photo of the young woman pointing angrily at the speaker. "We did create this mess; it's arrogant Western colonialism that's to blame. But what most people fail to realize is these refugees, whom you so passionately defend, are the unwitting pawns in a much bigger game of global terror perpetrated by shadowy people with no morals at all. They won't be fighting in a conventional manner for political or religious rights. They will be systematically murdering innocent women and children, office workers and shop attendants, restaurant staff, Israelis, Arabs, Palestinians, Christians, Muslims, Jews, Europeans, and even Americans. One day it may even happen on American soil. And there will be no warning. Just a massive explosion or a burst of machine-gun fire. They are mass murderers whose only motive is greed, and right now the displaced and disheartened Palestinians are their cannon fodder."

"Professor Fisher?" Brian Walker stood up. "Or should I call you 007? This sounds like another one of those righteous speeches that the rich capitalists give to justify keeping the rest of the world permanently in the Stone Age. Are you dudes looking for another Vietnam? I doubt if you'll do any better here than you're doing over there. And all in the name of freedom, or so you say."

The speaker smiled. "Let's have this discussion at the end of the school year, Mr. Walker, after you've been here awhile. I'd be curious to see if any of your views have been altered by living in the real world, and not just on an American university campus."

"Well," Dr. Thomas said, coming up on the podium at the end of William Fisher's presentation. "It looks like this year promises to be quite different from a normal junior year in the States. Mr. Fisher will be conducting four more workshops over the next two weeks, which is a part of your Junior Year Abroad orientation process. In addition, one professor from each of the academic departments, as well as the schools of Medicine, Pharmacy and Nursing will be giving you short and informative presentations. We believe that by the end of the month, you will all better understand the Middle East and Lebanon, where you will be spending your academic year."

"I could use a beer," said Matt loudly as the meeting broke up and everyone mingled outside on the front steps of College Hall. "Anyone care to join me?"

It was the beginning of an exciting school year for Matt, a year of discoveries and new friendships. By the end of the first month, in addition to his core of American friends, Matt's social group included Maha Hammad, Samir Hussein and his girlfriend Bedouina, and Demetrie Antonopolis, a somewhat older rich Greek student with a long pony tail. He knew all the interesting places to go in Lebanon and had even rented a large apartment in the mountains for ski weekends. Nobody knew much about Demetrie, but he was outgoing, popular, obviously with a rich father somewhere, and would never say no to a party.

They were together nearly every weekend for seven months, until the explosion that killed Samir, Bedouina and Maha, and turned Matt's life upside down.

Chapter Five

London

"AH, MY FAVORITE MEMBER OF THE ST. JAMES'S CLUB. Welcome back, Mr. Nagib." Andrew, the well-groomed club manager, beamed with delight. "It's been quite some time since you last blessed us with a visit here in London."

The stylish and very private St. James' Club and Casino, housed in an 18th century marble-columned building near Piccadilly, had something the rest of London coveted: freedom from gawking tourists. An exclusive membership list, healthy annual membership fee, fabulous nouvelle cuisine, and a large casino made the club the luncheon choice for diamond-laden ladies of leisure. It was also a discreet haven for international business dinners late into the evening. And tonight was no exception.

Mohammad al Nagib grunted, finally shedding his size XXL overcoat. "You're as charming and as full of bullshit as ever, Andrew. I assume my guests have been well taken care? I would have been here earlier, but important business needed my personal attention."

Andrew beamed. "Everything is as you requested, sir." The staff were trained to lavish personal attention on their private members. Like a handful of other exclusive dining clubs around the world, the St. James Club was a place where superior service was both expected and delivered.

"Excellent. Then bring a bottle of Fallet-Dart champagne to the table."

"Of course, Mr. Nagib. It will be my honor to deliver it personally to your table." Andrew discreetly signaled that the guests in the walnut-paneled cocktail lounge should be escorted to the dining room.

He then bowed, repeating an ancient blessing: "May you be the father of 100 sons, Mr. Nagib."

"Sons? Who the hell wants sons? They are weak and easily influenced. Haven't you learned yet, young man, that women are by far the more effective of the species? It is daughters we should develop, not sons." He waved his hand in dismissal. "I will be along in a moment."

Mohammed al Nagib strode into the gentlemen's washroom. He stood in front of the marble sink and oversized antique mirror. A half smile broke the permanent scowl. He carefully combed his thinning silver hair. The confident face in the mirror echoed his thoughts. *Three decades of planning, manipulating, bribing, threatening, and even a few disappearances. Now we are ready.* The clock on the wall ticked. He checked the time against his gold Rolex, then strode toward the dining room.

"Ah, there you are my good friend." Achilles Antonopolis stood up as Mohammed al Nagib walked through the large double doors into the formal dining room. They embraced warmly, kissing once on each cheek. The other two members of tonight's special dinner meeting, a Swiss and a Brazilian, each took turns hugging and kissing their host and business partner. Warm greetings were exchanged all around in French and English. The champagne glasses were full and the ever-bowing Andrew had withdrawn. They were at a corner table, slightly away from the rest of the guests.

Nagib briskly raised his glass to Jorge Molinas, sitting directly opposite. "Congratulations on your success."

The short, neatly dressed Brazilian returned the toast. "Sometimes the best strategy is to let your opponent believe you have failed while your plan is proceeding." He nodded to the others as they all drank deeply of the vintage champagne.

"Now that we are on schedule," Nagib went on, "I can report that within one week, two at most, our asset will be securely *in situ* and waiting for the signal."

"It is truly exhilarating to have destiny in our hands—and to be in control of the timetable." The diminutive Helmut Hofer adjusted his thin wire-rimmed glasses, never making direct eye contact.

"And when the timing suits our needs, we can act at will," added Antonopolis.

Nagib raised his bubbling flute of champagne. "For over thirty years we have pledged our lives together. Planning, testing, and revising our overall plans. I remember the old days when we would loan each other money during tough times. But thanks to all of your hard work and sacrifices, our business empires are not only expanding, but highly profitable. To our most ambitious project ever."

"My mining and logging conglomerate would have never survived without your assistance." The Brazilian bowed his bald head. "But now it's profitable beyond my wildest dreams."

Herr Hofer spoke just above a whisper. "My little bank has benefited handsomely from our long-term business dealings. And it's benefited those who know a Swiss bank is the safest place for their money."

"Ah, here comes the head chef himself," Nagib announced. Lowering his voice, he added, "I suggest we change the conversation, gentlemen. All plans for the next phase are available through the secure network." He looked up at the celebrity chef, decked out in a white smock, chef's hat and colorful bowtie. Everyone stood up, shook hands all around and the pleasantries began.

The Tonight Show

"I'm no longer allowed to tell ethnic or political jokes," the venerable late-night host quipped toward the end of his opening monologue. "The network brass get too many threatening phone calls from senators and congressmen. So tonight my writers have opted for a more scientific approach." He shuffled his feet as if in deep thought. "Let's see, the subject is ... oh yeah, genetics." The live audience broke into organized clapping, encouraging him on. "Okay, okay, patience. You don't get a scientific degree overnight, you know, these things take awhile."

A wry grin spread across his elongated face, making his chin look even more prominent than it was. He stared straight into the camera. "What do you get when you cross an Arab woman with a stick of dynamite?

" ... Nothing."

Blue Ridge Private Clinic and Hospital

A soft noise pierced the foggy veil of his mind. "Muzak. God, I hate Muzak." Matt fell back into a narcotic-induced sleep. For the past several weeks, he had been drifting in and out of consciousness. It was strange. In the mornings he would wake up to a set of electrodes placed on his arms and legs, stimulating his muscles, keeping atrophy at bay. He was just barely conscious as the machine kept up its steady rhythm of muscle contraction and relaxation. He could also feel a thick material covering his face, like large bandages. Then as soon as the machines were unplugged, he would fall into a deep sleep. More like a zombie than a living being.

But today, amid a collage of bizarre dreams, he surfaced into semi-consciousness again.

"No. No." The crisp bed sheet jerked uncontrollably. The dream came back. In and out of a vague blackness floated a face— her face. The same face captured on television. The suicide attack on the president. Bedouina Missoumi. It was her—he was sure of it. The image skimmed across his drug-fogged mind, smiling, snarling, laughing, brooding, beckoning. Soon more figures began to appear, misty, facing away from him. But each time they turned the face was always the same, Bedouina. Samir's long-dead girlfriend wafted closer and closer. He reached out with an invisible hand. She melted away. He sat up, trying to reach the evaporating form, then fell back into the soft pillow. More Muzak.

Again he awoke with a start. Another face.

"Who are you?" he called aloud. "Go away. Don't look at me. Go away." He didn't want to know. He wanted the screen of his mind to go blank, but it glowed even brighter as the fragments of images coalesced. His mind reached out. He could feel every contour of her face as if it were etched into his DNA. Matt closed his eyes tight.

"Oh, God." He let out a low moan. It was her. The red-haired beauty he comforted so many years ago during a thunderstorm in the skies. The goddess he had fallen in love with—Maha.

"Calm down now; take a few deep breaths." A soothing male voice came from directly overhead. "You must have been having a nightmare or a vivid hallucination. They're common with concussions and injuries of your type." Flashes of light moved back and forth across his eyes. The doctor held his lids apart and peered at his pupils.

"He's regaining consciousness. The swelling of the lining of the brain seems to be going down as a result of the drugs. It looks like your patient is making a speedy and complete recovery. But he still needs rest." The doctor turned slowly to face two men standing just behind him. Then all three men peered at the figure lying on the hospital bed. White bandages encircled head and face. Only the eyes were visible, with small holes for the nostrils.

"When will he be recovered enough for us to talk to him, doc?"

Matt flinched, but his eyes remained closed.

"Speak quietly. His ears are very sensitive at this stage."

"When? We can't wait much longer." A hushed voice, with a heavy accent.

"Not now. He still needs his daily exercise and then his rest. And it will be at least one more week before we can take the bandages off."

"But it's been five weeks already. We need to talk with him, time is running out." The other man moved into the bright light hanging over the steel-framed bed. His bald head glistened with sweat. They were in a small, elaborately equipped recovery room that was sealed off from the rest of the clinic by large doors and armed guards.

"Maybe by the end of the week, perhaps sooner. I've told you a hundred times, medicine and politics don't work on the same timetable—I'll let you know as soon as he's fully recovered." And with that the surgeon ushered the two men out of the hospital room. Slowly he returned, staring at the vital signs flashing on the machines in the otherwise darkened room. Matt could sense his presence, watching, waiting.

"WHERE AM I?" Matt aimed his words at three out-of-focus faces staring down at him.

"You're in a private clinic, Dr. Richards. And, I might add, you're recovering very nicely. Today I can take the bandages off."

Matt slowly felt his face. Shaky hands moved cautiously back and forth, then up and down. His entire head was bandaged. "Must have been a hell of an accident." He vaguely recalled screaming tires and Kelly slamming on the brakes. Everything else was lost behind a dense mental fog.

"Can't you get rid of that damned Muzak? It's driving me crazy, and God knows what it does to the rest of the patients." The two visitors turned to each other.

"So, do I look like a codfish? And you still haven't answered my first question. Where am I?"

"Dr. Weissman is leaving now, but we'll be able to answer all your questions." A heavy-set olive-skinned man faced the doctor. "We'll call you when we need you, doctor. Stay close at hand."

"Very well." He left without looking back. The door secured itself automatically with a faint hydraulic hiss.

"You're in a private hospital in the Blue Ridge mountains," the stranger said, pulling a chair next to the bed. "It's reserved for only the most special patients." The motor whirred as he lowered the height of the bed so they could talk face to face. The other man, younger and taller, grabbed another chair. He slammed it down next to his partner. The heavy metal legs struck the bed frame. Matt winced at the noise.

"What's happening ….." Matt stuttered, as his mushy mind slowly came to grips with the conversation.

"Oh, I'm so sorry. You haven't seen the headlines, have you?" The younger man unlatched his briefcase. "Here, let me read it to you. It's the *Washington Post,* dated February 23, the morning after."

"After?" he muttered.

"After the accident."

Matt tried to sit up. His body barely moved. He grunted. After a few attempts, he finally got himself propped against the thick foam hospital pillow. Closing his eyes, he listened carefully as the stranger spoke slowly and distinctly.

"Daughter of Senator Mason Stevens Killed in Drunk Driving Accident." Matt groaned through the layers of gauze. "That's the head-lines, front page no less. Now I'll read you the story." He held the paper in Matt's direct field of vision.

> Ms. *Kelly Stevens, 22, only child of U.S. Senator and Mrs. Mason T. Stevens of Virginia, died in a tragic single-car accident on the George Washington Parkway at approximately 11:15 P.M. last night. According to the D.C. Metro police, who arrived a short time after the accident, Ms. Stevens's yellow Porsche Boxter apparently went out of con-trol and swerved across the highway, crashed through a guard rail and struck a large tree. Police estimate the small sports car was traveling at exces-sive speed. Ms. Stevens died instantly.*
>
> *Kelly Stevens, a senior at Sweet Briar College in Lynchburg, Virginia, was attending a reception for newly appointed personal physician to President Pierce, Dr. Noubar Melikian. She was accompanied by a friend, Dr. Matthew Richards, assistant professor of biology and anatomy at Sweet Briar. Dr. Richards, who was driving at the time, was also pronounced dead at the scene....*

"What the hell?" Matt jerked into an upright position and tried to grab the newspaper. The other man shoved him back, restraining his arms. "Goddamn it. What's going on here? And let me go, you big ape." Matt's head exploded with pain. He collapsed back onto the pillow.

"Relax, doc, we haven't finished." He cracked a tight smile. His dark-skinned face seemed to glow.

> *Matthew Richards, 54, son of famous heart surgeon Dr. Wilson Richards, and disbarred from practicing medicine several years ago in an alcohol-related incident, had a blood alcohol content of 0.25% at the time of the accident, nearly three times the legal driving limit.*

Matt grabbed the paper, the print wavering before his weak eyes as his mind absorbed the words. *Shit*. The pages fluttered to the floor. Somewhere in the dark distance an intercom crackled.

"Not only are you a drunk and a murderer, Dr. Richards, but you're also legally dead. Your past is pretty messed up, and I'd say your future doesn't look too bright either." The older man stood up. Matt noticed coarse black hair growing out of his ears.

Matt gathered his strength, fighting back the pain. "Okay. You got my attention. Now what do you want from me? This is some sort of setup. I should have known something was up when that black car kept trying to ram us from behind."

"Yes, that was unfortunate. We lost two good men that evening, but they did their job, forcing you to speed up for our little reception party ahead."

"What do you want from me?" Thinking and moving were taking their toll. He felt nauseous.

The younger man got up and put his ear against the door, gave the okay signal, then sat down again. Hairy Ears spoke again. "We need your help."

"Go to hell."

"We want you to help us track down a terrorist cell –"

"A terrorist cell!"

"Yes. A group that has placed highly trained assassins in deep cover, right here in the U.S."

Matt's head pounded. He formed his words distinctly through the bandages. "Man, have you got the wrong guy."

"We think not, doc."

"Oh? And what twisted logic leads you two idiots to choose me?"

The younger man's face hardened. "Our sources tell us this cell was organized by a group of radical students who went to the American University of Beirut."

Bedouina's intense face shimmered. Unbidden, Maha swirled, auburn hair glowing, then Samir's smiling face…*But they're dead. Dead….* Matt kept quiet.

"So? What's going on, doc? You checking out again?"

"No. Just thinking this is some kind of sick joke."

Hairy Ears was leaning close to Matt's face. "Guess what year these students were at the American University? 1966 to 1970. Ring any bells?"

"Go to hell."

"You were there."

"Sure, I was there. But I was only twenty-one years old, a naïve college student from the States. I just wanted to experience a new culture, drink some beer and get laid. I had no interest in politics or political causes then, and I don't now. Besides, I'm not a detective or a secret agent, and now I'm just an ex-doctor and a two-bit college anatomy professor, for Christ's sake."

"You're also a stinking drunk." The younger man leaned over the bed. A jagged white scar ran from his left cheek down to his chin. "And a doctor who couldn't handle the pressure. Luckily your license was revoked before you killed someone on the operating table."

Hairy Ears watched the eyes beneath the bandages. He gauged their anger. "Is he right, doc?"

"I drank more than I should. I won't deny it."

"How nice. More than I should. What a crock. You were, and still are, a lousy drunk." Hairy Ears sat back in the chair. "There are two types of alcoholics, Dr. Richards. The unfortunate person who has a genetic predisposition toward alcoholism, and the coward who tries to hide from the past, present and future inside a bottle. You're not a real alcoholic, doctor. You're just a miserable wimp running away from a failed career, dozens of failed relationships, and a legend of a father you could never measure up to." The words cut into Matt like the double-edged sword of truth that it was. He closed his eyes, wondering where this was heading. What he really wanted was just to drift off to sleep. Forever.

Scarface stood up abruptly, the metal chair tipped onto the floor. Matt jumped at the noise.

"Okay. As you so eloquently put it, I'm not cut out for much of anything. So why me?"

"Two reasons," Scarface said. "First, we believe you came into contact with several of the suspected members of this cell while you were in Beirut."

"Like who?" Again Maha's green eyes.

"What I'm about to say is highly classified, known to only a few individuals. For the past several years we've been keeping an eye on a radical law professor from Berkeley, Dr. Brian Walker. You were at AUB with him between 1968 and 1969, weren't you?"

Matt nodded, not having thought about Brian in many years.

"We have reason to believe that during that time, Walker, who we suspect may be the leader of this cell, recruited several other students, both American and Arab. How well did you know Brian Walker?"

"Jesus Christ, that was over thirty years ago. We were just kids on a junior year abroad program."

"But you did know him." Hairy Ears said.

"Of course I knew Brian, as well as a dozen other students who were my friends that year."

Scarface watched him.

Matt explored his bandages. "Quit staring. There's nothing to this. I haven't spoken to any of them since 1969."

"I see."

"Fact is, three of my Arabic friends were killed in a bomb explosion near the end of the last semester. Things changed. I came home. No letters, no Christmas cards. Nothing." Images of the explosion came roaring back. He could taste the ashes and feel the scorching heat—could still see Samir Hussein incinerated before his eyes. The nightmare was etched into his skin. A permanent searing of his psyche. Matt lay against the pillow, exhausted.

"Did you see the CNN footage of the suicide bomb attack on the president?" Scarface again.

"Yeah, I saw it."

"Did you recognize the woman's face?" He leaned in, looking straight into Matt's eyes.

"Nope." It didn't seem right to tell them the woman looked like Bedouina Missoumi. After all, it couldn't be—she died in the explosion at the restaurant. Besides, he didn't trust these people. There was something ugly and dangerous going on. "Look, I haven't seen or spoken to any of them since we left Beirut. So I'd say I'm the wrong guy for your little clandestine assignment, wouldn't you?"

"Ah, yes, well that brings me to the second reason we've anoint-
ed you, Dr. Richards." Hairy Ears picked the newspaper up from the
floor, carefully folded it and laid it on the white hospital sheet.

"Which is?"

"You're all we've got," he said simply. "And you're expendable.
After all, you're dead, as reported in all the newspapers and on television. They even held a funeral for you. Pretty sparsely attended, I might
add. Your father didn't even show up."

"And if I refuse?"

He bent down close to Matt's bandaged face. The smell of garlic
made Matt nauseous. "You're officially listed as dead. So who's going to
care if you die twice?" The words uncoiled slowly, like a serpent.

"Okay, I get the message. But haven't you dimwits overlooked
one important point? I can't go around looking up old college friends if
I'm dead. Wouldn't it look a little suspicious, a corpse suddenly spring-
ing back to life?"

Scarface walked over to a wall phone and pressed the intercom.
"We need you in the safe room, Dr. Weissman." He turned toward
Matt. "The good doctor will make your decision a little easier."

Minutes later, the last of the long cotton bandages was carefully lifted from around his head. He felt the movement of air against
his face and on the matted hair follicles on his head. He felt ten times
lighter as Dr. Weissman began removing gauze squares from his cheeks,
chin, nose and around his eyes.

The accented words of Hairy Ears pulled Matt from his thoughts.
"You suffered terrible facial lacerations as a result of the accident, Dr.
Richards. Someone had to make a quick decision, so we asked Dr.
Weissman here to give us a hand. He's a very talented plastic surgeon
and our little hospital has quite an array of sophisticated equipment for
just such contingencies." The man stared at Matt's face with interest.
"Well, well, well."

He turned to the surgeon, busy putting the piles of cotton and
gauze in the waste bin near the sink. "Where's the mirror? It's time Dr.
Richards had a look at himself."

A slow fear coursed through Matt's body. He was perspiring. In
that instant, Dr. Matthew Richards realized he was helpless. A prisoner. A pawn in some twisted political game where people could murder

and kidnap at will, manipulate the press and possibly even governments. Who are these people, and what do they want? With shaking
hands he took the oval mirror from Dr. Weissman, gripping the smooth
clinical handle with both hands. It wavered back and forth as he slowly turned it around.

"Oh my God… That's not me, that's not my face—you fucking
bastards, you had no right, you had no right." Matt stared at the
stranger in the mirror. The hair color was the same, but the shape of
the face was totally wrong. Matt's face was lean and creased with deep
lines, with an almost boyish upturned mouth. This new face was round,
the cheeks fuller, the nose more prominent and slightly bent. The
mouth was definitely not his. Thin, stern, joyless. The beard, though
nearly all gray like his, was thicker and denser. The distorted image of
an aging prize fighter wavered before him.

"What have you done?" was all he could manage. His body
shook.

"Actually," Dr. Weissman responded while watching the facial
muscles move easily and naturally, "it's a relatively new procedure. As
a result of my recent research on nerve regeneration and facial muscle
attachment, I have finally been able to perfect the technique of a full
facial transplant. And we are able to achieve complete healing and full
facial control in just six weeks, seven at the most."

Matt threw the mirror as hard as he could, catching Scarface on
the temple. The mirror ricocheted, bounced on the floor, the glass
splintering. No one moved.

Bleeding from the temple, Scarface pressed the barrel of a pistol
into Matt's face. It felt odd, numb on his new skin. "Maybe we should
just end your miserable life here and now, asshole. You really don't get
it, do you? You've got no choice in this matter. You belong to us, and
you'll do exactly what we want you to do. It's as simple as that. So stop
trying to act like someone with a semblance of dignity and self-respect.
You've been a coward and a weakling all your life. You should be
thankful we're giving you a second chance to finally do something with
your miserable little life." He released Matt and stepped back. The pistol slid back smoothly into the hand-tooled shoulder holster. "We'll be
back after you've had a chance to sleep on it." He nodded to the doctor. The syringe was already inserted into the IV tube.

Matt started to panic, his heart racing. "So what if I go along with your plan?"

"Several very important people will be extremely grateful, Dr. Richards. That, and your life won't have been a total waste after all. But we're not impressed with your sudden change of heart. It's the only option you've got." They walked out.

Dr. Weissman pulled out the empty syringe. In less than thirty seconds Matt drifted into another drug-induced sleep. The dreams came again.

Beirut, December 29, 1968

THE BECKONING AROMA OF THICK ARABIC COFFEE floated into the bedroom of the ski chalet in the snow-covered mountains above Beirut. The soft mattress shook. Still half asleep, he sensed Maha's presence. Her warmth. Her essence. Inhaling the scent of her perfumed skin, he recalled last evening's lovemaking. His eyes slowly opened. She was over him, the tips of her long red hair tickling his face and eyelids. Matt closed his eyes again, committing every part of her to memory. He wanted to remember this moment forever. Eyes, hair, musky ....

"Last night I took the most wonderful journey of my life. I went straight to heaven." Her sweet breath was warm as her lips caressed his cheek. "I am changed, Matthew. Forever. Now I am a woman. Your woman. I have given to you everything that is sacred to me, willingly and with joy. And what you gave me was fantastic." They kissed, and he drank her in, only to feel her body move quickly off the bed. "Now," she giggled, as her large, firm breasts bounced up and down. "Let's see if you can ski as well as you make love."

The mountains of Lebanon formed a giant barrier running the length of the narrow country, separating the fertile coastal plain edging the warm Mediterranean from the high desert expanses of the Bekka Valley. In Phoenician times, the entire 161-kilometer-long mountain range was covered with a dense forest of cedar trees, known in Arabic as *Arz-ar-Rab*, the Trees of the Lord. The huge trees became a valuable source of lumber for building the massive temples of Egypt. Trade with Egypt was brisk, and while the Phoenicians flourished, the cedars rapidly dwindled. Only a small stand of fewer than four hundred trees—some over a thousand years old—now remained. They were the survivors, a lonely reminder of how easily something so noble and beautiful can be lost forever.

"Aren't these mountains exquisite? A paradise of virgin white snow. And just think, it lasts until May, sometimes later." Maha laughed with delight as she strapped on her skis just outside the chalet door. It was midweek. The pristine slopes nearly deserted. Matt and Maha had slipped away to spend two days at the large chalet their friend Demetrie had rented for the season. This was their first extended time alone, and their first experience as lovers.

Tears filled her eyes. "Have you ever seen such an inspiring view?" Nearly out of breath she came to a stop, the edges of her Rossignol skis sending up a shower of snow. She was at the beginning of a steep run, about half a kilometer from where the lift had deposited them. Matt was also breathing heavily, having a difficult time keeping up with this woman as she snaked across the slope, her skis perfectly parallel. Being from Seattle, Matt had grown up skiing, but next to Maha he felt like a rock tumbling down a bumpy hillside. He came to a showering stop alongside her, but his sharp edges struck a small rock and sent him flying onto his back. He looked up and laughed.

"Stop clowning around, Matthew. You must see this view. It's magnificent. Imagine how the invading armies felt when they reached the mountaintop and looked out."

Stretched out below them, well over thirty-five kilometers away, lay the city of Beirut. It glowed in the early-morning sunlight. The blue Mediterranean danced and shimmered. Several gray tankers slowly exited the harbor, plodding ahead of their frothy wakes. The Phoenician legacy was still as vibrant as ever. Where the lower end of Saint George's Bay curved around, they could just make out the red-tiled roofs and lush gardens of the American University of Beirut.

"Wow," Matt exclaimed, when he'd pulled himself back up. "It's like we're gods on Mount Olympus looking down on the world." Besides biology and math classes, Matt was taking a course in ancient mythology taught by Professor Richmond Hathron, as eccentric as he was famous. Dr. Hathron, an American, had lived in the Middle East for many years. In their classes twice a week, he would often read passages from Homer's *Iliad*, from the original Greek, translating the flowery text as he went. It was this class that had opened Matt's eyes to the profound soul of the Middle East, where first the Greeks, and then the Romans, had such a strong and lasting influence on the culture.

"Hey," he said, squinting into the sun, "what's all that smoke over there? Isn't that Beirut Airport?"

Maha didn't hear him. "If you can catch me, you can kiss me." she yelled, leaping off the snowy ledge. She tore down the steep face, gracefully carving a sinuous trail. Snow erupted at each turn.

Matt was about to race off after her when he noticed two skiers in dark clothing emerge from the left side of a snow bowl and head directly for Maha. They raced closer and closer, flying straight toward their target. She looked over her shoulder, expecting to see Matt. Instead she saw the two men. She slowed down, her skiing more rigid, jerking from side to side as she awkwardly turned. She looked tense and frightened. Matt watched, not knowing what to do. He looked closer. They were on a course that would take them by her. He relaxed.

But suddenly they veered directly in front of Maha and stopped. She tried to swerve out of the way, but her ski tips crossed. She tumbled down into the snow, face first. Both skis flew off in opposite directions like feathers from a gunshot bird. He watched in horror as she slid for twenty yards before coming to a stop next to a small mound of snow.

Matt catapulted off the ledge shouting, "Get away from her," but they were too far away to hear. Or else they just ignored him. As he headed straight down, the two skiers closed in on either side of Maha, just sitting up and brushing off the snow. One of the men reached down to help her up, but she resisted, lashing out with a ski pole. In a few mad seconds Matt was within earshot. Maha was screaming in Arabic. Matt crouched down and headed straight for the nearest intruder—a human missile flying down the steep slope.

Looking up, Maha saw Matt barreling down towards them. "No, Matt, it's all right. Don't—"

The taller of the two skiers stood directly in his path. Grabbing the hood of the stranger as he flew past, Matt jerked him to the ground, then dug his ski edges and swished to a stop a few feet downhill. He yelled at the other man. "Get away from her, you sonofabitch." Matt began sidestepping up the slope, frantic to reach Maha. The man he'd downed reached into his parka. A Damascus knife glittered in the sun. Matt stared at the deadly curved blade.

"Matt. Watch out." The skier with the knife lunged at Matt's back. She moved swiftly, reaching out. The deflected blade bit into the back of her hand. Bright red blood splattered across the snow.

"Stop it right now—stop it, all of you." Maha screamed at the men, then clutched her hand in pain. Matt scooped up a handful of cold snow, packed it down over her wound, then wrapped it tightly with his bandanna. The two Arabic men had come up alongside, the taller one threatening Matt with the knife.

"What are you doing, Saleem?" Maha screamed. "Are you crazy?"

"You should be ashamed of yourself, sneaking around with this man. We've been looking for you all night." Suddenly he fell to his knees, sobbing. "Father's dead."

All color drained from her face. "What?" She was shaking as she gripped her older brother by the arm. "Oh God. What happened?"

"He was at the airport late last night for a flight to Amman when Israeli commandos attacked. They blew up several planes on the runway and shot up the main building. Father tried to duck down behind a ticket counter...." When he looked up, a fierce hatred burned in his dark eyes.

"Zionist pigs. They shot him in the back. He bled to death. And where was the cowardly Lebanese army during all this? Their barracks are only five kilometers away." He spit into the snow. "I will kill them all."

His vow fell on deaf ears. Maha fainted into Matt's arms, her warm blood melting the snow.

Chapter Six

The Tonight Show

As the host began to wind up his opening monologue, the live audience was in an exceptionally festive and jovial mood. "Well, I see you people are really wound up, and just as well. We have a great show for you tonight. Of course, unlike Bill Clinton, we can't get our current president on the show. In fact, I don't know of anyone who's even heard from him lately. And speaking of the president," he said, with a wink, "I've been continuing my study of genetics. I find the subject fascinating." Several in the audience jeered loudly, recalling his earlier jokes.

"My recent studies have led me to some startling discoveries. As you know, genes control such things as hair color, eye color, and even, I have recently discovered, behavior. Why just this afternoon I made a startling discovery while comparing the DNA of an ostrich and the president. They both contain the same gene for putting one's head in the sand."

The Oval Office, 7a.m.

Horns from early morning traffic blared along 17th Street. President Ross Pierce, sheltered by thick glass from the outside noise and outside threats, sat alone at his desk in the West Wing. He looked straight ahead. A bust of Abraham Lincoln, sitting on the fireplace mantle, stared back. *I wonder which is better, Mr. Lincoln, to know you're an assassination target, or to be taken by surprise?* Lincoln just kept staring.

Nearly three months after the suicide attack that killed Dr. Andrew Norman and so many others, he was still troubled. His minor flesh wounds were healed, but he still ached for all the people slaughtered. Even more troubling was how to respond. Congress, the press, the American people—indeed, the entire world—clamored for an official U.S. response to the attack, as well as a major policy statement on terrorism. Everyone demanded some type of action.

The hidden door next to the office of the Chief of Staff opened slowly. "You wanted to talk with me, Mr. President?"

Ross Pierce stood up and motioned to a chair. "Yes, Karl. I do. I thought maybe we could talk a little before the day really hits."

Karl van Ness sat comfortably in the massive wing chair. "What about?"

"Why don't you sit over here, out of the sunlight. It shows off your wrinkles, and reminds me of mine."

"Both sets earned in the service of our country, Mr. President," van Ness said gravely.

"Mine were earned getting my ass in a sling, and yours were earned saving it. For which I'm eternally grateful, Karl."

"So, how can I help?" Van Ness sat uneasily now.

"Coffee?"

"Thank you."

Ross poured his mentor a cup of coffee, a touch of deference reserved only for this man he both trusted and needed.

"I want to talk about that female terrorist attack, how things are shaping up."

Van Ness waited. His coffee was hot, and bitter.

"As you know, I've made dozens of speeches since the attack. I've promised the American people, and the world, that the United States would not stand for such cowardly acts."

"And they've been good speeches, Mr. President. People can feel your conviction and...."

"My string is running out, Karl. I know it and you know it.

People want action, not talk." Pierce set down his coffee mug on the desk, careful to place it on the coaster.

"And what are you not telling me?"

Ross stared, startled at the blunt question. Then he nodded. "Something big is afoot, something evil. I don't know what, but some-one tried to kill me once, and I don't think they will stop. I got into this seat on promises of bringing about peace, one way or another. Now they bring the issue right to my doorstep, and I still don't have a fuck-ing plan of action I can believe in."

"I understand, Mr. President. And I wouldn't advise an approach like your predecessor launched in the wake of September 11. Costly and unfortunately ineffective."

"I know. That's one of the reasons I'm sitting in this chair today. However, in the eyes of the world it looks as if the war on terrorism is being lost, not won."

Van Ness continued to listen. The coffee cup sat on the side table, untouched.

"Let me spell it out for you. The polls tell us the American peo-ple are fed up with the fear and uncertainty. Not knowing when and where the next attack will come. They're afraid terrorism will reach into their local communities. No one feels safe anymore. And I don't blame them. I'm practically a prisoner of this office. I can hardly go out and meet the people." President Pierce stood up, clutching the large coffee.

"And the protesters. Have you seen those slogans, Karl? *Nuke the Bomber Bitches, Fight Back Now Before It's Too Late,* and *Don't Wait for Another Pearl Harbor.*"

"They're difficult to miss." Van Ness watched the president move toward the windows facing the south lawn.

"I'm getting thousands of letters and e-mails demanding America take a firm stand to protect itself. Most of them want us to launch a retaliatory strike right now." He shook his head. "In all my years as a governor, senator, and now president, I've never seen such vitriolic displays of public anger."

"From my discussions, Mr. President, it appears the military, along with the CIA, fully support the public demands for all-out retal-iation."

"I know. I've been briefed until I can't look at another slide. They keep saying they have the targets and the means. All they need is a thumbs-up from me and the righteous force of America's high-tech weaponry will put the terrorists out of action forever." He glanced at his mentor. "That's a direct quote."

Karl van Ness nodded. "The major defense contractors are pressing their congressmen. And several senior politicians are afraid of losing their hefty PAC contributions. It's not pretty on the hill, Mr. President." He stood by the fireplace, waiting for the name he knew would come up.

"And that arrogant asshole, Mason Stevens, chairman of the Senate Select Committee on Intelligence, has been meeting with the press almost daily. He's leading the crusade for retaliation. Shit, his office phones here just about every hour for another meeting to press his case."

"He has a point," van Ness said. "If there is fresh intelligence data identifying the nations harboring and actively supporting terrorist networks, it could become obsolete if we don't strike soon."

"I know it, Karl, that's what worries me. And he's whipping the American people into a frenzy. Just watch this tape of the Larry King Show last night." Ross Pierce walked over to the wall unit and grabbed the remote control. A large flat screen TV boomed to life. The tanned face of Senator Stevens emerged.

"Watch this sonofabitch. And look at that hairdo. Coiffed for the occasion."

"The reason we're confronted with increasingly bold and bloody acts of terrorism is because terrorism works," the senator barked. "Blatant acts of murder and mayhem get these cowards an enormous amount of attention from the liberal media and catapult them onto the world stage."

"Whoa, senator," replied King, pushing back his chair. "Are you saying terrorism is also a propaganda tool?"

"That's right. Then the ineffective United Nations and certain cowardly members of the international community go soft whenever there is an opportunity to prosecute and put the terrorists in jail." Senator Stevens tapped his fingertips on the table. "Their lame excuse is that they need to better understand the causes of terrorism. Some governments even express the opinion that these groups must have some validity to their grievances if they engage in such open displays of violence. It's all just rhetoric—what they're doing is avoiding the real issues."

"And your solution, Senator?"

"The time for talk is over, Larry. These murderers grow bolder by the minute. If the president doesn't strike now, and strike hard, I fear that American soil will become a prime target for every half-crazed terrorist on the planet. Some of whom our intelligence tells us already have access to deadly biological weapons and makeshift dirty bombs."

The senator, his face red, gazed directly into the camera. "Swift and severe reprisal is the only language these international criminals can understand. It's time President Pierce showed some backbone. We've got to convince the terrorist organizations and their backers— not to mention those spineless nations hiding within the United Nations—that we mean business."

Ross Pierce threw down the remote control. "I'm not a coward, Karl. And by God I do have the force of character and courage to unleash the wrath of America's military and technological might on these bastards. I'm even willing to support targeted covert operations and assassinations if necessary."

"But...?" Karl van Ness watched his protégé.

"When I was in Vietnam I saw first hand the senseless futility of war. No outsider can really force a country into submission. Hate and violence only breed more hate and violence, never peace."

"But this isn't a conventional war."

"I know. The terrorists have moved well beyond seeking recognition or understanding for their cause. By amassing body counts, their goal now seems to be to destabilize the global economy and weaken the willpower of the West."

"So what keeps you from letting the military strike?"

"A couple of things. For one, the polls are pretty evenly split. While half of the American people favor retaliation, the other half demand a peaceful solution. They believe it's time the United States took a stand for what is right. To stop the global escalation of terrorism, retaliation, more terrorism, and more retaliation. Look at the mess the Israelis are in. Tit for tat, bodies for bodies. And it spills over to other parts of the world as well." President Pierce sat back down in his chair again and closed his eyes.

Karl van Ness waited, his coffee cup still untouched. "Let's have your views, Mr. President."

Ross Pierce spoke again, much calmer now. "Okay. Recognize the State of Palestine and stop giving support to Israeli aggressiveness."

Beyond the bulletproof glass traffic honked on 17th Street, and protesters chanted and carried signs in front of the White House. Van Ness listened, trying to make out the words, but only the anger came through clearly. "That wouldn't be a very wise political move."

"I know that, Karl. But a growing percentage of Americans feel that Israel's true purpose is not self-defense, but territorial expansion. And full recognition would immediately erode Arab sympathy for the terrorists, whose stated aim, after all, is recognition of the rights of the Palestinian people." Ross took a sip of coffee. "Once we've recognized Palestine, the Arab nations will have to withdraw their support of terrorism, or face being branded by the U.N. as terrorists themselves."

Van Ness nodded. "Believe it or not, Mr. President, I do see the logic of this approach. For years the United States and the international community have seen the recognition of Palestine as the only real solution, the only path to lasting peace. The problem was, none of our politicians and elected officials had the courage to make the final decision. In fact, as we both know, several times over the past fifty years the United States, on the verge of official recognition, has pulled out at the last hour. Always for political reasons."

"I know, Karl. But it is the right decision. If we hope to maintain a position of positive influence in the world, then we must take the high road in times of international crisis. Especially now."

"You may be right, Mr. President. But you certainly won't be very popular with the supporters of Israel. You know as well as anyone the financial muscle and political strength of the Jewish lobby. And the fundamentalist Christians, another strong lobby, also back a strong Israel."

"So what's your advice, Karl?"

"The peaceful path might work. But if you chose to follow it, you need more political ammunition than you have at the moment. A lot more. You also need some leverage. Big leverage. Against Israel.

Against the Arabs. And here in the U.S. Otherwise, you won't survive your first term in office." Karl van Ness now stood directly in front of the president.

The intercom buzzed, breaking the mood. "Your next appointment is waiting, Mr. President."

"Have them wait a little longer." He watched his mentor.

"Not only would recognition be political suicide, Mr. President, but there's no telling what the Israeli secret service would do if they got wind of it. Many influential and powerful people depend on America's financial and military support of Israel. A third of our annual foreign aid—close to seven billion dollars—goes to Israel, a country no bigger than the state of Kentucky. They definitely wouldn't take it lying down."

The deadly Mossad. "Yes, I'm aware of that. But I've got another reason for seeking a peaceful solution."

Van Ness remained quiet.

"Oil. And the oil lobby is even bigger than the Jewish lobby." Pierce stood up and came around the wide desk. "Think of the potential, Karl. With skillful negotiations, we could obtain massive concessions, even partial ownership of vast oil fields. And to complicate matters, these same oil fields have long been coveted by the Russians. It would definitely be in the long-term interests of the United States to keep the Russians away from the Middle East's massive oil deposits."

"Then you are going to need some very big leverage."

"Just what kind of leverage, Karl?"

"I might have a few ideas. If you will excuse me, Mr. President, I have some work to do."

Long Beach, California

"THANK GOD I ARRIVED LAST NIGHT." Brian Walker was being escorted through the basement from the hotel to the main hall of the Long Beach Convention Center. "What do you make of the mobs out there?" he asked the two heavyset security guards assigned to deliver him safely for his speech. Walker, who had a resume a mile long—among other things, he was a professor of law at the University of California, Berkeley, an internationally recognized expert on terrorism, and a renowned criminal defense lawyer—was scheduled to give the keynote address at the Southern California Convention of Palestinian-Americans.

"I've been working as a security guard at the convention center for nearly ten years, and this is the biggest and meanest crowd of protesters I've ever seen," said one of the guards, fingering his holstered gun. "I'm expecting that mob to come rushing through these underground corridors any minute now."

"You sure picked a crappy time to give a speech, mister," the other guard said. "I hope you got a helicopter waiting."

Hundreds of protesters had begun arriving the day before. Campers, vans, rented buses and motor homes were filled with people from all walks of life who had an opinion to express about terrorism and America. Some traveled for days to reach the southern California beach community. By 9 A.M., the official start of the convention, over four thousand people were pressed together in the grounds surrounding the convention building. And more spilled over onto Ocean Boulevard. The undermanned and inexperienced Long Beach police force had given up trying to control the swelling throng. At the moment, they were just waiting, and hoping the day wouldn't turn ugly.

"Support Israel," shouted some. "Recognize Palestine," shouted others. The mob had separated into two camps. On one side were those deeply concerned about terrorism on American soil and blindly opposed to anything Arab. This noisy, unruly group included rednecks, bikers and NRA supporters hoisting incendiary placards. *Get a Free Carpet, Kill a Rug-Head*, one screamed out. On the same side were zealous, vociferous supporters of Israel carrying equally inflammatory banners: *God Chose the Jews—Not the Palestinians* and *Support Israel, Attack Now.*

And strangely, nestled within this camp, was a large contingent of fundamentalist Christians, clean-cut God Bless America types led by a charismatic minister, who loudly sang out "Onward Christian Soldiers." They carried their own posters: *Jesus Died for Our Sins—It's Time the Arabs Died for Theirs.*

In a small bricked area in front of the brightly painted convention center, the smaller half of the crowd, mothers with young children, college students, liberal ministers with congregations from numerous faiths, as well as Arab-Americans of many backgrounds, were equally loud and committed to the ideas indicated by their placards: *We're American Citizens, Not Terrorists; Stop the Madness— Recognize Palestine; Support Peace—Not Israel;* and *Down with Zionist Imperialism.* There were numerous women's rights advocates protesting the exploitation of women in both America and the Muslim countries.

Inside the round, tall convention hall gathered nearly six hundred of southern California's most prominent Palestinian-Americans. During the 1970s when Israel shoved Palestinians out of their homeland and neighboring Arab nations failed to offer them refuge—in the Arab world, the Palestinians are looked down upon as dirty, uneducated troublemakers, common laborers, housemaids, and garbage collectors—a large number of wealthy and educated Palestinians had moved to southern California. The group assembled inside the convention center were the elite, doctors, pharmacists and successful business people. A large number were Armenian Christians. No matter what their faith, all the delegates that morning were committed to one objective, the restoration of the State of Palestine and an end to conflict in the Middle East.

It was hoped that this convention would help raise awareness and understanding among the American people that Palestine was not a terrorist state. Terrorism was the desperate act of a handful of deranged people. The overwhelming majority of Palestinians were willing to find a way to live with their new neighbor, Israel. All they wanted was their country back.

"Ladies and gentlemen. It is time to begin." As the chairman of the convention welcomed the attendees, the muffled chants from the growing crowds outside formed an eerie backdrop, a faint threat rising and falling against the walls. Dr. Ahmed Khoury quickly finished his welcoming remarks and introduced the keynote speaker. Thunderous applause momentarily drowned out the chanting outside.

Dr. Brian Walker strode confidently up to the lectern, shook hands with his host and acknowledged the enthusiastic applause of the crowd with a nod of his head. At fifty-five years of age, Brian Walker portrayed a commanding presence. His long black hair, tied in a pony-tail, showed striking silver streaks at the temples. He still had the easy gait of an athlete. Accustomed to controversy as a result of his radical views on freedom and international law, he had accepted this speech as an opportunity to address not just these Palestinian expatriates but also the American people. Numerous reporters from the major print media were in the audience, as were camera crews from CNN and the other major networks. A team of reporters from the Arabic news network, Al Jazeera, had their TV cameras ready. With all the exposure, Dr. Walker was looking forward to helping America understand the gravity of the country's growing tide of hostility toward foreigners.

"During my lectures at Berkeley, I'm used to the angry mob being on the inside instead of the outside." The crowd laughed nervously.

He stared at the audience filling the circular hall, then his voice boomed out. "We hold these truths to be self-evident—that all men are created equal, that they are endowed by their creator with certain unalienable rights, and that among these are life, liberty and the pursuit of happiness." After a long pause, during which the only sound was the muffled chanting outside, Dr. Walker continued. "So begins the second paragraph of one of the most important political documents concerning human freedom ever written. The Declaration of Independence, signed on July 4, 1776, by fifty-six courageous individuals representing the original thirteen United States of America.

"What a powerful and visionary document," he declared, his voice gaining in intensity. "It's a shame America won't live up to it." Many in the audience gasped, several murmured angrily. "And I'm not talking about those people outside. I'm talking about our elected officials, the supposedly courageous upholders of our sacred Constitution. The Declaration of Independence, the Constitution of the United States of America, and the Bill of Rights were intended to be guidelines to help this nation live its values. But they have become a collection of highly malleable words that can be interpreted to fit the needs of whoever is in power at the time. Let me explain. And listen closely, because it is about to happen again.

"It is early 1942. The days following the Japanese attack on Pearl Harbor witnessed a great drop in American resolve. Unable to strike back effectively against the mighty Japanese empire, America instead lashed out at fellow U.S. citizens and peaceful resident aliens of Japanese descent. Executive Order 9066, signed by President Franklin D. Roosevelt on February 19, 1942, called for the deporting of all Japanese and Americans of Japanese ancestry from the Western coastal regions of the United States to concentration camps in the interior. Canvas-tented camps ringed with barbed wire and armed guard towers were hastily erected in such garden spots as Posten, Arizona, Manzanar, in the cold and bleak California high desert, and Topaz, Utah.

"The sad truth, as this deplorable act proves, is that constitutions and laws are not sufficient of themselves to protect the citizens of a nation from their own government. Despite the clear and concise language in the U.S. Constitution that writ of habeas corpus shall not be suspended, and despite the Fifth Amendment's statement that no person shall be deprived of life, liberty or property without due process of law, these constitutional safeguards, these inalienable rights, were denied to over 110,000 people, many of whom were American citizens, under Executive Order 9066.

"Then in 1944 this travesty, born out of fear, was upheld by our Supreme Court in a 6-3 decision against an American citizen, Fred T. Korematsu, convicted in a federal court in 1942 for refusing to report to a relocation center, instead remaining at his home in San Leandro, California, a designated 'military area' at the time." Dr. Walker paused, sweeping the room with his dark eyes. Suddenly, as if on cue, the assembled throng outside the convention center let out an angry roar. "In the not too distant future," Dr. Walker went on, unfazed, "I suggest our Constitution will again be grossly violated, except the names will not be Korematsu, Kodani or Yamamoto, but Hussein, Mohammed, or Markarian.

"Let me be perfectly clear. Even though all of you here today are American citizens, some naturalized and some born in this country, you must stand up for your constitutional rights. If you don't, the crown on the Statue of Liberty will be tarnished once again by the fear and ignorance of our elected officials. As you know, attacks on those of Arab descent in the United States are dramatically escalating. Some Americans, in their ignorance and insecurity, are lashing out at anybody with dark skin and an Arab-sounding name. Just as in 1942, the first attacks will come from frightened citizens in local communities. These will be followed by military intervention, and then an executive order."

A woman in the audience began to weep. The chants from the angry mob outside swelled to a frightening crescendo.

"You think it can't happen? That America has learned from its prior mistakes? Well, think again. It can happen again, and it will." Professor Walker's voice, strident at the microphone, was drowning out the noise of the crowd outside. His hands clutched the lectern.

"And who are these people who will trample on your constitutional rights? They are the individuals, the political organizations, and the nations who profit from terrorism. The Palestinian people are not terrorists, they just want their homes back. No, I am talking about greedy elected officials, entire countries, and highly sophisticated criminal organizations who profit from war and international upheaval. They don't want peace and will do whatever they can to perpetrate unrest, generate fear, and provoke conflict. And, believe it or not, one of those countries is the United States." Walker coughed, then paused for a drink of water from the cold, sweating tumbler atop the lectern.

"Yes, our country is no longer free, but held hostage by special interest groups—the Jewish lobby, the fundamentalist Christian lobby, the defense and aerospace industry lobbies. All pour massive amounts of money into the coffers of politicians across the nation, many of whom are now so deeply indebted that they no longer represent the will of the American people. Our elected representatives have become political pawns of special interest groups, and if unchecked, these servants of the people will take away your inalienable rights to life, liberty, and the pursuit of happiness."

Dr. Brian Walker paused to sip some water. All at once the heavy double doors to the convention hall crashed open, startling him. "What the hell?" he exclaimed, as the water glass slipped through his fingers and shattered on the stage.

For a few frozen moments, no one moved. An eerie stillness gripped the convention hall as it dawned on both groups that an ugly scene was about to explode. The emotional venting outside had gone unchecked for too long. Someone hurled a flaming Molotov cocktail up onto the stage. In a panic, one of the security guards drew his pistol and fired in the direction of a tattooed biker, poised to throw a second gasoline-filled cocktail. Before the biker released it, the bullet struck, spraying flaming gasoline all over him, instantly igniting his long greasy hair and beard. He dove to the floor, screaming and rolling, while people nearby backed away, protesters and delegates alike, shoving each other in an attempt to flee to safety. The shoving quickly escalated to shouting, then physical blows.

For a select group of well-paid men posing as protestors, the moment for action had arrived. Knives, brass knuckles, lead-filled pipes and hammers suddenly appeared. Their first targets were television cameras. Each was expertly put out of action. Then they turned their attention to the Palestinian-Americans and the protesters, tearing into the defenseless men and women with ruthless efficiency. Many of the elderly delegates never saw the clubs that struck the deadly blow on the back of their head, or the knife that punctured a heart. In less than ten minutes, fifty of the delegates and two dozen protesters were strewn about the convention hall, most of them already dead.

With two short blasts from a small whistle, the men dropped their weapons and melted away into the crowd. By the time they slipped out into the relative calm of the convention parking lot, sirens were blaring as police raced to the scene. Invisible in the turmoil, the provocateurs climbed into several large 4X4's and sped away among other vehicles fleeing the scene. Their thin rubber gloves, which left no fingerprints on the weapons, would be incinerated later. "Pretty easy way to make a couple of thousand bucks," one of the men marveled as he clicked the radio, a heavy metal station blaring out a savage beat.

Back in the hall Dr. Walker, crouching behind the lectern, glanced nervously from side to side. Just then one of the security guards ran up and crouched down behind the lectern. "You need to go, Dr. Walker." he shouted over the noise of chairs being overturned, fists flying, and people screaming.

Walker nodded, expecting the guard to lead him to safety. Instead the man, his hand covered in a thin latex glove, reached inside his coat pocket and pulled out a small-caliber pistol. "What I mean, asshole," he hissed, "is you need to go, *permanently*." He pumped a bullet into Dr. Brian Walker's forehead, tossed the gun out into the roiling crowd, and joining his partner, the other fake security guard. Both vanished in the turmoil. With the money now in an account in the Cayman Islands, they were set for life. The bodies of the two real security guards would never be found.

Chapter Seven

Blue Ridge Substance Abuse Clinic and Private Hospital

THE DOOR OPENED AND THE LONE FIGURE SLIPPED IN. It was time to check on his patient—just a quick look at his vital signs while the sedative was still working. Whatever else he'd become, he was still, first and foremost, a man of healing.

As the pneumatic door hissed closed, Dr. Weissman walked lightly to the bank of monitors, awash with red lights and blinking numbers. "What on earth," he exclaimed, stopping halfway there. A flat line was etched across the heart monitor screen. The oxygen level registered zero. His head snapped around. The sheet was pulled up over the patient. He went over to the bed and as he began lifting the sheet, a low, muffled voice came from underneath

"Act normal, Doctor, and don't say anything or I'll sever your femoral artery with this scalpel. Remember, I'm a doctor too. You'll bleed out in seconds."

Dr. Weissman stood still as he felt the surgical steel pressing against his leg. "What do you want?"

"I want to get out of here, and you're going to help me." Matt said, emerging from under the bed and leading the surgeon by his white gown into the shadows behind the bank of monitors.

"But there are CCTV cameras everywhere, even in this room. You'll be spotted in no time." Weissman's voice trembled. He felt tired and oddly lost. "I can't get you out of here. There are guards patrolling the corridors of this wing constantly. I'm afraid, Dr. Richards, we're both trapped in here."

"Tell me," said Matt, "whose face do I have? And who are these people?"

The elderly doctor put his finger to his lips. "I honestly don't know who they are, but I can tell you that the face you have, and it's a masterful job of a transplant if I do say so myself, belonged to an international contract killer, an assassin. He killed for the Mossad, KGB, CIA and others. He was just about to join Al-Qaeda when he was killed by a female Mossad operative. Al-Qaeda offered better pay, I guess."

An international assassin? "How do you know all this?"

"I overheard the two men you met earlier talking about it just before the surgery. It was his body they buried in the closed casket at your funeral."

"And you don't know who these people are?"

"No. I was brought here two years ago from Israel by the director of this clinic. I was promised enough money and equipment to rapidly advance my research in facial transplants. Mostly I work on private patients with badly disfigured faces. You're one of two patients to be put in this secure area of the hospital and given a full facial transplant."

"Well, you're my only hope at the moment, doc, so let's figure out a way for me to get out of here. Otherwise we both might wind up dead. Did this dead guy have any documents on him? Passports, identification, stuff like that?"

"There's a box of his personal effects in the storage closet. They left it there, along with a suitcase of clothes. I think in all the activity surrounding the operations they just forgot about it." He touched Matt's arm. "Will you please put that scalpel away?"

"Okay. Give me your lab coat and I'll pass myself off as you. You crawl around the back and climb into the bed while I shield it from the CCTV camera, then I'll tie you up. You can tell them I overpowered you, gave you a sleeping drug, and escaped." Matt paused. *How to escape?* "Where's your car?"

"It's a white VW Passat, and it's in the private staff parking lot right next to this wing." Dr. Weissman fumbled around. "The keys are here in my pocket, but you'll be seen by the guards and the cameras. It won't work."

"It's better than staying here. Now, take off your coat and get into the bed." Matt put on the white surgeon's smock and stood up beside the bed. Using cabling from the monitors, he bound the doctor's arms and legs. "If you lie here and give me a chance to escape, we both might live a little longer." The elderly surgeon nodded.

Matt opened the closet. He stared at a single piece of leather carry-on luggage, Hartman. It contained a few shirts, some pants, a sports coat and a pair of Italian leather shoes. His eyes registered on a green surgeon's cap on a shelf. Putting it on and draping several clean lab coats over the valise to hide it, Matt made his way out into the hall. It was clear for now. Like the doctor he was, he confidently strode down the hall toward the rear exit sign.

A voice rang out. "What are you doing, doctor?" A security guard.

"Making rounds," replied Matt. "Would you like to help me change a few dressings and bedpans?" He opened the door on his left and strode in.

"All doctors are arrogant assholes." The guard strode back up the hallway, muttering to himself.

Inside the room Matt leaned against the door, sweating and trying to calm his racing heart. He hadn't had a drop of alcohol since the accident, which must have been over seven weeks ago. He'd always wondered what going cold turkey would be like, but never had the courage or desire to quit drinking. *I guess every cloud has a silver lining.* Could he remain sober once he was free—if he got free?

After a few minutes to calm down, he scanned the room. It was nearly identical to his, but without the security door or a CCTV camera. There was a single bed in the center with a short figure under the sheets. A female voice moaned. He stepped over to the bed and carefully lifted the sheet. It was a young woman, about twenty years old, obviously under heavy sedation. In the faint light from the instruments on the wall he noticed the nearly healed stitches around the edge of her face. He was replacing the sheet when suddenly her hand sprang out like a claw and gripped his arm.

"No, Daddy, no." she moaned, then fell quiet. Her grip loosened. Her arm dangled over the side of the bed. She was asleep again. Matt reached down and gently placed her arm back on the bed. The white hospital tag around her wrist was blank except for the blood type, O-positive, with two capital letters, like initials, next to it.

Matt's medical mind began to wonder about this strange woman, but survival instincts pulled him away. The guard could be making his rounds now. How long would he have to wait inside this room? Sweat broke out on his forehead. He cracked open the door.

Nothing. He opened the door a little further, trying to get a view up and down the corridor without being seen. *Now or never.* Summoning some long forgotten reservoir of courage, he strode out of the room as if he were the staff doctor moving on to his next patient. He turned left, the red exit sign clearly visible just twenty paces away.

Reaching the door, Matt looked back up the dimly lit hallway. The guard must have returned to his desk, probably for a few moments of sleep. He reached for the door handle, but his hand froze just above the knob. The sign shimmered in the shadows. "Door locked and alarmed at all times. For staff use only."

Matt swallowed hard. His heart pounded. *Being sober does have its plusses.* Reaching into the lab coat, he produced Dr. Weissman's keys. One was obviously a VW key, the logo prominently embossed on the top. Several others looked like house keys. One stood out as plain and unmarked, like the key to an office or business. Matt slowly inserted the key into the lock. It fit, but when he gently tried to turn it, it wouldn't move. Then he remembered that this was a new wing. Perhaps the locks and keys weren't well worn yet. He applied more force. The key turned. He pushed the door open, revealing the brightly lit parking lot. The VW Passat was only three spaces from the door.

Here goes nothing. Half wishing he were in a drunken stupor, Matt moved to the car. His hands shook. As he climbed in and shut the door, a battered Ford Taurus pulled into the lot and parked just opposite Dr. Weissman's car. Matt ducked down onto the passenger seat, fighting the urge to throw up. He breathed deeply, trying desperately to calm his nerves and stomach. The drugs he had been given for the past few weeks were still very much in control of his system. He closed his eyes to keep from blacking out. A car door slammed. He heard the crunch of footsteps on gravel.

Matt sat up. He scanned the parking lot, then noticed the clock on the dash. 4:45 am. They would soon discover Dr. Weissman. He reached up to adjust the rear view mirror.

"Oh God." A strange face stared back at him. "How long will it take to get used to this face?" He reached up to feel the prominent nose and strong square chin. It was a handsome face, refined yet rugged. He had read medical journals about patients whose entire personalities changed after getting major facial surgery. Maybe that was a good thing for him. So far his life had been a failure.

Pulling the green surgeon cap down as far as possible, Matt drove the car toward the front gate, barely controlling his urge to jam down on the accelerator and flee this evil place. Slowing down, he lowered the window, raised his arm and waved.

"Leaving early, Dr. Weissman?" The guard reached inside to push the button for the gate. Matt rolled up the window, keeping his head down, as if looking for something. The gate slowly swung open. He accelerated briskly, narrowly missing one side of the gate. To his right was a large ornate sign: *Blue Ridge Substance Abuse Clinic and Private Hospital, Admittance by Appointment Only.*

"Or kidnapping," he muttered, heading down the road toward what he hoped would be the main highway.

Safe, but for how long? About a mile down the asphalt lane he came to the Blue Ridge Parkway, which wound along the backbone of the Blue Ridge Mountains. He knew it ran for nearly 460 miles, all the way from Shenandoah National Park in northern Virginia down to Great Smoky Mountains National Park in North Carolina.

"Before I go much further, I'd better look at these documents and see who the hell I am," he said, listening to his voice. It sounded disembodied in the car's confines. "At least I still sound like me." Pulling into a turnout overlooking the lowlands of Virginia, Matt stopped the car and reached for the carry-on bag. The clothes, he was relieved to discover, were nearly his size, though the man must have been a little more muscular. He tried on a shirt—a little loose, but it would do for the time being. The pants needed to be tightened with a belt. He dressed in the darkened car, then turned on the overhead light. Taking out the wallet first, he noticed it was fine-grain calfskin Pierre Cardin. *Not a pauper.*

The wallet contained a valid Maryland driver's license in the name of William Stubbs, age forty-seven. Matt didn't recognize the address, but it was his new face staring back from the plastic card.

There were also several Visa cards and an American Express Platinum Card, all in the name of William Stubbs, and all current. Nestled in the wallet were a large number of one-hundred-dollar bills, some tens and twenties. He gripped the money tight, his new life line, while his mind raced. *How to stay alive? Who to talk to?* He reached into the bag again.

What he found next shocked him—twelve valid passports from various countries, all with different names. Two were U.S. passports, one in the name of Stubbs and the other Scott. Each carried the same photo but a separate selection of credit cards, driver's licenses and identity cards. The other nationalities included France, Germany, Britain, Russia, and Switzerland, as well as Brazil, South Africa, Egypt, Morocco and Lebanon. At the bottom of the bag, in a bulging zippered wallet, was a small fortune in currency matching each of the countries.

Matt sat back, perspiring heavily. Bile rose up, sour in his throat. His new face belonged to a hired assassin who was no doubt known by nearly every major government. *A perfect target.*

Blue lights flashed behind him. Gravel crunched under tires coming to an abrupt halt. Matt jumped, realizing that a Virginia state trooper vehicle had came to a stop directly behind him. Quickly he shoved the documents back into the leather valise, threw it on the floor, and opened the car door.

"Stay in the vehicle, sir," a voice boomed over a loudspeaker. "Please have your driver's license ready for inspection."

The passenger door of the police car opened and a large black man emerged in a round-brimmed felt hat. Keeping his right hand on his pistol holster, he walked up to the white VW.

Matt's hand was shaking as he jabbed at the button which operated the window. "You woke me up, officer. I was trying to catch a few winks before continuing my drive."

"That's sensible of you. May I see your license, sir?" The trooper seemed relieved, if still somewhat suspicious. Every police officer in the country was aware of incidents where policemen were killed during routine traffic stops by lunatics or junkies.

"Stubbs, officer. William Stubbs. I'm coming home from a business meeting at the Greenbriar Hotel. Wanted to get home before my kids went off to school." Matt dug into the wallet and handed the license through the window to the officer. "Don't think I'll make it though. I just had to stop and rest." His hands shook.

Shining his large flashlight first on the license, then on Matt's face, he stepped back and signaled to his partner that everything was okay. The other officer started up the police vehicle. Routinely passing his flashlight into the driver's compartment and then over the back seat, the officer seemed satisfied. "Rest as long as you need to, Mr. Stubbs. And have a safe journey home."

In a few moments the police cruiser pulled out of the overlook and headed back up the mountain. Matt slumped over the steering wheel, his entire body shook. *Will the rest of my life be filled with lies?* Racked with a fear he'd never experienced before, he turned on the ignition and jammed the accelerator to the floor. Tires squealing, he spun around in the gravel turnout and shot back onto the dark highway.

"Get a grip, Matthew – William," he said to himself, trying to regulate his breathing. Over the next several minutes he willed himself to calm down. The speedometer fell to just below the speed limit. The added oxygen relieved his anxiety and soon he was back in control. He settled in for the three-hour drive to Sweet Briar College.

As his brain cleared, it occurred to him that his captors had probably decided to keep his disappearance quiet. They wouldn't risk exposure. Instead, whoever they were would probably come after him. And they had a huge advantage—they knew his face while he had no idea who they were. At least he had a head start.

Baltimore-Washington International Airport

Faint streaks of orange and gold exploded across the eastern horizon, chasing away the blackness but not the bitter cold. The silver Jaguar XJS slid into an empty space in the four-level parking garage in front of BWI's curved terminal. The airport, built in 1950 and first named Friendship International, was modernized and enlarged in the 1970s to serve Washington, D.C., to the south, and Baltimore to the north. As on any weekday morning, the parking complex was alive with business travelers scrambling out of their vehicles and heading for flights in the early morning darkness. No one would notice two men talking inside a car in the parking lot, especially since the entire level was now full. The long line of incoming cars kept climbing up the ramp to the levels above.

"It is good to see you again, my friend," said Mohammed Al Nagib as the rear door opened and the tall man from the Jaguar settled down. They were nestled in the plush leather seats of a Rolls Royce Silver Cloud. A soundproof, tinted-glass barrier separated them from the chauffeur.

"You flatter yourself, Mr. Nagib. I am neither your friend, nor am I pleased to see you. The less we meet, the better, as far as I am concerned." His guest was elegantly dressed in a black business suit. "Let's make this quick. What problem is so great that we couldn't talk on secure phone lines?"

"Actually, there is no problem, Mr. Fisher. On the contrary, everything is on schedule and running according to plan."

"So why the urgent meeting?"

"There is an old passage from the Koran: 'Trust in God, but tie your camel.' I just wanted to look you in the eyes and hear firsthand that you are still in position to get the information we need. Telephones are wonderful inventions, but nothing beats a direct, face-to-face conversation." The Egyptian smiled.

"I am not amused, nor do I have all day." William Fisher, director of Middle Eastern intelligence at the National Security Agency, glared in the gloomy interior.

"Of course," Nagib said. "The fact is, we've spent years carefully developing our contacts. I must be certain that you'll be able to deliver us the right information before anyone else knows about it. We must know the president's decision before it is made public. The future depends on it."

"President Pierce has called a special meeting for today." William Fisher was a member of the president's Special Task Force on Terrorism and the Middle East, along with Senator Mason Stevens, the director of the CIA, secretary of state, national security advisor, secretary of defense, and the chairman of the Joint Chiefs of Staff. "He needs to decide on an official course of action in response to the suicide bombing attack, and he's running out of time. And the Israelis keep pressuring everyone for more arms, more money and more support against the Arabs. Senator Stevens seems to be firmly on their side—in every meeting he pushes their security issues." Fisher looked around at the parked cars and the occasional hurrying traveler.

"But it shouldn't be much longer. Soon I should know what course of action the United States will pursue. As soon as I find out, you'll know," Fisher caught al Nagib's eye. "Just remember our agreement—I'm counting on you to eliminate the Israeli bastard who led the raid that killed my wife. Now, unless you have any more stray camels that need tying, I must get to my office."

"I do so look forward to hearing from you at your earliest convenience." Nagib murmered. William Fisher slammed the door and returned to his Jaguar.

The tinted barrier slowly descended and the liveried driver turned around. Demetrie Antonopolis took off his chauffeur hat, his long ponytail falling out. "I don't trust him."

"Neither do I, Demetrie." Nagib lit a Cuban cigar, his first of many for the day. "But I still feel sorry for him."

"I don't understand."

"It's a shallow man who acts only out of revenge. Because of his hatred and bitterness he is harmless. When this affair is over he will slink away into the darkness with his fat Swiss bank account."

"So why feel sorry for him?"

"Because he will never find the peace he desperately seeks. Revenge never brings peace. There's an ancient proverb: *When a man goes for revenge, he must first dig two graves.* Remember Demetrie, the truly dangerous men are those who act with forethought and meticulous planning, driven by a vision and burning desire. Those who dream of a new future and are committed to pursue that vision are the ones to fear. Men like Fisher are simply pawns in a global chess game, and I control their every move."

The elegant Rolls Royce exited the BWI parking garage. A nondescript gray car kept a safe distance behind.

Washington, D.C.

"Our practice has certainly picked up since you became personal physician to the president," Dr. Margaret Khalid said. She was the only other physician in Dr. Noubar Melikian's small medical practice. "Guess everyone is hoping they will hear the latest gossip about the president—or else they want bragging rights." she said, studying the appointments listed on her computer screen.

"The good news is most of President Pierce's medical issues are handled at Walter Reed Military Hospital. We're just around for general checkups and the occasional bad fish dinner." Dr. Melikian sat at his desk reviewing the same screen. "Remember to keep your evenings free whenever I'm invited to political or social dinners. You may have to stand in for me in case the president has a medical emergency."

"So much for my personal life," she said. "It's hard enough getting a date with a decent man in this town without having to spend most of my evenings sitting by the telephone waiting for the president to have indigestion or choke on a pretzel."

"I'm sorry, Maggie." Dr. Melikian smiled, looking over at his associate. "I know it's been hard starting over. In any other country in the world, you'd be a senior medical officer and probably have a large staff of your own. That's why I took you into my practice. You're one of the most experienced GPs I've ever met. It was difficult for me as well, coming from Switzerland and settling into the medical profession in the United States. My only advantage is I came here in my late twenties, so I've had longer to get established. And I guess I got a few breaks along the way as well. I still thank my lucky stars that my father's employer took such an interest in me and supported my education and career."

Noubar Melikian walked over to where his associate was standing, a pile of patient files in her hands. "As far as I'm concerned, you can stand in for me anytime, even with the president. In fact, I'm going to send a letter to the White House making certain that if I'm not available, you're my stand-in, no questions asked."

"So I still have to sit by the telephone, only this time it's official," her brown eyes watched him. "Why don't you find me a husband instead? Preferably one with tons of money in the bank so I never have to work again." They both laughed. "In the meantime, I guess we'd better get our schedules coordinated and attack another busy day."

Life had been pretty hectic for Dr. Melikian following his appointment as personal physician to the president of the United States, what with security checks, briefings on protocol, training on how to respond to the press, and additional training to cover possible biological or chemical attacks on the president. To make matters worse, he was now at the top of every Washington socialite's list for dinner parties and social functions. Not that it wasn't exciting and even flattering. But at his age, he wouldn't have minded a few quiet evenings reading.

"Who will you be rubbing shoulders with this month?" Maggie asked.

After a few strokes on the keyboard, Dr. Melikian's Epson printer came to life. "Here it is, the complete social life of the personal physician to the president of the United States." He frowned and handed her a two-page printout. She scanned the pages with exaggerated awe.

Dr. Melikian, a modest man, was embarrassed. "Enough of this foolishness. We've got patients to look after—and another Secret Service security check of our offices."

The Oval Office

"WELCOME, MASON," PRESIDENT PIERCE SAID, waving for him to join the others around the antique coffee table in front of the fireplace. "Coffee? There's sugar over there."

"Of course, Mr. President. Everyone knows the best coffee in Washington is served in the Oval Office. But it always comes with a high price tag." Muffled chuckling broke out among the small group, all members of the president's Special Task Force on Terrorism and the Middle East.

"I think you can afford it," Pierce responded. As chairman of the powerful Senate Select Committee on Intelligence and one of the longest-serving U.S. senators, Mason T. Stevens had assembled a massive war chest, which he spent freely during his re-election bids every six years. For a hefty campaign donation, businesses with ties to Virginia could get Senator Stevens's solid backing for their interests. And his backing meant big bucks in government contracts.

"My family send their condolences, Senator," the president remarked, turning serious.

"Yes, we all send our condolences," echoed General Ernie Reese, chairman of the Joint Chiefs. "How's your wife?"

"Thank you, gentlemen. We're doing as well as can be expected—God moves in mysterious ways."

An awkward silence filled the room. The president broke it. "Yes, well, I've asked you here this morning to get all the options out in the open, and your personal views, concerning our official response to the terrorist menace. It's time we laid out our position to the American people and the world. We'll meet every Tuesday and Thursday morning to tackle this damn situation until we come up with some viable solutions. Here's the main problem: the public seems to be evenly split on the issue. It would be easier if there was a solid majority opinion one way or the other."

The individuals seated around the table nodded. Senator Stevens continued to sip his coffee, watching the others closely. "However, this situation may also be to our advantage. With the polls evenly split, once we decide on our course of action, we can engage in a little positive propaganda to build up support for our position. At least we won't have to overcome overwhelming opposition. Your thoughts?"

"With all due respect, Mr. President, there's only one course of action," General Reese said. "Bomb the hell out of the sonsofbitches and cut the balls off any left alive. These fanatics don't play by any rules other than the murder of innocent people. We'd better take care of them quick before someone gets his hands on a nuclear or biological bomb and uses it."

"In this instance," said Senator Stevens, gently returning his coffee cup to itsmatching saucer, "I happen to agree fully with General Reese. Unfortunately, the time for a peaceful approach has long passed. Europe has given in to the demands of terrorists for so long they're practically a legitimate special interest group now. No, the world's been too soft on these maniacs. The only option left is massive and deadly force. Somebody has to start making terrorism severely unattractive as a political option." He looked at the others, flashing his practiced smile.

"And thanks to the dedicated work of the NSA and CIA, we now have ample intelligence concerning the whereabouts of certain senior terrorist leaders as well as major training camps. This information, gathered at great expense and unfortunate loss of life, won't be current forever. We need to strike now."

Director of the CIA Terry Finch, a man of few words whose organization had benefited over the past several years from the vociferous support of Senator Stevens and his intelligence committee, looked around the table and nodded in agreement. A brilliant academician and a former professor of international policy at Harvard University, Dr. Finch administered the CIA as if it were a government think tank. "Mason's right. I'm not certain how long this intelligence will remain current, but it's high quality at the present time."

"Senator Stevens and the military-industrial complex are very persuasive," said Secretary of State Nathan Vance, a long time senior statesman and former U.S. ambassador to the UN, "and I do agree that the world has been far too soft on terrorism. Every two-bit fanatic with a political or religious grievance now sees terrorism as a legitimate way of getting the world to take notice. Unfortunately, we're no longer dealing with small-time fanatics. September 11 has proven just how organized and deadly this game has become. Nonetheless, I don't believe direct attacks or all-out war will solve the problem."

"So what are your thoughts, Nathan?" the president asked. "And don't hold back."

Vance colored a little. "Well, I've been traveling constantly for the past several months since the suicide attack, talking face to face with all the major foreign leaders. Most don't have the stomach or the support at home for a full-scale war on terrorism. And those in the Middle East, I must tell you, are still extremely sympathetic to the issues of Palestinian statehood and curtailing Israeli expansion. Besides, most of our European allies are getting pretty fed up with Israel. It's universally understood that if it weren't for massive U.S. aid, Israel would be forced to get along with their neighbors or perish."

"What are you driving at, Nathan?" Pierce said.

"Simply put, direct war won't work. Overt attacks and massive use of force will only intensify the terrorists' resolve and lead to increased reprisal attacks. By waging direct war, in one fell swoop we'll be creating more terrorists and alienating the entire Muslim world." Vance looked around at the Task Force members. Several gave him cold looks. He pressed on. "It's like trying to fight the Hydra—cut off one head, and three more grow back to take its place. Anyway, it's been proven that we can't fully defend ourselves against terrorists. No matter how much we spend on homeland defense, they still slip through."

"And what is your solution?"

"We've got to figure out a way to recognize Palestine as a legitimate country and tone down the Israelis. At the same time we need to make it perfectly clear to the terrorists that we aren't giving in to them. We need some leverage to get all the parties to move in the direction of a lasting and peaceful solution. But I'm not sure yet what that leverage is." The secretary of state looked sallow and tired from his marathon travels. "But a solution should surface if we continue open dialogue with the Arab nations and our allies."

"If I may add to that point, Mr. President?" National Security Advisor Caroline Black interjected cautiously. "Women in this country and around the world are beginning to protest in massive numbers against terrorism and global unrest. Their collective voice is becoming louder and louder. The graphic television footage of the death of a female suicide bomber on American soil has galvanized them. They're tired of seeing women used as tools for terrorists."

"For Christ's sake," exclaimed Senator Stevens, his face reddening. "I can't believe the drivel I'm hearing. Who gives a damn if it's a man, a woman, or a dog that carried the bomb? The fact is, little lady, this is war. We didn't start it, but by God we're in the middle of it and we have to respond—now."

The senator stood up, spreading his arms for effect. "Let me remind you all of the facts: The beginning of this whole mess was the hijacking of an El Al airliner on July 22, 1968. The hostages were released in exchange for sixteen Arab prisoners held in Israeli jails. The hijackers were also released. I'd say that was a successful operation. So success spawned repetition. And...."

"We know the history, Senator," Nathan Vance murmured.

"Seems to me everyone has forgotten it. Between 1968 and 1975, there were 204 terrorists arrested after hijackings and other attacks, and every one of the bastards was eventually released—even those involved in the murders of the Israeli athletes at the 1972 Olympics. Thanks to the sniveling German government. Not surprisingly, the rate and intensity of terrorist attacks and the death toll has continued to rise. In 1985 a TWA airliner was hijacked and flown to Beirut; an American passenger murdered and his body dumped out onto the tarmac. And then there was poor Leon Klinghoffer, the man in the wheelchair killed by terrorists aboard the cruise ship *Achille Lauro*. And again the terrorists were released. Are you getting the picture here?"

Stevens was shouting now. "At least three terrorists have been awarded the Nobel Peace Prize and several have received honorary degrees from leading American universities. How's that for legitimizing terrorism?"

Senator Mason Stevens sat down, his voice calmer. "The message is clear: If you believe strongly enough in your cause to kill civilians in cold blood, then you must be justified and we should try and understand your position. Bullshit. The only possible solution is just the opposite: We have to make it clear that if anyone resorts to terrorism to promote their cause, not only will their cause be hindered, but they will be hunted down and killed."

"But all that changed after September 11," protested National Security Adviser Black. "They went too far that time—now the majority of the world condemns acts of terrorism."

"That's just political rhetoric to placate us," Stevens snapped. "We have evidence of terrorist buildups in the Sudan and Malaysia, and of terrorist leaders freely walking around in France and Italy. Meanwhile, Hezbollah training camps, in the jungle where Argentina, Brazil and Paraguay intersect, are well funded and pumping out hundreds of assassins and suicide bombers every month. We suspect that the Arab woman who attacked the president came from one of those camps. Look, we have the targets and we know which countries are supporting and funding these bastards. The time to strike is now." Meaty hands gripped the arms of his chair.

"The problem with suicide bombers," CIA Director Finch said softly, "is that the threat of retaliation against them is useless. They're already dead." He pulled his pipe out, ceremoniously tamped down the tobacco, and looked at the president, who nodded his approval. With a sleek silver lighter, Finch took a few long puffs.

"However," he resumed, waving his hand through the smoke, "there is one way to dramatically reduce the number of individuals willing to become suicide bombers. And that is by retaliating with massive prejudice against their families. Many families of suicide bombers become minor celebrities in their countries. They receive sizable amounts of money from the terrorist organizations as remuneration for the loss of their sons and daughters. It's very simple. We can send a powerful, clear-cut message to the terrorist community: Become a suicide bomber, and we kill your entire family."

A stunned silence fell over the Oval Office.

"But that's immoral," Carrie Black protested, dumbfounded. "And illegal."

"Tell that to the families of the people buried under the rubble of the Twin Towers," Senator Stevens said in an acid tone. "This is war. Why should we play by the rules when they don't? Now you are talking sense, Dr. Finch. I like it."

"But the U.N. would totally condemn us."

The senator looked at her, his voice cold with disgust. "Are you referring to that same stellar organization that appointed Libya as the head of the Human Rights Council? What kind of a farce is that? The U.N. is so mired in politics its members can't even take a piss without a resolution."

"What do you think, Will?" President Pierce said, turning to the NSA's director of Middle Eastern intelligence. William Fisher adjusted his tie, getting his thoughts together. The Task Force, with its polar opposite views was difficult for him to navigate safely.

"As you all know, I've lived in the Middle East for years," Fisher began. He sat on the small sofa next to Carrie Black and took some comfort from her presence. "On the whole, the Arabs are pretty much like everyone else—they don't like war any more than the rest of us. However, they've been backed into a corner on this Palestinian issue by their religious leaders. They don't like the Palestinians any more than the Israelis do, but it's become a *Catch-22* for them. Supporting Palestine is the only way to save face. The radical clerics are the ones we should really be worrying about. They not only stir the pot, they finance, recruit and harbor the terrorists. Our organization is monitoring several of these right-wing clerics who preach out of mosques in London, Kuala Lampur, Yemen, Saudi Arabia, France and Lebanon. If it were possible to neutralize them, most of the direct connections to the terrorists would be severed." He looked at the president, who stared back, his face blank.

Fisher continued. "We're also monitoring a remarkable surge of terrorist recruitment in Southeast Asia. As you know, there are 250 million Muslims in that region, and they're even less predictable than the Arab Muslims. Unless we put an end to being soft on terrorism, I'm afraid we're going to have to do battle there as well."

"So, you support the retaliation approach outlined by Senator Stevens and Dr. Finch?" said Pierce.

"On this issue, we agree, Mr. President," replied Fisher, conscious of Carrie Black's cold look.

"And what about you, Ron?" Pierce said, addressing Secretary of Defense Ronald Burns.

"Mr. President, we've got the greatest military force in the history of the world, and if it comes to war, we'll throw everything we've got into it. But I'm not certain we're ready for an all-out war against an enemy that's so elusive, so fluid, and spread all over the globe. I'd be happier if we had more allies willing to step up to bat and commit their troops and technology. But the fact is, the Europeans are hiding in the corners, and Britain, our only ready ally, doesn't have all that much international muscle." The secretary of defense paused, casting about for the right words. "In principle, I agree with Senator Stevens and General Reese, but I just don't know how we can pull it off and still defend our own soil at the same time. I know I should be the guy waving the flag and charging up the hill, but I'm inclined to agree with Secretary of State Vance—we've got to find more ways to exert influence on the Arab countries, and Israel as well."

Abruptly, President Pierce stood up. "Thank you, gentlemen, and Ms. Black," he added, nodding toward the national security adviser. "Thank you all for coming. I'll be in touch with each of you privately for further input. And we'll meet again on Thursday, same time. I'd like each of you to work out your best and worst-case scenarios for our next meeting."

As the members of the Special Task Force gathered their papers and headed out, President Pierce asked Carrie Black to stay behind for a few moments.

"So what's eating you?" he asked, as soon as the door was closed.

"Do you really trust these guys, Mr. President?" Black said. "It's as if everyone has multiple hidden agendas." She sighed, plunking herself down on the sofa. "Frankly, I get tired of trying to figure out who is doing what to whom and why."

"Let me tell you something, Carrie," Pierce said, sipping his now cold coffee. "I learned a valuable lesson when I was eighteen. My father sent me for the summer to work on a cattle ranch in Mexico. My job was to break the wild mustangs. Some days I swear they almost broke me instead. One of my daddy's favorite sayings was, 'What doesn't kill you makes you stronger.' During my time there I worked with an old Mexican *vaquero* about four feet tall with no teeth. He was the foreman of the operation. He didn't speak English and my Spanish was pretty basic, but somehow we communicated. It was him and the horses who taught me about trust."

He smiled at her. "I trust everyone and no one, Carrie. Oh, I'm prepared to listen to anyone, but I never believe what they say, at least not fully. The truth, like fine wine, country music and good-looking women, is a matter of opinion. I've found that listening is the best policy, but I prefer to decide for myself what is the truth and just whom to trust." He took another sip of coffee. "Mason was right. It needs warming up, but we do have the best coffee in Washington."

"I prefer decaf," she said.

"I'll make a note of that for our next meeting. Anyway, as a general rule in politics—and you may want to remember this—I've found it doesn't pay to trust the newcomers or the old timers. The newcomers are too easily swayed and haven't yet formed their own opinions. They are much too eager to kiss ass and get reelected or reappointed. As for the old timers, the fact that they've survived in Washington for any length of time means they've sold their soul to the highest bidder, or bidders. It's the mid-career politicians I find most trustworthy. They've weathered the freshman temptations of corruption and bribery but haven't been around long enough to be totally corrupted by special interests." The president stood up and turned to stare out the window. With spring still in the wings, the Rose Garden looked bleak and desolate, the thorny bushes severely trimmed.

"And what about Senator Stevens?"

"If you follow my rule, the senior senator from the great State of Virginia is definitely not to be trusted. To flourish on the Hill as long as he has means he must be pretty deep in someone's pocketbook, and he probably has a blackmail dossier on nearly every politician of any importance. Including you and me."

The President turned back to face her. "But what I can't figure out about Senator Stevens is how he's able to get hold of such current intelligence on the terrorists. Everyone knows the American intelligence community is still organized for a cold war. It's going to take them another ten years to fully adjust to the realities of terrorism and the new world order." President Pierce shook his head, wondering how the United States of America had made it this far without being decimated from the inside out. "It's the mountain of information he has at his fingertips that I don't trust. If I were a betting man, I'd say he's been bought by a very powerful interest. The question is, which one?"

Caroline Black gathered her briefing papers, and with an approving nod from the president, headed for the door. With her hand on the doorknob, she asked, "And what about me, Mr. President?"

"Well, you fall into the newcomer category, Carrie. If you ever graduate, I'll let you know." President Pierce sat down behind his desk and watched the door close behind her.

A small door on the left side of the Oval Office opened. "Come in Karl. Did you hear the proceedings this morning?"

"Yes Mr. President. Very interesting."

"I only have a few moments. What have you got?"

"Just a few thoughts on your dilemma. May I continue?"

President Pierce switched on his intercom. "Hold my next appointment for a few moments, will you, Miriam?"

The Hart Senate Office Building

"HE'S BEGINNING TO WAVER," said Senator Stevens into his private cell phone. "Now he's trying to decide which path to choose. And he's actually listening to input from all sides for Chrissakes."

"Is that all you have to report?" The voice at the other end was synthesized and scrambled. "I wish you had more information for me, because we have a problem."

"Now what?" Stevens said, sitting down in his armchair. "You people always create problems and then blame the world for not helping you out."

"He escaped from the hospital sometime in the early morning."

"Escaped? Shit. Well, it's your problem. My job was to bring you the doctor for a change of identity, so you could use him to track down his old Beirut friends and the terrorist cell. I did my job, and quite frankly I couldn't care less if you've gone and messed up your job."

"But he could draw attention to us, and ultimately to you."

"Then put out an alert to the police. After all, he has the face of a known assassin."

"And when they find him and he divulges his true identity?" the voice said. "Someone is certain to start an investigation. And the terrorist cell may accelerate their timetable before we can find out who they are. No, we'll have to find him quickly, and if we can't capture him, then we'll eliminate him. In the meantime, my people will try and track down all the American students who were at AUB that year and put pressure on them. One of them must know something about the terrorists."

"If you're going to hunt him down, use some of the money we keep lavishing on you people and hire some professionals. I don't want you implicated. If the government finds out about your activities on our soil, it might tip the opinion polls the wrong way." Senator Stevens paused, hearing only silence in his receiver. "Are you still there? Have you fainted or just shit in your pants?"

"I'm still here, Senator. I was just thinking about what this little incident might do to your illustrious career…."

"Don't threaten me, you bastard—go find your lost doctor." He clicked his cell phone shut and tossed in onto the sofa. Muttering, he returned to his desk. "They're all the same. Too much religion and definitely too much inbreeding."

Chapter Eight

Sweet Briar College

THE BRICK BUILDINGS AND GROUNDS LOOKED THE SAME. So did the coeds walking to class in the cold air, or sharing cigarettes in the parking lot next to the library. Everything seemed the same, except him. Not only did he have the face of someone else, he was no longer a part of this place. Professor Matthew Richards was dead.

Was it foolish to come back? It was the first place pursuers would look for him. No, his mind reasoned. He needed that diary. The one Samir helped him buy that day in the bazaar. If there was any hope of making sense of what is happening, he'd have to remember his experiences in Beirut. The problem was, his memory was a bit foggy about that period. Actually, his memory was a bit foggy about nearly everything. But then that was the purpose for making Scotch his sole liquid intake. To dull his memories and the pain of the past, present and future.

He calculated that it had been six or seven weeks since he'd had a drink. And he did feel better physically. He couldn't recall ever feeling so light and energetic, except maybe in his teens when his body was hard and his hormones were on the rampage. Matt parked the stolen car at the far end of the faculty parking lot.

"May I help you, sir?" An attractive young student looked up from behind the counter in the faculty office. He recognized her immediately. One of his senior biology students, a bright African-American who studied hard and held down several jobs on campus. Sweet Briar College attracted two types: the daughters of the rich and famous for whom money was no object, and bright students from middle- and lower-income families who helped defray the $26,000 tuition through scholarships. Even though she had a large scholarship, this student still had to work.

Her "sir" caught him in mid-stride. He had almost forgotten, he was a stranger. Would he ever get used to being himself on the inside and someone else on the outside? "Actually," he said hesitantly, "my name is William Stubbs. I'm Dr. Matthew Richards's cousin. Is there someone I can speak to about picking up his personal effects?"

The student's eyes registered sorrow. "I'll go get Ms. Parsons, the assistant dean of faculty affairs," she said. "Please have a seat, I'll be right back."

Wonder who they got to take over my classes? Matt sat and fidgeted in the chair. As the seconds ticked by he grew more and more uncomfortable. *How soon before they started looking for him?* Fear descended. He shouldn't have come back.

"Hello, Mr. Stubbs? My name is Fiona Parsons, assistant dean of faculty affairs. Sara tells me you were inquiring about Professor Richards?" She was a slightly overweight woman whom Matt had met once before, at the infamous faculty party where he drank more than usual.

"Yes." Matt stood and shook her hand. "I'm William Stubbs, Matthew's cousin. His father, Dr. Wilson Richards, is away in South America and asked me to collect Matthew's personal effects. I have some identification if you need it," he said, reaching for his wallet.

"That won't be necessary, Mr. Stubbs. I'm sorry to tell you this, but—but just a few days after Professor Richards's accident, the faculty house he lived in caught fire and burned down. We've been trying to reach his next of kin. I don't enjoy being the bearer of bad news. I'm certain there were mementos and personal effects his family would have wanted. Professor Richards was an unusual man, so ... so full of life, shall we say?"

They're way ahead of me. So someone had probably burgled his residence and burned it down to destroy any possible evidence. He tried to remain calm. "What about his office here on campus?" Matt smiled, wiping the sweat off his forehead. "Maybe he kept some personal effects there?"

"Why yes. Some of the students helped pack up his books and papers. A few pictures, boots, umbrellas, cardboard boxes, that sort of thing. They're stored over at the campus maintenance shed. I'll call and tell them you're coming over. Shall I say right away?" she asked, picking up the phone.

Matt nodded. *Just books, umbrellas and boots?* He tried to recall what had been stored in his office. There was a chance one of the boxes contained the diary. At least he would have a look. When Ms. Parsons put down the phone, Matt thanked her and turned toward the door.

"Do you want to know where the building is located, Mr. Stubbs?" she said.

"I think I can find it. Thanks for your help. I'll just load up the car and be on my way." Smiling, he exited the small building.

"That whole family is weird," remarked the dean as she returned to her office.

Matt walked up the tree-lined asphalt road toward the maintenance shed. The brick and corrugated iron building was located at the rear of the campus. Snow still piled over much of the campus, and the bare branches of maple and elm trees defined themselves against the slate sky. "Bizarre," he muttered to himself, raising the collar of his coat—the other guy's coat. Not only did he not recognize himself in the mirror, now he was a stranger on a college campus where just a few weeks before he was recognized by everyone.

Jesus, can't people see beyond the face!

He passed several students during his walk up the road. They kept their heads down against the wind. As he approached the senior bench he spotted a woman. He'd never seen her on campus before, but she looked familiar. Tall and attractive, she was deep in conversation with one of the women teachers from the biology department.

Then he remembered. The outspoken reporter from the *International Herald Tribune*, the reception for Dr. Melikian. This time her auburn hair was flowing around her shoulders, not piled up on top of her head. He recognized her athletic figure, confident gait, prominent nose, and light-olive skin. Caution tightened his gut. *What is she doing here?*

The two women, deep in conversation, drifted across the large open quadrangle that formed the center of the campus. Matt followed. When they arrived at the library building, the women shook hands, then the biology teacher disappeared inside.

Matt took the calculated risk and approached the reporter. "This is a strange coincidence," he said, smiling. "Didn't I see you at the reception for Dr. Melikian several weeks ago? I'm William Stubbs, Dr. Matt Richards's cousin. I've come to collect his belongings." Matt stuck out his hand, which she took and shook lightly. She stepped back for a good look at him in the morning light. "So what brings you to Sweet Briar, Ms. …? I'm sorry, I recognize the face, but not the name."

"Delacluse. Nicole Delacluse from the *International Herald Tribune*. Did you say you were Dr. Richards's cousin?" She stared at him closely, reporter's instincts in play.

Can she really see me? "Yes. Matthew's father, Dr. Wilson Richards is in South America and asked me to come when I could to collect his personal effects. But not much is left. Seems his house burned down just after the accident."

Matt decided to press his own questions. "And what are you doing here? Not much international news in a little out-of-the-way woman's college, is there?"

Her eyes stayed on him, burrowing deeper. "What say we move out of this cold wind and get some hot chocolate at the campus bistro? Or would you like something stronger?"

"Lead the way," said Matt, checking Stubbs' watch. It was mid-morning. Plenty of time before the maintenance shed closed for lunch, and he was curious about what this reporter was up to.

In the bistro, Nicole Delacluse continued to study him. "There's something about you that I can't quite figure out," she said after a long silence, then shook off the thought and took a sip from the piping hot mug.

"You *were* at that reception for Dr. Melikian, weren't you?" Matt said.

"Hell yeah, I was at the reception—in fact, I saw your cousin, who happened to be drunk as a skunk, being dutifully escorted out by the Marines. Seems he fired a big roundhouse hook into Senator Mason Stevens's fat face."

She grinned, then caught herself. "Hey, no offense—I'm sorry about your cousin…."

"Yeah, well, he was on a collision course—it was just a matter of time."

She studied him again. "Anyway, I decided there was a big story brewing, so I took a few pictures with my mini-digital camera. Nice photos of the unconscious senator. Then I headed for the front driveway." She sipped her hot chocolate, still staring at Matt. "I saw Dr. Matthews with Senator Steven's buxom daughter. The good doctor was being strapped into the passenger seat of her Porsche. He was so drunk he passed out as soon as he hit the bucket seat. The parking attendant had to fasten his seat belt. I got a picture of that too." The hot chocolate was rich, frothy, and comforting. She cupped the mug in her hands. "This is nice. And the chocolate as well."

"Yeah, nice against the cold," Matt said. "As I said, he was on a collision course with life. It seems you think he was a bit of an asshole?"

"No, I only met him briefly at the reception. But from what I've heard here on campus he was a tortured soul—as well as quite a rascal."

"And just why are you poking around asking questions about my cousin?"

"Well, first of all, the feds, or whoever they were, confiscated my mini-camera. They told me it was a matter of national security. Then I read the report in the *Washington Post* the next day about the accident. It stated that Dr. Richards was driving. But that's impossible. He was passed out in the passenger seat. No one could recover that quickly and drive."

"That makes sense."

"Then when I told my boss at the *Tribune* about all this, he told me to drop it. He said it was old news and to stay away from the Richards affair." She shrugged.

"And it looks like you did exactly as you were told." He couldn't keep from grinning.

"No one tells me what I can and can't investigate," she said, her eyes hot. "I follow my instincts. And there's something wrong about this whole affair. So I came to Sweet Briar to talk to a few of the teachers and students about the notorious Dr. Richards."

"Found out anything?"

"Not much. Your cousin was a drunk and a womanizer. He was having a heated affair with one of his students, who just happened to be Senator Mason Stevens's buxom daughter. And I've also found out she was a pothead, and a cocaine addict as well. She even supplied some of the girls in her dorm with coke. Word is, she couldn't function without a hit at least every 30 minutes. So what about you, Mr. Stubbs? Did you find any of your cousin's things?"

Matt felt an anger. *Kelly was buxom, so what? She took a hit now and then, so what?* His messed-up life suddenly came rushing back at him. "Nothing left of the burned-out house," he said. "But he did keep some personal effects in his office at the biology department. They were packed up and stored in the maintenance shed. I was just on my way there when I ran into you. Care to join me?"

Matt knew the source of her questions. She was a professional reporter and tenacious. She knew he hadn't been driving the car, and that meant a lot to him. He needed someone on his side. He felt incredibly alone at the moment, and ruthless men were after him. *I need to trust someone.*

"Join you? Only if you pick up the tab," she replied. "I never go to second base with a man who doesn't pay the check." They walked out of the cozy bistro and headed for the maintenance shed.

"You certainly know your way around," said Nicole, pulling up the hood of her quilted parka against the wind. She took in his rather thin jacket.

"They gave me directions in the Faculty office," Matt said. He walked briskly to stay warm. This would be his last visit to the beautiful Sweet Briar College campus. Yet his mind was screaming it was time to leave, to get out of there while it was still safe.

An hour and a half later, they approached the faculty parking lot. Nicole had been giving him odd looks ever since they left the maintenance shed. "Okay," she said, firmly grabbing Matt's arm. "What the hell is going on? You said you came for Dr. Richards' belongings, yet all you did was rummage through a few boxes and take an old leather journal. Who are you, and what are you really after?"

Matt yanked his arm away. "Still working for the *Tribune*?"

"No. I'm on my own. I tried to get Dr. Richard's death out of my mind and couldn't, so I went to my editor and told him I wanted to investigate the Richards's affair. He said no. I said yes. He said hell no. I said hell yes, and told him to go fuck himself."

"And?"

"He shit-canned me."

"Do you always talk like a sailor?"

"Only when I'm drunk or angry. And I'm still pissed off at that SOB for sacking me." She grinned sheepishly, cheeks colored in the cold wind. "So here I am investigating it on my own. But I'm open for a good partnership. Assuming you level with me first."

They resumed their walk, and by the time they reached the VW Passat Matt had made his decision. His whole adult life had been a twisted tangle of drunken lies. It was time for a change. Matt stopped.

"What is it?" Nicole asked.

"I'm wondering two things: if you can stand the truth and how you just might have a terrific story – if it's ever allowed in print."

"Meaning what?"

"Okay. First, I'm trusting you with the truth."

"I'm waiting. Spit it out."

"I'm Matt Richards. And you're right. I wasn't driving that night, Kelly Stevens was."

Her eyes were bright with disdain in the cold air. "Bullshit. Go turn yourself in to some clinic. You may be nice, but you definitely need help."

Matt looked straight at her, wondering how to convince her. He smiled weakly.

"Something…." Nicole said, a professional gaze cutting into him.

"What? Something?"

"You're not crazy. Something's going on."

Matt smiled and let out a long sigh. "Thank Christ for good reporter's instincts."

"So talk. The news reported Dr. Richards dead. It made the front page of the Washington papers and all the television stations—they even held a funeral." She paused. "You don't even look like him. Although I must admit, there is something familiar about you. But you're definitely not Matthew Richards. So who are you and what's going on?"

"Give me your hands. Come on, trust me. Give me your hands."

Her hands were tense in his, ready to pull free. Slowly he directed them to the stitches under the hairline. "Feel the scars?"

As dispassionately as he could Matt told her what had happened after he had hit Senator Stevens. Everything from the car chase to waking up with a new face at the Blue Ridge Clinic. He took his hands from hers, watching the concentration in her eyes. Her fingertips were delicate. "You might recall my voice," Matt said.

"Shut up." She shook. "You were drunk that night. You spoke differently, if it was you." The hands moved, fingertips now softly probing the scars around his hairline.

"Well?"

"It's not your voice. Your eyes."

"You remember my eyes?"

"I do believe you, weird as it sounds." She lowered her hands. They still shook. "How did you get here?"

"I escaped late last night. I came back to Sweet Briar to find my old diary from my year in Beirut."

"What about the car that was forcing you off the road?"

Matt winced. "We braked hard and sent them over the edge and into the river. I assume they drowned."

"Funny, there was no mention of any other car crash that evening in the police report. I got a hold of the police file on the accident."

"Looks like they fixed that, like they fixed the phony accident."

She shook her head. "Things certainly aren't adding up. I'm still having a hard time believing the full facial transplant."

Matt sucked in the cold air and looked around. No one seemed to be paying attention to them. "Well, I'm a doctor. I can tell you it's a highly experimental procedure, not yet perfected here in the U.S., but the work is first class. Dr. Weissman said he was brought to the clinic so he could finish his transplant research. Somehow the bastards decided on me as a guinea pig."

"Can I touch it again?" She traced her fingertips along the jaw line, around the hairline and the neck. "Yeah...."

"What?" Matt pulled back.

"Faint, but I can feel the scar tissue underneath. God, it's like a Frankenstein movie."

"It gets worse. The face belongs to an international contract killer. He was used by numerous governments till he fell out with one of them. So I don't know what's happening, yet I've got the face of a known assassin. Not a long life expectancy, I'd say." Matt turned toward the car. He fumbled in his pocket for the keys.

Nicole put a gentle hand on his shoulder. "Look....Matt? Are you all right? I do want to help. And I do believe you."

"At first I was a little unsteady from the drugs they were giving me, but that's all cleared up—and I'm off the booze. In fact, I feel better than I have in years, though I'm not so sure I like this face."

"It's a funny thing, but when I met you briefly at the reception for Dr. Melikian, I instantly noticed your eyes, how light blue they were. To be honest I kind of fancied you, but then I saw you were, how should I say, attached?"

"That wasn't one of my better evenings, and as you know, it got a lot worse."

"When you came up to me this morning in the campus yard, the first thing I noticed was your eyes. I recalled the enchanting eyes, but the face didn't match. It's amazing, I thought face transplants were something out of science fiction. But it looks perfect. Quite swarthy and equally handsome as before."

"Anyway," Matt shrugged, "it's mine now. But I came back to find my diary and here it is. Maybe it'll contain some details that will lead to this terrorist group before they strike again. *If* they even exist."

Nicole watched him.

"In or out, Nicole?"

"In. I'm in. Definitely."

"A great freelance story if we come through it alive."

"Don't patronize me, Matthew Richards." She glared at him. "You've got yourself a partner, not a tagalong bimbo."

Matt unlocked the car door.

Loud voices rang out. A group of students dodged between the parked cars, chasing each other, laughing in the bright cold air. They both relaxed.

"Shit, if we're late again for class the witch will kill us," one of them squealed, dashing past Matt and Nicole, who flattened themselves against the car door to let her by. Matt reached for the door handle.

Blood splattered across the hood of the Passat. The window exploded. Shards of glass flew. The dead weight of the young student crashed against the front of the car. Nicole pulled Matt to the asphalt. No sooner had they hit the ground than they heard the sharp pings ricocheting off the metal door frame where Matt's head had just been.

The young coed lay unmoving on the ground next to them, her neck gushing blood. The other girls screamed. Nicole grabbed the journal off the pavement and pulled Matt around to the other side of the car.

"We're getting out of here," she yelled over the screaming. "There's a sniper out there trying to kill you. Follow me and run for your life." Then she was up and away, sprinting and zigzagging behind parked cars toward a small wooded ravine at the edge of the parking lot. Several car windshields exploded behind her.

But Matt stayed where he was, his medical training kicking in. He crawled around the car toward the young woman, intent on checking her pulse. His heart sank. He yelled at the others to lie down, then followed Nicole, doubling over as he ran. In less than a minute they were both at the bottom of the ravine.

"Okay, professor," she said, breathing hard, "this is your campus—which way now?"

Matt got his bearings. "There's faculty housing at the end of this ravine. Come on." He jumped up and ran at a full sprint.

Had the sniper moved to another hidden location? *We can't outrun a bullet.* He stumbled over the frozen ground, suddenly weak. *I'm a target, not a candidate anymore.* He looked around. It wouldn't be too much longer before they got a clean shot and his miserable life would be over. If not today, then tomorrow, next week, or next month.

Well, maybe he could do a little damage before they blew his head off. The big problem was, he really didn't know who they were. The best plan, so far, was to try and find a connection to the terrorist cell through his old Beirut friends. *If I can locate them.*

Minutes later, winded and cold, his legs shaking from exhaustion, Matt emerged from the ravine and stepped into the backyard of a small wooden house. His foot slipped on a patch of melting snow. He crashed onto the frozen lawn. Nicole, close behind and not breathing nearly as heavily, helped him to his feet. They scrambled up to the back door. "Stay here," Matt whispered, breath heaving as he glanced around nervously. "I'll only be a moment." He slipped inside.

The house belonged to a faculty buddy he often spent the evening drinking Scotch with. He knew the layout well, and when he entered the kitchen a sense of relief flooded through his senses. Hanging from a familiar nail in the wall were the keys to a battered Jeep Cherokee.

Two minutes later, Matt and Nicole were bouncing along a snowy track at the back side of the Sweet Briar campus. "This is a service road that comes out next to the Briar Patch Bar, near the town of Amherst."

"Do you know all the bars around here?"

"That's a low blow. I thought we were partners."

"You asked if I could stomach the truth. Well, what about you?"

"It's a bar the students and some horny faculty often frequent. It's also right near the highway. I vote we head for the Charlottesville airport, drop this car off, pick up a rental, and get the hell out of this area."

Nicole looked shaken. She remained silent.

"Are you okay?"

"Aftershock, I guess. I'll be fine."

Matt glanced at her. "Hey, partner, you were pretty great back there. You sprang right into action." He paused. "Thanks for saving my life. I guess I froze."

"To be honest, I was scared out of my wits. But I've covered conflicts and been caught in crossfire before, so I just reacted. Self-preservation is my middle name. But I got the journal," she said, brandishing the leather volume. "What about that young woman?"

"Dead. The bullet must have passed through her neck, severing the carotid artery before it shattered the car window. Jesus Christ. Those bastards. They can't just kill innocent people like that."

"Look, Dr. Richards," Nicole said, examining a torn fingernail. "Sweet Briar College is definitely not the real world. The world is a fucking jungle these days. Teenagers high on crack shooting their friends, corporate greed, political upheaval, state-sponsored terrorism, third rate countries with nuclear arsenals, and the Middle East pushing everyone toward global war. Terrorists kill innocent people all the time and get away with it. And I'll tell you this, whoever they are, they must have a lot to lose." Silence filled the interior of the Jeep, broken only by the mushy hum of the tires. Soon they were on US 29, heading north in the direction of Charlottesville.

"If we rent a Hertz car at the airport," Nicole said, "I can use my corporate card from the newspaper. They won't mind. Besides, if we live through this, it'll be one hell of a story and they'll probably make me managing editor." She paused. "From Charlottesville we can drive to Washington. I know an ex-CIA guy who will help us. He's retired. Got eased out about fifteen years ago during another round of budget cuts. Been doing freelance work ever since. And believe it or not, I trust him."

"Is that an order or a suggestion?" Nicole punched him in the arm and snuggled down into the passenger seat, warmed by the blasting heater.

"Nicole?"

"Yeah?"

"Thank you."

"Look, I ...."

"No, I mean it. For being smart on your feet and keeping us alive back there. But mainly, for believing me." He looked ahead as the Jeep sped down the highway.

"I do believe you, Matt. Frankly, I wish I were covering a local garden festival. Definitely safer. But I do want to help."

"And another thing."

"What?"

"I need those journalistic skills of yours."

Nicole smiled. "I don't know. You escaped from that clinic, stole a car and made it back to Sweet Briar. Looks like you can manage quite well on your own."

Matt shook his head. "I need you." *Don't think I've ever said that to anyone.*

The Oval Office

"COME IN, DOCTOR." President Pierce was seated behind the massive Resolute Desk, made from the tough timber of HMS *Resolute* and presented to President Rutherford Hayes by the Queen of England. The walls on either side of him were adorned with paintings and photographs by Frederick Remington, Georgia O'Keefe, and Ansel Adams. Ross Pierce was proud of his Southwestern heritage. "Can I get you anything? Coffee, tea, something a little stronger?"

"No thank you, Mr. President." Dr. Noubar Melikian stepped into the Oval Office for the first time. He was immediately struck by the presidential seal in the ceiling. Looking down, he noticed a matching seal woven into the large carpet that entirely covered the oval-shaped room.

"This isn't a medical emergency, doc. I need your advice about something." President Ross Pierce rose and motioned his guest over to the sofa.

"I hope it's not politics, Mr. President. What I know in that department wouldn't fill a #25-gauge needle."

"When I need political input, Dr. Melikian, I've got a dozen spin doctors, analysts, and Ph.Ds waiting by the phone. Most have an axe to grind or an agenda to push, and the rest just want to kiss ass. What I want from you is a reality check. You're from the Middle East—I want to know how you see the situation there. And I want the naked truth—don't sugarcoat it just because of my position. I'm a big boy, I can take it, and I always listen carefully to everyone's point of view before making a decision. So fire away."

Ross Pierce sat back and watched Dr. Melikian. The briefing file he had read earlier expounded on the doctor's tireless efforts to find a peaceful solution to the crisis in the Middle East. "Okay, Mr. President, if you really want my opinion, I'll give it. The situation in the Middle East might be the catalyst that sets off a nuclear holocaust. It could be sparked in the West Bank or Palestine, but I suspect it's more likely to start in Pakistan or India or some other peripheral country. Tensions are running high. Every country has something to lose, and more to gain, with each day that the impasse and bloodshed continues."

"So if you were the man in charge, what would you do?" Pierce sat back in his large executive chair, his hands grasping the carved lion heads on the arms.

"It's not that simple. I only know one small piece of what might be the solution. But since you asked, I'll give it my best. Besides, I've got a funny feeling if anyone can pull off a miracle, it might just be you." Ross Pierce didn't smile.

"Get on with it, Dr. Melikian."

"First, I would officially recognize the state of Palestine. But before making the announcement, I would go to every one of the Arab nations involved—Syria, Jordan, Egypt, Saudi Arabia, Iran, Iraq, the entire lot, one by one—and let them know what the United States was about to do. And then I would secure a commitment from each one to do something spectacular to ensure a lasting peace. For example, Syria and Jordan might donate land to give the Palestinians more room to breathe, which would take the land pressure off Israel. Others would deliver Osama bin Laden and his chief lieutenants in Al-Qaeda to the United States for trial. Or better yet, just bring in their dead bodies and save the expense and hassle of trials."

President Pierce stared. "Shit, Noubar, I said I wanted to hear a different point of view, but I didn't realize you were going to give me the whole enchilada. Keep going, you're doing fine."

"Okay. I'd also go to all the Arab nations with a big shopping list. And I'd remind them that they have all said many times to the world that the only reason they support terrorism is because of the Palestine issue. Recognize Palestine, and you've taken away their excuse. Then pressure them to support global peace and stop supporting the terrorists. Get a commitment to shut down all terrorist support and funding, inside their own countries and abroad. And make them come to the United Nations, stand before the world, and show what they've done to eliminate terrorism." Dr. Melikian stopped to take a sip from the glass of water on the coffee table.

Ross Pierce waited.

"The truth is, Mr. President, Israel is a pain in the ass. They gobble up billions in U.S. foreign aid money but don't support us globally. My father had a saying: Why buy a cow when the milk's free? Israel has yet to shoulder any responsibility for the mess the world is in. All the Israelis have to do is cry, and the Americans come running with a bucketful of dollars. Meanwhile, Israel is illegally occupying the West Bank and the Gaza Strip. I'd say it's time to make Israel a responsible and accountable world citizen and make them stand on their own two feet. If they're going to have a Jewish state in the middle of an Arab region, they should learn to get along with their neighbors."

"How would that be accomplished, Dr. Melikian?"

"Cut off all but a reasonable amount of aid to the Israelis, say $200 million a year, contingent upon them demonstrating their commitment to peace. And give an equal amount of aid to the surrounding Arab states as well. Besides reducing our national debt by several billion dollars, the taxpayers would love you. Spend some of that money to get the U.S. economy cranked up again."

Dr. Melikian hesitated. "May I ask you a question, Mr. President?"

"Fire away."

"Do I still have a job?"

The president laughed. "Well, not having been treated by you, I'm not sure about your medical skills. So your position as my personal physician is still hanging in the balance. But you've always got a job as unofficial adviser." Pierce got up and walked over to the picture window facing the south lawn of the White House. He felt trapped in the nation's capitol and found himself yearning more and more for the wide open spaces of New Mexico. But the roses were just beginning to show the first new shoots of the year and he felt a little lighter. "Anything else?"

"One more suggestion."

President Pierce slowly turned around.

"Why not make Jerusalem an international city? Owned by the world and not any one country? That was the original intent of the 1948 resolution that established Israel in the first place, only no one had the balls to make it stick. That way all the bullshit about religion and religious rights would be taken away. It would be a city for all faiths, with its own government, answerable only to the United Nations."

President Pierce stared at his personal physician. The man was sweating and pale. In the past half hour this outstanding humanitarian had spilled all—his fears, his ideas, his dreams for the future. The danger in sharing one's dreams, as Ross Pierce knew all too well, was that others might grind them to dust.

"My father had a saying too, doctor," he said quietly. "Cows got lots of smarts, they know there's a time for eatin' and a time for ruminatin'. This is my time for ruminating." He stepped forward to shake his guest's hand. "Thank you for your valuable insight. I may call on you again, and hopefully it won't be because of some rotten fish. Meanwhile, I assume I can count on your discretion. Let's agree that this discussion never took place."

"Take two aspirin and call me in the morning," smiled Dr. Melikian. "My lips are sealed."

When the door closed behind him, President Pierce buzzed his secretary. "Miriam? Cancel all my appointments for the rest of the day. And tell Mr. van Ness I want to see him right away."

Chapter Nine

Charlottesville Airport

"Do you have a pen and a piece of paper?" Matt looked at Nicole after parking the car in the long term lot at Charlottesville Airport. "I need to tell Jeremy where his car is." His new partner dug into her purse. Matt scribbled a short note: "Jerry, Your car is at Charlottesville Airport. Keys inside the left front bumper. Keep mum and I'll explain someday. Thanks for the wheels and the Scotch, doc."

Thirty minutes later they were on the road in a new Pontiac Firebird, heading north for Washington, D.C.

In the airport terminal Nicole used a pay phone to call her contact, the former CIA operative. "So what did your friend say?" Matt asked.

"Well, to tell you the truth, he asked me how I was and why I hadn't called him for two years," she said. "And he said Uncle Bob retired last year. Then he wanted to know if I was serious about this guy I was bringing around."

"He's not your *father?*"

"Yes, he's my father. You got a problem with that? I told you I trusted him. He's about the only man I do trust, though my mother certainly doesn't. They divorced when I was young and she hardly ever let me visit him. Said he was a loner, a womanizer and a drunk. Remind you of anyone?"

"Don't provoke me, woman. I'm at the wheel of a dangerous vehicle and I know how to use it."

They lapsed into silence.

"Penny for them," Nicole said.

Am I ready to tell her about Maha's death? "Thinking about the death of my brother. Seems I lost faith in the future when it happened. And right now, everything seems confusing in my mind."

"You're sober, probably for the first time in years."

"True."

"But?"

He glanced at her. "I was just wondering if it's not too late to make something positive of my life."

"I have no doubt, Matt." As she glanced out the window her smile changed to horror.

"Matt, look out!" Nicole screamed as a big green car roared up alongside and swerved into them, jolting the little Firebird. There was a sickening crunch of metal, and then the attacker veered away.

"Shit," he yelled, seeing the Buick with two familiar male occupants. *Hairy Ears and Scarface.* "They're going to ram us again." He jammed his foot on the accelerator. The rented Firebird shot ahead, but quickly reached the engine's limit.

"We can't outrun them," Nicole yelled. "Matt, what are you doing?"

"Trying to save our lives," as he watched the black car loom in the rear view mirror. "Come on, assholes, floor it. You can do it. You can catch us." Both cars were at nearly 100 miles per hour. The Buick pulled alongside. He could clearly see Scarface sneering from the passenger seat. A shotgun appeared as the window rolled down.

Matt swerved at the Buick, which jerked away. Matt jammed down hard on the breaks, struggling to keep the Firebird in a straight line. The Buick shot past, but a second later braked hard. The heavy vehicle skidded on its mushy suspension. Smoking tires slid on the asphalt. Both cars entered the sharp bend at the same time, the Firebird's traction holding up. The Buick's tires couldn't gain a grip. The car careened off the road, down into the median strip and up into the other lane. Head-on traffic hurtled toward them.

Matt watched the Buick frantically trying to avoid a head-on collision. It veered off the road, bounced over a concrete shoulder and slammed into an oak tree. There was a loud explosion as the car burst into flames. Matt gunned the Firebird.

"Matthew," screamed Nicole, shaking and pale. "What's happening? Why are people trying to kill you? How do they know where to find you?"

Matt brought the speed down to sixty. His hands shook on the wheel. The rear view mirror was filled with cars stopped on the highway near the burning wreck. *Please, not her.*

"They seem to know right where I am. Just who did you really call back there at the airport?"

"I told you, my father. You don't think I'm somehow connected with all this? That I'm leading them to you?" She hit him repeatedly on the arm. "Stop this goddamned car right now. I want out. You're not only crazy, you're paranoid. I'm the only friend you've got, asshole. Is this how you drive people away? No wonder you're a drunk and a loner. Now let me out." Tears blinded her.

"Okay, okay. Look, I'm sorry. But I've been kidnapped, given a face transplant, seen an innocent young girl slaughtered before my eyes, and nearly run off the road by two goons. Who am I supposed to trust? Every time I look in the mirror I see a stranger staring back at me. I don't even trust myself." He looked over at Nicole. She was huddled against the passenger door, bloodshot eyes staring at him. "Screw it," he said, watching the highway.

After twenty minutes, Matt tried again. "Look, I'm sorry. You're right, I don't have any friends, and from the way things are going, it looks like I've got a limited future. Thanks for trying to help me." Through his new face he managed what he hoped was a sincere smile. "The face may be artificial, but the sincerity isn't. I mean it. Thank you. And I need you to help me. I'm scared. What do you say?"

She wiped her nose. "Yeah. Well since I'm in this car, and I'm still alive, we might as well try and find some solution to this mess. But I swear to God, if you ever doubt me again, I'll turn you over to the CIA, Mossad, KGB, MI5 and even Osama bin Laden."

"There's not KGB anymore."

"Matt!"

"Okay. So, do you know why someone is trying to kill me and how they've been able to find me so easily?" Matt kept the Firebird just below the speed limit. "All I can figure out is that someone is trying to kill me because they think I know something I don't. But I'm going to find out. If they're going to snuff out my life, then I'm going to know what I'm dying for. I do know it has something to do with a terrorist cell and the suicide attack on the president."

Nicole stared. "What do you mean the suicide attack?"

"I've got no real proof."

"Tell me everything."

Matt slipped the car nimbly around an eighteen wheeler. *Where to begin.* "The woman suicide bomber, the one they keep showing on the news? Well, I know her. More accurately, I knew her, once." He explained how Bedouina died in the bombing incident at a Beirut restaurant in April 1969, along with his girlfriend and his roommate. "She died. And yet when I saw the newscast, I knew it was her—the same woman. Of course it couldn't be, could it?" Matt's composure crumbled. He blinked back the tears and concentrated on the traffic. "They were incinerated: Samir, Bedouina and Maha. Gone in an instant."

Nicole placed her hand on his shoulder. "I don't know, Matt, but something's wrong, terribly wrong. It's like you're an expendable pawn in a deadly game and it's way bigger than both of us."

Matt put his hand over hers. *God I'm scared. And tired.* "I can't do this, Nicole. I'm not a spook and I'm certainly not a hero—I'm just a washed-out doctor and recovering drunk. Look, when we get to Washington I'll drop you off at your father's place and then I'm going to the FBI to turn myself in. I'll be safe there. I'll tell them everything. They can play hero and stop these bastards."

"No, Matt. If you go to the FBI, the CIA or even the D.C. police, you'll be dead within hours. Think about it. How do you think these guys operate so freely inside the United States? They've bought somebody high up is my guess. I wouldn't trust anybody in an official capacity at this moment. And if they get to you they'll find out about me, one way or another. And I'm not ready to depart this planet yet. I don't have my required two and a half kids, a dog and a cat."

"But I can't embroil you in all of this."

"I'm already in it. I know too much and I've seen too much. We live or die together. And my vote is we live." Nicole smiled. "So you just drive like a normal commuter into Washington and we'll go see my father. Besides, you and he will probably get along famously."

Two hours later, Matt parked the Firebird on a side street in Georgetown, a trendy suburb of Washington. Matt locked the leather valise in the trunk. *Now what?* Nicole stopped at a phone booth in front of a small restaurant. She dialed the number quickly.

"He's expecting us," she said, emerging from the booth. After a short walk she abruptly cut through someone's backyard and into an alley. Presently they reached a rotting wooden fence with the gate open. Nicole headed for the back porch of a dilapidated brick row house. As she opened the screen door and reached under the sisal mat for the key, Matt realized he hadn't asked her father's name.

"He's got a bug on him." A rough voice sounded as if it was coming from inside a closet. "Tell him to lie down and remove his clothes."

"I've got ears, I can hear you," Matt called out.

"I don't give a shit about you. It's my daughter I'm concerned about. Now lie down on the kitchen floor and remove your clothes. I've got a scanner here picking up an implanted homing signal. We need to locate it and get it out of your body quickly, before they pinpoint our location. I just hope it's not in some messy place, like the last guy."

"What happened to him?" Matt said apprehensively, whipping off his shirt, shoes, pants and underwear.

"He exploded. It took me a week to get the stench of body parts off my skin." The closet door opened and out stepped an elderly man with shock white hair, olive skin and a prominent nose. He carried what looked like a miniature Geiger counter. Nicole stood at the far end of the kitchen. Her father proceeded to sweep the machine slowly and expertly over Matt's naked body.

"For Christ's sake, hurry up, this tile floor is freezing. I'm shriveling up," Matt cried.

"Well, if that's shriveled, then I am definitely impressed," Nicole grinned.

"Shut up, Nicole. You're just like your mother," her father said, "nothing but sex on the brain. I found it. Raise your left arm—Dr. Richards, isn't it? Do you have a scar under your armpit?"

Matt shook his head.

"I hate to tell you, but someone gave you one recently. My guess is they planted an XT3400 homing device just under the skin. Has a range of twenty-five miles and lasts for three months. You're life isn't exceptionally important to these people, it seems to me, otherwise they would have used the longer-lasting model." He smiled. "Now, get your pants on. If the nurse would oblige me, I need to extricate this little package and send it on its way. Do you want a shot of a mild anesthetic or a large belt of whiskey?"

"Neither. Just watch out for the brachial artery," Matt pulled on his underwear and pants. "Who normally uses this type of bug?"

"They're not easy to get hold of. Used quite a lot by the CIA, MI6, and some of the more sophisticated foreign intelligence agencies."

A quarter of an hour later Matt had a line of expertly sewn sutures in his armpit. Nicole handed him a pocket mirror. "You should have been a surgeon," he said.

The old man was placing a small metal broadcasting unit into a brightly colored Federal Express pack. "Nicole, I'll be back in about half an hour. There's a FedEx collection center not too far away. With any luck, our little package will arrive in Rio Grande, Tierra del Fuego early tomorrow morning. Whoever's monitoring this little homing device will go nuts tracking it." He waved and let the screen door slam shut.

"What's his name?" Matt asked Nicole as he put on his shirt. Nicole set a large pot of hot tea on the table.

"His legal name is Elijah Tajikian. His father was an Armenian diplomat in Paris. His mother was French. He's an only child. I don't know much about my father's life, other than his mother brought him to the States when he was just an infant. It seems that his father disappeared under strange circumstances in the mid-1930s and they never saw him again. My dad married a French Canadian from Quebec and I was born in 1960. By that time he was working for the CIA and rarely home, and when he was he couldn't talk about his work. After he and my mother split up, I hardly saw him. But he would always send me postcards and parcels from exotic locations. He's still somewhat of a stranger to me, but he's good at the spook stuff, and he's the only man I even remotely trust."

"And your last name, Delacluse?"

"My mother's maiden name. I grew up under her roof, so I took her name."

Matt finished dressing and looked around the kitchen. The faded linoleum floors and chipped Formica counters described the existence of a man for whom home life had never been a high priority.

"What are you thinking, Matt?"

He stared at her. "Your reporter instinct buzzing?"

"You were far away for a few seconds. What's up?"

"Oh, just wondering if I'll wind up like your father. Alone." *If I live that long.*

"Have some hot tea, Dr. Richards." Nicole smiled, pouring the fragrant Earl Grey into a mug.

"Tea would be great," he said, somewhat embarrassed that she had seen him totally naked. Even after all those years as a physician seeing countless people naked, he never got used to other people seeing him without clothes. "And I wouldn't mind a hot bath. I feel as if I've got a year's worth of grime all over me."

"Drink your tea. I'll go upstairs and run the tub. First floor, second door on the left when you're ready."

As Matt savored a mug of Earl Grey, he went over in his mind what had happened since he woke up in a private hospital with someone else's face. *Whoever they are, they've got a lot to lose – or a lot to gain.*

Unfortunately, wherever he went, he was leaving dead people. He said a silent prayer for the student killed by a sniper. He also mourned beautiful, vivacious Kelly Stevens, killed in the automobile accident. Both Harry Ears and Scarface were dead, toast actually. He smiled at the fact that there was still some justice left.

Who's chasing me? And why? His thoughts turned to Senator Stevens trying to avenge the death of his daughter. He sipped his tea. Or it could be the CIA. After all, it had to take some pretty well-placed people to establish a connection, even as farfetched as it was, between himself, his friends from Beirut in the 1960s and a cell of terrorists operating in the United States.

"Bath's ready," Nicole called.

He trudged up the stairs, suddenly overwhelmed with exhaustion. A door with a brass knob stood half open.

"Aren't you going to take a bath? The water's nice and hot." Nicole's voice came from deep inside the room.

He pushed through the door into a small guest room; saw another door beyond, steam pouring out. After slipping off his shoes and socks and unbuttoning his shirt, Matt headed for the bath. Just inside the door, he stopped.

"There's a water shortage in D.C. and the mayor is encouraging everyone to conserve. The official slogan is 'Share a bath with a friend,' so let's not let this nice hot water go to waste, shall we?" Nicole snuggled down inside the tub, a thick carpet of glistening bubbles covering her body. "And hurry up, my feet need a good scrubbing."

She was gentle as she touched him, her fingertips tracing the contoured scar next to his hairline. "It doesn't really show."

"I can feel it every time I move. You can't imagine. It's like an alien has infused itself onto me. And into my soul. Sometimes I just want to tear it off."

Nicole kissed him on the forehead. "One day, when all this is over, you'll feel more comfortable."

"I want my old face back. It was wrinkled and dissipated by booze, but it was mine. Now I'm even a stranger to myself." He shrugged. "Want to make love to an international assassin?"

"No. I want to make love to you."

The Hart Senate Office Building

SENATOR STEVENS COUNTED THE RINGS from his cell phone. As per instructions, he picked up on the fifth ring. "Yes?"

"The situation has gotten a little more complex," the scrambled voice said.

"Jesus, now what have you guys gone and fucked up?" the senator glanced across the room to make certain his door was closed. There wasn't much privacy in the Hart Senate Office Building on Constitution Avenue. Wearily he sat down on the leather sofa, putting his feet on the coffee table.

The voice came alive again. "The contractors we hired to track down our lost package met with an unfortunate accident. We've lost contact."

"Is this a joke? Are you telling me you're worse off than when this whole thing started? You people can't do anything right."

"Let me remind you, senator, we're in this together, up to our necks. If you start thinking differently, you can kiss your political career goodbye. We'll find our lost package. At the same time we are proceeding with the investigation of the others from Beirut who might be involved. You can either give us some assistance, or stay quiet and let us get on with our work. I understand you Americans have to talk tough in order to feel important, but it does get tedious. Besides, before too many more years China will be kicking your ass all over the globe. In the meantime I'm stuck with you, so if you have any brilliant ideas, which I very much doubt, give me a call. Otherwise, I'll let you know when we have things wrapped up and—."

Stevens kicked off his shoes. "Who's the other package?"

"A woman. Delacluse. Nicole Delacluse. She works for the *International Herald Tribune* as a political journalist. She's spent most of her career in Europe, although she's American by birth."

"Track her down. All her friends and relatives as well." Stevens glanced at his Rolex. In an hour he was scheduled to meet with Dr. Finch, director of the CIA. "Better yet, I'll get my spooks to check on this Delacluse woman. They owe me some big favors. I'll let you know if I find out anything. And try not to make things worse."

Chapter Ten

Georgetown

"You're late," Nicole watched her father come through the door and hang his overcoat on a hook.

"Not late, just giving you two a little time to get acquainted. Any tea left?" Elijah rubbed his hands together. "It's cold out there. Actually, I could do with a little nightcap. Care to join me, doctor?"

Matt sat at the kitchen table drinking hot tea with Nicole. Their lovemaking, born of fright and survival, had been both passionate and cathartic.

It's starting. "Care to join me, doctor?" Matt repeated the phrase outloud. "You can't believe how many times I've heard that."

"And what did you usually reply?" Eli asked, glancing at Nicole. She looked away.

"Make mine a double Scotch, neat." The words sprang so easily to his lips. This time, however, he hesitated. An old Robert Frost poem, a favorite of his mother's, floated into his mind: *Two roads diverged in a yellow wood, and I took the one least traveled by, and that has made all the difference in the world.*

Matt held up his tea mug. "This'll do fine."

"Suit yourself. I've got some great single malt Speyside Scotch. A high-quality distillery called Glenrothes. It's 1987 vintage Scotch." He moved toward a cupboard where he kept his special stash.

Matt's gaze followed hungrily. Elijah reached deep inside a cabinet and pulled out the pinch bottle of amber nectar.

Nicole headed out of the kitchen. "It's your life. What's left of it."

"Seriously. I'll take a rain check, Eli. I'm still not feeling quite right after the surgery and drugs." Matt finished his tea. "In fact, I think I'll turn in. Thanks for helping me out. I'm glad I didn't blow up."

"Me too, Dr. Richards. Any friend of Nicole's is a friend of mine." Elijah Tajikian poured himself a generous two fingers of Scotch. "Have you thought about what you're going to do next? They'll keep coming after you. You know that, don't you?"

"I really don't know what the hell I'm going to do."

"Listen, I've worked with these types for too many years. I know how they think and move. To them you're a dangerous and uncontrollable element. You know too much. They won't rest until they eliminate you."

Matt sat back down at the kitchen table. "What are you saying?"

Elijah gave a world weary smile. "Two things really. Personally, I'm going to sleep with one eye open tonight. But you need to realize, you're the only one who can stop them. You're the one person who has half a chance of finding this terrorist cell and exposing it. And you may be able to expose the bastards who stole your face as well."

Matt buried his face in his hands. *God, I need a drink.* "You're right. I can't help thinking that I might be able to save the life of the president—does that sound absurd?"

"It does. But in this case, it's probably accurate." Elijah said, sitting down across the table from Matt and swirling the warm, soothing nectar in his glass. "Let me give you some advice. The only way you'll think straight is to forget about the consequences. Forget someone might be trying to kill you. Dwell on that stuff and it'll interfere with any rational thought. It's like playing soccer. If your mind is cluttered up you won't perform at your peak. The great Brazilian star, Pele, once said, 'A full mind means an empty net.' You've got to treat this as a puzzle and simply go about solving it. Forget about everything else."

Nicole came back into the kitchen. "So if this were just a simple exercise to find your old Beirut friends, what's the first thing you would do?" she asked, sitting down next to him.

"Well, I'd probably visit Dr. Martin Thomas. He was our faculty adviser at AUB. His job was to make certain everyone behaved themselves and came back in one piece. He got to know all of us pretty well. And funny enough, I just saw him before ….." Matt touched his face. "He hosted the reception for the new personal physician to the president."

Elijah finished his Scotch. "So why not drop in on him? See if you can learn something useful about your fellow students at AUB."

Nicole nodded. "You can review your Beirut diary. I'll drive you over to the National Institutes of Health. I'll call up first thing in the morning, make an appointment under my name. As a reporter, I can almost always con my way into an interview."

Matt felt suddenly uncomfortable. "Yeah. Good idea. But for now I think I'll turn in."

When the door closed upstairs, Elijah Tajikian turned to his daughter. "That man's got problems," he said, pouring himself another two fingers of Scotch. "And I don't just mean his face transplant or the people who are after him. He's got a deeper problem. Something's eating at him. It's in his eyes. There's incredible talent, yet it seems encased in an unnatural amount of insecurity and fear. Like he's running away from something." The old man shrugged, "But I like him. He's solid at the core, just frayed at the edges."

"Can we keep him alive?"

Elijah sipped the Scotch. "Let's hope so."

Nicole moved to where her father was sitting and leaned her head on his shoulder. "I know I haven't been the greatest daughter, but I'd appreciate it if you could help Matt. He has no idea what he's caught up in. And he's totally inexperienced and naïve."

"In the ugly side of politics perhaps. But his love life seems to be on target."

Nicole smiled. "And how would you know?"

Her father raised his eyebrows.

"Okay. So I like him. Don't ask why, because I don't know. Maybe he's just quirky enough to be the man for me." She gave her father a kiss on the cheek.

"I'll do some checking around," Elijah said. "Talk to some old spooks. See if I can't find out something. But we need to be careful. If not tonight, then certainly by tomorrow, they'll be looking for you."

"Good night, Dad," Nicole said. He locked up his house. Inside one of the kitchen cupboards he flicked a small, nondescript switch, activating sensor pads installed around the property. He took the receiver unit upstairs to his bedroom. He checked his .45 caliber semi-automatic pistol and placed in on the nightstand.

"Matt," Nicole whispered, "can I come in?"

"Sure."

She walked over to the side of the bed, paused, and then crawled in beside him. Her lithe body touched his, and a momentary charge passed between them. "You're warm," she said.

"And you feel really good."

"But something is wrong."

"Wrong?"

"Matt, you must believe me. I'm on your side, but – "

"But what?"

"I can't help notice you've been avoiding reading your diary."

He stroked her long hair. "True."

"Want to talk about it?"

Matt's hand moved tenderly across her silk night gown. "That's a lovely fragrance you're wearing."

"Matthew Richards."

His hand withdrew. "I'm afraid to read the diary because of what I was then, and what I am now."

"But you were young. Having big dreams and idealistic notions are normal at that age."

His smile was bitter. "And now?"

"Okay, let's hit it head on: back then you were cocky and brash. Today you're worn and cynical. Is that what you're trying to say?"

"I've made a mess of my life, Nicole. It's hard to face. And reading that diary will make it pretty clear what a jerk I've become." He buried his head next to her shoulder.

She stroked his forehead. "Did you ever hear the story of the Scotsman who went out partying one night and was so drunk he fell asleep under a tree on his way home?"

"What?"

"Well, you obviously haven't. Anyway, about an hour later along came sweet Mary down the lane. She sees this big bloke passed out under a tree, with his kilt up around his neck. So she took off one of her hair ribbons and tied it around his big Willy. The next morning he woke up, staggered over to the side of the lane to take a pee and noticed a blue ribbon tied around his rather large member. At first he was amazed, then he thought for a moment. 'I don' know where ye been, laddie, but I'm pleased ta see ya won first prize.'"

"What the hell are you talking about?" he laughed.

"What I'm trying to say, Dr. Matthew Richards, is that you're a great man."

Matt smiled. "That's laying it on a bit thick."

"Not so. You've got courage and compassion, I've witnessed it. You also have a keen sense of right and wrong."

"So pluck up my courage and read the journal. Is that what this pep talk is all about?"

She kissed him. "I liked the way you turned down dad's double Scotch."

"It wasn't the easiest thing I've ever done."

"I know that. Now read the journal." She climbed out of the bed.

"Do you have to go just now?"

"We both need some real sleep. I'll see you in the morning."

For the first time in over thirty years, Matt opened the leather journal. He thumbed through the pages, barely recognizing the neat handwriting as his own. One page, three-quarters through the book, had a purposefully bent corner. He stopped there. The entry was dated February 3, 1969. *A fabulous weekend of skiing in the mountains above Beirut.* He read a few pages, devouring the details of a long-ago life in a faraway place. After about half an hour of reading he fell into a deep sleep beset by troubling dreams.

Beirut, February, 1969

"WHAT SAY WE STOP FOR COFFEE?" Demetrie Antonopolis pulled the silver Mercedes off the winding mountain road and into the village of Basharri. "We've skied hard all weekend. I need a pick-me-up before driving the rest of the way down the mountain."

"Fine with me," said Matt. Maha opened one eye and looked out to see where they were. Brian Walker and Susan Miller were fast asleep in the back seat. The big green land cruiser, carrying Samir, Bedouina, Todd Cummings and Anne-Marie Khoury pulled off the road just behind them.

"This is Basharri, isn't it?" Maha sat up fully awake.

Demetrie nodded. "Basharri. Birthplace of the mystical poet Khalil Gibran. There's also an ancient Maronite monastery carved into the side of the cliff."

"Who or what are Maronites?" asked Matt.

"Early Christians," Maha said. "They gathered around a priest named Maron and adopted his monastic way of life. They were connected to the Roman Catholic See, and even established a Maronite College in Rome. The Maronites were heavily persecuted by the Ottomans and the other non-Christian invaders of Lebanon, but the Pope didn't show much interest in their plight."

"Nothing new there," Matt said.

"As a result of their persecution, they retreated for several centuries into a 1,000-meter-deep gorge in the Kannoubine Valley, right below us. They built monasteries in the cliffs and grew crops on the valley floor. The history of the Maronites is one of struggle to preserve their Christian faith amid the growing influence of Islam."

"We can climb down to the monastery," said Demetrie. "I've been there before, it's fabulous—an entire complex carved into rock."

"I need some coffee first," Brian grumbled, waking up in the back seat.

After coffee they set off down a narrow path that negotiated the cliff face in ever tightening turns. They picked their way down about seventy meters to a small landing. A rock archway marked the entrance to the ancient monastery, long since abandoned. The last rays of the sun could be seen far out in the Mediterranean as darkness rolled over the tops of the mountains. Using flashlights, they lit the way through the arch and into the first series of elaborate caves.

Matt aimed his flashlight at the ceiling. Immediately, colorful murals of holy men, angels and a floating figure of Christ erupted before them.

"It's lovely," Maha gasped. "I've always read about how special these monasteries were; now I know why."

Anne-Marie grabbed Todd's hand. "Just imagine how difficult it must have been to carve these monasteries out of the cliff face—and while they were hiding from enemies."

"The more things change, the more they stay the same," said Bedouina. "There's still religious persecution, only this time it's the Jews persecuting the Palestinians. And the Palestinians don't have monasteries to hide in. Just dusty refugee camps with open-air toilets."

"Relax and have a beer, Bedouina," Matt said, breaking open a six pack of Amstel.

"I've got a better idea," Demetrie said, producing a leather pouch carried on a cord inside his shirt. Ceremoniously, he took out a dark block of hashish. Besides being a graduate student in biology, Demetrie was also the local supplier of "killer hash," which he smoked several times a day. Matt wondered how he could function as well as he did, let alone drive.

They all watched as Demetrie set the block down on the cold stone floor, drew his thumbs across the top, and peeled off a thin layer of the fibrous hallucinogenic weed. Rolling the wad of hemp between his fingers, he then wrapped a double-size cigarette paper around its moist oblong shape. In seconds it was lit and on its way around the group seated on the floor.

Maha and Bedouina were the only ones who abstained. Matt at first refused, arguing that a beer was good enough for him, but finally he gave in to the urging of Todd and Brian. He took a small puff and held it in his lungs. At first nothing happened and he gave the thumbs-up sign. In the next instant he was doubled over in a fit of coughing. "Look you guys, I'm a drinker, not a smoker," he protested. After more prodding from his friends, he finally inhaled deeply and tried to hold the pungent smoke inside his lungs, but it was no use—again he exhaled, his mouth spewing out thick white smoke, his lungs on fire, his eyes watering. "Shit," he managed between coughing and spitting. "And you call this cool?"

As the fat joint made its way around the circle, Demetrie was busily preparing a second one. Within minutes, a mellow mood descended on the nine students seated on the floor of the ancient monastery. Matt, recovered from his coughing spasm, downed two beers and tried to cool his throat.

"So what's this crazy world coming to?" said Todd, the first to speak up after a long lull. "I mean, is the Middle East going to be the crucible for world destruction?"

"If you believe that spook William Fisher, we're all doomed to be dragged into a holy mega-war." Brian Walker reached for a beer. "God, this shit makes me thirsty."

"It's all right for you Americans to have a few joints, drink and complain about conditions here in the Middle East," Bedouina said. "Because it won't be long before you jump on a plane and fly back to America and your safe lives. In the meantime, we're stuck here waiting for the Israelis to attack again, like they did at the airport in December. Only this time they'll probably drop a nuclear bomb."

Matt could barely understand the conversation as it bounced back and forth. His ears were ringing and his mind had morphed into a nonsensical kaleidoscope of sights, sounds, smells and images. He downed another beer, trying to stop the onslaught, as Maha rocked him back and forth in her arms. Matt vaguely saw the images of Karl Mitchell and T. J. swimming among the sea of faces, but everything seemed surreal and disjointed. Sometime later, he opened his eyes as two older men joined the group. The next day, trying to recall the events of that evening, he couldn't determine whether they had been real or just drug-induced hallucinations. The strangers were introduced by Demetrie as true patriots of the struggle of the Palestinian people. Matt vaguely recalled something about an organization, a red and white keffiyeh, and two names—Mohammed and Yassar.

THE CLOCK ON THE NIGHTSTAND registered 6 A.M. when Nicole slipped into bed with him. "I couldn't sleep very well without you," she confessed, wrapping her arms around his warm body.

"I tried to read my journal," Matt said groggily, rolling over and caressing her hair. "I must have fallen asleep. I don't recall much."

They kissed, seeking each other, then a few moments later Matt fell back asleep. "Boy, have I got a great effect on men," she murmured, climbing out of bed. Her toe struck the leather journal on the floor. She picked it up and silently closed the door.

Elijah was rummaging around in the kitchen. "So how's Prince Charming?" He put a pot of coffee on the table. Nicole tightened her bathrobe to ward off the early morning chill.

"Comatose," she smiled, pouring herself a steaming hot mug and wrapping her hands around its warmth.

"It's nice having you here," Eli said, avoiding her eyes. "It's like things used to be…."

"Thanks for the sentiment, but we're both a little old to be playing family," Nicole said. "And in case you don't remember, it was never like this. You were always gone. Mom worried you'd disappear during one of your clandestine forays." Nicole caught herself too late—she could see the hurt in the old man's face. He turned toward the sink and rattled a few dishes.

Nicole went to him. "I'm sorry, Dad. That just came out. You're right. We can enjoy the fact that we're together now. Like I said to Matt, the past should be filed in a dusty folder called ancient history." She kissed him on the cheek.

"I'm going to have my coffee and skim Matt's journal. Why don't you take a shower and get dressed? I'll whip up some bacon and eggs for breakfast. Then I want you to read some of this stuff before he wakes up." Nicole gave him a gentle push out of the kitchen.

Instead of leaving, Eli walked over to the kitchen cupboard and reached in the back.

"I hope you're not having Sotch at this hour."

He withdrew a manila envelope closed with tape. Her name was written on it. "This is for you to open and read in case anything ever happens to me," he said. "I suggest you put it in a safe deposit box somewhere, but only open it after I'm dead."

Tears welled up. "What's this all about, Dad?"

"It's my life. I've written it all down over the past few years since I left the agency. There aren't many national secrets in there, at least not anymore. I wanted you to know where I was and what I was doing during those times I wasn't there for you and your mother. You should know. There are also a few other things in there that could be useful." He turned to go.

"Well it's gonna be a long time before I ever need to read this." She watched him walk up the stairs. The manila envelope bulged as it lay on the table.

Later that morning, Matt strolled into the kitchen, clean and dressed. "I feel like a new man." He sat down at the table and accepted a cup of coffee from Nicole. His eyes darkened as he noticed Eli reading his journal.

Eli looked up. "Hope you don't mind, Matt? That was quite a year you spent in Beirut. There are several big names in here—Martin Thomas, William Fisher, Brian Walker. Thomas is head of the National Institutes of Health, Fisher's one of the top guys at the National Security Agency, and Walker's a radical law professor at Berkeley. At least he was. He was killed about a month ago while giving a speech."

Matt's coffee mug hit the table hard. "Brian's dead—what happened?"

"It was in all the newspapers. It happened during a protest demonstration about a month after the suicide attack on the president. Professor Walker was addressing a meeting of Palestinian-Americans at the Long Beach Convention Center. There was a large group of protesters gathered outside the building. They were pretty evenly divided into two opposing camps. Anyway, at some point the crowd got out of hand and broke into the convention center. Some of the demonstrators had clubs and knives and quite a few people were killed. Shots were fired. His body was found lying behind the lectern, a bullet hole in his head."

Matt sat still, remembering his young friend, the energy and idealism he exuded. *Please let it be a coincidence.*

"Matt?"

"Yeah?"

"Are you okay? I shouldn't have unloaded like that."

"No, Eli. I needed to know."

"There's more."

Oh shit. "So, let's hear it."

"I hang out occasionally with some retired FBI types. We have a drink now and then, swap bullshit stories and try to keep abreast of things. For old times sake."

Matt nodded.

"Seems the two security guards assigned to Professor Walker mysteriously disappeared. Their families don't even know where they are," Eli said.

Matt rubbed his forehead. The stitches itched worse at the moment, and his head throbbed.

"After reading this journal and hearing your story, Matt, somehow I don't think Brian Walker's death was an accident, or a coincidence."

"So you think someone may be trying to eliminate all the people I was with in Beirut?"

"Looks like it." Elijah sneaked a glance at his daughter.

"Do you think Brian was a member of a terrorist cell?"

"No Matt, I don't. But he may have known enough from his Beirut days to get himself killed."

"That means others could be singled out. I have to find them – warn them."

"But there's a chance one or more of them are a part of this cell," Nicole put in.

"And," Eli added, "there could be more than one group after you and your friends; the terrorist cell which doesn't want to be exposed, and those hunting them."

"After thirty years, how can I know which of my old friends might be involved in this?"

"Look, Matt," Nicole said. "It's impossible to know whom to trust. You could be walking right into a trap. You don't have to do this. Right Dad? Isn't there someone in the agency we could go to? Matt's not equipped for this."

"No." Eli paused. "There's a good chance the CIA's involved, or at least some piece of it. And someone high up in the other agencies may be part of their network as well. You have to understand that trust is a commodity with these people—it's regularly bought and sold, according to the vagaries of global politics and the highest bidder. You've got to trust your instincts."

Matt nodded. "Eli, I've been thinking about this. The best person to start with is Dr. Thomas. And he lives and works right here in Washington."

"I called his office at the NIH this morning." Nicole replied. "When I pressed for an appointment, his secretary blew me off."

"Give me the phone." Matt dialed the number and waited. He sipped his now-cold coffee. "Hello, I'd like to get an important message to Dr. Martin Thomas…yes… Tell him that Dr. Wilson Richards, an old colleague of his, is in town just for the day.…" Matt listened while he made circles with his finger on the table. "Yes, the heart surgeon…Dr. Richards would like to speak with him about the death of his son, Matthew…yes.…" Matt put his hand over the mouthpiece. "She told me to wait for a few moments."

The doctor's secretary came back on the line. Matt perked up. "Fine. Seven-thirty this evening. Thank you very much," He punched the red button and handed the unit back to Nicole.

"Okay," Matt said. "Now let's see if we can't track down some of the others. The easiest should be Todd Cummings. His parents lived in Pittsburgh, so perhaps he moved back there after school. He was also the type of person to keep in touch with people. Except me of course. We drifted apart after the explosion at the restaurant."

Elijah looked at Nicole. "Sounds like a job for a good investigative journalist."

Matt managed a smile. *She's very good.*

"Thanks for the vote of confidence, Dad. I'll get on the internet. Most folks don't even know they're listed on some internet databases."

"Even me?" Matt's eyes darkened.

"I looked up your name, Matt, when I began snooping around. It was pretty easy to learn about your past."

"And you're still speaking to me?"

"She's a saint—she even speaks to her old man."

Over the next half hour, Nicole dug up the names and telephone numbers for five T. Cummings living in and around the Pittsburgh area. A Google search identified one as senior legal council for Monument Oil and Gas Corporation, as well as a member of the board of directors for the Pittsburgh Children's Hospital and the Pennsylvania United Way Campaign. Nicole, posing as a journalist doing a story on Beirut in the late 1960s, succeeded in reaching Todd Cummings at Monument Oil. He would be delighted to speak with her about Beirut, he said, and agreed to meet at 11:30 tomorrow morning.

Eli stood up. "Good work. I need to go out for a while."

"What's going on, Dad?"

"Just a few errands. Plus there's a man I used to work for, unofficially. He may have something on this. If not, he'll know who will." He reached for his coat and wool hat.

"Are you sure you can trust him?" Nicole looked over at Matt.

"Trust him?" Elijah paused in the hallway. "I've trusted him with my life more than once, and I'm still here."

For the next several hours Matt made a list of old acquaintances he could recall and those he found browsing through the leather journal. They then tried the Internet search engines again.

"I've got an idea."

"Yes, doctor?" Nicole looked up from the computer screen.

"What if I claim to be Dr. Richard's cousin? Just like I did at Sweet Briar. Then I can tell them I may have found something among Matt's personal effects with their name on it."

"That would give us an excuse to deliver to them in person," Nicole said, nodding.

"So what do you think?"

"Pretty sneaky. Must be the assassin in you." She ducked as he threw his pencil.

They both started as the door opened.

"Whoa. You two are jumpy." Elijah walked into the library with his coat half off.

"You were pretty quiet coming in. Something up?"

Her father turned to face his daughter as he hung up his coat. "I may have found something interesting." His smile was fleeting. A loud crash resounded from the front door. Elijah flung himself towards them. All three hit the floor.

"Dad!"

"We got unwanted company. Stay down. Stay down!"

Something hard bounced into the hallway. "Tear gas. I'd know that fucking sound anywhere." A loud hiss was followed by white smoke seeping under the door. He bolted the lock as a second canister banged up against the door. "Close the shutters and lock them. Don't talk."

CROUCHING DOWN, Eli folded back the corner of the carpet to reveal a trap door. Matt helped him pull on the cast-iron ring. The door creaked open. Eli and Nicole vanished down a narrow stairway as Matt grabbed his journal and notes.

Boots echoed loudly in the hallway. Matt ducked down the opening as the library door exploded in a shower of splinters and bent metal. The spit from suppressor-equipped MAC-10s wheezed into the room. More splinters showered Matt as he reached up to pull the heavy trap closed. Blood from several cuts on his face fell onto the wooden steps.

"Bolt it! Bolt it now!" Elijah reached up. Matt threw the bolt hard.

Nicole shook, "Jesus...."

"Are you hurt?" her father asked.

"Who are they, Dad? Who are they?"

"They're pros. That's all I know."

"And what is this place?" Matt looked around in the dim light. The blood was warm on his face. The stubble on his face was slippery. *It may not be mine, but it still hurts*.

"It's my escape route. Just in case.... There's a tunnel here that connects with an underground utility conduit and surfaces a couple of blocks away. Follow me." Elijah ducked into a hole in the wall. About three hundred yards into the tunnel he stopped and looked back at the other two, crawling on all fours.

Thrusting his hand into a small recess in the wall, the old man felt around and pulled out a small device resembling a garage door opener. It was sealed inside a zip-lock bag. "Ready?" Without waiting for a reply, he pushed the red button. Two seconds later there was a dull thud overhead, immediately followed by a huge explosion that rocked the tunnel and showered them with dirt.

"What the hell is *that?*" Nicole exclaimed.

"It's designed to look like a gas leak—I'll collect the insurance money later."

"Are they dead?" Grime mixed with the blood on Matt's face.

"Yes." Elijah started crawling forward again.

"But Dad, what about all your belongings? Your clothes, your furniture, your books?"

This guy's a professional too. Matt looked at Nicole, who stared open-mouthed at her father.

"I have a safe house where I've stashed most of my important things. We'll hole up there."

A few hundred yards along a ladder came into view. They clambered up, one after the other. Sirens blared just a few blocks away. Before emerging into broad daylight, they brushed the dirt off their hair and faces. Nicole used a handkerchief on Matt's cuts.

An aluminum conduit cover, bolted from the inside, lead out to the street. Eli cracked it, and then motioned for them to follow. They scrambled out into the bright winter sunlight and walked several blocks to the rental car. In minutes they were approaching downtown Washington and a small apartment in a run-down area northwest of Union Station.

Matt looked out at the run-down buildings.

"So how are you two feeling?" Elijah said.

"Shaken up and very scared." Nicole snuggled next to her father. "Tear gas. Guns. And they were so quiet, no loud ratta tat. Were those silencers?"

"Suppressors actually. They keep the noise level down to 40dB sound reduction. Lower on .223 calibers, but these were throwing nine mills."

Nicole stared at him. "At times like this you frighten me, Dad."

"It's what drove your mother and me apart." He turned away.

"Well at this point I'm glad you're on our side." Matt slowed down for a traffic light. "Eli? You talked earlier about going to meet someone you trusted…."

"I was able to talk to him. I told him what we suspect is happening."

"And?"

"All he said was 'Thank You.' Which in spook speak means; I'd just given him a key piece to a very big puzzle."

"I have no idea what you are talking about," said Nicole, looking at the father she barely knew. "Anything else?"

"Yes, but it's water under the bridge now. Just that there seems to have been a stakeout car parked up the street from the house. Guess I don't have to tell you that we're lucky to be alive." Eli shook his head and wiped his brow. "I'm too old for this shit."

"Thanks Dad." Nicole kissed him on the cheek.

The Hart Senate Building

SENATOR STEVENS SPOKE QUIETLY into his private cell phone. "Look, this evening is not a good time to meet. I've got an important dinner engagement. You know the less we meet the better for everyone concerned."

"I realize the risks, senator, but we've got a situation that needs your immediate support. I'm having a function at the Embassy this evening; you could stop by for a quick drink on your way to your dinner. It won't take long."

"Can't I just deal with it here and now? Obviously your people have screwed up again."

"Actually, it's good news. Our problems were eliminated in a freak explosion caused by a gas leak. The contractors got caught in the blast as well. I just need a little support from you to put a lid on anything the fire department or police may find in the rubble. It wouldn't do for too many people to be asking questions."

"I'll get on it right away. It's about time you people got something right. I'll be there at 7:15." The senator snapped his cell phone closed and chuckled.

Potomac, Maryland

NICOLE NUDGED HIM. "Ring the doorbell, Matt, we're committed now." They stood in front of the large double doors of Dr. Thomas's Potomac residence. Matt felt odd coming back here again. This was where it all started. The reception for Dr. Melikian, the accident, young Kelly's death, and everything else.

He pressed the buzzer.

The door opened right away, taking them by surprise. A butler stood before them, hand on the doorknob. "Yes?"

"Dr. Thomas is expecting me. I'm Dr. Wilson Richards, and this is Ms. Nicole Delacluse."

"Yes sir. This way, please." The elderly butler led them into Dr. Thomas's library and took their coats. "I'll announce your arrival. Dr.

Thomas is taking a phone call at the moment, it shouldn't be too long. Would you care for tea or coffee while you're waiting?"

"Coffee please." Matt glanced around where several weeks ago he had punched Senator Stevens. He rubbed his hand unconsciously. Photos of Dr. Martin J. Thomas with various dignitaries, including heads of state and several former presidents, filled the desk and coffee table. Floor-to-ceiling bookcases offered elegant bindings. A diploma from Yale University held the place of honor, on the wall behind a carved Jefferson-style desk.

The butler returned with a silver coffee service. "Dr. Thomas will be right down." He departed with a quick bow.

Nicole poured two cups of coffee. "Oh, I'm sorry," she said as the spoon slipped from her hand and dropped on the carpet. Bending down to retrieve it, she deftly placed the small listening device Eli had given her on the underside of Dr. Thomas' desk.

A few moments later the door opened. Nicole turned around, spoon in hand. Dr. Martin Thomas walked in. As soon as he saw his visitors, he stopped. "You're not Wilson Richards."

"No, sir. I'm not."

"Just what are you doing here – both of you?"

"Dr. Thomas, listen to me carefully. We don't mean you any harm, and I regret the subterfuge in coming here, but you must hear me out. And the truth may be little hard to take."

Dr. Thomas stood still and watched them. "Try me."

"Very well. My name is Matthew Richards. Dr. Matthew Richards."

"That's preposterous. I know Matthew Richards."

"Look at the scars on his face, Dr. Thomas," Nicole said, pleading.

"What?"

"The scars around his hairline. He's been given a face transplant."

Matt nodded. "Go ahead, Dr. Thomas. It really is me."

Martin Thomas hesitated, then stepped forward and examined Matt's hairline. "Dear God. What....? Who...?"

"It's a full face transplant, sir," Matt said, as professional fingers examined him. "They did it to me just after the party you held for the new personal physician to the president. Right after I was reported dead."

"You were killed in a car crash with Senator Steven's daughter that night. How....?" Dr. Thomas slowly lowered himself into an arm-chair, still staring at Matt.

"I was kidnapped, reported as dead, and given this new face." Matt sat in the opposite facing chair.

Dr. Thomas stared. "This doesn't mean you are Matthew Richards. It only proves you have a new face."

Matt laughed; an open innocent sound that spread a look of bewilderment across Thomas' own face. "Okay. Fair enough. How about this? I was at the reception for Dr. Melikian. You and I spoke briefly in the receiving line. You asked about my father and then said you were sorry to hear about the death of my brother, Sam. Later that evening I flattened Senator Stevens, right here in this room, and left with his daughter."

Dr. Thomas nodded thoughtfully. "And remember the time I came to your office at AUB asking for advice about medical school? You told me that just because I came from a long line of prominent physicians that was no guarantee it was the life for me. You said a per-son had to have it in their blood, otherwise they wouldn't be happy with such a demanding career." Matt smiled ruefully. "I should have lis-tened to your advice, Dr. Thomas. I didn't turn out to be a very good physician."

"What are you thinking, Dr. Thomas?" asked Nicole.

"I'm thinking about the transplant and the stitches and how the healing process would fit into the time frame. It fits." He looked from Nicole to Matt. "What have they done to you? And why?"

"Are you ready for more hard news?"

"Can I have some coffee first?" Nicole handed him a cup.

"Whoever did this to me believes there is a terrorist cell here in Washington actively plotting to kill the president, and that one or more of the students we knew at AUB are involved."

"The suicide bomber that killed Dr. Norman ...?"

"Probably the same group," said Matt. "That's why I'm here, why I came to you. To find out who among our group might be involved."

"But that doesn't explain your face transplant, Matt."

"I was going to be used to track down my old AUB friends. But I escaped from the hospital where I was being held. I'm trying to figure this out, but there are a lot of missing pieces."

Dr. Thomas sat back, lost in thought. "That's quite a story. Why don't we just call the FBI and let them get to the bottom of this? The deputy commissioner is a good friend of mine." He walked over to his desk. "And it's our duty to warn the president if he really is in danger."

"Dr. Thomas?" Nicole jumped up from the sofa and wedged herself between him and the desk. "Someone's trying to kill Matt. They've made several attempts on his life already, and innocent people have been killed. Anyway, the president's adequately protected, especially following the recent attempt on his life."

"I don't believe I got your name, Ms. ...?"

"Delacluse, Nicole Delacluse of the *International Herald Tribune*. I'm on a special investigative assignment following the suicide attack on the president. Don't you think it's a little too coincidental that Dr. Brian Walker was killed recently? He was one of Matt's best friends at AUB. And from what's happened to us in the past few days we know the people trying to kill Matt must have connections high up in our government. Either that, or some friendly foreign country, or both. Please—don't make that call."

"Kill Matt?"

"There have been several attempts on my life," Matt said. "And innocent bystanders have been murdered. These people are ruthless and determined."

"Alright, it may be too dangerous to involve the authorities at this time. But what on earth can I do?"

"I need your help locating all the junior year abroad students," Matt replied. "I also recall a graduate student, William Fisher I believe. He was much older than the rest of us, but he also came over with our group. He gave some terrific lectures about the Middle East. Could he be somehow involved?"

"There's no way it could be Will Fisher. He's now one of the top directors at the National Security Agency. In fact, he's on the President's Special Task Force on Terrorism and the Middle East. He's a genius at synthesizing information and drawing conclusions from it. The NSA and the president are fortunate to have him. In fact, maybe he could shed some light on all of this. I can probably get you a meeting with him."

"Maybe in a few days—right now, I don't want to send anyone on a wild goose chase."

"Dr. Thomas," Nicole said, "I've never heard of a face *transplant* before. That's super-advanced medical technology, isn't it?"

"It used to be," Dr. Thomas said. "But in the last year the techniques have advanced greatly. The Israelis seem to be the leaders in this procedure at the moment, but the Austrians, Swiss and Germans aren't far behind. Where did you say this clinic was?" he said, turning to Matt.

"I'm not sure," Matt lied. "Somewhere outside of Washington. But I was so drugged up, I doubt that I could ever find it again. Doctor, do you have your old AUB yearbook for 1968-69? Maybe that will jog my memory. And have you kept in touch with any of the students from that period?"

"Not a one. When I came back at the end of that year, I was pursuing my genetics research at Yale. Then NIH called a few years later and asked me to join their management team. Since then it's been a steady round of work and speeches. But retirement is only a year away." Weariness entered his voice.

"There's more to this position than just trying to provide for the health of the nation. In fact, too much politics for me." Dr. Thomas shrugged. "My yearbook should be on the bookshelf, just over here," he said, getting up. "Ah yes, there it is. American University of Beirut, 1969."

For the next twenty minutes, Matt and Martin Thomas pored over the pictures in the yearbook. Nicole took notes in her reporter's shorthand. The doctor's memory was better than Matt's, but then he hadn't worked his way through a tanker load of Scotch in the last thirty-some years.

"I'm sorry to break this off, Matthew, but I've got a dinner guest due to arrive in a few minutes." His hand came up and reexamined Matt's surgery. "Whoever did it, Matt, it's very good work."

"I'm not sure my mother would approve," Matt said, pulling back.

Dr. Thomas winced. "I'm sorry. That was uncalled for. Are you sure you don't want me to make a call and get you both into a safe house or something?"

"No thanks. But I would like your private cell phone number, just in case."

Dr. Thomas plucked a business card from a silver holder on his desk and wrote on the back. "Now I really must see to my guest. It's too important for me to cancel at the last minute. He's probably arrived by now. Please keep in touch. And good luck."

"You will keep this just between us for the time being, won't you?" said Matt, reaching for the card.

"Of course." They shook hands firmly. "Take care Matt, and you too, Ms. Delacluse. Anderson will show you out. Now, you really must excuse me."

The butler appeared. As they were gathering their coats from a closest in the hallway, a small door opened. Senator Mason T. Stevens stepped out, smoothing his tie and adjusting a tight vest.

"Oh, I didn't know Martin had guests. I was just freshening up. Haven't we met before? I'm Senator Stevens," he said, holding out a fleshy hand to Matt. He smiled approvingly at Nicole.

"It's a pleasure to meet you again, Senator Stevens." Matt gripped his hand equally hard. "I'm Dr. Hunter and this is my wife, Veronica. We're NIH researchers in plastic surgery. I never forget a face. A carryover from my profession. We met about three months ago at the reception for Dr. Melikian. Nice meeting you again, senator."

As they got into the car and headed down the driveway, Nicole turned and looked at Matt. "If we live through this, Matthew Richards, I'm going to marry you."

When they were a block away, Nicole touched his arm. "This is a good spot."

Matt watched her unwrap the small digital recorder and battery operated receiver. "What if it rains?"

"Haven't a clue. Dad didn't mention that. Let's hope the weather stays good. I'll just be a moment. She stepped out of the car and set the recorder in a dense hedge bordering a large residence.

"How long is it good for?"

"Dad said up to six hours. We should at least be able to hear what the senator has to say. If they talk in the library, that is."

Matt and Nicole walked, arm in arm, into Eli's safe house. Matt used one of the fake IDs and a credit card from the collection in his valise to book the first flight out of Washington's Ronald Reagan National Airport for Pittsburgh. Tomorrow was their appointment with Todd Cummings.

"This ain't the Ritz," said Elijah, "but it does have a small guest room. You guys figure out how to arrange yourselves; I'm going to bed. We'll listen to the recording first thing in the morning."

"Don't worry about us, Dad, and by the way...." She pulled out the distinctive pinch bottle of Glenrothes Single Malt Scotch. "Sweet dreams."

Matt and Nicole crawled into the small twin bed and slipped into each other's arms. They were exhausted but Matt's mind kept churning. Past and present bombarding him with images. Somewhere in the assault of images, he slept.

Cairo, early December 1968

THE SOOT-COVERED TRAIN from Aswan to Cairo pulled into the station. It was early morning hours after a nighttime run along the Nile River. This was the end of their educational trip to the monuments and museums of ancient Egypt. In two days they would be on a plane heading back to the American University of Beirut.

Most of the seventeen American students hadn't slept that night. Instead, the journey on the train was an excuse for a party, with beer and liquor flowing freely. Twice during the night Dr. Martin Thomas, their chaperone, had tried to confine their revelry to one car and stop them roaming and yelling through the train. When the train finally did pull into the Cairo station, several of the bedrooms stunk of vomit and booze.

Matt and Todd Cummings wearily dumped their luggage onto the bed of their shared hotel room. "What should we do with our last day in Cairo?"

"I'm gonna sleep." Todd crashed heavily onto the bed. "You do what you want." Matt bathed and changed into something loose and comfortable. He was also tired, but the covered bazaar, the famous Souk of Cairo, was where he wanted to be.

It was an easy ten-minute walk from the Sheraton Hotel on the banks of the Nile River to the exotic alleys and merchant districts of the bazaar. The ancient market in Cairo was many times larger than the one in Beirut.

He stood beneath the great arched portico, staring at dark passageways running in all directions. Pungent smells from the spice vendors assaulted his nostrils. *I could find them blindfolded.* Arabs, still dressed as they had for thousands of years, eyed him curiously. Their bags were full of food and other merchandise bought at the morning market somewhere deep inside the souk. Matt wandered about aimlessly, every once in a while coming across the central courtyard of a mosque.

He found a food stall and ordered a cup of grainy Arabic coffee, a bowl of yogurt with honey and a pita bread sandwich filled with roast lamb. *If only Maha were beside me now.* Her face filled his memory, sweet and innocent.

They didn't see him as they hurried by, but Matt noticed the two men right away—William Fisher and a Middle Eastern man in an expensive western business suit. They talked in rapid Arabic.

What is Fisher doing here? Curious, Matt left several bills on the table and followed at a safe distance.

"You are American, yes?" A high-pitched voice. A dirty Egyptian boy came up beside him, walking in lockstep. He smiled, showing rotten teeth. He was young, but his eyes knew more than his age.

"That's right." Matt smiled down at him. "And who are you?"

"My name is Saleem. Allah in his infinite wisdom has chosen me to be your guide today." The boy bowed. "Where would you like to go and what would you like to see?"

Matt glanced after Fisher and his companion. "Your English is very good, Saleem. Where did you learn it?"

"My mother is a maid for a woman who teaches at the American University in Cairo. I also learned some English at school," he said, beaming.

"And shouldn't you be in school now?"

"Oh no. Allah said it is my duty to help you. So here I am." The eyes hardened. "Why are you following those men?"

"Is it that obvious?" Matt said. "Actually, I know one of them. I was just curious where they were going."

"Follow me. I know where they are going, and we will get there before them." Saleem disappeared around the next corner. "Are you coming?" he said, poking his head back around.

Matt weaved and ran through the dark lanes of the covered bazaar, lagging behind his guide. Abruptly they came upon a lavish nightclub at the edge of the bazaar. Matt stared at the carved door and the immense white sign announcing the entrance to the Hidden Veils Nightclub.

Saleem pulled hard on his sleeve. Matt found himself in the dark recesses of a carpet shop just across from the nightclub. He watched as William Fisher and the older man walked by and disappeared into the nightclub.

"Would you like me to take a look for you?" asked Saleem. "I can get in and out without being seen. It would be fun."

"Yes. But be careful," said Matt. "And come out in five minutes and tell me what you see. Then I'll let you guide me around the city for a few hours."

"It will be a great honor to be your esteemed guide. I shall return shortly."

Matt stood in a dark alley a few shops away from the entrance to the nightclub and waited. Several elderly men came and went over the next few minutes. Matt looked at his watch. Ten minutes passed, and no Saleem. Matt looked around. *Shit.*

Matt waited a few more minutes, then stepped out of the shadows and headed for the nightclub.

"Watch where you're going!" Matt said, regaining his balance after being nearly knocked over by someone from behind.

"Oh, a thousand pardons, Sir. I was late for a meeting and didn't see you. Are you all right?" A young man, a few years younger than Matt, looked up, again making apologies.

"I'm okay," said Matt. "Your English is very good."

"Why thank you. I am a student. My benefactor insists I become

fluent in English. He says it will be important for my future success."
The boy looked at his watch. "Now if you will excuse me, I must hurry.
May Allah protect you." He hurried toward the nightclub, opened the
door, and slipped inside.

Later that afternoon, at a food stall near the giant Heliopolis
obelisk on the banks of the Nile in downtown Cairo, Saleem told Matt
what he had seen in the nightclub. The American had been seated
with a large Egyptian man, watching the belly dancers and drinking
Arabic coffee. A man in a Palestinian headdress joined them. The
three of them talked very quietly to each other.

"Can you describe them?" asked Matt.

"The man in the red keffiyeh had a hooked nose, large lips, and
hadn't shaved, like my brothers sometimes." Saleem laughed as he
looked around, street smart. "He was a Palestinian. That is all I can
tell. And just before I left, another man, not much older than you,
joined them. He looked like a college student. I have seen many of
them at the house where my mother works. And he had an Armenian
accent."

ELI GENTLY SHOOK NICOLE AND MATT. "Better wake up."

Matt stirred, then sat up. Tension hardened his eyes. "What's
happened?"

"Nicole, both you get dressed. We need to talk. Right away."

"What is it, Dad?"

"Dr. Martin Thomas is dead."

"Oh, God." Nicole drew the bedcover up to her neck.

"It's on the morning news. He died of an apparent heart attack
in bed last night. His butler found him."

Matt dressed quickly. "Were there any signs of violence?"

"If there were, it wasn't reported in the news. All they said is the
butler heard noises coming from his room. It seems he died after a
coughing fit that was too much for his heart. He had been taking heart
medication for the past year."

Nicole talked as she dressed. "We've got to retrieve that recorder.

Maybe we can find out something about his death."

Matt pulled on his trousers and reached for his shoes.

Nicole stood in the doorway. "I'll go get it. Make some coffee will you?"

"Watch yourself," Elijah said.

"Just have the coffee ready."

When Nicole returned Matt was on his third rerun of the Dr. Thomas story on CNN. "Nothing new. Did anyone see you?"

"No. Believe me, I was careful. I parked a block away and walked to the hedge. Dad?" Nicole handed the recording device to her father.

"Gimme a few minutes." Elijah produced a set of headphones and began listening. Matt and Nicole waited, watching as he sat hunched over, listening, eyes fixed in time and space.

"Okay. He made two calls. Most of it's blank, but the two calls had him phoning his son, a physician in California, and one to William Fisher in Baltimore."

"Fisher?"

"What did he and Fisher talk about?" Nicole asked, an impatient edge in her voice.

"I couldn't hear clearly what he was saying to Fisher."

"Did he mention my name?"

"He mentioned your name several times, Matt."

"That's all? No details about the conversation?"

"Sorry. It must have been a cordless phone and he must have moved away from the desk."

Nicole stepped close to Matt. "What time were the calls?"

Eli scanned the digital readout. "Just before midnight."

"Matt? Stevens was obviously gone by then. Shit. I wish we had more."

Chapter Eleven

Pittsburgh

ONCE DOMINATED BY STEEL MILLS and buried under black smoke, Pittsburgh had transformed itself into a renaissance city. The riverfront was transformed into malls and tree-lined parks. With several major league sports teams and world class universities, the city had become well known for its innovative medical, computer and software expertise.

Monument Oil and Gas Company occupied the top ten floors of a magnificent high rise that soared above the downtown skyline. Todd Cummings, chief legal counsel and corporate secretary, had his office in the executive suite just below the boardroom and executive dining rooms. While executive dining rooms were going out of fashion in corporate America, they were a necessity for Monument Oil. It was there that foreign dignitaries and the heads of major oil and gas companies from around the world, especially the Middle East, were entertained. The corporate dining rooms were not only a quiet place to talk business. They were also secure.

Nicole's interview with Todd Cummings had been scheduled for 11:30 A.M., and her eyes widened as they were shown into the anteroom of Cumming's office. It was lushly appointed with dark mahogany paneling, Persian carpets, and a large oil painting by Thomas Hart Benson depicting Pittsburgh during the 1920s. "There's more money tied up in the furnishings here than I'll ever see in a lifetime," she murmured to Matt as they sat down on a sofa. "Look at this: real damask."

"If you got it, flaunt it. That's the motto of corporate America," Matt said, preoccupied by what he was going to say to his old friend Todd. *What am I going to say?*

Nicole noticed Matt's frown. "Are you worried?"

He nodded.

"You did well with Dr. Thomas. Cummings is no physician, so he may be tougher to convince. I'll back you up." She squeezed his hand.

"Mr. Cummings is ready to see you now," said the secretary, her dark hair elegantly arranged in a chignon. Her smile was big and practiced. "You'll be having lunch with Mr. Cummings. Are there any special dietary requirements for either of you? Our chefs are used to special needs."

Nicole shook her head. "No alcohol for either of us," Matt said, "but other than that, we'll eat anything." Nicole gave him a quick smile.

The secretary ushered them into a spacious corner office overlooking the Allegheny River.

"Ah, Ms. Delacluse," said a trim man with a closely cropped beard and neatly styled salt and pepper hair, "I've been looking forward to your visit. It's not every day I get an opportunity to talk about something other than oil and gas." He smiled, extending his hand.

"I hope you don't mind, Mr. Cummings, but I brought one of my colleagues along. It's his first assignment with our paper and I'm showing him the ropes. This is, ah… Sam Parsons."

Matt studied the sleek features obviously maintained by an active outdoor life. *He's aged well. Better than me.* As Matt watched him from behind his new face, he recalled Beirut. Splashing azure blue water, intense conversations, Maha….

"Nice to meet you, Mr. Parsons," Cummings said, extending his tanned hand.

Matt just nodded as they shook hands. *Three decades. Where did it all go?*

"We'll soon go upstairs for lunch," Cummings went on, "but we can begin here." He motioned them over to a sofa while he sat down in a large wing chair. "It was Beirut in the late 1960s you were interested in, wasn't it?"

For the next half hour Nicole was the consummate journalist, starting out with questions that allowed Cummings to brag a little about his career, then when he seemed relaxed, posing interesting but superficial questions about Beirut, his first impressions, special things he remembered vividly, any people he still kept in contact with.

"Actually, I've not kept in touch with many from those days," Cummings said, fingers touching his neatly trimmed beard. "I do stay in touch with a couple of old friends, Anne-Marie Khoury, a brilliant artist, and another good friend, Theodore Janus."

"Good friends from our early days are to be treasured," Nicole said, closing her notebook, offering no threat.

"Yes indeed. In fact, I've just lost two friends from the old days. Brian Walker – perhaps you read of his death at that Palestinian rally – an appalling business. And then Matt Richards." Cummings leaned back in his chair. "Odd the paths our lives take. Matt was a brilliant student, great promise all around. But I hear drink got him pretty bad." He waved his hand. "Sorry, I'm drifting off the subject, Ms. Delacluse."

Matt doodled in his reporter's notebook. *He's still a pompous ass.*

Todd Cummings rose abruptly. "Time for lunch."

After lunch had been served in one of the small private dining rooms on the top floor and the waiter had left them, Matt knew it was time to begin. *Here goes nothing.*

"There's something I must say to you."

Cummings paused, his fork in mid-arc. "I beg your pardon, Mr. Parsons?"

"Brace yourself, Toad." Matt gazed intently in his eyes. "I'm not Sam Parsons. It's me, Matt—Matt Richards."

"That's a sick joke. Just what the hell is going on here, Ms. Delacluse?"

Nicole reached over and touched Cumming's hand. "You should listen, Mr. Cummings."

Matt noticed the eyes change. The corporate animal was on alert. No telling what he would do next.

"I suggest you explain yourself."

"Of course. I called you Toad because that's what I always called you. Remember? Back at Harvard. And at AUB."

Cummings stood up. Nicole pulled hard on his sleeve. He settled silently back into his chair.

"I suggest you listen, Toad." Matt leaned forward. "Listen to my voice. You can't deny it's my voice."

Cummings stared. His eyes darted between Matt and Nicole. "What in God's name are you two doing…?"

"I had surgery. A face transplant. And it wasn't my idea. And they faked my death as well. It's me, Toad."

"Dear God. I don't believe it."

"He's telling the truth, Mr. Cummings. You can check his stitches," Nicole said.

"That won't be necessary. Okay. So if you are Matt. Which I still very much doubt. What do you want?"

"Matt's in big trouble. He desperately needs your help. That's why we are here." Nicole stopped talking.

They all sat quietly while the waiter refilled the wine glasses and left.

"Tell me exactly what is going on," Cummings said. "And tell me everything. And don't think I won't call the security guards if…."

Matt nodded. "You were right about my drinking, I went downhill fast. But I'm recovering now. Only things are happening which I don't understand. I really need your help, Todd."

Tension left the table. "How can I help?"

"I'm going to tell you everything I know. I only hope you will believe me, because it's pretty farfetched."

"Try me. What you've already said is farfetched." Cummings' voice was cold. He was a practiced negotiator.

"I was kidnapped, portrayed as dead, and given a face transplant. Someone wants to use me as a ferret to track down a terrorist cell planning to kill the President of the United States."

"That's the biggest crock of shit…."

"Listen to him!" Nicole interjected.

"I escaped from the clinic where I was held prisoner and am trying to find out who these people are. They have tried to kill me twice already. I have to find out why." Matt leaned forward. "Look, Todd. We didn't always see eye to eye during college, but we trusted each other once. And I'm asking you to trust me again."

"Why?"

"Because I'm afraid they may try to eliminate those who were at AUB with me that year. And that means you might be in danger as well." *He doesn't believe a word I'm saying.* Matt plunged in again. "Look don't you think the deaths of both me and Brian are a strange coincidence in timing? Well, I've got worse news—Dr. Martin Thomas died last night of an apparent heart attack, just a few hours after Nicole and I visited with him. Someone is systematically eliminating all the people we went to Beirut with."

"Okay, okay—if you really *are* Matt Richards, then why don't you just go to the FBI? Why talk to me under false pretenses?" He reached for his water glass. His hand trembled.

"Because we have reason to believe someone high up in the federal government might be involved," Nicole said.

Matt debated with himself. *One last chance.* "Todd, you saw the television pictures of the assassination attempt on the president. Did you happen to look closely at the face of the bomber?"

"Of course, they only showed it a thousand times. Why do you ask?"

"You tell me."

"Well, I did think for a second that she resembled Bedouina…but it couldn't have been. What are you driving at?"

"I'm not sure. I've been thinking this over and over in my mind for years, all with no answers – except one."

"Which is?"

"The only person I actually saw killed that night at the restaurant in Beirut was Samir."

Todd Cummings went white. "You are Matt Richards."

Matt lost it, nerves snapping. "Jesus Christ, Toad! I thought we were past that…."

"Yeah, well you expect too much, like always. You come in here unrecognizable, with a reporter, notebooks, and lies. I need time."

"I need time, too. But I haven't got much. They're trying to kill me!" Matt's sweeping arm knocked his plate on the floor. They froze as the waiter opened the door.

"No problem, Charles. Close the door please." Cummings pushed back his chair and studied Matt and Nicole. "So what you are saying is that Maha and Bedouina may not have died that night. Then where did they go?"

"I don't know, but it was Bedouina who…."

"You don't know that. It may have been someone who looked like her."

"I feel it. It was her."

"Look, Matt. You were in love with a beautiful redheaded Jordanian, deeply in love." Cummings glanced at Nicole. She nodded for him to continue. "The human mind is pretty complicated. I can understand your yearning for Maha to be alive, but it's just a romantic delusion. And there's no evidence about either Maha or Bedouina." Cummings stood up. "There's nothing I can do for you. I want you both to leave right this moment. This is sickening."

"You think losing my face isn't sickening?"

Todd Cummings glared at Matt. "I don't doubt that something is going on, something violent and ugly. But take a look around you. I'm a senior officer here. I'm not putting my firm at risk, jeopardizing my career, because of a college acquaintance I knew over thirty years ago." He paused. "Sorry, you're on your own. Now get out."

"Mr. Cummings..?"

"I'll show you both to the express elevator. If you're still in the building after five minutes, I'll call security. They're armed."

At the elevator, Matt stared at his old friend. "You can't just walk away from this, Toad."

"Just watch me."

As the elevator door closed, Matt held the door open for a few moments. "Hey, Todd? Watch your back old friend." The door hissed shut.

OPENING HIS OFFICE DOOR, Todd Cummings growled to his secretary. "No calls."

"Was lunch satisfactory, Mr. Cummings?"

"Fine. I need some quiet time to think about the upcoming direc-tor's meeting." He smiled coldly. "Hold back the hordes for me."

"Yes, sir."

The ice crackled as he poured a large straight bourbon and sat behind his desk. He swung his leather chair to face the view over the river. Cummings had risen high. He had worked hard, with talent, patience, and some ruthless decisions. He was a professional problem solver. He was about to put those skills to work.

"What is that bastard up to?" he said, swirling the bourbon in the glass. "Suppose there is a terrorist cell operating in the U.S. planning on killing the president?"

Cummings stood up. He always thought best by talking out loud. "But if there is a terrorist plot on the life of the president… Trace the repercussions. …m 1: this cell tries to kill Pierce, even if they miss, almost certainly the U.S. would … mor I full retaliation. Item 2: If war breaks out, Monument Oil and Gas, and its delicate negotiations for oil concessions in the Middle East, would be ruined. Shit! We need peace, not war if we are to secure those oil reserves for ourselves. But with that deranged Matt Richards running around…."

He paused by the television, tuning it to CNN. He scanned the running ticker tape. Then it came….

"We're interrupting this portion of Inside Asia with a special late-breaking headline news report from Washington, D.C. Metropolitan police have now confirmed that they are looking for a possible suspect in the death late last night of Dr. Martin J. Thomas, retired director of the National Institutes of Health. The suspect, known by the FBI and CIA as a contract assassin, was identified by both Dr. Thomas's personal butler and Senator Mason Stevens, who had had dinner with Dr. Thomas earlier in the evening. According to the butler the suspect, posing as Dr. Wilson Richards, was accompanied by a woman whom authorities have identified as Nicole Delacluse, formerly an investigative journalist for the *International Herald Tribune*. Both Senator Stevens and the butler gave identical descriptions. The two are wanted for questioning and are believed to be somewhere in the greater metropolitan D.C. area."

A full-face photograph flashed up on the screen. "The male suspect, seen here in this CIA photo, may be armed and should be considered extremely dangerous." Todd Cummings leaned forward and stared at the image of the man he'd just had lunch with.

"Matt, you sorry sonofabitch, you're in a heap of trouble. And it's time to make that phone call." He returned to his desk.

MATT JUMPED AT THE SOUND of Nicole's cell phone chirping inside her purse.

"Yes? Oh, hi Dad. We're driving back to the Pittsburgh airport. What's up?" Her face turned ashen. "Okay, we'll call you from a service area in about an hour. I love you, too."

Nicole turned to Matt. "Well, we're famous now. CNN has just shown our photos on Headline News. We've been named as possible suspects in the death of Dr. Thomas. And to top it off, the CIA has identified you as an international contract assassin, armed and dangerous. Dad suggests we drive back to Washington instead of flying, ditch the rental car in the suburbs and take the metro back to his safe house."

They were both quiet as the rental car continued down the Pennsylvania Turnpike.

"Maybe it's time we turned ourselves in, Matt, and told them the truth? Besides, they didn't alter your fingerprints, did they? You can still convince them you're really Matthew Richards. They've got to believe you."

"Just how long do you think we'll live if I do that?" Matt replied. He pulled the car into a service area. "There's another way to do this. Remember Cummings talking about Anne-Marie Khoury?"

"The artist?"

"That she is. And if anyone knows what all the old gang is doing, she's the one. Maybe it will shed some light on who might be involved with the terrorists."

"What's she like?"

"Well, it's been a long time. But she was warm, fun-loving, sensitive. She was well liked by everyone at AUB. It's worth a try." Matt recalled some of the fun they had that year. A fleeting smile crossed his new face, an odd congruence of past and present.

"And if she's not home?"

"Damn it, Nicole, work with me, please. I haven't got much hope left."

"But we can't just drive all over the country looking up your old Beirut pals. Someone will recognize us."

Matt nodded. "You're right. But we've got to talk with her, in person. It's our only chance. Then we'll get back to Washington, I promise." He leaned over and kissed her.

"Hold it there, cowboy. Not while I'm driving. Are you hungry?"

"Now that you mention it, I'm starved. I didn't eat much back there in the executive dining room. I could murder for a Big Mac right now."

"Okay. I'll park at the next services area. But you stay in the car. We stand a better change of not being recognized that way. What do you want on your hamburger?"

An hour later they were headed for Massachusetts. Matt gestured at the cell phone. When he heard her voice his mind relaxed. Her soothing hello spanned decades and continents. He kept the conversation brief, just as they had planned. He was Matt's cousin who found a few things in his effects with her name on them. They agreed to meet up at her home in the morning.

Nicole smiled. "Tomorrow, then?"

Matt nodded. "Best bet is to find an out of the way motel where we can spend the night and make the final drive early in the morning."

"Okay." Nicole stared ahead at the turnpike.

Matt looked at her. "What is it?"

"I shouldn't say anything. Just fatigue, I guess."

"We're partners, remember? And I do care for you, Nicole."

"Tell me about her."

"Who, Anne-Marie?"

"No. Todd Cummings talked about Maha. The redhead. He said you were deeply in love. I need to know, Matt, because I care for you, too." She swallowed hard.

Matt looked away. The tires rattled on the center markers as the car changed lanes. *Maha.* The name brought back memories both painful and exhilarating. He kept his emotion in check. Nicole deserved that.

"My first real love, the only woman I guess I ever loved. It wasn't just a heady combination of adolescent love and lust, but a deep, powerful, and lasting love—or so I thought. But in the years following her death I often wondered if it was her I loved, or just the idealized vision of a woman I could never spend a life with."

And so Matt began telling Nicole about the first and only love of his life. Had it been reality, or just a myth built in the sand of his personal loneliness and despair? "She was Jordanian, a third year pharmacy student at AUB." He went on and on, sparing no details, the meeting on the plane, the ski weekends, the visits to historic sites, the parties, and even their love-making. He was just about to relate events leading up to the restaurant explosion when he stopped in mid-sentence. *That's it.* Something at the back of his mind, clearer now since he hadn't had a drink in several months, began to pull at him.

"I'm sorry," Nicole said quietly, "I didn't mean to pry into your personal life. Let's just drop it."

"Wait a minute." Matt breathed. "I remember now. After the death of her father, she changed. In my lovesick memory she was always the same loving girl, full of life, optimism and sensuality. But the truth is—I can see it clearly now, I guess I didn't want to admit it to myself earlier—the truth is, she gradually became more and more cynical about the future."

"What do you mean?"

"She started making off-the-cuff comments about life in the Middle East, the Palestinian situation, even our relationship. At one point, just before the bomb explosion, I remember her saying that her future was already chosen. She seemed sad and far away." Matt fell silent, his mind racing. Finally he murmured something.

"What's that?" Nicole said.

"I said maybe it *is* possible—maybe her death was faked, and Bedouina's too. Maybe it was all part of a long-term plot. But what could make two young girls turn into cold-blooded murderers? And suicide bombers?"

"You really don't know much about women, do you?" Nicole said. "All women feel alienated from their true selves by the rules and stereotypes that prevail in male-dominated societies. And the alienation is proportional to the degree of repression. Did you know that even today, in Jordan, there's a law that allows a father to kill his daughter if she is seen walking in the street with a man not approved by the family? And it really happens. Imagine living with absolutely no rights? Like chattel. And yet they watch television programs from other parts of the world showing women in powerful positions, being able to speak their minds. It's easy to see why most of the women in the Middle East are unsure of themselves, and highly susceptible to male pressure."

"You're saying young women can easily become suicide bombers?"

"Yes. And the terrorists take full advantage. It's not difficult to convince a young girl that by giving her life for a noble cause, she can gain the respect and adulation normally only accorded to men. She can finally be on an equal footing, and her family will gain a measure of stature because of her sacrifice. And if she's suffered some trauma already—rape by a relative, the death of a loved one—then that sense of hopelessness might make her even more susceptible."

"Maha's father was killed at the airport." Matt turned to look out the window.

"Okay. Then add to that a little incentive—terrorists usually promise a sizable monetary reward to the family—and bingo, you've got a candidate ready and willing to blow herself to bits for Allah." Nicole shuddered. "Think of how many bright Muslim women have been turned into bomb-carrying zombies by these madmen. Just recently a suicide bombing was completed by a young woman Arab lawyer. An educated woman with much to contribute."

"Didn't the Israelis kill her brother earlier?"

Nicole kept driving.

"Guess that makes both Bedouina and Maha likely candidates?" said Matt, subdued, the magnitude of their suffering and loneliness etched across his face. *God I'm tired.*

After a few miles of awkward silence, his words were faint and hesitant. "Do you think it's too late for her? Maha, I mean, if she's really alive?"

Nicole stared at him incredulously. "After all you've been through in your life, you still ask about a woman you haven't seen for over thirty years? You must have loved her deeply, Matt. You may not realize this, but it's every woman's dream to have a man love her forever. You are a very special man, Matthew Richards. Very special indeed." She stared into the rearview mirror. Nothing.

The St. James Club, London

THEY WERE TOGETHER AGAIN for the second time in two months, unprecedented for the four businessmen. Yet these were unprecedented times. A light snowfall deadened the sounds of traffic slowly moving up St. James' Street. The lights from the men's clothing stores on Jermyn Street were bright against the falling snow.

"The time is rapidly approaching when our planning will bear fruit," Mohammed al Nagib said. They were seated at a quiet corner table at one end of the dark mahogany paneled dining room. "But we need to accelerate our plans, gentlemen."

"What do you mean, accelerate?" asked the Brazilian, Jorge Molinas. "This is supposed to be an opportunistic timetable, not a forced one. We will only have one chance."

"I agree. However, new developments have taken place which we need to discuss. I'm certain after all the facts are known we will arrive at the best decision." Nagib slowly lit a Cuban cigar. The meal had been outstanding, the service impeccable, the wine nectar.

"Waiter?" Nagib beckoned. "Tell the head chef I have a complaint."

"Right away, Mr. Nagib." The tall Swiss-German girl looked worried as she hurried away.

Within moments, Claude Villiers in his spotless white culinary jacket and floral bow tie strode up to the table. "Don't tell me. My wife always complains that I overcook the beans," he said, bowing.

"Oh, no. The meal was fabulous as usual. I won't live long enough to wait for you to make a mistake in the kitchen, my old friend. But I am disappointed with the champagne. Last time I was here you gave me the name of the makers, Daniel and Gerald Fallet, two brothers from outside Drachy, as I recall. Well, my personal assistant rang them up and ordered five hundred cases. They told him no. They said they have a limited number of private clients who have been with them for generations, and since they only produce a small number of bottles a year, they aren't taking any new clients.

"Can you imagine that? I even offered to buy the entire production at a premium price—and still they said no." Nagib gave the tall slim chef a quizzical look. "Is this your sly handiwork, making us come to your club in order to sample this outstanding bubbly?"

"I wish it were true," Villiers said, sighing histrionically. "However, I am allowed very little myself, and it is reserved for my favorite guests. Shall I bring you another bottle, then?" He bowed and backed away, then stopped briefly at a nearby table to greet the other guests.

Once they were alone again, Achille Antonopolis spoke. "Please enlighten us about this little situation."

"It seems that someone well connected with the intelligence community in the U.S. believes that a deep-cover cell is in place in the United States. They're attempting to uncover it." He looked at each of them.

"But how could anyone know about our plan? You don't suspect a leak in our group, do you?" The Swiss banker looked at the others suspiciously.

"I don't know," Nagib flicked white ash from the Cuban cigar. "But what I do know is that somehow they've gotten hold of a list of Americans attending the American University of Beirut during 1968-69, and they believe that one or more of them is involved. In fact, they seem to be using one of the former students to search out the others."

The Greek shipping magnate began to perspire. "And their objective?"

"If it were me," said Herr Hofer, "I wouldn't want to eliminate the cell. I'd want to control it. For example, depending upon the potential benefits, I would either expose it and reap the rewards, or help it finish its job and reap a different set of rewards. Or maybe even use it for my own political and financial purposes." He sat back, polishing Dickensian tiny spectacles. "Interesting situation we have here, very interesting."

"That's why you've been such a good partner all these years, Helmut," Nagib said. "You think of all the ways to profit from any situation."

"What have you done about this so far?" asked the Brazilian.

"So far, our associate in one of the major U.S. intelligence agencies has assisted in thwarting their efforts. But it's only a matter of time. My suggestion is that we accelerate our plan and in the next week or so, find the best opportunity available to put our asset into action. In the meantime, if we can eliminate or contain the individual they're using as a ferret, it would be helpful."

The Swiss banker frowned. "But will this acceleration negatively impact our profits?"

"Perhaps, Helmut, perhaps. But only by a few million—minor compared to the billions we stand to gain when America goes to war against the entire Muslim world. After all, we supply a great deal of the chemicals, arms, equipment, and make the loans to finance those poor Middle Eastern nations being attacked. We can settle for being fortunate, we don't have to be greedy." With that, the Egyptian-American raised his flute of bubbling Fallet-Dart Millesime in a toast. He said no more. At this point, the less the others knew about his ultimate plans, the better.

At 11:30pm al Nagib and his party left the dining table and took the elevator up to the casino. Waiters quickly cleared the table. A few minutes later a small recording device, previously concealed beneath al Nagib's table, was slipped into a cashmere overcoat as it was being opened for its owner. The distinguished gentleman buttoned his coat, turned up the collar, and slipped a small wad of bills into the hand of the cloakroom manager.

"My best to your family, Robert."

"Good evening, Mr. van Ness."

Chapter Twelve

Concord, Massachusetts

"THAT'S HER HOUSE," SAID NICOLE, pointing to a white Cape Cod. It stood alone at the end of a long lane overlooking a frozen lake. The two-story cottage was surrounded by pine trees. Several other houses fringed the lake.

Elijah had filled them in on Anne-Marie Khoury's background. He had surfed the Internet and talked with private sources until late into the night. "It's an artist's life," he told them, as they listened on the phone in a motel room not far from Concord.

"After returning from Beirut, she finished her senior year at Boston College as an art major and married a medical student. He became a renowned medical researcher, but about eight years ago died of leukemia. Childless and widowed, she threw herself into art and established a reputation for watercolors. It seems she travels extensively, using bleak landscapes around the globe as a backdrop for her paintings. There are a few posted on her personal website."

"Anything that could connect her to the terrorists?" Matt felt tired and frustrated.

"I'm getting there. A good agent gathers every scrap of detail, no matter how trivial. It may save your life one day."

"Sorry."

Elijah continued his story. "Anyway, most of her paintings are exhibited at a posh gallery in Boston, and she donates a great deal from the sale of her paintings to a charity for orphaned Palestinian children." His words quickened. "And get this. She's also on the board of advisers of the Halaby Foundation, established in the early 1980s by a wealthy Lebanese businessman and his wife. It provides scholarships for Middle Eastern students to study in the United States and Canada. Interestingly, Dr. Noubar Melikian serves on the foundation's board of directors. And, surprise, surprise. So does Mohammed al Nagib..."

Matt knocked on the door and waited. What would Anne-Marie look like? What would he see from behind his new face? A widow, shorn of companionship without children. She would pour herself into her art, of that he was certain. Had she lost herself in her world of pigment, just as he had lost himself in Scotch? Or would she be the same fun-loving girl he remembered?

When the door opened Matt strove to keep his new face friendly and anonymous. She was just as he remembered. Long black hair now streaked with grey. A fuller face, but the eyes still twinkled.

"You must be Matt's cousin. Please come in."

"Thank you, Ms. Khoury. This is my wife Veronica. Please call me Tom." They followed her into the warm and comfortable home.

"I hope you like herbal tea? Fennel actually. It's all I have on hand." She disappeared into the kitchen. Her pleasant voice echoed through the large rooms. "Please sit down. I'll be right out with the tea. It's been a busy morning already. The people from the gas company were here earlier checking the meter in the basement. They just left about an hour ago. Usually I don't get many visitors, but that's the way I like it."

Soon the tea was being poured. "Since your call yesterday," Anne-Marie said, "I've found myself thinking a lot about Matt. We had such great times together that year with our small circle of friends. It was a magical time for all of us. Not without its heartbreaks, I might add, but still a pivotal time in my life. It was during that year I decided to dedicate my life to painting and to helping Palestinian orphans. I've been doing it ever since." She took a long, slow sip from the pungent herbal tea. "And we had some pretty crazy times as well." Her eyes sparkled over the cup as she looked at Matt.

"Like the time you wrapped our heads in toilet paper to make us look as if we were wearing turbans?" Matt smiled.

"What did you say?"

"Don't be alarmed, Anne-Marie. It's me, Matt."

She stood up, her face contorted with confusion and anger. "Get out. Now!"

"Please listen to him, Ms. Khoury. I beg you," Nicole said.

"Actually, I'm getting used to this reaction," Matt said, still smiling. "After a while, as you show people your new face and tell them who you are, you develop a pretty thick skin. So I'll say it one more time. I'm Matt Richards. And I really like that painting over there, the seascape with the rich violet tint. It's where we used to gather after class, isn't it. You captured the mood and light really well."

Anne-Marie sat down. Paint smears decorated her smock.

"Are you all right?" Nicole asked, putting her hand on Anne-Marie's shoulder.

"She's all right," Matt said. "She's already using that artistic eye on my face. The scars are hidden under the hairline, Anne-Marie. What do you think? Am I still a handsome stud?"

A tentative smile bent her mouth upwards. "Whoever said you were good looking?"

Matt laughed and sat next to her. They hugged. Her cheek was salty as he kissed her.

Her hand came up to her cheek. "That was very strange…." She recovered. "I really missed you all these years, Matt. Every time I spoke with Todd he was always running you down. But we had such fun. You were so alive then." She leaned back and examined his face. "What has happened to you?"

"Look, Anne-Marie. I'm in big trouble and I need your help. People are trying to kill me and they appear to be going after some of our friends as well. Did you know Dr. Thomas died two nights ago?"

She collapsed into her chair, stunned, as he explained the possible connection between that death, Brian Walker's, and his own kidnapping.

"Mia, do you remember that night we went to the Maronite monastery near Basharri on our way back from skiing? My diary puts it in early March."

"How could I forget?" she replied. "All those murals on the ceiling and the whole thing carved out of the cliff…."

"We were smoking hash and I must have passed out because I don't remember much. What do you recall about that night?"

"I remember you coughed a lot, and then drank quite a few beers." Her smile faded as she probed into the past. "You're right; we did get stoned, thanks to Demetrie and his ever-present hash block. Let me think now… No doubt we talked about politics in the Middle East, we always did. That might have been the night—come to think of it, yes, it was. *That* was the night we made a pact to try and stop the madness. Brian swore he would become a famous lawyer and defend oppressed people's rights. And he did—poor Brian. I can't believe he's dead."

She squeezed Matt's hand, then pointed across the room to a tiny alcove. "I painted the Maronite Monastery. I had to; it was such a pivotal place in my life, a holy place that inspired me beyond words. I'm not happy with the painting. I could never get the real feel of the place." She gave a lopsided smile. "Anyway, I promised that night I would raise money for Palestinian orphans. Karl Mitchell and T.J. …."

Matt jumped. "They were there? I don't remember them going skiing with us."

"They arrived at the monastery later—I guess it was after you passed out." She stared at the teapot.

"Did some other people show up, two Arab men maybe?"

"Yeah, those two were weird."

Just then the phone rang. Anne-Marie went into the kitchen to answer it. She called back. "I have to take this call, guys. Won't be long. Why don't you go out and take a look at the lake? It's beautiful this time of year."

Matt and Nicole put on their overcoats and strolled down the neat gravel path to the frozen lake. A flat gray light hit the surface, accenting the frozen, rippled texture. Cold air swept off the lake in gusts. Matt pulled his collar up. "Perfect place to inspire a painter," he said. Nicole pressed close.

They trod the worn planks of the wooden dock, soaking up the peaceful surroundings after days of fear. Canadian geese honked overhead. Matt smelled smoke from a nearby cottage. "Someone is enjoying a leisurely morning by a warm fire," he thought.

A massive explosion turned the grey light into an orange hell. Splinters of wood and debris flew past them as if expelled from a cannon. The shock wave threw them from the dock onto the frozen lake. Matt landed on his hands. Screaming in pain, he grabbed his wrist and twisted onto his back. The house was a wall of flames and billowing smoke. Burning shingles rained down on all sides, sizzling as they hit the lake ice. Samir Hussein's blazing body seared through his mind. "Not again," Matt groaned, but this time he forcefully pushed the paralyzing image away. "Nicole! Nicole!" He grabbed at her.

"Get down! Crawl along the edge of the lake," he yelled in her ear. "They might still be watching. Keep hidden beneath the weeds along the bank. We need them to think we were inside."

They dragged themselves toward the weedy bank. From there they rose into a half-crouch and skirted the lake until they reached the next boat dock, 200 yards away.

Matt stopped. "I've got to go back." He was turning around when Nicole gripped his arm.

"Don't play the hero now, Matt. I need you alive, with me."

"But I'm a doctor, I've got to try and—"

"You're a doctor, not a miracle worker. She's *dead.*" Nicole held him close, her body absorbing his pain. In a few moments he stopped shaking.

Sirens blared across the small community of Concord. "The volunteer firemen are responding," said Matt. "They'll be here soon. We've got to get away."

They sprinted a short distance to a neighbor's dock, scrambled through the reeds and up onto a snow-covered lawn. In seconds they stood panting alongside a wooden garage.

"What is it?" Nicole asked, feeling Matt jerk as if struck by an electric shock.

"A phony gas company serviceman must have rigged the house. The timer was probably detonated remotely. They must have been watching the house." Matt slid down onto the cold ground. "To top it all off, I left my leather journal on the coffee table."

"Not quite," said Nicole. "Call it habit or reporter's instinct, but I always carry important papers with me, even when I go to the bathroom. I crammed your journal inside my bag just before we stepped outside," she pulled it out and held it up.

"Thank Christ!" he said. "Now what?"

"Let's see what's inside this garage. Maybe we'll be lucky."

Matt broke a window in the garage door with his elbow. He reached in and opened the door. A shiny 1956 Packard caught the light.

"Matt, I can hotwire this antique. You'll have to decide where we go." In less than a minute she had found a screwdriver, pried open the steering column and was arching two wires together. The motor purred to life and the gas gauge showed half full. She looked at Matt, some of the strain leaving her face.

The wail of the fire engines grew louder. "You are definitely your father's daughter, Nicole," he said, climbing into the passenger seat. "Let's pay a visit to Dr. Karl Mitchell. He's all we've got. Our research had him pinpointed as a retired professor of geology at the University of Rhode Island. That's on the way back to Washington. When we get clear of here, call your father and ask him to track down Karl's most recent address and phone number."

The old Packard lumbered from the garage. The sirens were closer now. They watched the mirrors. They checked the road ahead. No one had any interest in them.

Rock Creek Parkway, Washington, D.C.

THE USUAL JOGGERS WERE OUT in the late afternoon, braving the cold and wind in the canyon of Washington's Rock Creek Parkway, intent on getting their exercise fix for the day. "Running is one of the few positive addictions," said the slim doctor, slightly winded as she approached her halfway mark and the endorphins began to kick in. Every day Dr. Margaret Khalid took a 5 mile run in the mid-afternoon and then went back to work for the rest of the day, usually late into the evening. It was a good thing her apartment was only a few blocks away from the office; daily runs helped keep her sane.

As she ran along the asphalt path that wound through the canyon, a lean male runner in blue leggings and a dark hooded jersey slowly overtook her.

"Just keep your natural pace," he said. His breathing was easy and relaxed. "We're moving the timetable forward. You must be ready to act within the next seven days. Go to an Internet café every morning for the next week. Log into www.beirut69.com and sign on as 'asset1.' We'll send you instructions about the exact date." He sprinted away, opening a large gap between them, then took one of the many uphill trails to the main streets lining both sides of the narrow canyon. In less than a minute, he had vanished.

Maggie Khalid finished her run, added another tube of black rinse to her hair while showering, cleaned and reinserted her brown-tinted contact lenses, and was back in Dr. Melikian's office in less than an hour.

Kingston, Rhode Island

"I'M LOOKING FOR DR. KARL MITCHELL." A thin, attractive man answered the door of a two-story home on a street next to the University of Rhode Island campus. Matt recognized the man right away—Theodore Janus. But everyone always called him T. J.

"Are you the person who called about Matt Richards—his cousin?"

"Yes, I'm Thomas Black, and this is my wife Veronica. It's good of Dr. Mitchell to see us on such short notice."

"I'll tell Karl you're here. Come on in. You're in luck; he's having one of his better days." T. J. led the way through a living room adorned with white rugs and marble statues. It had the look of a boudoir. Matt glanced at Nicole, raising his eyebrows. They emerged onto a south-facing sun porch where a fragile-looking man with a ponytail was sitting up in a hospital bed, reading Stephen Hawking's *Brief History of Time.*

"This is the man who phoned yesterday, Matt's cousin," said T. J., arranging a blanket over Karl's feet. "Keep your feet covered or you'll get pneumonia again."

Dr. Mitchell studied his guests over the rims of his bifocals. "I've been reading Hawking's book. Funny thing about time. There are moments when it seems as if the past and the present are the same, only separated by the blink of an eye. Like now, wouldn't you say, Matt?"

"No, Karl," T. J. sighed, "this is Matt's *cousin*, not—"

"Karl knows what he's talking about, T. J.," Matt said. *Still sharp as a tack.*

"Who did the work, Matt?"

"Wish I knew. I was kidnapped and the surgery performed against my will."

"Your face has been on the news. Every hour."

"Just what I need." Matt waited as T.J. stepped closer.

"Jesus. How does that feel? Does it hurt?"

Matt smiled. "Actually, it itches more than it hurts."

"How can I help you, Matt?" Karl Mitchell closed the book and tossed it on the floor.

"I'm in big trouble, Karl. The people who did this to me are now trying to kill me. I escaped from the hospital and for the past several days I've been running for my life. And to find out why."

"Why come here?"

"Because I think there's a link to that night in the monastery, near Basharri."

"Basharri. That was quite a night."

"Someone was there, Karl, someone from outside our AUB group. Do you remember who?" Matt moved closer to the elevated hospital bed.

"How much do you know about AIDS, Dr. Richards? Not what it says in the medical books. The real life and death of it? The pain, the hopelessness, the guilt.... Herpes is something you live with, Matt. AIDs is something you die with. And more often than not, something you give to others, even your loved ones." He reached out for T.J.'s thin hand.

"I just have to look at you, Karl, and then look at T.J. It maybe about suffering and death, but it's also about love and partnership."

T.J. looked at Matt. "We had to get out of Beirut. Gays are not very well accepted in the Middle East, especially back in the late '60s."

"As I look back over my life I realize I was terminally irresponsible," the scientist went on, his mind drifting a little. "At least you have a chance to make up for your mistakes. I don't have the time or energy to even try. I'll die soon, knowing I could have prevented this and didn't. Brains I had, but wisdom?" He coughed again. This time bright red blood drizzled from the corner of his mouth.

"The fact is, Dr. Mitchell, none of us has much time," Nicole said. "This goes as high up as the president of the United States."

"Ah, yes. The suicide bomber. Bedouina."

"So it was her?"

"Of course. So she didn't die in the explosion? And Maha?"

"I wish I knew."

Karl Mitchell looked over at Nicole. "I'm glad to see you've finally found someone who loves you, Matt. As I grow older I realize what a true blessing love is. Let's see…Basharri." He closed his eyes. "Everyone was stoned when T. J. and I arrived, but it didn't take us long to get into the groove. Demetrie certainly had the best hash."

"Why did you show up in the first place?" Matt pressed. "It seemed to me like a spontaneous decision for us to stop in Basharri that night and visit the monastery."

"We were invited by Demetrie," T.J. said. "He'd met a man who was trying to organize a group to help the Palestinians. It sounded interesting, so we drove up that afternoon and arrived a little after you guys. The others drifted in later."

"What others?" asked Matt, looking from T.J. to Karl.

"An elderly Egyptian businessman," Karl said, "Mohammed al Nagib. And another Arab wrapped in a red keffiyeh who didn't speak or show his face. I've forgotten his name."

"Yassar?" Matt said.

"That may have been it. Anyway, Nagib spoke that evening about a special organization he was helping organize. Its mission was to take a stand for the Palestinians and their right of statehood. As I recall, the more influential and wealthy Arab countries were less than supportive of the Palestinian cause, still are. But the Israelis were growing in strength and presented a threat to Islam. He painted a graphic picture of the refugee camps, the suffering of women and children, the torture and humiliation of Palestinian men at the hands of Zionist aggressors. He even read some poems written by refugee children from the Chatilla camp. The longer he went on, the more interested everyone seemed—unless I'm mistaking being stoned for being interested."

Matt glanced at Nicole. "What happened after that?"

"I don't know if anyone ever joined his fledgling organization. I never saw him again, and no one in the group ever spoke about it to me...."

T.J. signaled that Karl was growing sleepy. It was time to leave.

"Just one more question, Karl," Matt said. "Has anyone else from the old AUB days been in touch with you recently?"

Karl Mitchell lay still. Matt glanced back at Nicole. As the silence lengthened, they moved out of the sunroom toward the front door.

Matt gave T.J. a hug, then reached out for the door. Karl's reed thin voice echoed into the hallway. "Just one person.... Todd Cummings. He called—was it yesterday, T. J.? Yes, called and wanted to know what I remembered about that night. He also asked if I'd spoken to William Fisher recently. Will was at the monastery that night as well. In fact, it was Will who organized the entire meeting—not Demetrie." Dr. Mitchell paused, trying to rally his limited strength. "Be careful, Matt. You deserve a second chance to make things right."

CNN Headline News

THE CNN ANCHORMAN, seated in front of a large bank of monitors, spoke quickly. "Sometime within the next week, President Roswell Pierce will be making a major policy speech. According to an announcement just made by the White House press secretary, President Pierce has been working on a strategy for responding to the suicide bomber attack on his life over three months ago. When asked by reporters why this official response has been so long in coming, Press Secretary Sheila Morgan replied that President Pierce would not be goaded into rash action by threats or acts of terrorism. His response would be well thought out, prudent, and comprehensive.

"CNN will keep you informed as soon as we know the date and time of this important policy statement by the president."

Washington, D.C.

"I CERTAINLY AM GLAD to see the two of you," Elijah said as Matt and Nicole sat down on the sofa in the small living room of his hideaway apartment. "What did you do with the car you stole in Concord?"

"We parked it in a long-term lot at BWI Airport, wiped off our fingerprints and then took the train back into town," replied Nicole. "What a great old car, that Packard. We parked it out of the way. I hope no one will touch it. Maybe after this thing is all over we'll drive it back to its rightful owner."

"Our lives may be over if we don't figure out what the hell is going on," Matt said, tired and frustrated. "Anne-Marie and Dr. Thomas are dead, and it's my fault."

Eli poured himself another two fingers of Glenrothes. "We need to think this through. Look at things from a fresh perspective."

"Dad, what did you find out about Mohammed al Nagib and William Fisher?"

"Quite a bit," Eli said. "William Fisher's had a very unusual career. I still haven't found out how he wound up as one of the top dogs at the National Security Agency. His first assignment was as an embassy attaché posted in Beirut, where he stayed until 1982, the year his wife was killed."

"What?" said Matt, coming out of his funk. "How did she die?"

"She was killed in one of the Palestinian refugee camps in southern Lebanon during an Israeli raid. She was a volunteer nurse. Every so often the Israeli commandos would sneak into southern Lebanon, either across the border or from the sea, looking for Arab terrorists hiding out in the camps. She was shot in the back by an Israeli colonel who was leading the raid. Word among the intelligence community is Fisher took it pretty hard and became a recluse. Then about a year later, he landed a plum job at the National Security Agency and steadily rose through the ranks."

"What exactly is the NSA?" Nicole asked.

"It's the communications and research arm of the U.S. intelligence network. Originally NSA staff were code breakers; now they're also experts on terrorism and clandestine communications used by hostile foreign governments and political groups. Fisher was recently promoted to director of Middle Eastern affairs for the NSA and is a standing member of President Pierce's Special Task Force on Terrorism. He never remarried, and is known to be dedicated, hard working, intelligent—and highly opinionated."

"Sounds like the same jerk I met in Beirut thirty years ago," replied Matt. "But why did he arrange that meeting at the monastery? And how did he know the Egyptian, al Nagib?"

Eli savored his Scotch, ignoring the look on his daughter's face. "You don't have time to read all there is about Mohammed al Nagib. Not only is he fabulously wealthy, he also shows up at high-society functions up and down the East Coast and in Europe. He has homes in London, Zurich, Athens, Rio de Janeiro, Bermuda and Cairo, plus a large estate up in the Blue Ridge Mountains, where he often entertains dignitaries from other countries. And he's a big contributor to both the Republican and Democratic parties."

"Sounds like a real slime ball," Nicole said sourly.

"That and more. Al Nagib immigrated to the United States in the early 1970s from Egypt and somehow bought his way into the computer business. He's now chairman of one of the biggest technology and software conglomerates in the United States. It's based just outside Washington, near Dulles Airport, where a large number of defense and military technology companies are headquartered. He's regularly seen in the company of a wealthy Greek shipping magnate."

"Don't tell me," Matt said. "His last name is Antonopolis, right?"

"How did you know that?" Eli said, raising his eyebrows.

"One of the regulars in our AUB group was Demetrie Antonopolis, playboy son of some Greek industrialist. Demetrie's father must be mixed up in all this, and probably Demetrie as well. Anything known about al Nagib's early days?"

"Absolutely nothing is known about him before he arrived in the United States. The record is a blank," said Eli.

"So," Matt mused, "he shows up in Beirut in early 1969 trying to organize a radical group, and then the next year winds up in the United States in 1970. You say he immigrated—he's an American citizen?"

Eli nodded. "Quite the patriot—known for throwing elaborate Fourth of July parties and lavishing thousands of dollars on fireworks."

"Cut to the chase, Dad," said Nicole. "What's the unofficial word on this bastard?"

"Well, it's never been proven, but he's suspected of being an international arms dealer and global financier. Some people believe he's been responsible for putting people into key positions of power. Like a few heads of state, African dictators, and even some elected officials in Europe and the United States. And then, when it suits him financially, he helps remove them. Think of all the recent leadership changes in the Congo and other African countries.... At any rate, he earns his money during times of war, not peace. And his close business ties to a Brazilian mining industrialist named Jorge Molinas are suspect—Molinas supports Hezbollah terrorist camps in the tri-border region of Paraguay, Argentina and Brazil."

Matt drummed his fingers on the table, something tugging at his thoughts. *A name, a face, a fact. What is it?*

"I've made a fresh pot of tea," said Nicole, reaching across the table to pour the piping hot herbal tea into Matt's mug. Opening his eyes, he stared at the diamond tennis bracelet around her wrist. He'd never really paid much attention to it before. It glimmered in the overhead lights of the kitchen.

"I've got it! Your bracelet— it just reminded me of the wrist band—it was there all along in the back of my mind."

"What the hell are you talking about, Matt?" Nicole exclaimed. She looked at her bracelet, trying to read its secrets.

"When I was escaping from the hospital, I ducked into a darkroom to avoid one of the guards. I was still a little groggy, but there was a young woman lying on the hospital bed. I looked at her face but didn't recognize her. She had scars like mine, another face transplant. She must have been having a bad dream because her hand shot out and grabbed my arm. I remember her saying something like, 'No, Daddy, No.' When I put her hand back on the bed, I noticed the hospital tag around her wrist. It caught the light from the ceiling. There was no name. Only a blood type, A-negative, and two small letters. I didn't register those letters at the time, but now I can see them clear as day: K.S. Kelly Stevens."

Eli's face clouded. "If the press reported both of you dead," he said slowly, "it suggests that Senator Mason Stevens is somehow involved."

Matt sipped his piping hot tea. "What if he helped fake the accident in order to get his wayward daughter cleaned up, off of drugs, and out of sight? The last thing a powerful senator needs is a drug addict daughter. Maybe *that's* why he insisted Kelly come to the reception for Dr. Melikian—maybe he arranged the whole thing."

"With whom?" asked Nicole.

"Didn't Dr. Thomas say it was the Israelis who were the most advanced in facial transplant procedures?"

Nicole's face went white. "You don't think Senator Stevens is working with the Mossad, do you?"

"Whoa, young lady, you've been watching too many James Bond movies," said Eli, pouring another two fingers of Scotch. "First of all, foreign intelligence agencies aren't allowed to operate inside the United States, period. And second, it would be a treasonable offense—not to mention political suicide—for an elected official to be involved with any foreign government operating clandestinely on American soil."

"Are you saying this kind of thing doesn't happen?"

"It *can* happen—but certainly not with the chairman of the Senate Select Committee on Intelligence. He's cleaner than clean."

"My father had a sophisticated medical term for situations like this," Matt said. "Bullshit. Here's how I see it, farfetched as it may sound. The Israelis promise Stevens that his wayward daughter will get rehabilitated, a new face and a faraway job. And they probably give him a pile of cash to deposit in some Swiss bank account. All he has to do is help them get hold of me to use as their ferret, and make it look like an accident. With all his intelligence contacts, that should be pretty easy to arrange. So far, so good. However, the Mossad now have him perfectly positioned for blackmail, so he probably reports to them everything that goes on in the President's Special Advisory Council on Terrorism." Matt faced them, his excitement mounting. "Somehow the Israelis know a terrorist cell exists right here in Washington. And if they can find it, they might be able to control it. Even use it to their benefit."

"How so?" quizzed Nicole. "How would it benefit the Israelis to control this terrorist cell?"

"Why, to make certain it does its job," replied Eli. "Or, on the other hand, expose it to the U.S. authorities. The American people would really rally against the Arab world if they knew there was a terrorist cell about to kill the president. Either way, the Israelis win."

Matt nodded. "It's a clever gambit. After all, they don't want peace with the Arabs any more than the terrorists want the liberation of Palestine. It's moved way beyond those idealistic days. The Israelis, or at least a certain faction within Israel, wants the United States to wage a full-scale war on the Muslims, which means more dollars and more protection for Israel."

"But that's monstrous." Nicole looked at Matt, then her father.

"No," Eli said, swirling his glass. "That's global politics."

"What about al Nagib—how would he fit in?" Nicole asked.

"That's the easy part," Matt replied. "Al Nagib organized and financed the terrorist cell. He probably recruited the members over thirty years ago just for this special purpose. I'll bet Bedouina and Maha were taken out the back of the restaurant before the blast—I'll bet they went underground and became members of Nagib's terrorist organization. And, I'll bet Samir was supposed to accompany them. But the bomb went off too soon, and he died in front of my eyes. That night Bedouina lost the only love she had ever known. She would have been extremely vulnerable to al Nagib's propaganda. She became the perfect candidate for a suicide bomber."

"You don't think they planned to kill Samir in order to soften up Bedouina?" Nicole asked.

"It wouldn't be the first time someone was sacrificed for the greater good," Eli said. "I've seen it more than once."

"There's a pattern here," Matt said. "After Israeli commandos killed Maha's father at the Beirut Airport, her brothers must have hounded her unmercifully about being a slut and having an affair with an American. She was probably ostracized by her family, which would have made her susceptible to join the group along with Bedouina and Samir. Perhaps she's already been used as a human bomb—or maybe she's still alive and waiting for her call to glory." He looked at Nicole. "You think Maha's here in Washington, don't you?"

"And William Fisher?" Nicole came back quickly, avoiding Matt's eyes.

"That's easy enough," Elijah said. "After the senseless death of his wife at the hands of the Israelis, he could have been recruited by Nagib. He theorized about the rise in terrorism as early as 1967. But the State Department ignored him for many years. Then it all turned out exactly as he predicted. Now he's a celebrity. But, with no wife and a burning hatred for the Israelis, he would have been the perfect candidate to become a double agent. Maybe he was promised revenge on the man who killed his wife. Plus he undoubtedly got a mountain of cash. He's probably feeding evidence to al Nagib about what goes on at the President's Special Advisory Council meetings."

Matt felt sick. "Christ, the two of them—Mason Stevens feeding the Israelis, and William Fisher feeding al Nagib. And neither knows what the other is doing."

"But this is all speculation," Nicole said. "It could be a house of cards."

Matt watched her. "There may be two moles inside the president's inner circle."

"It wouldn't be the first time for that, either, Dr. Richards," Elijah said. "But I won't bore you with a history lesson." He drained his Scotch. "Wait a minute, now—what if the woman bomber wasn't supposed to kill the president at all, but his personal physician instead? Remember the president stood back to let Dr. Norman come front and center to face the press. The bomber had the president, but waited." Elijah stared at his empty glass then at Matt. "I'll be goddamned."

"But what purpose would that serve?" said Matt.

"No – that's clever." Nicole said. "Don't you see, Matt? That way they could get their own candidate endorsed as personal physician to the president—Dr. Noubar Melikian."

"Dr. Melikian is the terrorist?"

"Could be, Matt." Elijah went over the possibilities. "Who better to assassinate the president of the United States whenever it becomes convenient for Nagib and his organization? All Melikian has to do is call up the president and say he found something troubling in the last medical test and that he must see him right away. There are any number of ways the trusted personal physician could get into contact with the president on short notice. Hell, you're the doctor, Matt. Think of the numerous toxins, biological agents and drugs that can kill instantaneously or over a period of time."

"Eli?" Matt said. "Can you call in some IOUs; dig up some stats on the good doctor?"

"Can do easy. And, while I'm at it, I'll locate the Blue Ridge Substance Abuse Clinic and Private Hospital. Find out the address, who owns it, who's on the board of directors, what their expertise is, who goes there, everything. And if Kelly Stevens really is there, then that's how we'll put the squeeze on Senator Stevens."

Matt nodded, assessing Elijah Tajikian, a most dangerous gentleman. "Maybe we're getting somewhere. As for me, I've got to figure out a way to meet Dr. Melikian myself. If I can just get into his office, look around, speak to him… Easier said than done, however. I'm wanted by the police and the media have plastered the picture of an international assassin all over the place." He stared at Elijah. "Take a good look, Eli. Have you any idea how obscene it is having the face of a killer? I wish I could tear it off right now."

"Maybe we're just imagining all this," Nicole said quietly. "I honestly don't know. But the fact is, if we don't do something soon, they may strike before the president makes his policy statement to the nation."

They all nodded. Elijah Tajikian poured another Scotch. The tumbling ice cubes were loud in the silence.

The Oval Office

PRESIDENT PIERCE'S INTERCOM BUZZED. "Yes, Miriam?"

"I've done the best I can to juggle your schedule, Mr. President, but I could only squeeze in five minutes. He's here now, waiting." Her voice was courteous, but he caught the exasperation.

"Send him in. And thank you, Miriam."

He sported a closely cropped beard and neatly styled salt and pepper hair. "Thanks for seeing me on such short notice, Mr. President."

"This must be pretty damned important, Todd." Pierce fingered his tin cup.

"You know my position concerning the country's continuing dependence on foreign oil. It's critical for our future. And I'm certain you're aware of the fact that a war in the Middle East could greatly damage our prospects of continued access to the huge reserves held by the Arab nations."

"Tell me something I don't know, Todd, or don't waste my time." Pierce glared at his old friend.

"Okay. I have good reason to believe that one of your trusted advisers is actually working for a terrorist group. They've placed a deep cover cell here in this country for the purpose of assassinating you or some other high public official. If that happens, the American people will demand a full-scale war. Need I say more?" Todd Cummings stared back at his oil industry colleague and former golfing buddy.

The president put down his tin cup. His face darkened as he turned toward the window facing the Rose Garden. New shoots were just beginning to emerge from the trimmed stems. "That's a pretty serious accusation, Todd. Every person on my staff and in an advisory capacity has been thoroughly screened by the FBI. They've even had their assholes checked."

"I recognize that, Ross. But I'd say the consequences are too great to ignore the possibility. Let me tell you what I know, and then you can decide for yourself. Sometimes, Mr. President, self-interest and the interests of the nation coincide. This is one of those times."

Pierce flipped his intercom switch. "Change of plans, Miriam. I need some more time with Mr. Cummings. Do the best you can. And tell Mr. van Ness I must see him right away." He gestured at his old friend. "Sit down, Todd. And don't leave out one scrap of information or you'll find your ass transferred to Mongolia. The chairman of Monument Oil owes me a couple of big favors, and I won't hesitate to use them. By the way, I'm going to record this conversation."

For the next half hour, Todd Cummings filled the president of the United States in on his Beirut experiences of thirty years ago. He described his recent visit from Matt Richards, Matt's association with Senator Stevens's daughter, the phony account of his death, his kidnapping, face transplant, and someone's attempts to use him as a ferret.

"A face transplant?"

"Yes, Mr. President. Grotesque as it sounds."

"Dear God."

"Matt and I spent a year together in some pretty unusual circumstances and I haven't seen him in over thirty years until the other day," Todd went on. "He's a recovering alcoholic and a failed physician. But on the inside he's made of solid stuff."

"What I want to know is—do you trust him?"

"Yes. I do trust him. He's in big trouble and he came to me for help. And I know it cost him his pride to do that."

"Can you find him?"

"That I don't know. We didn't part under the best of circumstances the other day. And he's wanted by the D.C. Metro police in connection with the death of Dr. Martin Thomas, so he's probably gone into hiding. Although if I know Matt, he'll try to get to the bottom of this himself. He was with a woman, Nicole Delacluse of the *International Herald Tribune*. We could start there."

"I'll see what the spooks can find out. Now, there must be more. What about this mole in my council?"

Todd Cummings laid out all he knew about the complex web of relationships among the members of his old AUB circle and their acquaintances. President Pierce then cancelled all official appointments for the rest of the day. The only person allowed into the Oval Office was Karl van Ness.

Miriam took two ibuprofen to combat a splitting headache.

Chapter Thirteen

Elijah's Safe House

MATT LAID ALL THE PHONY PASSPORTS, credit cards and wads of money from the leather satchel out on the kitchen table. He began sifting through them. It was just before dawn.

"What are you doing, Matt?"

"I want to know more about the person whose face I've inherited, Nicole. He was one well-traveled guy." Matt scratched the thin scar under his hairline. "I wonder how many people he killed in his job as a free-lance assassin?" Plucking a passport from the pile, he studied a photo of his predecessor in a fake beard. "Here's an idea. Maybe I could alter my looks to get into Dr. Melikian's office."

Nicole picked up an expensive leather wallet lying on the table. Inside was a small black folder, resembling a bank deposit book. The cover was embossed in gold with the name Bahamas Overseas Bank, Ltd, in flowing script. Curious, she turned it over in her hand. An odd-shaped gray metal key fell out and bounced on the floor. They stared down at the worn linoleum.

"It looks like a safe deposit key," Matt said, reaching down and picking it up. "A 7-digit number. Look in that passbook and see if it matches this number: J-8317077."

Nicole opened the booklet and flipped through several pages. "Oh my God, Matt, there's over fifteen million dollars in here." Her hand shook as she handed him the thin booklet.

"The numbers don't match, but the deposit box must be in the same bank. Not only did he travel a lot, he was very well paid as well."

Elijah appeared in the kitchen doorway. Bloodshot eyes surveyed them both. "Fancy passports. Used to have a few myself, once."

"So, what did you find out?" said Nicole.

"I need a cup of coffee first."

"Dad, don't torture us."

"Alright," he took a sip from the hot mug of coffee Matt held out. "I went to an out-of-the-way watering hole last night where a number of old spooks hang out. We had a few drinks and shared old war stories. We also did some real talking. Turns out the Armenian-American doctor has led a charmed life. A veritable Cinderfella. Some big money paid for medical school in Switzerland. And somebody helped him get established in Washington. By all accounts he's an outstanding physician as well as a tireless spokesman for a peaceful solution in the Middle East."

"Anything suspicious?" asked Nicole.

"Only that his father, a low-level engineer in Cairo, worked for a cement company owned by a rich Egyptian family."

"Al Nagib," Matt said.

"That's correct. This whole thing stinks. Nagib is playing all sides against the middle. No matter which way it turns out, he wins big." Eli gulped his coffee. "This needs more sugar, or maybe some Scotch."

Matt put the key, the Bahamian bank book, and the wallet with thirteen hundred dollars in his pocket. He selected one of the passports. The rest of the documents he stuffed into the leather satchel. And stood up. "I'm going to hide the rest of this stuff in the bathroom closet. For safekeeping."

Elijah nodded. "And what was Nicole hollering about?"

"Just a bunch of zeros. She'll tell you. I'll be right back."

As Matt shut the bathroom door, the lights flickered and went out. Eli was up and moving, but too late.

A loud crash echoed down the hallway. The front door was blasted off its hinges. Eli grabbed his daughter and pulled her down onto the floor. Four men in black ski masks burst into the kitchen. Blinding light came from the M-3 Streamlights fitted to their Hechler and Koch 9 mm pistols. Laser beams pinned Elijah and Nicole.

"We're not armed." Elijah thrust his hands high into the air. Nicole did the same. Silenced rounds sent them crumpling to the floor.

Matt turned the lock on the bathroom door. A small window faced onto the fire escape. He yanked with all his might, but several layers of thick white paint held it shut. He picked up a small stool and flung it at the window. Glass flew outwards.

"Somebody's in the back!" Boots echoed down the hall. Seconds later two intruders turned the doorknob. Matt squeezed through the window, ignoring the glass shards as they cut into him. A blast from a shotgun splintered the bathroom door. Matt took the rusty fire escape four steps at a time. He jumped from the last rung as another blast from the shotgun ricocheted off the fire escape.

The alley was black, hidden from the encroaching dawn. He sprinted toward the street. He emerged onto N Street, then forced himself into a lazy walk, lungs heaving.

Moments later a beige sedan roared passed and swerved into the alley, sparks flying as the chassis scraped the curb. A second sedan skidded to a halt, blocking the alley entrance. Men in suits piled out with automatic weapons at the ready.

Matt blended into the stream of commuters headed for the metro. They were bundled up against the cold wind. The women wore tennis shoes, the official footwear for commuting to downtown office jobs. Matt followed the flow of bodies down into the station. He descended the stairs and caught a train heading toward the Kennedy Center and the west side of D.C. There he remained in the alleys and shadows until the shops opened, slipped into a clothing store, and emerged with a navy pea coat, a stocking cap and a pair of dark sunglasses. He pushed out the dark lenses and put on the black-rimmed frames. Then he got back onto the metro to Union Station and settled into a public telephone booth on the mezzanine level. He was well out of the way of the commuter crowds.

There in the telephone booth Matt let go, weeping into a dead phone. Everything caught up with him: Kelly Stevens imprisoned in her new face. The dead: Martin Thomas, Brian Walker. The dying: Karl Mitchell and T.J. Now Nicole and Elijah. Both dead. Anne-Marie's face erupted in his mind, grotesque in bold azure paint strokes. Matt grabbed at his cheeks, trying to pull off the foreign face bonded to his. Then his father's favorite phrase overpowered his fear. *It's time to shit or get off the pot, Matt. Suck it up, son.* He stood up. Air filled his lungs. His pounding heart calmed itself. He had loved only two women in his miserable life, and both had been ripped from his grasp. He wasn't much, he didn't have much in the way of skills. What he did have was anger, and the knowledge that it was his time. His time to fight back.

In that cold ugliness he looked around the station. But no one was interested in him. He was alone. Frighteningly alone this time. "What sort of God runs this fucking universe? What's wrong with love?" He rattled the folding door back and forth. Several people stared. He left the mezzanine, heading for the tracks. Was he being followed? He stopped several times to check, once bending down to tie his shoe. As he walked he steadied his breathing and rehearsed his lines. He found an empty bank of phone booths. He deposited the coins.

"Good morning. My name is Dr. William Summers. I'd like to speak with Dr. Melikian. Yes…Tell him I'm a close friend of Dr. Wilson Richards…Richards, yes, the heart surgeon." Matt looked up as people hurried for their trains. "I've just returned from Brazil and have an important message for Dr. Melikian from Dr. Richards. I've only got a few hours in town, but I'll only take a few moments of his time. Dr. Richards really wanted me to deliver the message in person." Matt waited as he was placed on hold by the receptionist. He scanned the crowds. Just people going about their private lives. Matt envied them.

"Thank you. Tell Dr. Melikian I'll be over within the hour."

His next call was to the American Airlines reservation desk. In a few minutes he had a booking under the name of Brian Scott, the name on the passport he'd pocketed back at Eli's. At least they had the same face. The flight for Nassau left at noon from Dulles Airport. Plenty of time.

For the past several days Matthew Richards had been pondering the situation he found himself in. Presumed dead, wearing the face of an international contract killer, wanted by the police and who knows who else, it was only a matter of time before a sniper or a police officer put a bullet through his head. When Nicole found the bank book and the key, it struck him as a golden opportunity to go into hiding before he was killed. All he had to do was catch a plane to Nassau, use the passport that matched the name on the bank book, transfer the money, fly to Argentina and buy a small ranch. Maybe in Tierra del Fuego, far enough away where nobody would care who he was. After all, Butch Cassidy and the Sundance Kid fled to Argentina and lived quite happily for several years. Until they got restless and returned to the business of robbing banks and trains. Now that Nicole was dead, his noble thoughts of saving the president and preventing world war three were a cruel joke.

Matt walked over to a corner kiosk and ordered a hot coffee and an almond croissant. Sacraments for sound decision-making.

The White House Situation Room

"THEY'RE COMING AROUND, SIR," said one of the Secret Service agents. The president strode through the door of the basement bunker in the White House. The Director of the CIA, Dr. Terry Finch, stood up.

"Any sign of the other one?" President Pierce walked over to a sofa where Elijah and Nicole were sprawled. A female agent handed him a cup of coffee.

"Not yet, Mr. President, but it shouldn't be long now. And these two should be able to give us some idea where he might be hiding. Anyway, Elijah will tell us what we need to know." Finch cleared his throat. "He was a loyal employee of the agency for quite a few years."

"Could you be any more naive?" President Pierce asked acidly. He took another long sip from his coffee mug.

Elijah Tajikian sat up, moved his head from side to side and slowly looking around. He glanced over at his daughter, also slowly coming out of her drug-induced stupor. "I always wondered what the aftertaste was from those knock-out pellets. Now I know. Like a mouthful of horse shit." He noticed the president of the United States towering over him. "Slumming, Mr. President?"

Karl van Ness whispered in President Pierce's ear.

"The rest of you are excused," the president said. No one in the room mistook his remarks for a suggestion. "Dr. Finch, one of the marine guards will escort you to a waiting room upstairs. I'll need to speak with you as soon as I'm finished here. And no telephone calls. Period."

Once the CIA director and the rest of the entourage had left the room, Ross Pierce pulled up a chair and sat down facing the sofa. Elijah and Nicole were now fully conscious.

"How are you, Ms. Delacluse?"

She stared blankly at the president, her eyes still drooping.

"She'll be okay in a few minutes, Mr. President," Elijah said. "Right now she thinks she's hallucinating."

"Nicole?"

"I'm here. Just give me a minute."

Pierce smiled at the former CIA case officer. "Karl says you were a good agent. And so does Finch."

"With all due respect, Mr. President. Dr. Finch is a bean counter. And a bonafide asshole. He couldn't care less if men and women of courage put their lives on the line every day for the safety and security of this great country. All he cares about is balancing his budget and getting more appropriations from Congress for research and technology. Electronic espionage, what a crock—"

"Thank you, Mr. Tajikian. You're apparently coming to faster than your daughter." The president focused on Nicole. "With us now, Ms. Delacluse?"

"Yes, Mr. President. As a reporter, I'm used to the unexpected. But I'm not prepared for this. What happened?"

"Well, first of all, let me apologize for kidnapping you and your father. It's not how we normally do things, entering private homes under force and ...." He cast about for words. "Look. I need your help. America needs your help. Shit, the entire goddamned world needs your help."

Nicole looked at her father.

"What can we do?" Elijah said.

"I want you to tell me, in as much detail as you can, what the hell is going on. I had a visit recently from a Mr. Todd Cummings. I think you know him, Ms. Delacluse. He convinced me that I'm in grave danger, and a Middle East war could break out soon. We don't have much time, and I'm prepared to move quickly if I need to."

"What about my daughter's safety?"

"As far as I can tell, neither of you have done anything wrong, though your daughter is wanted for questioning in the death of Dr. Martin Thomas. I'll see to it that she's exonerated if you give me the information I need," the president said. "If she's innocent, of course." Pierce smiled. "No pressure. Now, why don't you let your daughter start at the beginning and tell me everything that might be important? I'm going to have this conversation recorded; we might need it. Right now I'm most interested in what you know, Ms. Delacluse. Tell me about Dr. Matthew Richards and this deep-cover terrorist cell. And where the heck is he, anyway?"

"You mean he wasn't captured too?"

"If he was I wouldn't have bothered with you, now would I?"

Elijah interrupted. "He must have escaped out the bathroom window. He was headed that way before your goons broke down our door."

"I apologize for the theatrics," Pierce said. "Everything will be repaired. It was the only way I could get you here without anyone knowing—especially those who might be involved. Now, that's the last apology you're going to get from me. Are you going to tell me what the hell is going on, or am I going to have to do this the hard way?"

Eli motioned for his daughter to sit down. He had been in similar situations in his career and it was best to acknowledge reality. "Okay, let's get down to business." Elijah looked up at van Ness.

"I assume you two know each other," said President Pierce. "Now, if you two don't mind, I would very much like to hear what is going on in my country."

For the next forty-five minutes, Eli and Nicole told President Pierce, Karl van Ness, and the invisible tape machine everything they knew about Matt Richards. They documented what had transpired, and how it might be connected to the fate of the Middle East.

President Roswell Clayton Pierce stared into the sudden quiet. "I could use a drink."

"If you've got any Scotch, Mr. President, make mine a triple," Elijah said

Van Ness spoke quietly into the telephone.

"You say Dr. Matt Richards had a face transplant, against his will, and now has the identity of an international contract assassin?"

"As implausible as it may sound, yes."

"And you believe Senator Stevens's daughter is alive, also with a face transplant, and may still be in that clinic in the Blue Ridge Mountains?"

"That's right."

The president gestured to Karl van Ness. "Have someone research face transplants and their threat to national security."

Van Ness nodded, and then went back to his phone conversation.

"You do realize how well connected and important Mohammed al Nagib is? These are pretty serious accusations against such a prominent American citizen."

Nicole found his eyes on her.

"Would you stake your journalistic career on all you've just told me?"

"Frankly sir, right now I don't have a career to protect. But, yes, I believe what we have told you is the truth."

The drinks arrived. President Pierce watched Elijah gulp down his Scotch, hug his daughter, then face him. "Great Scotch, Mr. President."

"No slumming here, Mr. Tajikian."

Blue Ridge Mountains, Virginia

TWO MARINE HELICOPTERS DESCENDED onto the gravel driveway of the Blue Ridge Substance Abuse Clinic. Twelve armed secret service agents quickly entered the building while others rounded up the guards at the front gate near the highway. The telephone lines were disabled and the executive staff secured in the private wing of the hospital. Dr. Weissman, his white hair whipped up by the whirling rotors of the lead helicopter, escorted his patient, strapped to a collapsable hospital bed, into the chopper. It took off and headed directly for the south lawn of the White House.

An urgent message was sent to the office of Senator Mason T. Stevens, summoning him to the Oval Office for a private meeting with the President. The subject was national security, and he was to appear at 1:30 pm.

The White House

WHEN PRESIDENT PIERCE ENTERED THE SMALL ANTEROOM, down the hall from the Oval Office, CIA director Finch quickly stood. "Look Ross, I don't know what you think you're doing holding me here like this, but—"

"Sit down and shut up, Terry," Pierce said. "We've got a major situation here, and I need your full cooperation. If you give me that, you just might keep your job. But if I find out that you had anything to do with this mess, I guarantee you that I will personally hang you by the balls, if you have any, from the Capitol Rotunda."

Finch sat down.

"Do you remember that remark you made the other day in our meeting on terrorism?" the president said. "The one about an effective way to deter future suicide bombers?"

"You mean by eliminating their immediate families as a future disincentive?"

"Can that be done on the families of the last four or five major suicide bombers? And quickly? I know this is highly irregular and I'm not even going to think about what Congress might say, but I'm asking your opinion and I want a straight answer. No theory, just yes or no."

Dr. Finch nodded, his color coming back. "It can be done, Mr. President, and in such a way that we aren't even involved. The names and locations of the close families of the recent suicide bombers are known by most intelligence services. In particular Israel, Australia, and, of course, the United States. And there are highly qualified independent contractors who are not traceable to us."

Pierce's eyes turned cold. "You'll report directly to me, and tell no one else about this. I'll be calling a meeting of my Special Advisory Council on Terrorism at 7 A.M., three days from now, in my office. If you can't get this operation accomplished before then, tell me now."

"It can and will be done, Mr. President."

"All right. This is your opportunity to put in place one of the major planks in a platform that will bring about a lasting peace in the Middle East. It could also end organized global terrorism." Pierce felt as if he was back in his A6 Intruder, responding smoothly while everything was happening at once. "Oh, and I want the nations sponsoring those terrorist scum, and the terrorist leaders themselves, to clearly understand that the U.S. will no longer tolerate suicide bombings. There will be swift reprisals against the families of the terrorists. This will be the standard response from now on. Now get the message out, and put some teeth into it."

Finch stood up. Pierce noted the perspiration on his upper lip. A bean counter, Tajikian had said.

"Dr. Finch. You will personally make all necessary calls to the various people involved, and you will assure them the CIA will guarantee the funding for the contracts."

"Yes, sir."

"And when this is all over, you and I will sit down and discuss your future, assuming either of us still have one left by then."

The Medical Office of Dr. Noubar Melikian

"DR. MELIKIAN WILL SEE YOU NOW, Mr. Summers. His office is the first door on the left." Irene Leonard, the receptionist, pointed down the hall of the renovated townhouse.

"Thank you." Matt walked down the hall and paused in front of a white wooden door. He was sweating as he knocked lightly, just below the brass nameplate.

"Please come in."

A thick red and blue Persian carpet covered the floor. A built-in bookcase covered an entire wall. It was loaded with reference books. The medicinal smell and the comfortable feeling in the room transported Matt to his father's office in their home. As a boy he would often push open the heavy door and sit in his father's worn leather chair, pretending he was a famous surgeon. Matt had wasted his whole life pretending to be somebody he wasn't. Now he was at it again. This time in a false face. *What about Dr. Melikian—was he a pretender, too?*

A white-coated physician came around from behind the cluttered desk with his hand extended.

"Thank you for taking a few moments out of your busy schedule, Dr. Melikian," Matt said, shaking his hand. "I'm Dr. Bill Summers. I work for an international medical organization called Esperança."

"Ah, yes, the organization founded by that Franciscan friar. Father Luke Tupper, wasn't it? Don't you operate a hospital boat on the Amazon?"

"Actually, two hospital boats. We also provide primary and secondary medical care to impoverished people in the forests of Bolivia, Belize and several African nations. We also provide nurse and health worker training in developing countries. But I doubt if we're as busy as you are."

Dr. Melikian motioned for Matt to sit down. "To be honest, it's the social activities that really wear me out. I'm becoming allergic to rubber chicken dinners."

Matt smiled. "As I told your secretary, I have a message from Dr. Wilson Richards. I saw him in the Amazon a few weeks ago. He'd like to visit you when he returns to the States. He wanted me to wish you the best as you travel the thin line between the Hippocratic Oath and the pressures of political Washington. I'm not certain what he meant by that, but he asked me to deliver the message directly to you."

"I know all too well what Dr. Richards means. Tell him it would be an honor to meet him. He's one of the early pioneers in heart surgery, of course. But he's also a great humanitarian as well." Dr. Melikian glanced down at his watch.

"I'd appreciate it if you could give me a brief tour of your offices. I understand you're a specialist in both benign and malignant basil cell carcinomas, and that you do some advanced research right here in your own offices. We are seeing a growing number of skin cancers in the Amazon and some other tropical areas, and we're at a loss as to why."

The doctor nodded. "I can give you a quick tour, Dr. Summers, but then I really must be getting back to my patients. As for the growing incidence of skin cancer in the heavily forested tropics, I don't have a clue. I do know the increase in skin cancers in Australia has been traced to the degradation of the ozone layer and the resulting increase in solar radiation. I'd be interested in knowing more about your findings."

"I'll send you some of our findings on e-mail as soon as I can."

"A quick tour, then. Let's start with our small research laboratory upstairs."

Dr. Melikian moved with a surprisingly quick stride up the staircase to the second floor and, at the end of the hall, opened the laboratory door. Matt was about to follow him in when down the hall another door opened and an elderly patient emerged, followed by a tall woman in a white coat. She was a striking woman with thick black hair. Stunned, Matt stood at the threshold, drawing their attention. The woman doctor raised an eyebrow at him. Her eyes were a dark brown behind her glasses.

Matt smiled awkwardly, entered the lab and closed the door.

"That's my associate, Dr. Margaret Khalid," Dr. Melikian said, anticipating the question. "A brilliant physician recommended to me by my benefactor. She's a gold mine of intelligence and competence, and the patients adore her. It's been tough for her starting over in the States. Anywhere else she would be medical director. I'm fortunate to have her on my staff. And the president likes her too."

"Starting over, being your partner and having the favor of the president of the United States doesn't sound too bad."

Melikian laughed. "A good point. I'll tell her that."

Matt and Dr. Melikian made their way back down to the reception area and shook hands. "Tell Dr. Richards I look forward to his visit anytime."

"I certainly will. And thank you for your hospitality and the cook's tour." Matt put on his pea coat. "By the way, may I ask who your benefactor was?"

"You may have heard of him—Mohammed al Nagib?"

The Oval Office

"Have a drink, Howard. I think you're going to need it," President Pierce motioned with his tin cup toward the well-stocked liquor cabinet. FBI Director Howard Duncan poured himself a double Scotch, neat. Having been summoned to the Oval Office several times before under previous administrations, he knew that when the president said "have a drink," something big was coming down the pike.

Over the next hour, the tin cup occasionally resounded on the coffee table as President Pierce laid out the situation. "That's what we know so far. A deep cover terrorist cell operating inside the U.S. The kidnapping and face transplant of Dr. Matt Richards. The suspicious deaths of Dr. Martin J. Thomas, Professor Brian Walker, and Anne-Marie Khoury, all connected to each other during their time in Beirut in 1968-69." Pierce also mentioned his recent discussions with Todd Cummings of Monument Oil, and the possible connection between William Fisher and the international financier and industrialist, Mohammed al Nagib. Without naming his source, President Pierce also related some startling facts and the transcripts of a conversation held in London at the St. James Casino.

"May I have another drink, Mr. President?"

"Look Howard, time is short. And if people as high up as Mason Stevens and William Fisher are involved, I don't know whom to trust. So I'm going solo on this one. And I'm definitely not going through Congress. Don't have the time or the inclination. Besides, the longer we wait, the greater the risk that we'll lose the advantage of surprise."

FBI Director Duncan gulped his second drink.

"Very rarely does a man in my position get the opportunity I'm being presented with. I'm not a brilliant man, Howard, but I've been put into a position of global responsibility. And Lady Luck has just aligned the stars in our favor. By God, I'm not going to miss this chance to do something bold and lasting."

"What are you suggesting, Mr. President?"

"I want you to be here when Senator Stevens arrives. Which will be in about five minutes. I sent him an urgent message requesting a highly confidential meeting in my office at 1:30." The president checked the old clock on the fireplace mantle against his Gold Rolex

Oyster watch. "As you already know, agents have recovered his daughter from that clinic in Virginia. You'll never guess who its primary backer is."

"Mohammed al Nagib," the director smiled. "I've been doing a little digging of my own since you called a couple of hours ago. He's well hidden among all the legal entities. But in essence, the clinic is on land he owns, it's next to his private mountain estate, and one of his medical technology companies is the prime funding source. Oddly, there are prominent Israeli physicians and industrialists on the board of directors—even the Israeli ambassador to the United States. Not to mention our own esteemed senior senator, Mason T. Stevens."

"You *have* been busy, Howard," Pierce said. "Now, I have Senator Stevens' daughter waiting in the room next door. Why don't you go in and get acquainted with her, then bring her in when I buzz?" Pierce opened a door hidden in the paneling, and waved the FBI head through. "This is a distasteful affair, Howard. But if we do our job right, we may just save the world from a bloody and senseless war. And we might even secure a lasting peace at the same time."

"Let's hope so, Mr. President. I'd like to retire and do some fly fishing without worrying about being nuked or gassed in my own country."

The intercom buzzer sounded. "Mr. President, Senator Stevens is here for his 1:30 appointment."

Ross Pierce shut the door behind Howard Duncan and flipped the intercom switch. "Send him in, Miriam. And proceed with the arrangements we discussed."

Senator Stevens's bulk filled the doorway. "Good afternoon, Mr. President." His confident, convivial and practiced public voice boomed out. Not every Senator was summoned for a private meeting in the Oval Office. "I cleared my calendar as soon as I received your urgent message."

"Sit down, Senator Stevens." The president studied him. "As we speak, the FBI is entering your office in the Hart building, as well as your home office, and placing your entire staff and household under arrest. All your files and correspondence, as well as computer equipment, telephone logs and bank records are being confiscated. You are under arrest for high treason against the United States of America." He watched as Stevens blanched, his posture imploding upon itself. Fear inundated him.

"Mr. President. I don't understand...." Then the arrogance and confidence of years in the Senate returned. "Is this some sort of sick joke, Ross? Just what the fuck are you playing at?" Stevens boomed, in a voice usually reserved for the floor of Congress.

Off to the side of the oval office, a barely visible door opened. A young woman, pale and gaunt, entered the Oval Office, followed by the director of the FBI. No one spoke as she approached Senator Stevens. She stood in silence before her father.

"Daddy, it's me, Kelly. Why did you do this to me—and to Dr. Richards?" she tried to hold back her tears but failed. Trembling, she moved into the FBI director's arms.

Senator Stevens avoided her gaze. He looked first at the FBI Director, and then to President Pierce. "I don't know what you're after, Mr. President," he finally announced, "but of course I'll cooperate fully. And in return for my full cooperation, I'd like to be able to retire gracefully after this is all over."

"At the moment, Mason, I'm not in the mood to make deals, nor am I really concerned about what happens to your sorry ass. You got caught for a crime that men better than you have been hung for. Now, I suggest you sit right here with FBI Director Duncan and myself and tell us everything. And I mean everything—we're short on time."

"And what about my daughter? I was only trying to help with her drug problem. I don't want anything to happen to her."

Kelly flew at her father, screaming. The president restrained her at the last minute. "I hate you, Daddy. I hate you! You're only concern about me was whether or not I would embarrass you."

"Come on now, sweetheart, you know I was only trying to protect you from the ugliness of this world. I know I should have spent more time with you, but I just couldn't get away from my duties in Congress. I wanted so much to be someone you could look up to—someone you could be proud of."

"How can I be proud of someone I don't even know?" She stood her ground, perhaps for the first time.

Dr. Weissman entered the room with a marine guard. After a nod from the president, they escorted Kelly Stevens from the room. She held back for a moment and called to her father. "You never knew me. You don't know anything about me. And you have no idea how much pain you've caused. To be honest. I like my new face. It separates me from your crimes, and your ugly self-indulgence."

When the door closed, Ross Pierce stared at Senator Stevens, a political giant, now a broken man.

"Listen to me, Mason," the president said quietly. "You're going to tell us everything, right from the sordid beginning. I know you're in bed with the Israeli ambassador, and I want to know exactly what the two of you are up to. I have a feeling you probably don't know how much of a pawn you've been in whatever game they are playing, but we'll discuss your situation later." Stevens stared at the floor. The time for filibustering and goading was over. At least he was smart enough to know it.

"You can start with how much they paid you and where you've stashed the money," FBI Director Duncan said.

For the better part of two hours, the senator told them everything. He began with his growing concern over the past several years that the U.S. was going soft on Arab terrorists and how, in his opinion, Israel deserved additional military and financial assistance. The struggling little nation needed to be fully equipped to support the United States in a war of retaliation to wipe out the terrorists and their sponsoring regimes once and for all. As far as the senator was concerned, the only solution was a military one, and he had pledged his support to assist Israel through his position in Congress and from his seat on various committees.

"Several months ago, the Israeli ambassador had come to me with a means of helping my daughter. He would help her with her drug addiction by getting her into a special clinic for rehabilitation. He could arrange for a change in her identity and get her out of the country before she did me severe damage in the Senate. He would even arrange for a good job in one of the foreign embassies." His mouth formed a hard thin line, well known on the Senate floor. "She's my daughter. I had a responsibility to her. I did what I thought was right."

"Where does Dr. Matthew Richards fit in?" Duncan asked.

"Him? The Israelis knew about his disgusting affair with my daughter. I imagine he got her hooked on drugs in the first place. They said they could get rid of him. All they wanted in return was some advance information on our strategies against terrorism."

Pierce stood up. "That's enough for now, Mason. You'll be going with Director Duncan down to FBI headquarters to make an official statement."

"But I must call my wife...."

"I'll have someone call your wife and tell her not to expect you home for a few days."

"But what about the Senate? I've got meetings and responsibilities...."

"It will be taken care of. And after this is all over, you and I will sit down and decide what to do with you. And what would be in the best interests of the United States."

Senator Stevens stood up to his full height. "And what if I just tell you to fuck off and I go to the press instead? My life is ruined already, but I won't let you ruin this great country. You've already gone soft on these Arab bastards. I knew you were a broken man after your time as a POW, but no one would listen to me. You haven't got the stomach for a real fight."

"You only know one way to fight, Mason." The president turned and looked out at the rose garden. "Head-on, guns blazing and mouth roaring. There is a time and a place for that approach, but if the only tool you've got is a hammer, then everything looks like a nail. Democracy and the people of the United States of America will win this war, Senator. On that score you can be damned certain. But it will be done my way. In case you may have forgotten, the American people elected me to run this country, not you, and certainly not the Israelis. If you want, I can have you arrested for treason right now. Or we can do this the easy way for all of us."

Ross Pierce looked directly into the Senator's eyes. "Now dig deep, Senator. This may be the biggest decision of your life. You have served this great country for a long time. Don't stop now."

An ugly silence permeated the Oval Office. The director of the FBI stood back, immobile, a mere witness to the fate of a man, a presidency, and a nation.

"Do you play poker, Mr. President?"

"Only occasionally, Senator. And tonight I've got the stronger hand."

Senator Mason T. Stevens stepped back. "You have my full cooperation. May God bless America." A marine guard came in and escorted him down to the basement garage where Director Duncan's car waited.

Director Duncan exhaled. "Jesus. I'm glad that's over."

"Me too."

"Think he'll play?"

"He'll play. He's a professional politician."

"Maybe when this is over he should get one of those face transplants."

Pierce shook his head. "No need for that."

"Mr. President?"

"He's two-faced already. I've got one more job for you, Howard. I want your most trusted men to take William Fisher into custody and put the squeeze on him until he tells you everything concerning his association with Mohammed al Nagib. Use whatever method that works. I don't care how you do it, but I want every scrap of information out of him—names, dates, places, contacts, everything. And keep him hidden away. We may need him again. Tomorrow morning you and I are going to meet with the Israel ambassador and, how shall I say it? Gain his unequivocal cooperation in putting an end to this terrorist game once and for all."

"You're walking a fine line here, Mr. President," Duncan said, shaking his head. "Some of what you're asking me to do is illegal, or at least would be highly distasteful in the eyes of Americans. And I don't have to tell you that what you're about to do will probably put an end to your career."

"My career is the least of my worries at the moment, Mr. Director. Besides, being president doesn't pay that well. Now, are you with me or not?"

"It would be my personal pleasure to help you solve this mess, Mr. President. I have grandchildren who deserve to live their life free from the threat of terrorist attacks and those who want to curtail freedom of thought and choice. I'll call you this evening with an update on Mr. Fisher." Duncan moved to the door. He paused before opening it. "When I was stationed in the Far East many years ago, I heard a

Chinese curse that went something like this: 'May you live in interesting times.' I'd say we are both cursed, Mr. President."

"Let's review that in six months, Howard."

When the door closed, President Pierce called the secretary of state, the national security advisor, and the attorney general to an impromptu meeting in the Oval Office. Then he would get ready for his meeting with the Israeli Ambassador. After that, if fortune was still on his side, he would craft his policy statement on terrorism to the nation and the world.

The Streets of Washington, D. C.

THERE ARE NUMEROUS OBSCURE PLACES in the nation's capitol where people can find shelter and food for the night, away from prying eyes. The Greater Good Mission on Q Street gave Matt a hot meal and a warm place to sleep, and nobody asked any questions. As he lay on the dirty thin mattress, the only one asking questions was Matt. What did he really see in the hallway of Dr. Melikian's office? An elderly patient emerged first, then the woman. Tall, black hair, brown eyes, heavy frame glasses. Dr. Melikian said it was his assistant and partner. Dr. Margaret Khalid. She stood some distance away, in the darkness of the hallway. Like a dream. Like one of his drunken hallucinations, shimmering just beyond what was real, but close enough to hurt. How long since he'd had a drink? Weeks? Months? Could this all be real? He knew of cases of long-term alcoholics who continued to have hallucinations months and even years after they'd stopped drinking. Maybe that was it. That plus the stress and fear.

Matt Richards looked around the basement and wondered if he would wind up like these forgotten souls. Spread out across the floor, drunk, homeless and alone. When they were young and full of life, did they ever think they would end up here? *Shit. This could be me.*

A raspy voice whispered from the mattress next to him, "Try and get some sleep, young fella. Nighttime is worst. The gremlins take control of your head. You'll either learn to go to sleep, or they'll drive you crazy." Matthew Richards closed his eyes. He tried not to think about Maha—or Nicole.

Chapter Fourteen

Washington, D.C.

AT 8:30 THE NEXT MORNING, Matt Richards emerged from the homeless shelter, thinking again about his meeting with Dr. Noubar
Melikian. He was assaulted by the city noise and smell from the sidewalk garbage. People hurried by, eyes down at their feet.

As Matt walked, he reviewed the evidence against Dr. Melikian.
Item: he's in a perfect position to assassinate the president. Item: he
was plucked from obscurity in Cairo and given a first-class education
by a benefactor who just happens to be an international financier and
arms dealer. Item: strings are pulled to get him into medical school in
Switzerland. And the final item: the benefactor maneuvered Dr.
Melikian into the highly sought after post of Personal Physician to the
President of the United States.

Matt watched the morning traffic, surging and stopping, everyone going nowhere in a hurry. In reality, he had nothing. No real evidence. Only paranoid hunches.

It must be him. But something still bothered Matt about this
whole affair, something he couldn't put his finger on. He decided to
find an Internet café and do a little research on Dr. Melikian. He was
also uncertain of how he could warn the president, especially without
any real proof, and wearing a killer's face.

Inside a telephone booth, plastered with suggestive ads and various 1-900 numbers, he found a Bell Atlantic Yellow Pages book. The pages he needed were still intact. The nearest internet cafe was on 17th Street near Dupont Circle, about ten blocks away. After a brisk walk along Q Street he turned the corner and saw the entrance to the *cyberSTOP Café,* a block ahead. Still wary, he looked over his shoulder. A police car cruised up the street. He turned and gazed into a storefront window. The cruiser continued its patrol up the street and turned the corner.

Then he saw her. Walking out of the *cyberSTOP Café* wearing a brown fur coat. Her athletic stride took her swiftly to the curb, arm raised to hail a cab. Almost immediately a metro cab pulled up, and the black-haired woman climbed in.

It can't be. The other physician in Dr. Melikian's office. Why would a prominent physician go out of her way to use an Internet café when undoubtedly she had Internet access at the office and at home? The taxi moved off down the street. Still thinking about her, he walked into the café, buffeted by the warm air from the heating system. The heat triggered images of the white café overlooking the Mediterranean where Samir and the others had died.

He ordered a cappuccino and a blueberry muffin, then sat down in a cubicle with a large flat screen, a mouse and keyboard.

Dr. Melikian didn't have a personal or business website, so Matt went to Google and typed in Noubar Melikian, M.D. A surprising number of entries popped up onto the screen, most of them articles in newspapers, domestic and foreign. One article described his background and contained extensive information about his commitment to a peaceful solution to the Middle East crisis. *Camouflage for a deep cover assassin?* While he couldn't rely on his own intuition, especially after years as an alcoholic, he had to admit he'd been impressed with the sincerity of the doctor yesterday. Dr. Melikian certainly didn't seem like an assassin—but then, maybe that was the point.

After an hour of scanning articles, Matt started visiting websites searching for photos. There were numerous pictures of Dr. Melikian with President Pierce. He found family photos and even a few old grainy pictures of Noubar Melikian as a young boy. There was even a photo on his graduation day from medical school in Switzerland.

Why Switzerland? His mind wrestled with the alternatives. Why not the U.S.? What was al Nagib up to?

Frustrated with more questions than answers, Matt was about to log off when a picture of Dr. Melikian with his associate, Dr. Margaret Khalid, slowly took shape on the screen. "Good God!" The other users stared at him, not used to someone talking out loud to their computer terminal.

He studied her face. The glasses. The eyes. But something else about the picture bothered him. *What is going on here?* He leaned forward, studying the image. The more he stared at the image, the more it began to resemble Maha, only with glasses, brown eyes instead of green and black hair instead of red.

More images swirled. The café in Beirut, Anne-Marie in the monastery, Maha's red hair, her green eyes drawing him in. He was about to log off when he saw it. He peered closely at the image on the screen. Dr. Melikian and Dr. Khalid were shaking hands and waving to photographers. *What's that on her left hand?* The detail was too small to discern. He had to know more.

Matt got up and walked toward the front. He felt sick. It took all his effort to calm down. After a few minutes of deep breathing, he reached the counter. "Yes?" said a pasty-looking young man with multiple body piercing, wearing a name tag of Aubrey. "Something wrong with your machine?"

"Can you show me how to enlarge an Internet photo?" They both walked back to his cubicle. A couple of clicks of the mouse later, the image filled the screen.

"If you want better resolution, or you want to zoom in on an area, I know a website that has a really cool program," the young man said, glad to be doing something other than ringing up the cash register. "All we need to do is select this image, save it, then log into a certain website, transfer the picture, and bingo. There it is, with nearly a dozen zooming and enhancement tools."

"Can you enhance the woman's left hand?"

"No problem," Aubrey said. Matt got up and the young man slid into the seat like a veteran fighter pilot entering the cockpit. "How big do you want it?"

"What I want is a closeup of her face, and then one of her left hand." Matt watched as the screen evolved into a kaleidoscope of images.

"That's great. Perfect. Can I get a print of each of those?" he said, handing the young man a crisp $50 bill. "This should cover the prints and something extra." Matt sat back down in the warm chair and stared at the two enhanced sections of the original photograph. In a few minutes the young man returned with the two prints. He looked back over his shoulder as he walked away.

Matt managed to compose himself. His eyes grew hot, but he blinked back the emotion. The aches was unbearable. *The scar on the left hand. Where her brother's knife cut her that day up on the ski slope in the mountains high above Beirut.* He vividly recalled putting a ball of frozen snow on her bleeding hand, then wrapping it in a bandage.

This isn't an hallucination. Matt ran his fingers along the edge of the print. Maha's alive. He could barely form the thoughts. *She must be the terrorist.*

Matt grabbed his pea coat. When he stepped out of the small computer cubicle he froze. Two policemen were standing in the door-way of the café. Young Aubrey was pointing in his direction. "Metro Police, stay right where you are." A tall black policeman put his hand on his weapon.

Matt pushed hard on the top of his cubicle, sending it crashing to the floor, then raced down the rows to a rear door. *Don't be locked!* He reached the rear door but it wouldn't budge. Frantically looking up, he saw a slide bolt at the top and threw it. Outside, he ripped off his pea coat and threaded one of the bulky arms through the two handles of the double door and tied a thick knot with the two sleeves. He ran toward the end of the alley. Loud kicking came from the café door.

As he turned onto 18th Street, an empty taxi cruised by. Matt whistled loudly, waving his arms. The taxi stopped on the other side of the street. Matt raced over and yanked open the door. "My wife's been in a traffic accident. She's at a hospital in Georgetown. I'm so scared I can't remember which one. You must know. Just get me there quickly." He shoved a $100 bill through the slot in the thick Plexiglas security enclosure. The taxi driver, an Indian by his accent, floored his vehicle. Matt looked back to see the two policemen emerge onto the street. One pointed at the retreating taxi. The cab slid around the corner, and they were lost from view.

Matt made a gagging noise in the back seat. "I'm going to vomit." he yelled. "Stop the cab, I feel sick." The taxi driver looked back in disgust. He stopped the cab next to the Dupont Circle Metro station. Matt doubled over and moaned, then burst out of the taxi and sprinted down the steps into the metro station.

The taxi driver stared for a few moments, checked the back seat to see if there was any puke, then fingered the $100 bill and slowly drove away. "Crazy Americans."

The Oval Office

"THE ISRAELI AMBASSADOR IS HERE TO SEE YOU, MR. PRESIDENT."

"Thank you, Miriam." President Pierce flipped the switch, and picked up his tin cup, rolling it back and forth between his hands.

"I am honored to be invited to the Oval Office, Mr. President." Ibrahim Barak was a short stocky man with a rugged, suntanned face. He stood at attention. His years of desert fighting and covert operations gave him a strength of character his more political colleagues lacked. "The Prime Minister of Israel sends his personal greetings."

"Thank you, Mr. Ambassador."

"Please call me Ibrahim, Mr. President. It would be an honor."

"Certainly. Would you like some coffee, Ibrahim? Or perhaps something stronger? Please, you can sit here, in front of the tape recorder." The president pressed the buzzer on his desk. A discrete side door opened.

Barak watched as Senator Mason Stevens and William Fisher entered. He looked directly at the president, then at the man escorting the others.

"I'm certain you recognize Mr. Howard Duncan, Director of the FBI."

General Barak nodded. He waited, a trace of perspiration forming on his forehead.

After everyone was seated, the president continued. "Mr. Ambassador, you were accepted onto United States soil as a representative of the sovereign nation of Israel. As such you are free to remain in this country as long as you obey the laws of our great nation."

"Mr. President, I must protest…."

"When did your patriotism get twisted and corrupted, Ibrahim?"

Barak stood up. "With all due respect, Mr. President…."

"Sit down. If you want to leave this room, be my guest. However, the FBI and Secret Service will welcome you with open arms. You've broken just about every law of diplomacy on the books."

Ambassador Barak sat down. "I am an Israeli citizen. I am my nation's ambassador to the United States of America. I have diplomatic immunity."

"At this moment you've got squat. Take a look at the pathetic men beside you. Senator Mason T. Stevens for instance. What do you think he had to say about you and your espionage activities?"

Barak glanced at Stevens. "You have no evidence against me or the nation of Israel."

President Pierce slowly raised his tin cup, then slammed it down on the Resolute desk. "Look, you sorry sonofabitch. I know all about your sordid dealings with the senator here. Bribery and extortion are serious crimes in this country."

The former Israeli army officer again stood up, slowly and in control. "I am an Israeli citizen and my nation's ambassador to the United States. I have diplomatic immunity. I don't know what kind of game you are playing, but I will be leaving now and returning to my embassy at once."

"You will do no such thing." President Pierce watched him. "You're going to cooperate and I mean *fully*."

Barak hesitated, then sat down.

"Now, we know all about your relationship with Senator Stevens here. Like I said, bribery and extortion of a U.S. senator are pretty serious crimes in this country. We also know of your illegal intelligence-gathering operations in this country, partly through Senator Stevens, who is a member of my Special Advisory Council on Terrorism and the Middle East. Then there's your close association with an internationally known contract assassin wanted in connection with the murder of Dr. Martin J. Thomas."

The general's eyes went cold. "Are you trying to frame me for the death of Dr. Thomas? I had nothing to do with that. You're putting two and two together and coming up with a number that fits your needs. I'd say the guilty party here is Senator Stevens."

Mason Stevens' face turned beet red. "Why you sonofabitch...."

"Take it easy, both of you," the FBI director said.

"We were only trying to help the United States track down a deep-cover terrorist cell. Israel was actually trying to protect your country." Barak ignored Stevens. "Maybe we did go a little overboard in our efforts, but we were trying to save our two great nations from the fanatical and perverted terrorists who threaten world peace."

William Fisher's words were cold in the silence. "Is that what you were thinking when you shot my wife at point blank range in the Chatilla refugee camp in 1982?" Director Duncan stepped behind Fisher. "You called her a whore of the Palestinians, then killed her in cold blood and never even flinched. One day, when you're least expecting it, General, I will shoot you in the face." Fisher felt Howard Duncan's hands on his shaking shoulders. "What is it you say? An eye for an eye?"

"I am not on trial here," Barak said evenly. "Military actions of the State of Israel are none of your business. Now what do you want from me?"

"Information, Mr. Ambassador," President Pierce said. He walked across the room and stood directly in front of the Israeli ambassador. "I want to know about your unofficial meetings and dealings with the international arms dealer Mohammed al Nagib. Mr. Fisher here has given us his version; now I want your side of the story. You are aware, aren't you, Mr. Ambassador, that Mohammed al Nagib recruited, organized and personally ran the same deep-cover terrorist cell you say you were trying to locate?"

Ibrahim Barak looked ill. "Oh, God."

"Looks like you've been set up and double-crossed, Ibrahim."

"HELLO? WHITE HOUSE? This is Dr. Margaret Khalid, calling on behalf of Dr. Melikian, the president's physician. May I speak to Miriam, President Pierce's personal secretary? It's very important—Dr. Melikian needs to see him right away. Yes, of course, I'll wait." Glancing up from her desk she made certain her office door was locked; Maggie Khalid took a few deep breaths to calm her racing heart.

"Hello Miriam, this is Dr. Margaret Khalid calling from Dr. Melikian's office. The doctor has found something that concerns him in the president's last blood test. An abnormal high prostate specific antigen count." She heard a gasp on the other end of the line. "Yes, well, since the doctor is attending the White House dinner this evening for the Crown Prince of Saudi Arabia, he wondered if he could come a few minutes early and take another blood sample from the president. After all, these tests are often a little finicky; it may just be a false alarm. But it's better to be on the safe side. Thank you, he'll be there at 7:15 this evening. In the Oval Office? Fine. And thank you, Miriam. Sorry to trouble you with this, but it is important."

Dr. Khalid leaned back in her swivel chair. She closed her eyes. It was a few moments before the trembling subsided. In the beginning, she could not sleep, always frightened. The daily rituals had been the worst; putting in the brown contact lenses, making sure her dyed hair was just right. And always the fears. A brown lens dropping out, a haunting green eye looking around in horror at who might be looking. Wondering what else she was hiding.

But the biggest fear of all was being watched, being suspected. Like that man with Dr. Melikian at the clinic. And it was him again at the cyberSTOP café. But it couldn't be. The first man was well dressed, a professional. The second almost a derelict. Stubble on his face…The stress was unnerving her. Even the increased dosage of valium didn't help. But the end was near. It would soon all be over. She would martyr herself. Maha, not Margaret, would once again gain respect in the eyes of her family, united again with her father. Her courage and dedication returned.

"Now, time for Dr. Melikian to have a lunch that doesn't agree with him." She reached for her medical bag and pulled out the small bottle. A couple of drops in a coffee mug, and within an hour the recipient would have all the symptoms of a full-blown case of food poisoning. Vomiting. Diarrhea. Cold shivers. Two days in bed, guaranteed.

"You did eat lunch today, didn't you?" Dr. Khalid said as she entered the large office carrying two cups of fresh brewed coffee. It was three o'clock in the afternoon. Their usual time to review the day and talk over any pressing issues.

Dr. Melikian smiled. "Yes, Mother." He looked up from his pile of papers. "I took a walk down by the river and had a quick bite at the Memorial, my favorite delicatessen. Their roast beef sandwiches are marvelous. And the pickles are enormous. That's the one thing that always amazes me about America. The portions are so huge. It's a contest to see who can choke the most customers."

"Here's your coffee. I used the Starbucks' special blend that you like. As close as we can get to real Arabic coffee without going to a restaurant." She smiled, setting the mug with the presidential seal on his desk. For the next twenty minutes they discussed their cases and made plans for the rest of the week. "Don't forget, doctor, you have the state dinner at the White House for the Crown Prince of Saudi Arabia this evening. Eight o'clock sharp."

"I did forget. I was actually thinking about an early evening in bed with a bowl of popcorn and a good book."

"I wish *I* could go to the White House and hobnob with the Saudis," she said. "Maybe I'd find a wealthy man there to take me away from all of this." She waved her arms about. "I'll come back and check in on you about six o'clock—just to make certain you haven't slipped out the back door with a suitcase full of popcorn." She walked down the hall to her office, setting the timer on her Nike running watch.

At four o'clock, the intercom rang. "Maggie, can you go to Dr. Melikian's office right away? He just buzzed me and said he's not feeling well. Maybe you should check on him—and you might need to take his patients."

"I'll be right there, Irene." She fed the last of her papers into the shredder, tied up the black plastic bag and placed it in the special incineration can. It would be reduced to ashes at the end of the day.

The sound of retching and the sour smell of vomit came from the doctor's private bathroom. She found him on all fours, his head over the toilet bowl.

"I knocked, but you didn't answer, so I—are you all right?"

"I'd be better off dead." He slowly stood up and wiped his mouth with a towel. "After what I've just been through, I have a lot more empathy for our patients."

"Sit down and I'll take your temperature. You look awful, a U.S. Army green color." Dr. Khalid smiled, trying to inject some humor.

"One hundred and three. Between that and the shivering and vomiting, I'd say you've either got a bout of the flu or a classic case of food poisoning. What was that you ate for lunch?"

"Roast beef, and too much of it. Doesn't taste nearly so good on the way back up." He managed a wry smile before urgently returning to the toilet bowl.

Back in his chair, Dr. Melikian put his head on his desk, trying to slow down the spinning. "Have Irene reschedule as many patients as possible. You'll have to handle any others. It shouldn't be too heavy a load, since I was scheduled to go to that White House dinner."

"I'll have Irene call your wife. You can't drive in this condition. If it's food poisoning it will work itself out of your system in about twenty-four hours—but you have to rest."

"Very well. For my sins I will go home and rest. And for your sins, you will go to the White House in my place."

"Oh no. Besides, they'll probably seat me somewhere close to either the president or the crown prince. I'll have to stay awake and look interested."

"I'll call Miriam right now and arrange it," he said, about to reach for the phone. Instead, he grabbed his stomach and ran for the toilet.

"Alright, I'll go. And don't worry; I'll arrange everything with the president's office. But first I'll have Irene call your wife."

Within half an hour, Dr. Melikian was lying in the back of a taxi on his way home. Dr. Margaret Khalid struggled with his caseload, fighting down her fears, smiling through her brown eyes at patients, and thinking about killing the president.

At 6.15 she freed herself from the office and went home to change. She checked her black medical bag. The appointment with the president was scheduled for 7.15 in the Oval Office. The Oval Office, seat of aggression and oppression. She had been there only once, but she knew the layout perfectly. This night she would be so far from the sun-drenched city of Beirut, where once young students had passionately discussed politics and freedom. This night she would make history for their cause.

IRENE LEONARD STAYED LATE at Dr Melikian's office, frantically trying to rearrange his schedule for the next several days. When the phone rang she cursed under her breath. "No, I'm sorry; Dr. Melikian has left for the day. And he won't be in tomorrow or the next day, he's taken ill. Oh, yes, I remember you, Dr. Summers... Dr. Khalid? No, I'm sorry, you just missed her. She's standing in for Dr. Melikian at a function at the White House this evening. Yes, I'll tell him you called. Good night, Dr. Summers."

Matt's hand trembled as he put down the payphone. *Dear God. It's happening.* Who could he call? Who would believe him?

He approached the elderly Asian proprietor behind the counter. "Can you change this $5 bill for coins for the pay phone?" Noticing a bandage on the man's forearm, Matt forced a smile. "I'm a doctor. Are you okay?"

Was Maha already at the White House? Was she talking to President Pierce at this very moment? How would she do it? A poisoned tongue depressor? An injection? The Asian proprietor broke through his fears.

"It's a deep scratch from my cat, and it's not healing very well." He moved the bandage a little to expose a red and swollen gash.

"You've got an infection. If you have some iodine or betadine, swab it twice a day for several days, and let the air get to it. Cuts heal better with fresh air." His smile was brittle. "Oh, and could I have some change for the pay phone?"

Matt looked at the television above the cash register. The 6:30 news. A picture of the White House appeared behind a fast-talking female correspondent. "Tonight," she announced, "President Pierce and the secretary of state are hosting the crown prince of Saudi Arabia at an official state dinner here at the White House. This visit certainly comes at an auspicious time, as the president is in what appears to be the final stages of preparing his response to the nation and the world on the approach the United States will take toward the escalation of terror on American soil. We still don't have a date for the president's speech, but the White House press corps says we can expect it to come sometime within the week."

Matt thumbed a coin at the slot. It dropped to the floor. Coins rattled in his hand. He fed the rest into the payphone. The White House correspondent droned on, but Matt was playing his own scenario. They kill the president – that is Maha, beautiful Maha, kills the president. Then the United States, in rage and revenge, declares all-out war on terrorism and the nations who support and sponsor terrorism. And of course, billions more for defense and additional money and arms for Israel. But even greater profits for Mohammed al Nagib and his criminal financial organization. Providing arms to both sides was a very lucrative business.

The phone rang again at Dr. Melikian's office. Matt placed his shirt sleeve over the mouthpiece. He had a vague plan, which just might work. It had to, because it was his only plan at the moment.

"Hello? I must speak with Dr. Melikian right away. This is Dr. Schultz from the emergency room at George Washington Hospital. There's been a traffic accident involving a taxi that was carrying a Dr. Margaret Khalid. It's important I speak with Dr. Melikian right away, Ms. Khalid's life may depend up on it."

"Oh God. Not Maggie. The doctor's not here. He's gone home ill."

"Then give me his home number and his cell phone as well. I'll call him directly."

"But I'm not supposed to give out personal numbers—"

"Listen, miss, I know you're doing your duty, but this woman may die in the next half hour. I'm a doctor. My job is to save lives, now hurry up." Matt's urgency was all too real. He jotted down the two numbers, and then reached into his pocket for more coins. He froze. Slowly he lowered the handset.

A large white man in a dark suit walked into the store and asked for two cups of hot coffee. Matt picked up the phone and turned his face away. He pretended to be talking. Soon the bell in the front door jingled and the man was gone. Matt shook as the fear gripped his entire body. *Why am I reacting?* He filed away the description of the man. *Two coffees?* That could mean a stakeout car was watching Elijah's apartment. They were onto him. He was running out of time.

On the third ring, the automatic answering machine picked up the call. A recording came on. "You have reached the residence of Dr.

Noubar Melikian. Please leave a message and a number, and I will return your call as soon as possible." Matt fumbled for another set of coins and this time dialed the cell phone. He hoped that, like most physicians, Melikian would answer his private line day or night.

On the second ring, a scraggly voice answered. "Dr. Melikian."

"Dr. Melikian, listen to me carefully."

"Who is this?"

"Are you sick or incapacitated?"

"I have food poisoning, but I'll live. How did you get this number? And who the devil are you?"

"Dr. Khalid poisoned you. What was it, in your drink? Coffee, tea?"

Silence, then retching.

"Dr. Melikian, you are the only person who can save the president of the United States from being assassinated tonight. Right now, Dr. Khalid, if that's her name, is on her way to the Oval Office in your place. She is a terrorist. She plans to kill the president."

"I know your voice."

"Listen to me. She plans to kill the president."

"You're Dr. Summers, from the other day …."

"Will you listen to me? Dr. Khalid is on her way to kill the president. She made an appointment under your name for 7:15 this evening, knowing full well that you would be unable to attend."

"You're mad."

"I'm on my way to the White House right now. Get dressed and get over there if you want to save the president, and Dr. Khalid."

"Summers?" Melikian paused, his voice steady. "I can't go anywhere, I've got food poisoning. I can barely move."

"You don't have food poisoning. She probably gave you a large dose of Bethanechol. As you know it produces similar symptoms. If you have any atrophine in your medical bag, use it. The symptoms will quickly subside. It's an old trick we used to use in medical school."

"What did you say about Maggie?"

"She's a terrorist. Her real name is Maha Hammad. She's Jordanian and a close friend of the suicide bomber that killed Dr. Norman. It's all part of a plan to get Maha into the White House to kill the president."

"How do you know she's a terrorist?"

"Because she has a scar on her left wrist; I was there when she got it. And long ago I was in love with her. Now take the atrophine, get dressed, and I'll meet you at the first gate on Pennsylvania Ave, just in from 17th Street. There's no time to lose."

Matt hung up as the door bell jingled. He turned around, not knowing what to expect. *Oh, my God.* A face from the past. Demetrie Antonopolis. Older, with taut bronze skin and a graying ponytail.

He blocked the aisle leading to the door. "It's over, Matt. Let's go. Quietly if you don't mind." A pistol emerged from the pocket of his black overcoat.

"What do you mean, it's over?" Matt backed against the rack of canned vegetables.

"Think, man, think. Or are you still muddled from all that booze?"

"Ah, yes. How convenient. I'm the fall guy, and the real rats go free. And are you still a dope head, Demetrie? Can't you see you're being used, just like me?"

"Step over here. There's a car outside."

Reaching into his pocket, Matt brought out a can of warm diet soda. With slumped shoulders, the body language of the defeated, he walked slowly toward Demetrie.

"I thought you'd have a bottle of Scotch, not a soda can." He laughed at his own joke. The car honked. Demetrie turned to look.

Matt shook the can and quickly pulled the ring tab. Foam sprayed into the killer's face. His hands instinctively went up to protect his eyes. Matt grabbed two large peach cans off the shelf and slammed them into the side of Demetrie's head with all his might. Blood spurted out from both ears. Demetrie staggered, roaring in pain. Matt leapt feet first into the Greek's chest. The ponytail whipped as his head snapped to one side. Demetrie crashed into a wooden fruit container, his back impaled on one of the metal bars. His body hung quite still.

Desperately, Matt scanned the store for a way out. "Here! Here!" He heard a call from the back. The elderly Asian proprietor was holding open a door just beyond the bins of wilted lettuce. "Thanks," Matt said, squeezing his shoulder. "Call the cops. Tell them he tried to rob you. Shit, tell them anything." He ducked into the alley and sprinted toward the street.

A young black man was climbing into a dark maroon Mini Cooper with tinted windows. Matt jerked open the passenger door and dove in.

"What the fuck you doin' man? Get the hell out of here," the driver bunched up his fist and swung wildly. Matt pulled out a $100 bill and held it up. The man stared. "Okay, you got my attention, but I ain't into no queer stuff."

Matt ripped another bill from his wallet. "Listen, I've got to get to the White House right away; it's a national emergency. Unless you want to be responsible for another September 11, let's see how fast you can drive."

"Bullshit, but keep the C-notes coming." He put the Mini into gear. The tires screamed. The little car shot out into the street. "Shit, man, you some kind a James Muthafuckin' Bond?" He stomped on the accelerator. "There's a big car with an ugly looking white guy chasing us." He looked at Matt, then grinned. "Well Whitey, this is your lucky day. Because I'm the Rolf Schumacher of Washington, D.C. I know this town like my bitch's titties." The car slid into a narrow alleyway, knocking over garbage cans and crushing cardboard boxes.

Matt looked at his watch—6:45 P.M. The car chasing them was the least of his worries. How was he going to gain entry to the White House, uninvited and wearing the face of a killer? *God, Maha. Don't do this.*

What had Dr. Melikian said? Just phone the White House. That's right, simple as that. Get the Marine guards to charge down the halls and arrest her. So why hadn't he done that? He was putting the president at risk – why?

Maha. He needed to confront Maha. He needed to be there. Evil people had kidnapped him, robbed him of his face, and destroyed his life. And by God, he was going to stop them, and save Maha. He saw her wrist, packed in ice, the memory shimmering like her tears that day. Red blood pooled on the virgin snow at her feet, so innocent. But now…. The car hurtled through an intersection, horns blared in protest.

"We've lost the car." The Mini Cooper responded with a lurch as he downshifted.

"Either they already know where we're headed or they're not welcome there," Matt said. "Listen, when you get to the intersection of

Pennsylvania and 17th Street, just let me out and take off. There's no need for you to get involved in this."

The young driver nodded. Matt shoved three one hundred-dollar bills into the pocket of his leather jacket. "Are we gonna' win, mister?"

"Absolutely, my friend. Absofuckinglutely."

Ahead loomed the White House with its stately columns glowing in the huge spotlights. As the Mini roared down 17th Street, he could see the Old Executive Office Building. It marked the intersection with Pennsylvania Avenue. Matt got ready to flip the door handle and jump out. Some hundred yards away, a taxi screeched to a halt in front of the guard barrier blocking the entrance to the White House. The taxi driver got out and opened the rear door. A bent-over figure with white hair staggered out of the taxi and stumbled toward the entrance gate.

"How'd you like to earn some bragging rights?" asked Matt, turning to the young black man.

"What you got in mind?"

"Can you crash into that taxi? Not too hard, just hard enough to cause a commotion and distract the Marines? You'll get arrested, but don't worry; I'll see that you get released. And maybe a special citizenship award as well. Let me out here, and then give it your best shot."

"You crazy, you know that, dude?" he grinned, then stopped the car. "My mama's gonna kill me, but I'll do it." The boy gave Matt a broad grin and stomped on the accelerator. The little car gained speed, then quickly went into a controlled skid. It slid into the idling taxi. The cab driver began yelling and cursing, flailing his arms in the air. The young black man flung open the car door, staggered a few steps and collapsed on the sidewalk, screaming and rolling. Alarm bells blared on the big iron gates. Secret Service guards and Marines raced toward the young man, their guns drawn.

Matt sidled up to Dr. Melikian and supported him with an arm. "It's me," Matt said as they moved up to the entrance gate.

"Dr. Summers. Or are you an imposter as well?"

"In more ways than one. What made you decide to believe me?"

"I don't believe you. But if there's one chance in a million of preventing war in the Middle East, I'll do just about anything—even listen to a crazy man like you. Besides," the doctor smiled weakly, "your antidote, atropine, helped right away. It must have been Bethanechol she slipped in my coffee."

"Halt." A tall marine, hand on his side arm, stood just inside the heavy iron gate.

"I am Dr. Noubar Melikian, President Pierce's personal physician, and I have to see the president at once. It's a matter of national security. The president is in danger at this very moment." He held up his White House ID.

"Shoot us later if we're lying," Matt said. "We must get to the president at once. Escort us in or you may be responsible for the death of the president of the United States."

The marine was not to be pressured. He peered closely at Dr. Melikian's ID, then quietly spoke into his walkie-talkie. The gate opened and two other marines took Matt and Noubar by the arm. They quickly escorted them into the west wing of the White House, barking orders as they went. "Secure the president, secure the president. Where is he?" they demanded of a guard in the hallway.

"In the Oval Office with Dr. Khalid. She just went in."

DR. MARGARET KHALID KEPT HER SMILE IN PLACE as she watched him standing at the window. A big man, an attractive man, perhaps more relaxed than she had remembered. She was here, in the Oval Office, power center to a nation intent on destroying the entire Middle East. Her hands shook as she opened her black bag and reached in.

"Dr. Khalid?"

"Yes, Mr. President?"

He didn't turn around. "Most people who come into the Oval Office are eager to talk. I don't recall you being the shy type."

"I'm filling in for Dr. Melikian. I guess I'm a little unnerved and overwhelmed."

"Frankly, I'm used to the trappings now. Did you know that out there in the dark garden, new shoots are emerging from the thorny stalks of the roses? It's amazing. Even after a severe pruning in the fall, and the freezing temperatures of a harsh winter, the lengthening day-light of spring will again produce her miracle. In a couple of months we'll see big bright roses again."

"Really, sir?" She examined the tiny needle smeared with the deadly toxin.

"Speaking of seeing things again. I saw an old friend of yours the other day."

She stopped, the syringe held up to the light. "Of mine, Mr. President? I really don't think …"

"Matthew Richards."

The syringe fell onto the carpet. Her hand trembled as she reached down. After picking it up she found the president of the United States looking directly at her, unsmiling.

"Are you all right, doctor?"

"Of course." Where did her response come from? Her shocked heart? The twisted pit of her stomach?

"Let me tell you a story, doctor. And you might want to listen very closely. A long time ago, I was in love with a woman I couldn't have." Pierce stood with his hands behind his back. "She was the daughter of a wealthy Mexican rancher. If I close my eyes I still see her. Jet black hair, a fiery temper, and the bearing of a spirited mustang. I was shy and she was wild and free. Yet we fell deeply in love. For one fantastic summer we had a wild, forbidden love affair. Then she went away to school in Mexico City and I came back to the States to go to college. I never saw her again.

"I suppose I could have become bitter and angry over lost love. But instead I decided to use that experience as an example of what is possible between two different people. The memory of that love helped save my sanity when I was a POW in Vietnam. I believe the capacity to connect at a meaningful level with another human being is hard-wired into all people, doctor. No matter what their culture, race, religion, or political beliefs. And no degree of brainwashing can take that from us. It can be crusted over, but never eliminated."

"Mr. President …."

"By the way, Maha, Matt still loves you."

She knew she should charge him. Her trainers had recited it over and over. As a last resort, charge. The needle only has to scratch the skin for the toxin to take effect. Do it now. Now. She really should charge, lunge, drive the needle home. But instead she just walked slowly forward. Matt Richards. A name from another time, yet always deep within her. He had spoken his name. How fine it tasted in the air, spoken out loud, not locked away in some forbidden place. Good times, great times…the sound of the sea, the evening breeze on their faces, starlight. Bedouina and Samir laughing; Maha and Matt finding excuses to steal away in the moonlight. To be alone. To be lovers.

"Stop right there." A loud voice from the side of the room.

Her feet kept slowly moving. Odd, she didn't like the harsh lighting. Her contact lenses, awash in tears, gathered the bright light. "Some choices open up a great future, others seal one's fate forever," she said, moving toward the president, syringe raised. Just a prick on the skin with the coated needle and death would be irreversible.

"At first we thought Dr. Melikian might be the deep-cover assassin, after learning of his affiliation with Mohammed al Nagib. But when my secretary said you called earlier about my blood test, and that you were coming instead of Dr. Melikian, things just sort of fell into place for us. Didn't they Karl?"

Karl van Ness had come into the Oval Office through the side door. He looked first at Maha, then the president. When the young Marine behind him raised his 9mm Baretta pistol, van Ness stopped him.

"It's still not too late, Maha," Pierce said. "Never too late for love and understanding to conquer the bitterness of hate and sorrow." He looked into her face, but it was slack, blanked out, like some of the POWs in Hanoi. Maha took another faltering step. "If you move any closer, the guards will be forced to shoot. You can stop this madness now. We will help you."

The main door of the Oval Office opened. Noise from outside shattered the silence. Matt, Dr. Melikian and three marine guards stepped in.

"Maha?"

She turned toward Matt's voice. "Your face. What has happened to you?"

"It's still me."

Maha bent over and took out her contact lenses. They fell onto the carpet, landing on the head of the woven eagle. Her green eyes flooded with tears. "I want to see you clearly one last time." She smiled. Her face was serene.

"I loved you from that very first moment on the airplane."

"Matt, I can't see you behind that face. But I feel it really is you."

"Everything will be all right. Now put down the syringe, Maha. Just lay it down."

Her face returned to a smooth façade. Empty. She brought the needle to her arm. "It's time for me to leave, Matthew." For a brief moment she held his gaze. "May Allah in his infinite wisdom have mercy on my soul."

"No! Maha!"

The needle slid easily into the back of her left hand, next to the long scar. "My father will be waiting...."

Matt caught her as she fell. A marine quickly grabbed the syringe and stepped back. She looked up at him. "We have seen each other one last time, my darling. I hoped we would." Her breathing was short and labored.

"What's on the needle? Tell me," pleaded Matt. "We'll get the antidote."

"I'm sorry I left you so long ago," she said. "But at least I'll die in your arms." She coughed. Her face broke out in a cold sweat. "Perhaps something good will come of all this. You must remember all the days of your life, Matthew, that I loved you and only you, with all my heart."

"It doesn't have to end, Maha, please tell me. What's the toxin on the needle?" Her eyes dulled. Matt looked up at the others. "Help. Won't someone help?"

No one moved. "There is no antidote," Maha whispered. "That's the whole point to this game, Matthew. There is no going back. Forget the past and move forward."

"Maha, please."

"Your arms feel the same." She tried to touch his cheek but her hand fell back.

Dr. Melikian checked her pulse. "I'm sorry."

Matt shook her. "Oh, my God. Please....please." He held his former love tightly against his chest, feeling the life force flow out of her. He checked for a pulse.

Someone gently put an arm around his shoulder. "I'm sorry, Matt, I know this is painful." He found himself staring straight into the eyes of the other woman he thought was dead.

"Nicole?" He jerked when he saw Elijah standing at the back. "I don't understand." His arms remained around Maha.

She pulled her hand away, embarrassed.

A Marine brought Matt to his feet. "The president, sir."

President Pierce waited while Matt gathered his faculties. He tried not to look at Maha. Or Nicole.

"I'm very glad to meet you, Dr. Richards. I'm sorry it's like this."

"Yes, sir."

"We should leave the room now. Let those who know how to handle these things take over. I need you to come with me, Dr. Richards. I want to talk with you about the Middle East. Karl and I need to know what you know, and your ideas will also be welcome. Will you stay here at the White House for a few days? In fact Ms. Delacluse and Mr. Tajikian should stay also. You'll all be my personal guests, of course."

Matt nodded.

"I'll stay if you want me to, Matt," said Nicole.

He stared at Nicole. "Please stay."

The president was quiet as the marine guards picked up the body of Maha Hammad and carried her out of the Oval Office. "Noubar?" he said to Dr. Melikian. "I'm asking you to stay also. I have a feeling you may wind up playing a pivotal role."

"I'd stay anywhere I can get some rest, Mr. President."

"And Matt? Nicole?"

They waited, wondering what the president could possibly say.

"Give it time."

Pierce walked over to his desk and pressed the intercom. "Miriam? Tell the vice president to stand in for me at tonight's dinner. Tell them I'm not feeling well. Hell, tell them anything. And get Ms. Black, the secretary of state, the directors of the CIA and FBI, and the attorney general into the situation room at once." The president picked up his treasured tin cup. "Yes, it's time we made the decisions everyone has been avoiding. And I believe with what we have from

Senator Stevens, Ambassador Barak, and William Fisher, we may have a way to a lasting solution."

The President of the United States leaned over to the intercom and buzzed his secretary. "One more thing, Miriam. Tell the White House Press Secretary that my address to the nation will take place in five days, right here in the Oval Office." He looked up. "Now let's get out of here."

Chapter Fifteen

The Oval Office

THE SPEECH CAME five days after Maha Hammad's death.

Since that evening, the White House had seen Cabinet members, senators and congressmen who came and went at all hours, and lines of limousines filled with ambassadors and dignitaries from the world's nations. Extra phone lines were set up in the Oval Office so President Pierce could move efficiently from one conversation with a foreign leader to another. Time was the enemy now. Ross Pierce couldn't wait for the normal process of debates and consensus. He pressed hard for immediate decisions, and he got them. This was the opportunity the world had been waiting for, that peace-loving people had prayed for, that the supporters of terrorism had feared.

"Is my tie straight?" The president sat behind the massive Resolute desk in the Oval Office. President Pierce understood the power of visual imagery. He had personally placed a model of a Grumman A6 Intruder, the airplane he flew in Vietnam to his right. To his left were carefully arranged photos of his wife, three grown children, and grandchildren. At the edge of the desk stood an illuminated globe, turned so the Middle East could be seen by the cameras. Directly in front was his tin cup.

From behind the camera and cables crowded into the small office, someone respectfully said, "It's time, Mr. President."

"No, it's past time." President Roswell Clayton Pierce stared straight into the camera.

"Good evening, my fellow Americans and those of you from other nations around the world who may be listening this evening. Many of you have been waiting for me to make an official statement concerning the path the United States of America will take in helping eliminate terrorism, restoring peace to the Middle East, and stabilizing the world political situation. This evening I'd like to take the opportunity to update you on our efforts in this direction. As I said in my campaign speeches over a year ago and during my inaugural address, I am committed to bringing about peace in the Middle East. This was not just campaign rhetoric, but a solemn commitment that I intend to keep.

"As you can well understand, bringing about lasting peace is easier said than done. The reason I have been silent for the past several months since the tragic events surrounding the suicide bombing in Washington, is that I do not take my pledge to you, the American people and the world, lightly. So behind this apparent silence, my staff and I have been working day and night to find a workable and lasting solution." Reaching out to pick up his tin cup, the president continued. "I believe all the elements are now in place for the fulfillment of my commitment."

Matt, Nicole and Dr. Melikian stood off to one side, behind the cameras, cables and engineers who filled the Oval Office. They looked at each other, knowing full well what was coming next. Karl van Ness stood further back in the shadows. He nodded, briefly catching Pierce's glance, who nodded back. Quietly van Ness turned, closing the door as he left the Oval Office. He turned to one of the senior White House aides. "Call down and have my driver bring the car around. There's still some unfinished business."

The president followed the red light on the active camera. "The decisions I have had to make in the past few days have not been easy ones, and some will weigh heavily on my conscience for many years to come. However, I have made these decisions with the utmost thought and deliberation, and at all times for the greater good of all nations and the future of all our children and grandchildren." As he spoke the camera panned across the photos arranged on his desk.

"I have consulted with many foreign leaders and heads of influential government agencies, world organizations such as the United Nations, NATO, and the European Union, as well as trusted business, religious and academic advisers. I have followed American and world opinion polls and reviewed the mountain of e-mail I receive here at the White House every day. As I address you this evening, I am at peace with these decisions and I trust that you will support our actions for global peace and security for all peoples of the world.

"Let me begin. First, I must inform the American people that at the end of my term in just over two years, I will not be a candidate for re-election." The camera pulled back, revealing a wide-angle shot of the president at his desk, the presidential seal emblazoned on the oval carpet. Slowly, it zoomed in again.

"Why am I standing down? The reason is simple. Too many times elected officials avoid making the right decisions for fear that they will not be re-elected. The thirst for votes has turned many a good leader into a so-so follower. I have never been a follower and I won't start now. I am also not running for re-election because I want to assure all of you, no matter what your political affiliation, that I have absolutely no political agenda in the statements I am about to make and the decisions we have taken here at the White House. My only interest is for a lasting and peaceful solution to the terrible conflict in the Middle East and in putting a stop to the rise of global terrorism.

"For the past several decades, the Palestinian people have either been living in refugee camps on foreign territory or in their homes surrounded by soldiers. Like all people, they deserve the opportunity for a homeland, a nation, a place to raise their families, to worship their god and to pursue their dreams. Today, I have asked Congress to officially recognize the nation of Palestine and the rights of the Palestinian people for a homeland." The image on the screen switched to a picture of the Palestinian flag flying in the breeze.

"Having conferred with many of your representatives in Congress, I am assured that they will swiftly and overwhelmingly endorse such a proclamation. I have also conferred with the heads of the nations of Syria, Jordan, Lebanon and Egypt, who have all agreed to cede portions of their land to build the new state of Palestine. Palestine will be approximately the same geographical size as Israel, its neighbor along the western border.

"After extensive discussions with the Israeli ambassador to the United States and the prime minister of Israel, my administration has secured their agreement to support the development of a new Palestine and to withdraw all their forces from any occupied territories.

"With this recognition of the rights of the Palestinian people for a homeland, I am now formally calling on all Arab nations to immediately renounce any and all support for terrorist activities anywhere in the world." The tin cup turned in his hands. It looked out of place, yet so much a part of the man. "In earlier days, terrorism was designed to draw attention to the plight of the Palestinian people. Many of the Arab nations supported these activities, not wishing to abandon their Muslim cousins. While I do not agree with terrorist activities of any kind, nor the manner in which various Arab states have supported terrorist organizations, I do understand the Arab people's concern about the conditions in which the Palestinian people live." Again, the camera focused on a tight shot of the president's face.

"But now, the Palestinian people have what they want—a permanent homeland for their people. Thus there should be no more support, either overtly or covertly, for any acts of terrorism in the name of Palestine, or freedom in the Middle East.

"Let me be clear on this point. Those nations that do not immediately sever all support for terrorist organizations worldwide will be branded as terrorist states and will face the consequences. I have been assured that not only is the United Nations prepared to swiftly impose sanctions against these rogue nations, but it has also given the United States a firm commitment that more drastic measures will be taken for noncompliance, including embargoes, economic sanctions, immediate elimination from the United Nations, and possible use of force.

"Over the past weeks I have also conferred with many leaders in the Arab world who assure me that they will no longer support terrorism and in fact will begin immediately to arrest and bring to justice those individuals and organizations that continue to operate from within their borders. These Arab nations have even agreed to come before the United Nations individually and collectively to explain what has been done to shut down the terrorist networks for good."

Matt looked over to where Karl van Ness had been standing just moments ago. For the past week, in private and group meetings, van

Ness had been at the president's side as they hammered out this extraordinary set of events. Sometimes he would disappear for hours, only to return and whisper in the president's ear. Matt wondered just who he was.

"As a result of these decisions and the commitment given by the Arab leadership toward global peace, I have just this evening been informed by officials from Saudi Arabia that Osama bin Laden and several other top Al-Qaeda leaders have been killed in raids carried out by a coalition of Saudi Arabian and U.S. Special Forces. Al-Qaeda and its reign of terror on innocent people around the world has been seriously crippled, and if we all do our job correctly, it will soon be totally destroyed.

"Also, under the sponsorship of the Kingdom of Saudi Arabia, the Arab nations have agreed to form a task force, in conjunction with U.N. forces, to root out all known and suspected terrorists, as well as to shut down all terrorist funding activities. In addition, just yesterday, the government of Switzerland agreed in an unprecedented move of international cooperation to freeze the bank accounts of all known terrorist organizations and individuals. The global terrorist threat is being crushed at this very moment.

"I am committed to putting together the ingredients for a lasting solution to the Middle East crisis and an end to global terrorism, and making them stick. Therefore, the United States of America is realigning its allocation of foreign aid to the Middle East, beginning immediately. Many of you probably do not realize how many of your tax dollars have gone to this region for years, and yet we continue to be plagued with violence, terrorist activities, and even attacks on our own soil. Last year, for example, U.S. foreign aid, both economic and military, to the Middle East reached an unprecedented level of over eight billion dollars. This tax money flowed out with very little positive result to the United States or the world.

"That is why, with the support of key congressional leaders, I am proposing to drastically reduce the amount of foreign aid to the Middle East for one year. A good friend of mine once told me, 'Why buy a cow when the milk is free?' Middle Eastern countries have received a massive amount of foreign aid with no strings attached; they have not been held accountable for hindering, or failing to support, a peaceful solution. In fact, the State of Israel alone last year received over six billion dollars of aid, about 30 percent of total U.S. aid around the world and 75 percent of the aid to the Middle East. While in the past our government has seen such a large amount of aid as a means of stabilizing and thus reducing tensions in the Middle East, I think we can all agree it hasn't worked. For all the money we've spent, things have only gotten worse.

"The American people stand on their own two feet and work hard to get along peacefully with the nations of the world. It is time the nations of the Middle East, and especially Israel, did the same. If after one year, the Arab nations of the Middle East and Israel have continued to work together in peace, and have helped to snuff out terrorism and violence in their region and in the world, then reasonable and equitable amounts of U.S. foreign aid will again start flowing into the region. But only if peace is achieved and maintained.

"To ensure that various religious interests in the Middle East are respected, I have received a firm commitment from all the nations in the region to establish the City of Jerusalem, and surrounding religious sites, as an international holy city for all faiths. The freedom to worship freely at their respective holy places will be guaranteed to people of all faiths. As you all know, Jerusalem is a sacred city for Judaism, Christianity and Islam. In the not-too-distant past, Jews, Christians, and Muslims lived peacefully side by side in Jerusalem. It is my dream that this will again be the case."

Ross Pierce placed his tin cup to one side. "To govern this international city, each of the major faiths in the region has agreed to participate in setting up a ruling city council. My personal physician and good friend, Dr. Noubar Melikian, who has worked his entire life for a peaceful solution in the Middle East, has unselfishly agreed to be the interim mayor of the International Holy City of Jerusalem, while a structure for new citywide elections is being put into place." Nicole grasped Dr. Melikian's hand off camera while his picture was shown to the nation.

"There are many critics of the United States, in Europe and elsewhere, who say that America has it easy and that Americans are naïve. Let me put the record straight. They're wrong. Over the course of American history, thousands of our citizens have shed their blood in the name of freedom and peace on foreign soil, defending the freedoms of others. Americans aren't naive. We know that peace is a better option than war. And it's not an option for any country to bury its head in the sand and hope for peace while tyrants and terrorists kill innocent people out of hatred and greed. No. We will do whatever it takes to bring about lasting peace to the world."

The television screen switched to a live picture of the American flag waving over ground zero in New York City, then returned to the Oval Office. "With the decisions I have just announced, the United States is not running away from a fight with the terrorists and the bullies who want war for their own political and financial gain. On the contrary, we are stepping up the fight, with weapons more effective than bombs or bullets. The economic power of self-reliance and accountability."

"Peace in the Middle East cannot be imposed from without. We've seen that policy fail for the past 50 years. Peaceful coexistence must be a result of mutual commitments from within. That is why we have made these decisions to drastically reduce the amount of foreign aid. By stopping the handouts, we are urging the nations of the Middle East to take control of their own destiny, an intertwined destiny of mutual interdependence. I am asking all nations in the Middle East to once and for all make peace their highest priority."

President Pierce picked up the tin cup that had been with him through POW camp, on the campaign trail, and into the Oval Office. "Now, if you'll excuse me, I have work to do for the American people and the world." Slowly he tapped his cup on his desk, making a metallic sound, "Good night, God bless America, and may all the citizens of the globe live in peace and prosperity for many years to come."

As the picture of the president slowly faded away, replaced by a waving American flag, the sound of the little tin cup could still be heard.

CNN Headline News

"WHAT YOU AND I HAVE JUST WITNESSED, ladies and gentlemen, is one of the most extraordinary speeches from any world leader in recent memory," said the senior CNN newscaster. "If what he has told us really comes about, then President Roswell Clayton Pierce, in a selfless act of personal and political courage, has not only made the decisions everyone else has been avoiding, but has also gotten the leaders of the Middle East, especially Israel, to agree to them. What went on behind the scenes to bring about this unprecedented level of international cooperation we may never know. But on this my colleagues and I all agree. It must have been an extraordinary and heroic act of diplomacy."

The veteran newscaster cocked his head, intently listening to his earpiece. After a few moments of silence, a broad smile crossed his face. He looked directly into the camera. "I have just received word that in various cities and towns across the U.S., as well as in Europe and the Middle East, people everywhere are spilling out of their homes and banging on pots and pans in support of the president's new policy. I probably don't have to tell you, you can hear it for yourself. Just open your windows."

Scenes from cities across the United States began flashing onto the screen as people collected in parks, town squares, restaurants, baseball stadiums, anywhere they could gather and celebrate a new day with the sound of metal banging on metal. As the crowds swelled, the noise grew; a veritable symphony of homemade cymbals.

The newscaster came back on again. "I wonder if anyone, anywhere, is listening to this broadcast anymore?" he said with a wry smile. "It appears the whole world is out in the streets banging pots and pans in support of an unprecedented bid for lasting peace."

Chapter Sixteen

The Oval Office

"WHAT'S YOUR NAME, YOUNG MAN?" said the president of the United States to the young black man standing before him, wearing a suit and tie, his shoes polished to a high shine.

"William Jefferson Clinton, sir, but the guys just call me Jeff."

"Well," said President Pierce, laughing. "Would you mind if I called you Jeff as well? One Bill Clinton around here is enough for me."

"No, sir."

"Now Jeff, I want you to know that I appreciate very much what you did to help Dr. Richards here the other night, even though it got you in a lot of trouble with the Secret Service, the Metro Police, and more importantly, your mother."

"Yeah, she was mad as a—"

"Hush, boy," the heavyset woman whispered, knuckling him in the backside. Then she flashed her host a smile. "I was just acting like any concerned mother, Mr. President."

"Mrs. Clinton, I want you to know that your son is a true patriot, and that because of his courage and commitment, the world is a much safer place. You should be proud of your son."

"Oh, he's a great boy, Mr. President, and he works hard as a waiter at the Key Bridge Marriott Hotel. I only wish he could get into a trade school or something where he'd have a chance to earn a decent living and make something of himself."

"What trade are you interested in, Jeff?"

"Believe it or not, I've always wanted to work on the railroad, maybe as a conductor, or even drive the trains someday."

"I'll see what we can do." President Pierce thanked the young man and his mother. After the photographer took several pictures of young William Jefferson Clinton and the president, and before the marine guard escorted them out of the Oval Office and on to their private tour of the White House, Jeff looked at Matt. "Sure wish my girlfriend could have seen this."

"The one you know so well?" Matt said, straight-faced. He was rewarded with a street smile and a frown from Mrs. Clinton.

President Pierce sat down at his Resolute Desk. He picked up his battered tin cup, then looked at Matt, Nicole and Elijah.

"I know this would make the story of a lifetime, Ms. Delacluse. But I'm going to ask you to sign an affidavit swearing that you'll never reveal the events of the past several days. By the way, I've just been in communication with your former boss at the *International Herald Tribune*. He says you're a royal pain in the ass. That's a direct quote by the way. But he'll hire you back as soon as you're ready and able."

"I appreciate your support and assistance, Mr. President," Nicole said, reaching out and taking Matt's hand, "but I think I've got a better offer."

"Okay, I get the picture. But what about you, Dr. Richards? As you know, I need a new personal physician, at least for the next two years that I'm in office. Interested?"

"Under normal circumstances, Mr. President, it would be an honor. But I must respectfully decline. First I've got a little trip to take to Nassau, then I'd like to get rid of this face. It's not so bad, but sharing features with an international assassin is definitely a liability. Dr. Weissman has agreed to perform the operation. In a few months' time I hope to look like someone vaguely resembling the old Matt Richards. But as a result of what I've learned these past few weeks, I will never be the same. Someone once said looks can be deceiving, and in this case, they will be absolutely right."

President Pierce watched him. "I know about your little trip to the Bahamas. I'll have the FBI escort you personally there and back, just in case. After you get your old identity back, where will you be headed?"

"We're both going to join Esperança," Matt said. "The medical group that runs a surgical boat up the Amazon River. I spoke with my father at length the other night, and he's going to join us as well. My roommate in Beirut, Samir Hussein, used to say, 'The purpose of man is to be of service to mankind.' There's plenty of need for a good surgeon, make that two good surgeons, on the Amazon." Matt paused. "Can I ask you a question, Mr. President?"

"Fire away."

"What happened to Kelly Stevens? Is she all right?"

"Ms. Stevens and her mother have moved to London, where she'll begin her new career at the U.S. embassy as an assistant in the publications department. With the love and support of her mother, I'd say she'll be just fine."

"And who killed Brian Walker, Dr. Martin Thomas and Anne-Marie Khoury?"

"We have evidence—this is strictly off the record—that it was a person working directly for Mohammed al Nagib by the name of Demetrie Antonopolis. He was ordered to eliminate people from your Beirut days who might be able to place Nagib and William Fisher together."

"I knew him from my Beirut days. He was always smoking hashish and living a fast life," said Matt.

"His days of fast living are definitely over," said the president. "He was found dead in a market near Union Station. Something else off the record. We used a little creativity and convinced the Israelis that their ambassador to the United States was using an international assassin to kill people here in the United States, including me. As a result, I was able to put, shall we say, a considerable amount of pressure on the government of Israel to support my peace initiatives."

"Did you say a well-known international assassin?" said Matt, eyes widening. "You blackmailed the Israelis. They wanted to use me, with my new face, to hunt down the terrorist cell, and you made it look as if they were running an assassination plot on U.S. soil...."

"The fact that they bribed Senator Stevens, spied on my council meetings, and were in cahoots with al Nagib gave me additional leverage," the president said dryly. "At any rate, an assassin *did* infiltrate the White House—so it wasn't a complete lie."

"And what about Mohammed al Nagib?" asked Eli.

President Pierce crossed over to the window to admire the roses as the buds were breaking. "All I can tell you is the world will never again have to be concerned about Mr. Nagib or his three partners." He looked back at Matt. "I trust that is all we need to say."

"Word among the community is that several focused 'wet jobs' took place on the families of recent suicide bombers," Elijah said, looking at Dr. Finch.

"A few of our actions had an extraordinary affect on helping to reduce the threat of terrorism around the globe," said the president. The director of the CIA nodded.

CNN Headline News

"As tight-lipped as ever, President Roswell Clayton Pierce is giving no hints as to how he was able to orchestrate the extraordinary events that have culminated in his dramatic bid for a lasting peace in the Middle East and an end to terrorism. The remarkable concessions on the part of Israel and the Arab countries in the Middle East have brought about a completely different dynamic in the region. Peace is definitely in the air, with Jews and Muslims working together to make certain that peace endures."

The senior newscaster smiled into the camera, then continued with the major news stories of the day. "Citing ill health and depression following the death of his only child, U.S. Senator Mason T. Stevens of Virginia, chairman of the Senate Select Committee on Intelligence, has announced his retirement, effective immediately. Upon learning of the announcement of Senator Stevens's retirement, President Pierce described him as 'a man of strong character and a tenacious supporter of the American dream.' In a related story, we have also learned that Mrs. Stevens has just filed divorce papers, citing irreconcilable differences between herself and her husband. Mrs. Stevens has left the United States and is now living in London.

"On the international front, CNN correspondents in South America have just received word that suspected Hezbollah terrorist training camps in the tri-border region of Brazil, Paraguay and Argentina have been devastated by forest fires of unknown origin. The camps, rumored to be one of the main spawning grounds for international terrorists and suicide bombers, have, until recently, been hidden away in a remote section of the dense Amazon jungle. Sketchy reports from that remote region confirm that over seven major terrorist training camps, as well as mining and logging camps owned by the Brazilian millionaire Jorge Molinas, have been destroyed, reportedly by natural fires set off by unseasonably dry weather conditions and violent lightning storms.

"And we have additional news from the Middle East this evening," the newscaster went on. "The Israeli ambassador to the United States, General Ibrahim Barak, was found dead earlier today in his home in Tel Aviv. After he was recalled to Israel following President Pierce's peace initiative announcements, the ambassador's wife said he had been complaining of headaches and dizziness for the past several days. According to the ambulance crew who arrived on the scene, General Barak accidentally tripped down a flight of stairs in his home and broke his neck. He was pronounced dead at the scene."

The Tonight Show

THE MUSIC HAD STOPPED, the applause subsided, and the host had just walked out to face the live audience. It was time for the opening monologue, where nothing was off limits. For the next fifteen minutes, every public figure, politician, movie star and world leader was fair game. As usual, the live audience was well primed.

"Ladies and gentlemen," the host began, "as you know, I usually use this segment to poke fun at our elected officials, especially the president of the United States. What can I say? I have an irreverent streak.

"But this evening I don't have a prepared monologue. The times are too extraordinary and the mood of the world is, for the first time that I can remember in my lifetime, optimistic. I sat in my office all day thinking about what to say this evening. And—if you can believe this—for the first time in my life I couldn't find the right words. There are times when words fail to describe the significance of an event. One such time was December 7, 1941. Another was November, 22, 1963, the day John F. Kennedy was assassinated. And another, September 11.

"Then there was the other night. As I watched the speech by President Roswell Pierce, I knew that day would rank right up there as one of the most important days in the history of the United States, and the world.

"I have made fun of President Pierce for the past two years, not because I dislike the man, but because it's my job. But tonight, I'm not going to poke fun at anyone.

"As you know, it was easy to get Bill Clinton on the show. But President Roswell Clayton Pierce has proven much more elusive. So, since I can't get the man himself, I've got his alter ego instead." Reaching into his suit coat pocket, the famous host of the Tonight Show pulled out a small tin cup and held it up for the audience, and the nation to see.

Slowly he walked over to his desk and began to gently tap the little tin cup up and down. As if on cue, the audience clapped, keeping measured time with the sounds coming from the tin cup ringing out from the desk up on the stage.

Looking into the camera, his words rang out clearly. "Well done, Mr. President. Well done."

Beirut, two weeks later

RUE BLISS, ONCE RAVAGED by decades of civil war, was once again paved smooth and brightly lit. Boisterous crowds made their way towards the many restaurants, dodging the taxis and shiny new cars.

"It's lovely to see this ancient city booming again, isn't it Helmut?"

"I only wish our coffers were as robust and full of life. I fear we won't see the robust sales of weapons and explosives we had hoped for since our plan was discovered." Helmut Hofer stepped up onto the sidewalk, quickly following his friend and lifelong partner.

"Then it is good that we have many plans." Mohammed al Nagib, his large girth draped in a long white kaftan, walked leisurely down the street. His long black cane tapped rhythmically. Amber worry beads clicked as his fingers moved them back and forth. He nodded as several elderly men greeted him in passing.

"But why come back here to Beirut?" Herr Hofer looked around nervously. "I'm a little uncomfortable being out in the open like this. Especially after what happened to Jorge in Brazil."

"We are perfectly safe in this city, my friend. I'm not normally one to brag, but I practically own this town. At least all the important and most expensive properties. Not to mention the influential government officials."

"And we do own a bank here as well." His Swiss companion relaxed a little. "So what's the big surprise? What have you got planned?"

They continued down the street. Ten-thirty and another night of vibrant social activity was about to begin in the city once known as the Paris of the Middle East. At the bottom of the street, the cliffs of Ras Beirut overlooked the dark Mediterranean. A small restaurant stood at the very edge. Red and yellow bougainvillea flowers covered a rooftop terrace.

"The place looks empty. Are you sure it's open?"

"Of course it's open. For us that is. I own this little gem. Some of the best mezzas and seafood in all of Beirut. I bought it in the late '60s. There was an unexplained explosion that destroyed the former café and the old man who owned it didn't have the heart or the money to rebuild. It's been an excellent investment, as well as a very private meeting place." Mohammad al Nagib laughed. "And the irony is so perfect."

"What was that?"

"Nothing. Just a private moment. Now, to quench your curiosity, we are having dinner tonight with one of my best placed informers. A top person at the NSA. I've done numerous favors for him over the years. And of course he has reciprocated."

"I never cease to be amazed at your capabilities, my friend." The Swiss banker began to feel more confident with each step. "I assume you have another plan that will continue to increase our profits?"

"The best, and boldest yet. Now, I am starving and since we have the entire restaurant and staff to ourselves tonight, I suggest we quicken the pace. Our guest is undoubtedly waiting inside. And we are right on time."

Parked cars lined both sides of the busy street. Traffic honked at numerous groups of people crossing and entering the many upscale restaurants lining Rue Bliss. Several new Mercedes taxis stopped to let off diners for the evening. Mohammad al Nagib and Helmut Hofer negotiated a break in the traffic and briskly stepped up onto the sidewalk in front of the quiet, yet brilliantly lit restaurant. A blue neon sign glowed over the large double doors. *Restaurant Bliss.*

An apt name, thought Mohammad al Nagib. He stopped in front of the door. "Now where is the doorman? He should be outside waiting for us." Annoyed, he grabbed the ornate brass handle and tugged. "Damn thing must be stuck." He jerked at the handle.

The blast shook the tables of a dozen of the nearby restaurants. The empty Restaurant Bliss erupted. Mohammad al Nagib and Helmut Hofer were instantly incinerated. The very spot where Samir Hussein died 35 years ago.

Two blocks away, Karl van Ness sat in a parked car and placed an international call on his secure mobile phone.

The End

Check out these other fine titles by
Durban House at your local book store.

EXCEPTIONAL BOOKS
BY
EXCEPTIONAL WRITERS

FICTION

NONFICTION

BEHIND THE MOUNTAIN	Nick Williams
FISH HEADS, RICE, RICE WINE & WAR: A VIETNAM PARADOX	Lt. Col. Thomas G. Smith, Ret.
JIMMY CARTER AND THE RISE OF MILITANT ISLAM	Philip Pilevsky
MIDDLE ESSENCE- WOMEN OF WONDER YEARS	Landy Reed
SPORES, PLAGUES, AND HISTORY— THE STORY OF ANTHRAX	Chris Holmes
WHITE WITCH DOCTOR	Dr. John A. Hunt
PROTOCOL	Mary Jane McCaffree, Pauline Innis, and Richard Sand.

DURBAN HOUSE FICTION

A DREAM ACROSS TIME   Annie Rogers

Jamie Elliott arrives from New York onto the Itish Caribbean island of St. Lucia, and finds herself caught tip in Island forces, powerful across the centuries, which Find deep echoes in her recurring dreams.

AFTER LIFE LIFE   Doti Goldman

A hilarious murder mystery taking place in the afterlife. Andrew Law, Chief Justice of the Texas Supreme Court, is the picture of robust health when he suddenly dies. Upon arriving in the afterlife, Andy discovers he was murdered, and his untimely has death has soule some unexpected and far-reaching consequences—a worldwide depression, among others. Many diabolical plots are woven in this funny, fast-paced whodunit, with a surprising double-cross ending.

an-eye-for-an-eye.com   Dennis Powell

Jed Warren, Vietnam Peacenik, and Jeff Porter, ex-Airborne, were close friends and executives at Megafirst Bank. So when CFO McAlister crashes the company, creams off millions in bonuses, and wipes out Jed and Jeff, things began to happen.

If you wonder about corporate greed recorded in today's newspapers, read what one man did about it in this intricate, devious, and surprise-ending thriller

BASHA　　　John Hamilton Lewis

LA reviewer, Jeff Krieder's pick as "Easily my best read of the year." Set in the world of elite professional tennis, and rooted in ancient Middle East hatreds of identity and blood loyalties, Basha is charged with the fiercely competitive nature of professional sports, and the dangers of terrorism. An already simmering Middle East begins to boil, and CIA Station Chief Grant Corbet must track down the highly successful terrorist, Basha. In a deadly race against time Grant hunts the elusive killer only to see his worst nightmare realized.

THE BEIRUT CONSPIRACY　　John R. Childress

At some point every person is faced with a moral dilemma: the right choice or the easy choice. The Beirut Conspiracy is a fast-paced thriller torn from today's headlines. For newly elected US President Roswell Pierce, world peace or uncontrollable global terrorism wait his decision. For drunken and disbarred physician Matthew Richards, his time as a student in Beirut is about to catch up with him, forcing him into an equally difficult choice.

THE CORMORANT DOCUMENTS　　　Robert Middlemiss

Who is Cormorant, and why is his coded letter on Hitler's stationary found on a WWI Nazi bomber preserved in the Arctic? And why is the plane loadedwith Goering's plundered art treasures? Mallory must find out or die. On the run front the British Secret Service and CIA, he finds himself caught in a secret that dates back to 1945.

CRISIS PENDING　　　Stephen Cornell

When U.S. oil refineries blow up, the White House and the Feds move fast, but not fast enough. Sherman Nassar Ramsey, terrorist for hire, a loner, brilliant, multilingual, and skilled with knives, pistols, and bare hands, moves around the country with contempt, case and cunning.

As America's fuel system starts grinding to a halt, rioting breaks out for gasoline, and food becomes scarce, events draw Lee Hamilton's wife, Mary, into the crisis. And when Ramsey kidnaps her, the battle becomes very personal.

DANGER WITHIN　　　Mark Danielson

Over 100 feet down in cold ocean waters lies the wreck of pilot Kevin Hamilton's DC- 10. In it are secrets which someone is desperate to keep. When the Navy sends a team of divers from the Explosives Ordinance Division, a mysterious explosion from the wreck almost destroys the salvage ship. The FBI steps in with Special Agent Mike Pentaglia. Track the life and death of Global Express Flight 3217 inside the gritty world of aviation, and discover the shocking cargo that was hidden on its last flight.

DEADLY ILLUMINATION　　　Serena Stier

It's summer 1890 in New York City. A ebullient young woman, Florence Tod, must challenge financier, John Pierpont Morgan, to solve a possible murder. J.P's librarian has ingested poison embedded in an illumination of a unique Hildegard von Bingcn manuscript. Florence and her cousin, Isabella Stewart Gardner, discover the corpse. When Isabella secretly removes a gold tablet from the scene of the crime, she sets off a chain of events that will involve Florence and her in a dangerous conspiracy.

DESIGNED TO KILL   Chester D. Campbell

Award winning author Chester Campbell brings back Greg McKenzie and his wife, Jill, to the glistening white beaches at Perdido Key, Florida. Tim Gannon, son of the McKenzies's closest friends, has been found dead of a gunshot wound. 'Self-inflicted,' says the deputy who investigated, a clear case of remorse over the design flaw in a highrise beachfront condo that caused a balcony to collapse, killing two people. But, after two thugs work Greg over, he realizes Jill is in danger too, and if this is a murder case, he had better solve it fast.

HANDS OF VENGEANCE   Richard Sand

Private detective Lucas Rook returns still haunted by the murder of his twin brother. What seems like an easy case involving workplace violations, the former homicide detective finds himself locked in a life and death struggle with the deadly domestic terrorist group, The Brothers of the Half Moon. A must-read for lovers of dark mysteries.

HORIZON'S END   Andrew Lazarus

This wide-ranging international novel presents on man's long haunted pursuit of abandoned values on three continents—North America, Europe, and Asia. Through it all, the wartime sounds of Morse Code signals remind him of his journalist's mission to keep the faith and reveal the truth. Jack Lerner often finds himself in the arms of women who are brilliant, sultry, and enigmatic. He fights his fight facing tough decisions in honest news reporting and contending with a family's survival in a world that refuses to live up to his own personal moral standards.

HOUR OF THE WOIVES   Stephatic Daimlen-Völs

After more than three centuries, the Poisons Affair remains one of history's great, unsolved mysteries. The worst impulses of human nature—sordid sexual perversion, murderous intrigues, witchcraft, Satanic cults—thrive within the shadows of the Sun King's absolutism and will culminate in the darkest secret of his reign; the infamous Poisons Affair, a remarkably complex web of horror, masked by Baroque splendor, luxury and refinement.

A HOUSTON WEEKEND   Orville Palmer

Professor Edward Randall, not-yet-forty, divorced and separated from his daughters, is leading a solitary, cheerless existence in a university town. At a conference in Houston, he runs into his childhood sweetheart. Then she was poverty-stricken, American Indian. Now she's elegantly attired, driving an expensive Italian car and lives in a millionaires' enclave. Will their fortuitous encounter grow into anything meaningful?

THE INNOCENT NEVER KNEW   Mark W. Danielson

When Senator Sam Tinsdale's plane crashes short of the runway during a snowstorm and city-wide power failure, NTSB investigator is sent to Albuquerque to investigate. But when he arrives, he finds the crash site tampered with, evidence removed, and is threatened by men in snowsuits who refuse to provide I.D. When his boss, Ralph Dietz, issues a statement that the Cockpit Voice Recorder and Flight Data Recorder had failed, Stambler smells a cover-up.

JOHNNIE RAY AND MISS KILGALLEN   Bonnie Hearn Hill and Larry Hill

Based on the real-life love affair between 1950's singer Johnnie Ray and columnist Dorothy Kilgallen. They had everything—wealth, fame, celebrity. The last thing they needed was love. Johnnie Ray and Miss Kilgallen is a love story that travels at a dangerous, roaring speed. Driven close to death from their excesses, both try to regain their lives and careers in a novel that goes beyond the bounds of mere biography.

THE LAST COWBOYS   Robert E. Hollmann

What do you do when you have outlived your time?

Clint and Bubba, two aging cowboys, bodies worn out from rodeos and ranching, whose best days are behind them, try and survive in a citified world. Follow The Last Cowboys as they fight modern society in an attempt to hold on to the way of life they know and love.

THE LATERAL LINE   Robert Middlemiss

Kelly Travert was ready. She had the Israeli assassination pistol, she had coated the bullets with garlic, and tonight she would kill the woman agent who tortured and killed her father. When a negotiator for the CIA warns her, suddenly her father's death is not so simple anymore.

LETHAL CURE   Kurt Popke

Dr. Jake Prescott is a resident on duty in the emergency room when medics rush in with a double trauma involving patients sustaining injuries during a home invasion. Jake learns that one patient is the intruder, the other, his wife, Sara. He also learns that his four-year-old daughter, Kelly, is missing, and his patient may hold the key to her recovery.

THE MEDUSA STRAIN   Chris Holmes

Finalist for Fore Word Magazine's 'Book of the Year'. A gripping tale of bio-terrorism that stunningly portrays the dangers of chemical warfare. Mohammed Ali Ossman, a bitter Iraqi scientist who hates America, breeds a deadly form of anthrax, and develops a diabolical means to initiate an epidemic. It is a story of personal courage in the face of terror, and of lost love found.

MR. IRRELEVANT   Jerry Marshall

Booklist Star Review. Chesty Hake, the last man chosen in the NFL draft, has been dubbed Mr. Irrelevant. By every yardstick, he should not be playing pro football, but because of his heart and high threshold for pain, he endures. Then during his eighth and final season, he slides into paranoia, and football will never be the same.

NO ORDINARY TERROR   J. Brooks Van Dyke

In this elegant and meticulously researched Edwardian detective story, J. Brooks Van Dyke brings to life the stylized fashions and customs of the time, and weaves across them a story of treason, medicine, and murder. Follow Richard and Emma Watson, nephew and niece to the Watson of Sherlock Holmes fame, as they explore dangerous leads into aristocratic mansions and London's filthiest slums.

OPAL EYE DEVIL   John Hamilton Lewis

"Best historical thriller in decades." Good Books. In the age of the Robber Baron, Opal Eye Devil weaves an extraordinary tale about the brave men and women who risk everything as the discovery of oil rocks the world. The richness and pageantry of two great cultures, Great Britain and China, are brought together in a thrilling tale of adventure and human relationships.

PRIVATE JUSTICE   Richard Sand

Ben Franklin Award 'Best Mystery of the Year'. After taking brutal revenge for the murder of his twin brother, Lucas Rooks leaves the NYPD to become a private eye. A father turns to Rook to investigate the murder of his daughter. Rook's dark journey finds him racing to find the killer, who kills again and again as Private Justice careens toward a startling end.

ROADHOUSE BLUES Baron R. Birtchcr

From the suii-drenched sands of Santa Catalina Island to the smoky night clubs and back alleys of West Hollywood, Roadhouse Blues is a taut noir thriller. Newly retired Homicide detective Mike Travis is torn from the comfort of his chartered yacht business into the dark, bizarre underbelly of Los Angeles's music scene by a grisly string of murders.

RUBY TUESDAY   Baron R. Birtcher

When Mike Travis sails into the tropical harbor of Kona, Hawaii, he expects to put LA Homicide behind him. Instead, he finds the sometimes seamy back streets and dark underbelly of a tropical paradise and the world of music and high finance, where wealth and greed are steeped in sex, vengeance, and murder.

SAMSARA   John Hamilton Lewis

A thrilling tale of love and violence set in post-World War Hong Kong. Nick Ridley, a captain in the RAF, is captured and sent to the infamous Japanese prisoner-of-war canip, Changi, in Singapore. He survives brutal treatment at the hands of the camp commandant, Colonel Tetsuro Matashima. Nick moves to Hong Kong, where he reunites with the love of his life, Courtney, and builds a world-class airline. On the eve of having his company recognized at the Crown Colony's official carrier, Courtney is kidnapped, and people begin to die. Nick is pulled into the quagmire, and must once again face the demon of Changi.

SECRET OF THE SCROLL   Chester D. Campbell
Finalist 'Deadly Dagger' award, and ForeWord Magazine's 'Book of the Year' award. Deadly groups of Palestinians and Israelis struggle to gain possession of an ancient parchment that was unknowingly smuggled from Israel to the U.S. by a retired Air Force investigator. Col. Greg McKenzie finds himself mired in the duplicitous world of Middle East politics when his wife is taken hostage in an effort to force the return of the first century Hebrew scroll.

SECRETS ARE ANONYMOUS Frederick L. Cullen
A comic mystery with a cast of characters who weave multiple plots, puzzles, twists, and turns. A remarkable series of events unfold in the lives of a dozen residents of Bexley, Ohio. The journalism career of the principle character is derailed when her father shows up for her college graduation with his boyfriend on his way to a new life in California.

THE SEESAW SYNDROME   Michael Madden
A terrifying medical thriller that slices with a scalpel, exposing the greed and corruption that can happen when drug executives and medical researchers position thernselves for huge profits. Biosense Pharmaceuticals has produced a drug named Floragen, and now they need to test it on patients to gain FDA approval. But there's a problem with the new drug. One of the side effects included death.

THE SERIAL KILLER'S DIET BOOK   Kevin Postupack
Finalist ForeWord Magazine's 'Book of the Year' award. Fred Orbis is fat, but he dreams of being Frederico Orbisini, internationally known novelist, existential philosopher, raconteur, and lover of women. Both a satire and a reflection on morals, God and the Devil, beauty, literature, and the best-seller list, The Serial Killer's Diet Book is a delightful look at the universal human longing to become someone else.

THE STREET OF FOUR WINDS   Andrew Lazarus
Paris, just after World War II. A time for love, but also a time of political ferment. In the Left Bank section of the city, Tom Cortell, a tough, intellectual journalist, finally learns the meaning of love. Along with him is a gallery of fascinating characters who lead a merry and sometimes desperate chase between Paris, Switzerland, and Spain in search of themselves.

TAINTED ANGELS   Greg Crane
"One of the best mafia thrillers in years."
Tainted Angels tells the story of a Chicago crime family that defeats the Israeli underground's incursion into the New York drug market. After succeeding

in New York, Mario Paterlini, with the help of his three sons, expand their narcotics empire in California, where he must deal with the CIA, Mexican drug lords, an Italian narcotics broker, and Los Angeles gangs.

TERMINAL CARE   Arvin Chawla
Billionaire Thomas Poole, Sr., does not believe his son died from an overdose. As he watches the life support being pulled from Michael's body, he wants vengeance, and not on any street-level punks. A fast, scary thriller that will make you think twice about that next hospital stay.

TUNNEL RUNNER   Richard Sand
A fast, deadly espionage thriller peopled with quirky and sometimes vicious characters, Tunnel Runner tells of a dark world where murder is committed and no one is brought to account, where loyalties exist side by side with lies and extreme violence.

WHAT GOES AROUND   Don Goldman
Finalist ForeWord Magazine's 'Book of the Year' award. Ray Banno, a medical researcher, was wrongfully incarcerated for bank fraud. What Goes Around is a dazzling tale of deception, treachery, revenge, and nonstop action that resolves around money, sex, and power. The book's sharp insight and hard-hitting style builds a high level of suspense as Banno strives for redemption.

DURBAN HOUSE NONFICTION
BEHIND THE MOUNTAIN: Nick Williams
A CORPORATE SURVIVAL BOOK
A harrowing true story of courage and survival. Nick Williams is alone, and cut off in a blizzard bchind the mountain. In order to survive, Nick called upon his training and experience that made him a highly successful business executive. In Behind the Mountain: A Corporate Survival Book, you will find the finest practical advice on how to handle yourself in tough spots, be they life threatening to you, or threatening to your job performance or the company itself. Read and learn.

FISH HEADS, RICE, RICE WINE & WAR   LTC.   Thomas   G. Smith (Ret.)
A human, yet humorous, look at the strangest and most misunderstood war ever, in which American soldiers were committed. Readers are offered an insiders view ofAmerican life in the midst of highly deplorable conditions, which often lead to laughter.

JIMMY CARTER AND THE RISE   Philip Pilevsky
OF MILITANT ISLAM
One of America's foremost authorities oil the Middle East, Philip Pilevsky argues that President Jimmy Carter's fallure to support the Shah of Iran led to the

1979 revolution. That revolution legitimized and provided a base ofoperations for militant Islamists across the Middle East. A most thought provoking book.

MIDDLE ESSENCE...   Landy Reed
WOMEN OF WONDER YEARS

A wonderful book by renowned speaker Landy Reed that shows how real women in real circumstances have confronted and conquered the obstacles of midlife. This is a must have guide and companion to what can be the most significant and richest years of a woman's life.

PROTOCOL *(25th Anniversary Edition)* Mary Jane McCaffree, Pauline Innis, and Richard Sand

Protocol is a comprehensive guide to proper diplomatic, official and social usage. The Bible for foreign governments, embassies, corporations, public relations firms, and individuals wishing to do business with the Federal Government. "A wealth of detail on every conceivable question, from titles and forms of address to ceremonies and flag etiquette." Department of State Newsletter.

SPORES, PLAGUES, HISTORY: Chris Holmes
THE STORY OF ANTHRAX

"Much more than the story of a microbe. It is the tale of history and prophecy woven into a fabric of what was, what might have been and what might yet be. What you are about to read is real—your are not in the Twilight Zone—adjusting your TV set will not change the picture. However, it is not hopeless, and we are not helpless. The same technology used to create biological weapons can protect us with better vaccines and . CDR Ted J. Robinson, U.S. Navy Epidemiologist.

WHAT MAKES A MARRIAGE WORK?   Malcolm D. Mahr

You hear the phrase "marry and settle down," which implies life becomes more serene and peaceful after marriage. This simply isn't so. Living together is one long series of experiments in accommodation. What Makes a Marriage Work? is a collection of fifty insights reflecting one couple's searching, experimenting, screaming, pouting, nagging, whining, moping, blaming, and other dysfunctional behaviors that helped them successfully navigate the turbulent sea of matrimony for over fifty years. (Featuring 34 New Yorker cartoons of wit and wisdom.)

WHITE WITCH DOCTOR   John A. Hunt

A true story of life and death, hope and despair in apartheid-ruled South Africa. White Witch Doctor details white surgeon John Hunt's fight to save his beloved country in a time of social unrest and political upheaval, drawing readers into the world of South African culture, mores and folkways, superstitions, and race relations.